Elastun

Leo Black

ISBN-13: 978-1-7989-4089-1

Cover image by Blake Sullivan

For Charlotte and Sim

'Was there then, after all, something in the old heathen worship, something more than the mere deifying of men, animals and elements?'

William Hope Hodgson, *The House on the Borderland*

PROLOGUE

The South of England

Winter 1067

How could this be so? Both men agreed they had not strayed from the path through the forest since separating from their companions at the fork in the way earlier that morning. How could they have done it without noticing? Such a thing was not possible. Without doubt, they had followed the familiar route. Their horses had forded the same stretch of the river as they had in the past when traveling this way, and both men had even remarked on the fire blackened oak tree – lightning they supposed – that they remembered having ridden past the last time they made this journey. And that was only two months back. Perhaps less than that. They could not have forgotten the way in so short a time. However, after what must have been more than an hour of riding, they had still not reached the clearing, and the small group of thatch-roofed wooden huts that made up the settlement of Gyrtun. It should have been only a matter of a mile or so beyond the blackened oak. They had surely ridden much further than that by now, and it had still not appeared up ahead as they had expected.

"We must have lost the path. That has to be the truth of it, whatever we may think," said Turold. "There's no other explanation for it."

"How, though? And when?" asked Guy.

Turold shook his head. "It's a mystery to me too. All the same, we are not where we should be, are we? I say we retrace our steps. If we can get ourselves back to the river crossing, then we know that, at least, is correct. We ride from that point once more. Only with more care. Keep a look out for where we must have turned off. Make sure we don't repeat the same mistake."

Guy looked unconvinced.

"You think we should continue on, then?" asked Turold.

"No, of course not. This is clearly not the right way. Only, I really cannot see how we can have gone wrong."

"No, neither can I," admitted Turold. "We have, nonetheless. So going back the way we came seems to be the only option." He sighed. "You know the worst of it? This is going to make us late re-joining the captain. And I do not look forward to explaining to *him* just how we managed to lose our way from a straight path with not a single side turning offered from start to finish."

"If it will make us late, then why bother to go there?" asked Guy. "Think on it. Who or what is there worth the effort of checking up on in place such as Gyrtun? Gyrtun…it's barely even a village, it's so small. And so few of them. I'll wager there is not a man there who has ever held a weapon in anger in his life. What threat can they be to us? I know the captain orders it. I know it's all about making our presence felt. But in Gyrtun? In God's name, to what purpose? I tell you, Turold, I weary of watching over these cursed Saxons like ill-disciplined children. Leave that to the nursemaids, I say."

Turold was about to reply, when Guy silenced him with a gesture. "I know, I know. It's not our decision to make. Let's just get this done with then, shall we? This weather…it's not getting any warmer. The frost hasn't shifted all morning, and doesn't look to me like it will. The sooner I can get back to warming my arse by a fire back at the castle, the happier I will be."

"Only a fire? I can think of better things than that for keeping a man warm. In the meantime, however, we must attend to the Baron's business before we can attend to our own. As you say, let's get this over with, and get back to the others. So, it's back again to the river crossing then?"

"I suppose it must be," said Guy with a groan.

They turned their horses and rode, a little faster now, in the other direction. After a while Turold reined his horse to a halt and called for Guy to do the same.

"Something is still not right here, damn it! We should have come upon that tree by now…the burnt one. Surely by now? *Surely*?"

Guy looked back down the track.

"Could we have passed it and not have noticed?"

"Not possible. How could we miss something like that?"

"We were riding faster than before."

"I know, but to miss that tree would be difficult. So close to the path, burnt black as night… and *neither* of us sees it? I think not." Turold looked about at the surrounding forest. "No, damn it!" he said, with a shake of his head. "No. Nothing of this feels familiar. We are far wide of the mark for some reason. I can't understand it. Something is wrong here, Guy. It's almost as if…I don't know…as if there's trickery in it."

"Trickery? How so? By whom?" Guy gave his companion a good natured punch on the shoulder. "Come now, old friend. Trickery, indeed. Who by? There's been nobody in sight for hours now. How could it be so? You will be blaming witchcraft next!"

Turold attempted a smile.

"No, nothing of that sort. Nothing so fanciful. But think on it. How is it that we find ourselves lost when we have never stepped our horses from the track?" He shook his head again.

"Since we crossed the river it's been…" began Guy, but Turold held up a finger for silence. "Listen."

"I don't…"

"Listen!"

Guy heard it now. A faint, high-pitch keening from somewhere in the trees.

The horses heard it too. They became restless - their nostrils snorting anxious breaths that condensed as they mixed with the cold air, their hooves scuffing and stamping on the frozen earth of the track as they shifted about – and their riders struggled to control them.

"What is that?" asked Guy. "The wind…or a bird, maybe? Whatever it is, it's making the horses nervous."

Turold's eyes narrowed and he inclined forward in his saddle, listening harder. "Can't say. It could be a bird, I suppose." He sounded unconvinced.

The noise began to grow in volume, swelling out from the forest, reverberating among the trunks and branches.

"I think it's in the trees!" said Guy.

"Is it? I don't know. It seems on a level with us to me. And maybe coming from below us, too. Up from the bushes there. I'd say it's coming from all around us. Whatever it is, there has to be more than one."

The noise had now reached a level where it was necessary for them to raise their voices in order to be heard.

"Wolves?" asked Guy. Turold did not respond. "Turold, I'm asking you…"

"Huh?"

"Wolves?"

"No, that's not wolves. Doesn't sound right for wolves. Ever heard one make a noise that piercing?" He cocked his head, listening. "Oh, God save us. Is that human? A child's crying…more than one…children? What would they be doing out in this forest?"

"It's more like women," said Guy. "Women wailing. Dozens of them. I don't see anyone, though, so it couldn't be. That many, and we would see them all around us."

It grew louder still. Then, rolling beneath the high keening, came a deep roaring. The two sounds dissonant, jarring, creating a buzzing and throbbing that made the men wince. As the volume increased it became ever more uncomfortable. Grimacing hard, but resisting the urge to put their hands over their ears, both men now reacted in the way instilled by years of training and experience. They drew swords, hefted their shields at the ready, and braced themselves in saddle and stirrups. Guy turned his horse about, looked up and down the path, and into the treeline. He turned back to Turold, "Still nothing! How can it be so? There is absolutely nothing to see. Not in any direction," he bellowed. "I see nothing!"

Even as he shouted this, Guy looked up and beyond his companion. His expression moved quickly through incomprehension and alarm, to one of outright dread. His sword slipped from his grasp, and he fell from his horse onto the frozen earth of the forest path, pale and trembling.

Although he was a brave man, tested in battle, Turold could not bring himself to turn and look at whatever it was that Guy saw.

Then a voice spoke close to his ear. Whispering, but in some way distinct from the other noises around him.

Turold heard it say, "*Now he sees… He sees everything.*"

******

CHAPTER 1

Even at a distance, and through the trees, Eadwig could tell the riders were not from his people or his country. These were the men from across the water. Normans, carrying the long shields and riding the same deep chested warhorses they had used in battle to defeat the Saxon king, Harold. That was just over a year ago now, and since then their hold on this part of the country had become absolute. If the riders chose to spear a boy like him, cut him down with their swords, or simply ride over him, they could do so without fear of retaliation. At this thought he felt the fear take hold. His hands shook, and his legs seemed to become weak and unsteady – if he tried to stand, he was not convinced they would support him. His grandfather said that he *should* fear these men. Fear was a good thing, a warning not to be ignored, and would do him no harm providing he learned to master it. Not let it master him. At this moment he was not sure he could manage to do that.

He had seen these particular men before. They had been to his village, he was certain of it. Even then he had been afraid, despite being among his family and the other villagers. Right now he was alone, and in the forest. No one even knew where he had gone. He had ignored warnings, and crept out early, just before dawn, taking his father's old bow and Gra, his favourite of the hunting dogs, without permission.

Gra! What if he barked now? Eadwig called the dog to him as loudly as he dared, barely above a whisper, and was thankful for the dog's training and obedience, as Gra ran over and stood at his side. Even so, the dog was clearly agitated by the approach of the riders, quivering slightly and omitting a low, steady growl that Eadwig prayed would be too low to be heard above the rustle of the breeze through what leaves remained on the trees. He put an arm around Gra and crouched further down into the frost covered undergrowth, behind the trunk of a large beech tree. Using his free hand, he muzzled Gra's jaws as best he could. Low growls were one thing. A bark right now and they would be discovered for sure.

If these were the men he had seen before, it meant that the tall one at their head was Orderic, one of the captains of Baron de Varaville's guard. If that was so, the even larger man riding alongside him would be Walter, the one known as 'The Bear'. There was a story told of how Walter, mid-conversation with Orderic, had drawn his sword, and taken a nearby man's head off in punishment for some minor offence, without even breaking the flow of conversation with his captain. Eadwig's grandfather had said the story was foolish nonsense, an exaggeration by those who should know better. Just the same, he had added that Eadwig would do well to keep in mind that Orderic and all his men were very dangerous. Worse than bears, in fact.

******

The previous night had seen the heaviest frost of the year so far. The imprint of recent footfalls and cart tracks could be read in the mud of the path, still frozen to a hard cast, and a brittle ice now filled the spaces where yesterday there had been thin puddles of brown water. Orderic supposed that few of the horses whose hooves were recorded there would be a match for those now approaching the village on the path through the forest. He had ordered his men to ride their destriers - the muscular warhorses bred and raised from foals to be ridden into battle. Though there would be no battle today. Today the horses were merely for display. They made more of a show than the less impressive, although more practical, palfreys that were the usual mount for travel. And this journey, as were so many these days, was all about show.

Nonetheless, bloodshed was never entirely out of the question on any journey through this newly conquered England. Of course, for the most part, it was likely to be Saxon blood - at least in this part of the country. The southern regions had suffered the heaviest losses after that terrible battle near Hastings. Not only had they lost Harold, the man they hailed as king, but so great were the numbers of the Saxon ruling class - Earls and Thegns - and of the fighting men of the South to die in the fighting on that day, that the subsequent subjugation of the South was as good as complete within a year. The greater part of the South's spirit to resist had drained away into the mud with the Saxon blood shed near Hastings. Duke William was crowned King of all England in the Abbey at Westminster less than three months after that, on Christmas day. Even so, there were still those who would not yield, and the penalties imposed for spilling Norman blood needed to be, and always were, severe. Nothing could be taken for granted about these people. When among them, he and his men were always on their guard. Was anyone where they shouldn't be? Anyone looking around to see if they were observed? Or weapons in the possession of those who had no business to have them? Some of the surviving members of the Saxon ruling class had seen the wisdom of compromise, and had taken oaths of fealty to their Norman overlords in exchange for some residual degree of power among their own people. As a result - and against Orderic's advice - his brother the Baron had agreed that, for purposes of show, some of these Saxons of rank should be permitted to carry arms. However, experience had taught that there were ways of wearing a sword that betrayed a great deal about the intentions of the wearer. A blade soon to be drawn was not worn in the same fashion as one worn as a matter of costume. Perhaps, slightly more forward than was comfortable in order to be more readily accessible, the nervous wandering of the hand from pommel to hilt, the other hand instinctively steadying the scabbard for a smoother withdrawal, or the subtle, perhaps unconscious, shifting of the position of the feet, steadied and ready. But if Orderic and his men knew this, so could others. The real danger came from men like himself. Men trained to know what to look for, who would also know what to disguise or conceal.

Orderic sighed, leaned forward in his saddle, and patted Malleus, his stallion, on the neck. He then ran his hand along the crescent scar that ran down from the horse's neck to his shoulder. Healed now, the result of mistimed swing of a Saxon Housecarl's battle-axe. A fraction more to the left, Malleus would have been brought down, Orderic unseated and, without doubt, killed. As it was, the Saxon paid for his error with *his* life instead, lifted off his feet by a swing of Orderic's sword, and trampled under Malleus's mighty hooves. Yet not all of Orderic's comrades had been so fortunate. The Housecarls - the much feared elite fighting men of the Saxon army - with their heavy axes, expertly wielded, had been as impressive as they had been intimidating that day. Many a knight known to Orderic had perished having had his mount cut from under him. The cries of the maimed horses rising higher still than those of the men dying about them.

"See that?"

Orderic looked in the direction Walter had indicated.

"Nothing. What…?"

"There, rising from the dead bracken beyond that tree."

******

The men on horseback were closer now. From where he squatted, as low as possible, arm still clamped around Gra, it was possible for Eadwig to make out the horses' legs on the path. He counted ten animals. The men spoke in the unintelligible language he had come to recognize as that of the new King's soldiers, and he held his breath when he saw that they had stopped. He had to take his hand from the dog's muzzle to stifle his own cry when one the horses turned and began to move in his direction. He gave thought to running, but knew that to do so would put him directly in the horse's path. Gra was quivering violently, but remained obedient to Eadwig's restraining arm, even when the approaching rider drew within a just few yards of their hiding place. Even when the rider spoke.

******

"It's just a boy," Rollo said, laughing, and lowering his sword. "Perhaps ten, maybe twelve years. Hard to say. Bit of a mouse. Fine hunting dog with him, though."

"Tell him to stand up, show himself," said Orderic.

Rollo steadied his horse, and leaned out of his saddle in the direction of Eadwig's hiding place.

"Stand up lad. I see you. It's cold today. Your breath, it shows in the air, see..." Rollo huffed to demonstrate. "Gives away your hiding place. We saw you, even from the path." He waited a moment, and then continued. "I said *stand up*."

When Eadwig still refused to stand, Rollo's tone became harder. "We see you. Understand? Your breath. You steam like a turd, boy. May as well show yourself. Or I can just ride over there and drag you out. Better you just get up, eh? Who knows, I might not even eat you. Might let you go home to your bitch of a mother, if you have one. Or is that her growling next to you?" He turned back to Orderic. "Not sure if he's too brave or too scared to obey. Should I flush him out?"

Orderic sighed. "A boy you say? Hold there a moment." He turned to Walter. "Go take a look will you, old friend. If it really is a child, who could blame him for being afraid of

Rollo?"

Walter nodded, and rode over to join Rollo.

"It's neither courage nor fear that prevents him obeying your polite request, Rollo," Walter explained. "It's your language. He doesn't speak it. How long have we been here now, eh? More than a year. And yet you still forget that yours is not the language of these people."

"Well, it should be," growled Rollo. "Besides, it won't trouble me if I never talk with a single bloody one of these people. Especially if it requires my learning their clumsy tongue. Sounds like they have a mouthful of ..."

Rollo would have continued, were it not for Walter's expression urging caution, accompanied by the slightest shake of his head. Rollo realized his mistake and cursed under his breath, his long face growing pale.

"Fool!" Walter whispered.

"What should I say?"

"Nothing," Walter replied, still whispering. "For God's sake, say nothing. He won't, so why should you? Just bloody be quiet for a while... If you can, that is."

Walter rode forward until he was directly above Eadwig. Then in the language he knew the boy would understand, told him to show himself, and asked him what he was doing there.

The boy still did not step out from his hiding place. He merely shifted his position slightly, and mumbled something Walter could not hear.

"Look at me, boy. Do I look like someone interested in playing games?"

Eadwig looked up through a gap in the fronds of old bracken into the unblinking stare of a hard, ruddy face. There was the stubble of a few days' growth about the chin, but not a full beard like those worn by the men from Eadwig's village. The man wore chain mail, and a steel helmet. The helmet was dulled from years of use, but still bright enough that the pale morning sunlight bounced off it a little when he moved his head.

"What did I say, huh? Didn't I tell you to show yourself? So… do it! Stand up."

This time, Eadwig did as he was told, and got up. His legs were still shaky. He worried they might fail him. He still held on as best he could to Gra - as much for his own stability and reassurance as it was to control the dog, who was quivering with tension, and growling, although still obedient. Just.

Walter looked from boy to dog and back again. For a brief moment Eadwig thought he saw a look of amusement play across the big man's features. Then, just as quickly, they hardened again into the impassive inscrutability they had worn before.

"Your dog doesn't seem to like me very much, now does he? Doesn't trust me, I think. That's a wise animal you have there. Anyhow, what was it you said before, boy? You've stood up. Now speak up."

Eadwig breathed deeply, the breath shuddering in his chest, and spoke, as clearly and with as much control as he could manage. "I was…I was hiding."

"Better. I can hear you now. Hiding you say…from us?"

"Yes."

"Not very good at it though, eh? Still, apart from hiding from us, just what is it brings a young one like you out here so early? To be this far from anywhere, you must have left well before dawn. And what are you doing out on your own for God's sake? Out here…this time of day…it's not safe." He glanced again at Gra. "Ah… hunting I suppose?"

"The Baron allows my village to hunt in this part of the forest."

"Believe me boy, I know what the Baron does and does not allow. Lucky for you I already know your village has permission. That is, if you are from the village up ahead. Because if I thought you were not, I would slice you through with this." Walter turned his horse so he could show the sword hanging at his side. "Do not be misled by your age. Lack of years would not have saved you. Make no mistake about that. I've killed smaller than you for less reason."

Remembering the story of the beheaded man, Eadwig's breath shuddered in his chest again. He felt lightheaded for a moment, and did not hear what Walter said next. When the boy did not answer, Walter drew his sword, and then leaned forward, tapping him lightly on the shoulder with the side of the blade. "I asked you a question, boy?"

At the drawing of the sword, Eadwig had closed his eyes, waiting for the strike. Despite, to his surprise, receiving only a gentle tap, he had staggered back, barely managing to keep his balance.

"Open your eyes," Walter commanded. "You are still on earth. You'll see no angels today. Ah, come now…no need for that."

Eadwig did as he was told, and opened his eyes. The large man was no longer looking at his face. He appeared to be looking below his waist. Eadwig looked down too, and saw the dampness where he had emptied his bladder. Tears filled his eyes, in spite of his efforts to prevent them.

"Now, lad. No bawling," Walter said. He gestured towards the dampness, careful this time to use the hand not holding the sword. "No shame in that, now. I've seen grown men…big men like me…do worse. You have to learn…"

"To master it, my grandfather says," Eadwig said, and wiped his sleeve across his eyes.

"Does he now? Well, he is right. Takes learning, that's all. And you will, I'm sure. So, tell me, how was your luck?"

"Pardon? Luck? I don't know what…"

"Any luck with the hunt. You say you've been hunting. Did you catch anything? "

"No."

"No? Well, it can be that way sometimes. Still, that is a

fine dog you have with you. Even if he looks set to tear my throat out. Or try, at least. I've killed dogs before, too. Now, I dare say you will catch much with a beast like that at your side. *Next time*. Not today. You understand?"

"Next time? You mean I can go?"

"Yes, but remember, no more hunting today. You're to go home. Oh, and it's better not to hide from us, boy. Safer in the open. Where we can see you. Hmmm? Now, go home. Go!"

Eadwig hesitated, uncertain for a moment, then ran off, with Gra running close at his side.

Walter called after him. "Don't hide. Remember that."

******

CHAPTER 2

It was clear the village of Elastun had been warned the riders were coming. When the path took Orderic and his companions out from the trees, past some livestock pens, then in through the entrance gate in the wooden palisade, and into the village, its inhabitants were already waiting. They had gathered together in a group before the entrance to the largest building, a great wooden hall at centre of the village. The surrounding houses and huts appeared empty. The only movement was that of the animals, some in the pens, others foraging freely between the buildings, and occasional birds flitting between the trees that surrounded the village on three sides. Orderic halted his horse in front of the group, while the other riders fanned out in row behind him. He gave a slight bow, then addressed an old man standing with a woman Orderic knew to be the man's wife, at the front of the group.

"Greetings to you Eadred. Also to your wife…whose name I forget… that is if I ever knew it…"

"Ceolwin. Her name is Ceolwin," replied Eadred flatly.

"So it is," said Orderic, making it plain he was not actually interested. He glanced around the village, then back at Eadred and the villagers gathered behind him. "Well, Eadred, it seems you were prepared for our approach. All valuables safely hidden away I hope?"

"To what purpose? We have nothing left to hide. We have nothing that you would consider valuable these days. And you know that. Anything we had that you wanted your men have long since taken from us!"

Ceolwin put a restraining hand on Eadred's upper arm. "Careful, husband", she whispered, but it was already too late; the old man had said more than he intended. He tensed as he waited for Orderic's reaction. There was a pause, and then Orderic smiled.

"Don't feel so bad, old man. God knows there are more wealthy villages than just Elastun in this country. You are not the only sheep to be sheared. And certainly not the biggest. You say we have taken everything. Now is that true, I wonder? Let me see, what else might there be? Ah, I have it! What of the women and girls? Might we not steal something particularly precious from them?"

There were murmurs from the villagers, hands were held more tightly, loved ones huddled more closely.

Eadred cleared his throat. Ceolwin's hand had moved down from his upper arm into his hand. He reached his other hand around, laying it on top reassuringly. "That you do not, Orderic, is something for which we are very grateful," he said.

"Yes, but we may yet," Orderic replied, testing Eadred's resilience, and finding himself impressed by the fact that the old man seemed not to flinch at the implied threat, even as those around him did. "Not today, though. Just so you know; we had not planned to take you by surprise. Nevertheless, I feel I must congratulate you on your vigilance. We did not see your lookouts. You have taken care that they are well concealed. In the trees, perhaps?"

"Not lookouts. Just a young boy who disobeys his grandfather, but is swift of foot." The old man reached behind himself and pulled a boy forward from among the crowd. "My grandson. Hunting, now that his father and brother cannot."

Orderic heard a low grunt of recognition from Walter.

"It's the whelp from the forest."

"And what do they call you?" Orderic asked.

"We call him Eadwig," said Eadred

"I asked the boy," said Orderic. "Come lad, we know you can speak. Tell me your name."

"But Grandfather has told you?"

"Never mind what he may have told me. I asked you, boy. I want to hear it from you."

Eadred could not be certain, but it seemed to him his grandson looked to the one they called the Bear, who nodded, seemingly to indicate that the boy should answer.

"Eadwig. I am called Eadwig."

"I see," said Orderic. "Well, young Eadwig, your grandfather is right. You are indeed swift of foot. We had thought to arrive before you. Or is it perhaps that the track may not be the most direct route to this place?"

"It is, but I can run fast," replied Eadwig.

"So it seems."

His grandfather used a strong arm to hastily swing the boy back behind him.

"May I ask the purpose of your visit, my Lord?"

"Come now, Eadred. Must we go through this every time? I am *not* your Lord. That would be Baron de Varaville."

"Then what would you deem correct? How, then, should I address you?"

"With caution?"

"Always with that."

"Good."

"And by what title?"

"Oh, I believe 'sir' will suffice."

"Very well, sir. May I ask again the purpose of your visit?"

"Yes, you may. You have a church, do you not?"

Eadred was confused. This was unexpected. "We do. Yes, of course. A village such as ours…Though please be assured, it holds nothing of value to you."

"Oh? You know what is of value to me, then?"

"I know what has already been taken!"

"Where's your caution now?"

"I only meant..."

Orderic waved a hand to silence the old man. "Show me. Which of these…?"

"It cannot be seen from here. It lies a little beyond the

rest of our buildings, on the edge of the village, a little out of the way. At the start of the fields. Where the forest begins to open out. If you will permit me, I will lead you there."

"Very well, the rest of your people may go about their business… whatever that may be. My men will not harm them, so long as they stay where they can be seen. And no one is to leave the village until we ourselves have left. Understood?"

Eadred turned to the other villagers. "You all heard. Stay where you can be seen. You will be safe."

The villagers hesitated, only dispersing when Eadred strode forward, and waved them away. "Go. You heard what I told you. Stay where they can see you and you will not be harmed." He turned back to face Orderic. "It is this way. If you would follow me..."

"One moment," said Orderic. He looked around. "Let me see…Yes…Your Grandson there. Can he be trusted to hold my horse?"

"Eadwig? Hold a horse…Yes. Yes of course he can."

"Very well."

Orderic swung down from his saddle, and called to Eadwig, who by now had shrunk back into the doorway of the hall. When the boy came over, Orderic handed him Malleus's reins. "There boy, take these, be my squire for the morning. Can you do that?"

Eadwig nodded. He looked up at the big horse.

"His name is Malleus. Do you know what that means?" asked Orderic.

Eadwig shook his head.

"It means hammer," said Orderic. "Believe me, boy, when I tell you there is a reason for that choice of name. Stand to one side of him. Always to one side. Never in front. See those hooves? A horse like this will kick you lifeless if you don't take care. And keep close to me. Is that understood? He will tolerate you only if he sees that I do."

Eadwig looked up at the horse, saw the long scar.
"The man who gave him that is dead," said Orderic.

******

There were few flowers this time of year, but the berries from the holly sprigs she had collected would bring some colour to the inside of the church. Brother Theodric would not approve when next he visited, of course. But of what *did* he approve? That fat monk, he had misgivings about almost anything that was outside his narrow, monastic view of the world. Besides, the intervals between his visits had increased recently, so he might never see them. Perhaps he was caught up in all the work of bringing the Abbey at Menlac into line with the changes introduced since the new king had come to power? Perhaps. Then again, a less charitable interpretation of the increased lengths of his absences might be that it was no longer politic for him to be quite so involved with villages like hers since the installation of the new Abbot - a Norman, and a man who looked as much to his king for instruction, as he did to his God. Either way, it was of no concern to Alditha. What did she care what some fool of monk thought of her care of the church? It belonged to the village, not to the Abbey, whatever Abbot Robert might choose to believe, sat comfortably up there in Menlac, more than a day's ride away. It might as well be in Normandy. The villagers worshipped here with or without Brother Theodric present, or the Abbot's blessing. The truth of it was that their kind were a mystery to Alditha. Why were some men of this world so driven by the need to gain status and assert power, apparently for its own sake? Alditha would never understand this. Then again, neither could she understand the others, like Hakon, equally driven, but by some other, vaguer, notion of gaining what… Glory? And seemingly at whatever cost - to them or to others.

Like Hakon.

She immediately felt ashamed for having had the thought. But she could not entirely dismiss it. Not for the first time she pondered how much Hakon was complicit in the events that had led to his own death. She saw again the excitement and pride on her young husband's face on the day he rode out with his father to join King Harold in his fight with the Vikings under Hardrada. He had wanted so much to go. They would only be away for a few weeks at the most, Hakon had told her.

A few weeks? Forever, as it turned out. She had been told by Swein, a man of the village who had fought alongside them, that both men, Hakon and his father, had survived the glorious victory over Hardrada. The problem was that no one had expected to have to do the same thing all over again so soon. No one had expected Duke William to sail over from Normandy, appearing down south only days after the battle up north. A fresh army to face in a fresh battle. It was possible, of course, that Hakon had been excited by this prospect. Another invasion meant another great battle, and another great battle meant the chance of another great victory, bringing with it more of that precious glory. Or had the first taste of what fighting actually meant been enough? Had he been more afraid the second time, wondering if he could find the necessary courage within himself to do it all again? Even the Housecarls, the professional military men, must have been exhausted, brave and experienced though they might be. In the event, neither their skill in battle nor their courage had been sufficient to carry the day. All but a few died. King Harold himself among them.

From an early age Hakon had trained with the sword and battle axe alongside Wulfstan, his father, but neither man was a professional. He and Wulfstan were members of the Fyrd, the king's part-time army. It was an honour to serve in this way, Hakon had insisted. But all that really seemed to mean now was that, like his father, Hakon was good enough to die. Alditha wondered if he and his father were even together when that time had come. Did they get to stand and fall side by side, Wulfstan and Hakon? Perhaps back to back. Father and son, in a final display of courage and pride. Was it that way? Could it ever have been that way? The way Hakon imagined it. Or did they simply fall? Their last moments spent in the bewildered realisation that their deaths meant nothing, had achieved nothing. Was there even time for that? Maybe there was only fear and pain. Whatever the truth of it, both of them were now nothing more than part of some sundry heap of bones, deposited together in some place she would never know, and could never visit. Fallen together, or separated in the confusion of battle. Good enough to die.

Hakon's little brother, Eadwig, already both envious and proud when his father and older brother had left with other men of the village to fight alongside the king, now hero worshipped them even more than he had when they were alive. In death, to Eadwig, the two men had become faultless. Ideal versions of themselves. Hakon's grandfather too, always spoke with enormous pride when he spoke of his dead son and grandson, though his grief was plain. It was equally plain that the old man wished he had been young enough to have ridden out with them, died with them, and become a part of the same heap of bones. The glorious dead had it better than the subjugated living.

Hakon's mother, Godgifu, was also proud of how her men had died, despite struggling more than the rest of the family to come to terms with the pain of her loss. For Alditha, however, there was precious little pride. Most of the time there was only grief. In the beginning it had come in the form of an overwhelming wave of sorrow and panic. An almost physical pain in her breast that, on occasion, made it seem hard to breathe. Or want to breathe. So vast in its awfulness it could not be fully comprehended. These days that wave came and went, receding sometimes, and leaving in its place a numbing, grey, barrenness to existence.

If grief was uppermost, there was also another emotion, one that must always remain concealed, never to be spoken of. Anger.

Her foolish young husband had ridden off to die. Left her alone. Just so he could stand, gloriously, shoulder to shoulder with the other men in the shield wall. To be cut down. Gloriously. Gladly.

Stupidly.

No. She would not do this again. Unfair accusations against someone who was not there to defend themselves against them, and unresolvable questions that could only be made worse by dwelling upon them. Like knots of twine made worse by attempts to disentangle them. She had loved Hakon for almost as long as she could remember - like a brother for much of her life then later, differently, as a husband. She missed him, and that was what really mattered. That much was absolute, unqualified. And that was where she would leave it. That thought only. Anything else was partial, unhelpful, and unfair.

She sighed, sat down on a bench against the wall and looked about herself. Even as a child she had loved this building. Back then the priest, Father Adda, had lived among the villagers. An old man even then, Adda had welcomed her help keeping the place clean and well maintained. When Father Adda died, the Abbey at Menlac had sent Brother Theodric to take his place, but the aloof Theodric did not live in the village, and cared little for the building. So, through no conscious choice, but rather by default, Alditha had become the informal custodian of the building. An arrangement that seemed acceptable to both villagers and Abbey.

As she had from childhood, Alditha now found herself gazing into the shadows of the high ceiling. She had always found comfort in her faith, cherishing its strange and finely balanced blend of certainty and mystery. It made life more bearable, and even a little exciting, to think there were things beyond what it was possible to see or hear. Recent events had made maintaining her faith more difficult, but it was still there if she looked deep enough. And this old wooden building was where it was most likely to be found – particularly among the shadows. It was the oldest building in the village and had, for a long time, been the biggest, until Eadred had rebuilt his hall. He was the head man of the village back then. These days Alditha was not sure what his status was. Baron de Varaville had allowed him to stay in place, but not in power.

"Alditha." He had spoken gently so as not startle her. She knew his voice. She looked up and saw him in the doorway of the church. For a brief moment she wondered had she conjured him with her thoughts.

"Eadred."

"Alditha. You must leave, now."

"I can't…I still have to…"

"You can finish up here later. Now, leave us."

"Is someone with you?"

"Alditha! Enough! Leave now."

"Of course. Forgive me."

As she passed him, Alditha saw that Eadred wore an expression of barely concealed unease. She had mistaken the agitation in his tone for his usual irritability. This was something different. Although she knew better than to ask him what it was, the reason for Eadred's unease became clear when Alditha stepped past him into the pale light of the winter morning and saw Orderic. The Norman gave the slightest of nods.

"My lady."

Was there some deliberate irony in this choice of greeting and the tone of its delivery? More than likely with these people, Alditha thought. She was of appropriate status to be addressed as 'my lady' by the villagers, although she wondered for how much longer. From a man like this however, perhaps the best she could hope for was irony? Certainly, she dare not risk the same in response. Her "Good day, sir," was delivered with studied sincerity.

Orderic paused. He looked to Alditha as if he were trying to recall something. Then, after a moment, he asked, "You did not join your fellow villagers when they came out to receive us. You were not interested?...Not curious? Or is it that you were...?"

"Fearful?" offered Alditha.

"If you wish," said Orderic.

"I do not think fearfulness a matter of wishing."

"Were you, though?"

"Fearful?"

"Yes."

"Of course. We must all be."

"It is good that you are. Nevertheless, that was not the reason for your absence."

"No, in truth, it was not. I did not attend because I could not see what difference my presence would have made."

"I imagine you hoped you would not be disturbed here?"

"I had things to do."

"Things to do? Did you indeed? Well, yes, I believe I can understand that. After all, we all have things we must do, do we not? Tasks we must carry out," said Orderic. His eyes narrowed a little. "Although some of more consequence than others, I think." He smiled at her now, but it was perfunctory, and there was nothing of the smile in his eyes. "And yours is what...prettifying the church?" He pointed at Alditha's hand. To her surprise she saw she still clutched a spray of holly.

"Yes," continued Orderic, "I suppose the house of God must be maintained as best it can be."

There it was again, that tone, thought Alditha.

"The old man turn you out, did he?" asked Orderic.

"No, I had all but finished." She would not take this man's side against Eadred. Even in so light a matter. Even though what he suggested was true.

"*All but*, you say?" asked Orderic. "*Not* finished then. Now we must have the place pretty, mustn't we?"

"It is no matter. I can come back."

Until this moment Orderic's tone had been almost playful. Now it took on a harder edge.

"I do not ask that you return and do it, woman. It would please me, so I order it now. Do it now. Prettify the church."

Eadred must have been standing within earshot, just inside the doorway. He stepped out and said, "My dear… if you would continue your work inside…please." He motioned for her to return.

"Yes…please," Orderic echoed. This time the sarcasm was unmistakable. He gestured for her to enter ahead of him. Turning to Eadwig, who stood a few feet off, holding Malleus, he said, "Remember his name, and why he is called it. Always to the side. You have already survived Walter this day, and you may yet survive Malleus. Who can tell?"

Alditha gave Hakon's little brother a questioning look. He answered with a shrug.

******

"As you see, our church is wooden, like all our other buildings. Not grand. Not built in stone like some. Those of the towns."

Orderic, now sitting upon the bench where only a short while before Alditha had been sitting, looked up at the old Saxon, still standing despite his age, and pulled a mock sad face. Alditha felt the humiliation of seeing Eadred ridiculed almost as much as she felt her own humiliation at having to maintain the pretence of tidying the church around the two men like a servant. That mocking face made her want to break the brush with which she was sweeping the floor - a floor she had swept already that very morning - over the brutish man's head. Still, even if she had, it would simply shatter against the metal of his steel helmet. Everything shattered that came up against these damn men.

"Are you so very poor here, then, Eadred?" Orderic asked.

"No, not perhaps as poor as some. Then neither are we as wealthy as others. The towns, for example… they have much more…"

"If you say so. Still, let me tell you something, old man. My men and I ride through all the settlements hereabouts from time to time. There are a great many in the Baron's territory. And I would have to say Elastun seems to me nearer in size to a town than a village."

"Possibly, but…"

"And you, Eadred. Are you not a man of some importance?"

"Some… once…with things as they now are, however…"

"Let us forget *things as they now are* for the moment. Before now, this was your manor, was it not? That huge building everyone was gathered in front of when we rode in…the hall… that is yours, yes?"

"That is so, but…"

"*Your* hall, *your* village. I therefore suggest that you have indeed been a man of quite considerable importance here. If maybe not so much now…with things being as they now are." Orderic pulled the same sad face again. Alditha's grip on her brush was now so tight her hands had begun to ache. "Then answer me this, would you," Orderic continued. "Why only this wooden shit heap of a church?"

"May God damn you!" shouted Alditha, stepping towards him.

"Alditha!" Eadred held up a hand in warning. "Enough!"

She threw down her brush in frustration, stepped back.

"Please, my lord…sir…," Eadred said to Orderic. "I regret Alditha's behaviour very much. She does too, I am certain. She was not thinking. You must understand this place means a great deal to her." He turned to Alditha. "Girl, you will apologise. Right now!" Though this was a command, there was something that suggested pleading in his eyes. "You must," he added emphatically.

Alditha took a deep breath, steadied herself. She knew Eadred was right. She had been foolish - dangerously so, in fact. She must apologise, try to prevent things becoming any worse than they already were. She stepped forward again, only this time with her head bowed, arms at her sides, and hands, with an effort, no longer clenched into fists. However, before she could say anything, Orderic had waved her back. "No apology. It is not required."

Alditha realised with dismay that his tone was not one of forbearance. He was not being understanding or tolerant. The simple fact was that her outburst was of so little consequence to this man that he did not feel the need to make time to listen to any apology she might have to offer.

"*Alditha*. Yes, that's it," said Orderic. "I have seen you when previously I visited Elastun. I was trying to remember your name just now. Well, Alditha, with your permission, I will continue talking with your grandfather."

"He is not my…"

"It doesn't matter child," said Eadred. He turned back to Orderic. "Sir, I should explain. Unlike many villages, this church does not belong to the manor. It is belongs to the Abbey at Menlac. The building is theirs. An unusual arrangement these days, it is true. Particularly given they are so far from here, not even in this valley. However, the church here was established by them on this site long ago. We ourselves have no objection. Why should we?" Alditha snorted her disapproval of this last comment, but Eadred ignored her. "We have no objection," he continued. "And the brothers at Menlac certainly seem to consider the building suitable. I grant you it is old, and not very grand. Not stone, perhaps. Yet it has served us well here all this time. In Alditha's care it is always kept clean and decorated, as you can see for yourself. With or without the Abbey's assistance we carry out such small repairs as are necessary. As you can also see, it is dry, the roof and walls remain sturdy. As to anything major, however, we must defer to the Abbey. We would not have a say."

"Would you not? Well then, my time has been wasted in coming here. It will be for the Abbey to build the new church, it seems."

"New church?"

"A new building. I should tell you, the Baron is an extremely devout man. Prides himself on it, in fact. He does not like the idea of our Lord receiving the praise he is due from…well…shit heaps. And so the place comes down if it is not fitting, and a new building goes up. Be assured, this place would most definitely not be considered fitting in the eyes of the Baron de Varaville."

"The expense of such a thing…" said Eadred.

"Fortunately for you, if what you say is true, you need not trouble your grizzled head about that. Abbot Robert must worry his tonsured head instead. I wonder… do many of the churches in this valley come under the Abbey?"

"Some, I think."

"Would you happen to know which?"

"Not with any certainty."

"Then it would seem I must continue on my way. Visit every damn village. Spread the word to your neighbours. Make sure they understand that even the hairs of their heads are all numbered, eh?"

******

CHAPTER 3

When, a whole day having gone by, Turold and Guy did not re-join him and rest of his men, Orderic sent Walter and Rollo back to look for them. The route was simple enough. Taking the smaller of the two tracks presented at the fork in the way through the forest, Walter and Rollo rode straight ahead, splashed through the ford at the bend in the river when they came to it, carried on past a blackened oak and, within an hour of leaving the main track, they had reached Gyrtun.

Although the hardness of the frozen ground meant there would have been fewer obvious tracks than normal, they had expected to find at least some traces if riders had recently passed that way before them. They found none, however, and the people of Gyrtun claimed no knowledge of Turold and Guy having been there. Even after Walter threatened to arrange that the hamlet be razed to the ground and its inhabitants slain if it were to subsequently be discovered that they had lied to him, the people still denied ever setting eyes on the two men. So, frustrated, but inclined to believe them, Walter and Rollo turned their horses, and rode back out onto what was the only major track leading to and from Gyrtun, in due course turning onto the wider track that led up to Elastun. They did not stop when they entered the much larger village. Instead, they carried on riding, passing out of the gate at the far side. They then spent the next day and a half riding through a collection of similar villages - although none of them quite as large as Elastun - as they followed the route of the river up through to where the forest thinned, and the valley widened. Eventually, leaving the valley entirely, and entering a flat, open plain, they headed north towards the town of Menlac, with the stone Abbey at its centre. Once there, they joined Orderic and the others at the Abbey, where Orderic was in the process of breaking the unwelcome news of the expenses his Abbey would soon incur rebuilding its churches to an extremely agitated Abbot Robert.

Their business at Menlac complete, Orderic and his men began the long journey back to the Baron's castle on the coast at Rylemont.

******

The Baron was not listening. Orderic, knowing any further attempts to gain his brother's attention would be wasted, stepped back and waited. His face remained expressionless as he watched the Baron pace back and forth, occupied - as the Baron so often was these days - by some matter of his own imagining.

The day had broken grey and cold. And it had stayed that way. A bitter wind, blowing in from the sea that stretched away into the distance beyond the castle, cut across the courtyard. It watered the eyes and hunched the shoulders of Orderic's men who, despite being exhausted from long hours in the saddle, on reaching the castle at Rylemont, had been informed they must come to attention, and remain that way until Orderic had reported in full to the Baron. Only when the Baron was satisfied would they be permitted to retire to their quarters. The ride had been the end to almost a month of journeying around the villages and towns of the shire. Rest was what they deserved, not this treatment. Orderic glanced briefly in their direction. All but Walter looked straight ahead. Walter, as ever, was standing to one side, his troubled gaze shifting between Orderic and the Baron. Walter, like Orderic, knew what this was about. Turold and Guy, the two missing men.

Damn Bertrand, thought Orderic. His men's horses were already being seen to, for God's sake! Yet they themselves must stand out here in the frozen castle yard until his brother saw fit to dismiss them. Not for the first time

Orderic wondered about his half-brother's state of mind.

Minutes passed before Bertrand de Varaville at last spoke. Even then, he did not look directly at Orderic.

"This …" he said, raising a gauntleted hand towards the timber tower at the top of the motte - the great man-made hill at the center of the castle yard - "…will one day be replaced with one of stone. A stone keep. Like those of Normandy. That day is not so far off as you might imagine, Orderic. This wooden palisade, also. It too will become a stone wall. Soon. All of this. A castle of stone. Solid, and lasting. A symbol of our power and our permanence in this country. William's kingdom. A sea of Saxons could crash against it through the ages, and still such a rock as we will build here will remain standing. Stone walls around a stone keep."

"In time, yes. Still, I expect, given that our priority here is to…" Orderic began, only to be interrupted.

"Here…yes. Here…in England. Does the prospect of that not put you in mind of the glory of that great house of God, the Confessor's West Minster?"

It did not. How could it, out here in the mud-covered grounds of a comfortless wooden castle, hastily erected on a hill overlooking the dark and freezing sea of the English south coast on one side and, on the other, an unwelcoming forested valley whose Saxon inhabitants would surely have every Norman slaughtered to a man, were they to be given the opportunity? Life was hard here, pitiless, and frequently bloody. The contemplation of current and future glories - real or imagined - did not enter into things. That was a pastime reserved exclusively for a very privileged few. Those whose lifestyle afforded them the leisure for it. Orderic had witnessed that kind of privilege all his life. Unlike his brother, however, he had not often experienced much of it. Like Bertrand, Orderic had stood beneath the vast hammer beam roof of the West Minster. That *great house of God* of which his brother now spoke. He supposed that might be considered glorious. It was certainly impressive. He too had been there when Duke William was crowned King of all England in that place on Christmas day. The difference was that Orderic had not been there as an honoured guest, among the aristocrats and senior clergy, to witness that great, possibly even glorious, moment. He had there been there only as part of the guard, his role to keep those guests safe.

He would not say any of this to Bertrand. In fact, he wasted no effort providing an answer of any kind this time, beyond giving the slightest of nods. This, he knew, being all that was required of him.

"Without doubt," continued the Baron, answering his own question, as Orderic had guessed he would. "How could it not? Even when it was built, that was a Norman church." The unmistakable stress on the word Norman. "Without doubt, a clear demonstration... in stone …you see my point?..of the fact that King Edward, devout man that he was, intended us to claim this realm upon his death. He knew it to be the will of God."

Orderic glanced at the bleached streak of sea on the horizon. Somewhere beyond it lay Normandy. Any predestined association between what was out there, and where he stood now was as inconceivable to him as it was meaningless. He could comprehend no design.

His brother had followed Orderic's gaze, misinterpreting what lay behind it.

"That's correct," Bertrand said, confirming what he imagined to be Orderic's thoughts. "These two lands ruled as one." He smiled for a moment, more to himself than at Orderic, and looked back up at the tower. "Indeed," he said, with a satisfied nod, as if whatever it was he imagined would one day be there was already in place. "God's will be done."

God's will be done. Many of those nobles who had given their support to Duke William's conquest of England had, it was true, been more readily persuaded to do so upon discovering that his plans for the invasion of the island had the blessing of Pope Alexander. No one, however, would have supposed that the potential for rewards of new land and property had not been their prime motivation. Faith, however genuine, could also be convenient. Nevertheless, Orderic believed his brother might have been the exception. Certainly, Baron de Varaville himself insisted that he was. Duke William, so it seemed, had happened to want what God also wanted. And that God wanted England to fall to the Normans was what drove the Baron to add his forces to those of the Duke. After all, when the battle finally came, with William's forces arrayed beneath the banner of St Peter the apostle, had not the outcome more than demonstrated where God's favour lay? But then again, had it not been the Duke - now King of England - not God, who rewarded Bertrand de Varaville for his support with lands in the new kingdom far exceeding those he already possessed in Normandy? God's will be done. The Duke's will be done.

And what a will that was. The power of this man. Everyone knew the tales of Duke William. They knew of what he was capable. His personality a steel-hard alloy of the base metals of ruthlessness and cruelty, with the precious metals of courage and ability. The story of his rise from being the bastard son of Robert, Duke of Normandy, to being acknowledged Duke himself was well known. His having survived numerous attempts on his life as a child after the death of his father on pilgrimage to Jerusalem. His growing into a young man capable of crushing the conspiracies of disloyal and ambitious Barons. This all contributed to the aura that William created, and that created William.

And yet, behind his back, they still called him William the Bastard. Even now, when he was a king. Whatever claims might be made about anointing with holy oil, and a rightful claim to the throne, some things remained that were beyond legitimizing. King or not, he would always be the Bastard. You could rise above illegitimacy, but you could not alter the fact of it. Orderic understood this as well as any man might. After all, was he not himself Orderic the Bastard, illegitimate son of Baron Alberic de Varaville, the father he shared with Bertrand?

A father was all they shared. That they did not share the same mother was the cause of Orderic's bastardy. Bertrand's mother was Baron Alberic's wife, the Lady Alais. This made Bertrand rightful and acknowledged heir. Whereas Orderic's mother, Elfrida, had only been a mistress to the Baron.

Worse, Elfrida had been English. A Saxon. She had been part of the household of Edward, the late English king, known as the Confessor, when as a young man he had lived in exile in Normandy. It was in Edward's service there that she had met, and become mistress to, Baron Alberic. That Alberic had cared for Elfrida, there was no doubt. He supported her in bringing up their son. Even allowed her to name him, and teach him her native language. There were limits, however. Alberic gave his bastard son only as much acknowledgment and advancement as was possible without compromising the position of his legitimate son, Bertrand.

There had not been the same obstacle for Duke William. His father had died unmarried, leaving no legitimate sons to block William's progress towards gaining what might otherwise not have been his birthright. As it was, William, whose mother had been of far humbler stock than Orderic's, was his father's designated heir. An advantage Orderic could never have been given while Bertrand was alive. Orderic was a knight, yes. A knight, though, with no land to his name. A knight in service to his half-brother Bertrand. Bertrand, who had followed on from his father as the Baron de Varaville. A title that carried with it all the lands, and the men.

The Baron looked up at the tower a moment longer then, finally, turned and looked directly at his brother.

"So, Orderic, tell me how your news has been received in the shire? Not always well, I fancy. No matter. They will come to understand once the new buildings are in place. They can see then for themselves. Tell me, did you consider many churches in need of rebuilding? I imagine so. Few of the churches I have seen since coming here have impressed me as worthy of the name. How many must be replaced?"

"Fifteen, as I judged it," said Orderic.

"Fifteen? Really? So few? Your judgement…I can trust it? It was based on the standards I stressed… of what is fitting and what is not? Or need I ride out myself?"

"Be assured, I was rigorous. Possibly too rigorous. If there was any uncertainty, I condemned. It seemed prudent to do so."

"Yes, that would be prudent. Good. Fifteen it shall be."

"The figure includes three among those that come under Menlac. Abbot Robert was not pleased to discover it. His complexion became even more crimson than it usually is when I told him what would be required. He struggled to maintain any air of godliness, that is certain. "

"That is not a matter for levity!"

"Indeed it is not, my lord. Forgive me."

There was a pause while the Baron appeared to consider the credibility of his half-brother's contrition. "Very well," he said, apparently satisfied, although his expression remained one of disapproval. "All that aside, let us get to the point, shall we? You have been wondering why I have not allowed you to dismiss your men, have you not?"

Orderic was not wondering. This was about Turold and Guy. He nodded, nevertheless.

"Tell me then, Orderic. How is it you ride in with nine, when you rode out with eleven? Ah, I see you are less inclined to humour on this matter." The Baron began walking up and down in front of the line of men. "Nine where once there were eleven. Two dead. By who's hand? Do we know?"

"We do not. Nor do we have proof that they are in fact dead. I sent them… Guy and Turold …to Gyrtun… one of the smaller settlements …barely a hamlet. It did not require all of us. They did not return."

"Killed at this Gyrtun, then." The Baron held his hands out to his sides, palms up, as if explaining the obvious. "You know what must be done. Raze the place. Slaughter the people there. All of them. And let it be widely known why!"

"But it is not certain," replied Orderic. "My lord, there were no signs found that Guy and Turold had even travelled that way. And, as I say, no actual proof that they are dead."

"So where are they? Come now. They were killed, and the bodies were hidden. Hidden, that is all. We cannot tolerate the murder of our own. Examples must be made. Punishment must be meted out."

"Consider my lord. What if they are not dead? What if we punish a crime not, in fact, committed? No killing having actually taken place."

"So? Some dead Saxons. A useful example still made. What of it? You are not softening? What with you mother being…"

"It is not that! Never that. And you know it, brother!"

The Baron raised his eyebrows.

"Have a care how you address me, *Captain*."

Orderic paused. He took a deep breath.

"I would not hesitate to raze the village were it not for the risk of the impression given should Guy and Turold prove to be alive still. Would it not then appear that we could not properly keep track of our own people, much less theirs. We must show we are in control. It is vital while we are so few, and they are so many. It's about control. We cannot lose our reputation for that. These Saxons and their endless gossip. A Norman cannot fart without a Saxon comments on the smell. We must know what has become of my men before we act. If they are dead, then yes, it doesn't matter who among these people pays for it. Nor do I care. But we must know they are dead. My lord, there is something…I don't know…something *strange* about all this. Turold and Guy are good men. Men like that do not simply disappear, nor would they allow themselves to be taken or killed without there being something to show of the struggle. Allow me to look into it further before we act."

The Baron considered for a moment, and then nodded. "I see the sense of what you say. Very well, you may take your men back out there tomorrow and… look into it, as you say. No, wait…half your men. Take half. We are under strength here as it is. Mind you bring them all back this time."

"Thank you."

"Oh, and Orderic, someone *will* pay for this, you understand. Someone must be punished. Saxon… or Norman, if it comes to it."

"Norman, my lord?"

"Guy and…eh… the other one. If they are not dead, where are they? You tell me they are good men. We shall see. You said yourself we must show we can manage our own. Oh, and dismiss your men. They look dead on their feet to me."

******

At dawn, Orderic and four of his men, all wrapped in cloaks against the cold, rode out through the gates, and crossed the wooden bridge spanning the vast ditch surrounding the outer wall of Rylemont Castle. The guards in the gate tower looked on in silence, the only sound coming from the clopping of the horses' feet on the bridge, and the occasional shrieking of seagulls overhead. It had snowed in the night, and then frozen over, so the timbers of the bridge were made glassy and treacherous. One of the horses slipped, losing its footing, whinnying and skidding across the frozen surface before steadying itself again with heavy, jarring thuds and clacks if its hooves - the noise it made, and the shouts of its rider carrying out across the valley and echoing back, mingling with the sound of the gulls. When all five riders were safely across, Orderic turned and gestured for the sentries in the tower to close the gate. Among the men watching from the wooden ramparts was Richard, a captain like Orderic. Richard and his troop must have had the guard duty the previous night. The two captains exchanged brief nods. Then Orderic turned his horse, and led his men down the track that sloped away from the castle gate, through the village at the foot of the hill, and onto the road that ran along the base of the valley, following the course of the river for most of the way, and eventually leading back into the forest beyond.

******

CHAPTER 4

Penda was far too old for journeys like this one, he decided. It was all about the bones, it seemed to him. These days the cold always reached them and settled there, no matter how many layers he wore. Right now, those same old bones were being jolted and shaken by the movement of his horse on the frozen track. He ached all over. Looking down at Agatha, he suspected the hoary old mare felt the same.

"Good girl, Aggy," he said to the horse. "Take all the time you need. Slow and steady will do just fine. You go easy on me, and I'll go easy on you. What do you say old girl, do we have a bargain? Yes? I think we do. I know we do, you and I. We understand each other, don't we? Not that far to go now."

That Eadred sent him out on small errands like this one because he wanted him to feel he was still useful was not lost on Penda. He understood it, and part of him was grateful, even if the remaining part of him was just cold and tired. Maybe the time was approaching when he should try to explain to his old friend and master that he was not up to this sort of trip anymore. Maybe next time one of the younger lads could go fetch Aelfrith when Eadred needed to talk with him.

In the weeks since two of Baron de Varaville's men had gone missing, supposedly on route to Gyrtun, Eadred had met a number of times with Aelfrith, his head man out there at the hamlet, to talk over what might be done. Both men were very aware of the possible consequences if the Baron decided the people of Gyrtun, and maybe even Elastun too, were responsible. Or even if he knew they were not, but considered an example should be made, regardless of where responsibility actually lay. In the last year entire communities had been put to the sword for less.

Entire villages burned down. Particularly in the early days when pockets of resistance to Norman rule were widespread. Not so common these days. Not here in the south, at least.

Having delivered the message to Aelfrith, who promised to join Eadred early the following morning, Penda was now looking forward to getting back to Elastun, and spending what remained of the day by the fire in Cynric the Welshman's tavern. Not long now. The river crossing was just up ahead, and not far beyond that, the turn in the path that led to home.

"Sorry, old girl," he said to Agatha when they came to the water. "I know you don't like this. Must be freezing on those old legs of yours. Come on then…Let's get it done with, eh?"

Obediently, the horse stepped into the flowing water, but walking even more slowly than she already had been.

"Quicker would be better, girl," said Penda. "Get it over with, you know? Your choice, though. Take your time if you must. It will be your old legs freezing in there, not mine."

Penda sat back, resigned to the slow pace. He couldn't find it in himself to force the animal. He glanced upstream towards the bend in the river, then down in the other direction. He wondered just how many villages depended upon this river for their water. A good many, no doubt.

"Don't shit now, Aggy, whatever you do," he said with a chuckle.

It was then that the old horse stopped abruptly, her ears pricked up and back as if something were making her nervous.

"Ouch!" cried her old rider. "That was a bit too sudden for comfort! Made my ancient bones rattle, you did! And I thought we had reached an understanding about that? Anyway, come on now, you don't want to be stopping here, old girl." Penda looked around. "There's nothing to worry you that I can see. So, let's be moving on, eh?" He urged her on again. Her feet lifted and she took two or three faltering steps, as if she might continue forward, then she stopped and would walk no more, no matter how much Penda encouraged her. "Now look, don't be daft. We need to be on our way." He sighed, gave one of the horse's ears an affectionate tug. "I've never whipped you hard, and I'm not about to start now. Eadred's a good master to me, so I should be a good one to you. But please, Aggy. Do it for me. I don't want to die of cold out here. Who would take care of you then, huh?"

The horse began backing up.

"Oh, hey now! That's the wrong way. That's even worse. What do you think are you doing? Don't be trouble. Please." The horse halted, but would still not go forward. "Aggy? *Agatha*, don't be so stubborn. Will you please just behave…? What…?" Penda finally saw what was troubling the animal. "Oh…wait, what is that?" Something large and dark was lying on the opposite bank, half in and half out of the water. "So, it's that that has you all worked up is it, old girl? Hmm? What is it, I wonder? What do you think?"

The old man's eyes were not what they once were. He squinted. It looked like some old sacking or rags clumped together. Then again it might just be a dead deer. That would be worth having if it was not too far gone. There was another, more grisly, possibility, of course. The lump was big enough, after all, even if, from what he could see, it was not quite the right shape. Once he had convinced Aggy to cross to the other side, he would take a look.

"Whatever it is, there's nothing to worry about. If it was alive once, it isn't now. But we'll go wide of it, never fear. Maybe then we'll take a look…see what it is. No, you are right. On second thoughts, just me. *I'll* take a look. Don't want you getting all jittery on me again. Mind you," he added, "if it is what I hope it is, we'll have to think about what we do with it. Sorry, Aggy. You may have a bit more weight to carry…or drag, maybe. If it's the other thing…well, there will be no hurry for that. Eadred can send someone else for it. Not for us to sort *that* out, I think you would agree."

Having allowed Aggy to back up a little more, Penda rode her forward again. This time steering her as wide of whatever it was as the width of the ford would allow. He then rode down the path a little way before halting, dismounting, and tying the horse to a tree. As he walked back towards the river, crows cawed overhead, riding the chill breeze. If it was something dead up ahead, those dark birds would soon be down here making the most of it, if they hadn't already.

From this side of the river it was difficult to see anything. The half of the thing lying out of the water was obscured beyond a bramble covered hummock. Penda stepped to the water's edge and leaned forward, looking around the brambles, trying to get a better look at the half still in the water. The bend of the bank meant almost nothing was visible from this angle. For a moment he considered stepping into the water, wading around. He bent, testing the temperature with his old fingers. Absolutely not! Far too cold. He shivered at the thought, then stepped back, looked again at the tangle of brambles. So it would have to be through that way then. No other choice. Pulling out the small knife he wore at his belt - its blade little more than a stump, and nothing that would bother the Normans if they saw him with it - Penda walked over to a nearby sapling and cut off a branch. Returning to the hummock, he began to thrash at the brambles. When he had cleared enough, he stepped up and looked over the edge.

What he saw confused him at first. The thing was difficult to understand, even as close as this. It was shapeless, with bulges, dips, and knots like a large, misshapen grain sack. The edges were ragged and torn. But it wasn't a sack. The textures were wrong for that. It was smooth in places, coarser in others. Generally, it was various shades of grey with splashes of rusty brown. In places, though, it appeared blackened, scorched. He pulled away the last of the brambles, sought out a safe footing, and leaned in closer. Was there a pattern to some of the surface? To the greyer areas in particular? A pattern he was familiar with. Chain mail? Penda rubbed his old eyes. Looked again. Yes, definitely chain mail. Once he understood this, making sense of the rest of it came more easily. It was what was left of a man. A man in chain mail. A soldier. Of course! This must be what was left of one of the Baron's missing men. Had to be. As soon as he got back to Elastun, Penda would go straight to Eadred and let him know what he had found here. Odd that nobody had seen it before. The body must have washed down from somewhere upriver, got snagged up on this bend.

Penda's brows wrinkled as he squinted down at the body. "God save us," he mumbled, "what happened to you?"

Penda had not lived to be as old as he was without seeing his share of the dead. But this? The man was knotted up like a discarded corn dolly! His limbs were twisted inward, the bones snapped and turned at unnatural angles. A bare foot showed just above the water line, hanging down from the slightly raised ankle at an impossible slant, the bones splintered at the joint, no longer able to support it. Wrapped around the centre of the heap - what had to be the torso - was an arm in a horrid parody of an embrace, as if the dead man were trying to comfort himself in his own suffering. The fingers on the hand were merely stumps, the remaining flesh a sickeningly pale grey, almost white, as if there were no blood left in it. Also, it seemed to Penda as if the man had been burnt in places. Odd, localised, patches of it. This man been tortured before he died.

Penda knew it was wrong of him, ghoulish even, but for

some reason he felt he must see this poor man's face. His old eyes sought out, and soon found, the lump most in size and shape like a head. Yes, it had to be. There, just below the surface. Face down, still clad in the mail, and set at an angle as unnatural as the rest of the dead man's limbs. Penda squatted, used the branch he had cut to steady himself, and reached forward. He could not get a good enough hold with only one hand. He would have to let go of his branch. Reaching forward with both arms now, he cupped the head in both hands and lifted. Just an inch or two at first. Just to see if it would budge. As he had expected, it was heavy, with the weight and pull of the chain mail adding to the difficulty. Turning it sufficiently to see the face would require more of an effort. He had second thoughts for a moment. Then the compulsion to see returned, and Penda leaned in again, bent his old knees, braced himself as best he could, and pulled. Harder this time. When the weight finally shifted, and the head turned around to face him, Penda gasped, and dropped it. Recoiling at what he saw, he almost lost his balance. Most of what was left of the face, like the rest of the flesh, was a stomach-turning pale grey. The skin surrounding the eyes, which were sunken and closed, was much darker, almost black. The mouth, which was open, revealing the remnants of smashed teeth, drooled river water, now stained a reddish brown, as the head lolled back. The same liquid ran from holes where the nostrils had once been.

What he saw filled Penda with a mixture of revulsion and pity. The features of the face were pulled into what was, unmistakeably, an expression of utter agony. What on God's earth had this wretched man gone through before he died? What had he been made to suffer? Even a Norman should not have to…

The eyes opened, bloodshot, tormented. The lips drew back, the remaining stump of tongue twitched, then waggled slightly in the mouth, before it let out a half-choked sob of anguish.

Penda cried out. Slipped. Even in that briefest of moments he had time to realise that the river here was too shallow. The water would do nothing to break his fall. On impulse he put out an arm to stop himself. A mistake. He hit the riverbed with an agonising snap as his wrist fractured. *It was all about the bones.* He opened his mouth to cry out in pain, but only managed a high pitch gurgle as the freezing water filled his mouth. Rolling over, he put his hands out to right himself, and stand up out of the water. Another mistake. His right wrist would not respond as it should. It gave, with another excruciating pulse of pain, and he slumped back down into the icy flow. He tried again with the same result. He cursed his stupidity for making a second attempt. The shock of the cold and the pain must be affecting his capacity to think clearly. He knew he must get out of the water right now or he never would. He rolled over, and struggled up onto his knees, then tried to get himself up onto his feet without using his right arm. He could not manage it somehow. Kneeling there in the water, he began to sob. Panic was setting in.

"Enough!" he shouted at himself. "Think, you old fool! Think! You are on your knees, aren't you? So…"

Still on his knees, and shivering uncontrollably, he began to shuffle towards the bank, dragging each knee forward, one after the other. One small, juddering movement at a time. His thigh muscles ached with the effort. Once or twice he feared the force of the current might be enough to topple him. If that happened, he doubted he would have the necessary strength remaining to pull himself up again. Before he even died of the cold, he would drown in water shallow enough to stand up in. It struck him as odd that, even now, exhausted and in fear for his very his life, the humiliation of the whole thing troubled him almost as much as the danger itself. Eventually, however, after what may only have been a few minutes, but seemed much longer to Penda, he was near enough to allow his own weight to carry him forward onto the bank. Unable to prevent himself landing on his smashed wrist, he yelped in agony, rolled over onto his back, and cradled it in his other hand. But he was out of the water, thank God! He closed his eyes, allowing himself to rest a moment while the pain subsided. Only a moment, though. He was still far from out of danger. Although he had escaped the possibility of drowning, he could still freeze to death out here. If he could just reach a tree. Use it to haul himself up. Get to Aggy. He might yet make it back to the village.

He opened his eyes, looked up. Saw the mesh of tree branches overhead, shifting in the wind. Beyond them the empty grey sky. No, not empty. Flitting back and forth across that sky, the black shapes of crows. Wicked, unnatural, creatures. They might have a second body to feed on if things went badly for him. Out here. In this, dreadful, lonely place.

"Rest a moment," he said to himself. "Get your strength back, old fool. Yes, I will. Maybe close my eyes again. Only for moment, though. Only for a moment."

The other eyes had opened. The eyes on the face of a man who could not possibly be alive had opened.

Penda sat up. He would not stay here a moment more than he had to. He turned over onto his side. Then over onto his knees and elbows. His right hand hung lifeless from his wrist. The pain throbbing, but steady now. Bearable.

"Get it done, old fool!"

This time, without the added problem of the buffeting water, he did manage to stand up. Just. He nearly fell. Steadied himself. Then staggered down the track towards Aggy. Getting back up onto her was not going to be possible. He knew that, and was not going to waste time trying. Even so, she was warm, and she would support him.

******

"Will he live?"

For a moment Alditha misunderstood Eadred's question, and thought it odd. How could she possibly say if the Norman soldier would live or not until she had seen him, and knew the true nature of his wounds? When, eventually, he had been brought back to the village, Penda had spoken of coming across what he believed to be one of the Baron's men while riding back from Gyrtun. He claimed the man's injuries had been so terrible he should have been dead. Yet, by some means Penda could not comprehend, the man was still alive when he found him. So, once Alditha had tended to Penda, who was himself in a very bad way, Eadred had insisted she accompany him to the place where the old man claimed to have found the injured Norman. She would be needed there. Since the death of her mother, Alditha was now the village healer - the art passed down through generations of women in her family - and if there were any prospect that the man could be saved, everything must be done to help him as soon as possible. The villages of Elastun and Gyrtun might yet escape the Baron's retribution if the truth of what happened to his men were to be established. Even if the man died, the fact of their having done all that they could have to help him might count for something in the Baron's eyes. So, despite it being late at night, Alditha found herself riding through the darkness of the forest, on the path to Gyrtun, in the company of Eadred and two other men from her village, Swein and Alfred.

After Eadred, Swein was the next most senior man in Elastun. He had been a close friend of Eadred's son and, like him, had ridden out to fight against the Normans the previous year. A strong, proud man, he had survived the wound that had left him permanently lame, a wound that would have killed some men. He had not coped so well with the shame of surviving. Injured in the battle, he had been carried to the back, so had not been there when the Housecarls made their last stand. There were some things for which Alditha's healing arts had no remedy. In Swein's case, she thought, not even time would do much to help him.

The other man was the village blacksmith, Alfred. It had been he who discovered Penda, and brought him back to the village.

"Alditha. Will he live?" Eadred asked her again. "I am to blame. I should not have sent him. He is not as strong as he once was." She understood now that Eadred was asking about Penda.

The light was already fading, and it was beginning to snow when Agatha had wandered into the village without her rider. Alfred had recognised the horse immediately. Assuming Penda must have fallen off somewhere back down the track, he had ridden off in search of him, having first sent his boy with a message for Eadred. The old servant was lying unconscious on the track about half a mile from the village when the blacksmith found him, his damp garments beginning to freeze, and his prone figure already gathering a dusting of snowflakes. Alfred had thrown him over his horse and hurried back to the village. Nearing the outskirts he was met by Eadred coming the other way. Alditha had been preparing for bed when Eadred and the blacksmith called at her house, and between them carried in the old man. He had regained consciousness for a time, and it was then that he had told them about finding the Norman at the ford. It might have been taken as a product of his fever were he not so insistent that it was true, and apparently lucid, when he told them.

"It is as you say, Eadred," replied Alditha. "Penda is not as strong as he once was. He was freezing when you brought him to me. Most likely close to death already had Alfred not found him when he did. His fever is very high."

Eadred nodded. "I am to blame," he said again.

"Though not so strong, nor is he as frail as he might be. His wrist will mend, given time. The fever is the real worry," said Alditha, then added, "Still, there is always hope. I believe we will know for certain by daybreak." But she already knew. Penda would not be alive come the following morning.

Eadred sighed, looked away. "Daybreak, then," he said, more to himself than to Alditha.

"So, how far is it now?" Alditha asked.

"Huh?" Eadred turned back to her.

"How far until our path crosses the river…the ford there... where Penda says he found this man?"

"Not long. It's just up ahead now. If he is there, that is. If he is one of the Baron's men."

"You still doubt Penda?"

"I do not know. I doubt the man still lives, whatever Penda may have claimed."

"If he is in the water still, and has been after all this time, then he is past my help. The cold alone…That length of time… Nobody could survive."

"I know it," agreed Eadred. "At least we may swear to the Baron that we rode out as soon as we knew. If he is dead… and I too believe he will be… we will, if nothing else, have the corpse to show the Baron's men when they return. Which they will."

"What is to stop them saying we killed him?"

"You imagine I don't know there is that risk, Alditha? We will most likely be held answerable either way. Body or no body. Our only sure defence against an accusation of involvement in the disappearance of the two riders would be if this one lives, and can tell the truth of what happened to him. And there is no hope of that. We ride to the aid of a dead man. A corpse, nothing more." He sighed again. "And yet…Perhaps the corpse may tell us something of what befell him. If it does, we show the Baron's man. Besides, if we were to blame, why would we produce it if it could point to our guilt in the matter? He must understand that much."

"*The Baron's man.* We venture a great deal on what the *Baron's man* does or does not understand," said Alditha.

"Orderic," said Eadred. "It will be him that is sent. The missing men were among his party. At least he is the cleverest of them."

"Orderic? You think him clever?"

"He is who I would send if I were the Baron. We must share what the corpse tells us with him. If there is one with wit enough to understand, it is him. "

"Wit enough to interpret the facts to suit his purpose too!"

"Perhaps so, but this body is all we have. We must make the most of it."

"Perhaps," said Alditha.

"*Perhaps* is all we have right now. Ah, there we are, up ahead…the river. There it is."

Swein, riding at the head of the group, carried a torch. The way would have been clear even without it as the moon was bright, and the path white with the fresh snow. Alditha had demanded they bring light, nevertheless. It would be necessary if she were to see enough to tend the man's wounds. As they drew nearer to the water, the flames from Swein's torch were reflected back from the surface.

"Light the other torch," ordered Eadred. "Quickly, now! If he is here we must find him. Half in the water… Penda said he was half in the water. Look along the edge there."

The search did not take long.

"Damn!" cried Alfred, staggering back, a hand over his mouth. "He's over here. Wasn't sure at first. Then I moved some of the snow …The smell of the poor bastard…urgh!"

Eadred went over, grabbed the torch from Alfred's hand, and held it over the body. He crouched down and brushed what remained of the snow from the half not in the water. He did not cry out like the blacksmith, but when he spoke, his voice was deliberate, controlled. "Penda was mistaken," he said. "He had to be. It was the fever talking. It could not have been otherwise. This man cannot have survived. Not like that. Been dead for several days to judge from the look of him. You should be glad it is cold, Alfred. The smell could have been worse than it is." He stood up. "You will not be needed here, Alditha."

"You are certain of that?"

"Come see... if you must."

Alditha could not supress a small cry when she looked. Even though the shifting shadows cast by the flames of the torch, and the play of light on the flowing water lent the scene a superficial sense of movement, there was no doubting the stillness of the dead man's twisted and broken remains. He was dead, and that was a blessing. The pain he must have endured beforehand was unimaginable.

"As I said. Nothing you can do for this man."

"Pray for him?" suggested Alditha, knowing immediately she had said it that Eadred would object.

"Do you think any of his kind prayed over my son, or your husband, my grandson?"

"What can do that to a man?" asked Alfred, his question breaking the tension between Eadred and Alditha. "What twists a man up like that? Something twisted and snapped him. Seared him too, it looked like. Melted the chain mail right onto him. I'm a blacksmith, I know about fire and heat, and what it can do."

"No single man, that much is certain," said Eadred. "Whoever did this..."

"Or *wha*tever," interrupted Alfred.

Eadred turned on the blacksmith. "What are you talking about? What do you mean by that?"

"I'm just saying...It seems to me dark magic might be at work here."

"Dark magic? Nonsense, Alfred! We'll have none of

that, understand me?"

"But you can't deny…"

"It is not so difficult to imagine how this could be done. What I was saying was that whoever did this..*who*ever… worked in a group. Once you have three or four men determined to do it, then it is more than possible. Overpower him, hold him down over something hard…an anvil perhaps, and you can burn and break his limbs like…well, a blacksmith working metal. You said it yourself."

Swein was now holding his torch over the body. Having examined it for a moment he nodded his head, then re-joined the others. "What Eadred says it correct, Alfred. With assistance, and the right tools, I believe it would be possible to do this to a man."

"And the will," added Eadred. "You would need the will to do it. That is what does make this out of the ordinary. Somebody possessed the will."

"The will to do it? The man is a Norman, damn it!" exclaimed Swein. "How much provocation is needed beyond that?"

"I understand the provocation, Swein! You know that I do! We all do. That's not what I meant. The will I'm referring to is not the will for revenge. I'm talking about the will to do something quite so extraordinarily elaborate to exact that revenge. Something like this would have taken considerable determination. Seclusion too. This man would not have died quietly. And time... They would have needed time. Why not simply kill him quickly and get away fast?"

"*Revenge*, for heaven's sake!" said Swein, as if it were obvious, and sufficient to answer any questions. "You said it yourself."

"You are not listening to me, Swein," replied Eadred, becoming irritated. "He's a Norman, so make the wretch suffer. Take revenge. I understand all that. Naturally I do. But still I ask, why all this…? This was too much… Far too much." Sensing Swein about make the same point once again, Eadred held up a hand to silence him. "I mean too much to remain secure from discovery. A swift kill is always better. Less chance of discovery. Fewer indications left behind of who might be responsible." Eadred raised his torch and looked about. "And why was the body brought all the way out here?"

"It was not done out here, then?" asked Alfred.

"No, definitely not."

"How can you know that?"

"Not possible that it could have been," said Eadred.

"Why not?"

"Eadred is right, Alfred," said Alditha. "Just look about you."

Alfred shook his head. "I don't…"

"Think about it, man!" said Swein. "There would have been tracks. Signs of a struggle, perhaps. Most of all, there would be blood. A lake of it. Do you see any trace? A drop of it, even? You imagine you can do something like this to a man without spilling his blood? You cut a man open like that…it gets everywhere. Blood… and worse."

"There is fresh snow on the ground," objected Alfred.

"Not enough yet to hide the signs of something like that," said Eadred. "Not if you know what to look for. Besides, by the look of the flesh on him…what there is of it…this was done some time ago… *Days* ago in my opinion…And still he was not found until today? Not possible that he could have lain out here all this time and not have been found before now. No, this was done somewhere else. Then he was brought here. To a river crossing, of all places. He was meant to be found. Just not until now."

"What about what Penda said…about him still being alive?" asked Alfred.

"I told you, it was the fever in Penda talking. This man could not possibly have lived so long."

"He seemed so certain. The man opened his eyes, he said. Why would Penda say that if it were not true? I don't understand. Why would he lie about something like that?"

"The fever, damn it!" said Eadred.

"I am not trying to anger you, Eadred. It's just he did not strike me as being confused when he said it. And the old man never was a storyteller. No. Penda, a liar? I won't have it said of the old man!"

"Look again, Alfred. If your stomach is up to it. Tell me if you still believe that wreck of a man could have opened its eyes any time in the last few days." Eadred frowned, studied the blacksmith. "Or is it that you are still looking for the involvement of the black arts in this?"

"Listen, Alfred," said Alditha. "Penda was not being dishonest. None of us think that of him. What he told us was what he believed to be true. But he was mistaken, confused. A fever can make a person see things, and then repeat them in a way that makes them seem quite credible. Seem true. And yet they are not. You know that, Alfred. Penda is unwell."

"He is my friend," said Alfred.

"He is mine too," said Eadred, his tone now softened.

"There is another possibility," said Alditha. "A person can be dead before all of the body quite knows it. What I mean is that sometimes a body does not die all at once. Limbs twitch, chests give out breath. You've seen it with the slaughter of animals, haven't you? It's possible something of life remained in the eyelids. Some trace that Penda witnessed being spent for the last time. It is just possible."

"What Alditha says is true," agreed Swein. "I've seen as much on the battlefield."

"No magic there, Alfred," said Eadred. "All wrought by human hand. Just as what we found here has been. You understand?"

The blacksmith nodded. "Forgive me, Eadred."

"Come, Alfred" said Alditha, taking him by the arm. "Escort me back to the village, would you please? I want to look in on Penda. And I definitely do not wish to ride back through this dark forest alone. I'm sure Eadred and Swein can fetch the corpse back without your help. Isn't that so, Eadred?"

******

"Will you succeed where your companion failed, I wonder? I promise you will know as much pain as he did before we discover which it will be. Perhaps more of it. Such pain. You heard him for yourself. You know I speak the truth. Was it worse not seeing, I wonder? Only hearing? Imagining? I think so. You see, more than pain, you will know fear. Such fear. That is where we discover your quality, after all. Oh, don't trouble to tell me you are a warrior, and you have known both fear and pain before now. Your companion believed the same. I know you have stood among the torn and the smashed on the battlefield. Some of them brought to that state by your very own hand. You have stood there. You have breathed in the mud, blood, urine, ordure stench. Stood among the dead and dying. Some you called your companions, some your enemies – however it is that men choose to define these things. I know you have known this. How? Perhaps I have watched you there? But this is different. This is something else entirely. Take my word for it.

And yet you remain determined to show me how courageous you can be. That is what you tell yourself. But how is it that you can still cling to this impossible notion in the face of all you know to be true? All you just heard your companion endure? Despite the shaking of your limbs, and your fear soiled garments, still you persist in making your quivering, trembling attempts at curses. Inside you still counsel yourself to master your fear. I hear it even now, master your fear, master your fear, master your fear. I hear it, even above your heartbeat. And your heart hammers does it not? The thundering hooves of a warhorse. Charging or retreating, I wonder? And those sudden, quivering breathes rising from chest to throat. Despite all this, you will master your fear? Die with honour?

Die with honour. What can that really mean? Can it truly be done? In those battles you are so proud to have taken part in, tell me, what was the worst part? The part that you cannot reconcile to the songs and stories of heroic deeds. Was it not the screaming, and the pitiful, infantile crying of men who moments earlier were as strong and as bold as any there? That's never in the tales told, now is it? Ah, but you will be different. You Turold – yes I know your name – will face it all valiantly. Never a scream. Well, perhaps a scream or two, let us not ask too much. But no sobbing, no whimpering. And never, never begging for mercy. What do we think about cursing, though? Yes, cursing, that's good. Cursing it shall be then. A death with honour then. Oh, but wait now. Surely such a death needs to be known to the world before it can be honourable? Honour is not what you take with you, it is what you leave behind. To be judged by others as honourable or not - however it is men choose to define these things – it surely requires to be known? Do you see the problem? Who will know how you face your death but you? Death with honour has no meaning here, Turold.

You may remember, however, how I began. I questioned whether you might succeed where Guy failed. Have you asked yourself what this can mean? You may yet discover. You must prove yourself worthy to me first. Which brings us to the matter in hand. How shall it be described? A journey to the depths of your despair?"

******

CHAPTER 5

Eadwig was not the first to see the riders this time. The village of Elastun knew to expect their return, so had set men in the forest to await them, and run back to the village with warning. There was no opportunity to sneak out early with Gra and go hunting either. His grandfather had made it plain that, until the business of the missing men was done with, nobody was to leave the village without coming to him for permission beforehand - least of all young boys who should know better. Making this rule known to the assembled villagers in the great hall, Eadred had stressed the word *nobody* and, it had seemed to Eadwig, looked directly at him. His grandfather was not a cruel man, but Eadwig knew he would get a whipping if he disobeyed this time. Besides, the truth was, he was not as inclined to disobey as he might once have been.

At first, he and his friends had been excited by the sense of things happening. Things the adults were taking care not to talk about in their hearing were nearly always the most interesting things to hear. Knowing his grandfather would not say more - and would more than likely box his ears for asking - Eadwig had gone to his mother for an explanation. There was talk of a pack of wolves in the valley, she had said. They were coming closer in to the villages than was their usual habit. Perhaps that was what was worrying her father-in-law? Could the missing Normans have fallen prey to the wolves?

Eadwig could not tell if his mother was sincere or merely telling him something she thought would satisfy his curiosity. Either way, he knew better. He had already heard the rumours about the wolves in the forest. They had been going about for weeks now, but this was some fresh cause for concern. Besides, tales of wolves killing humans were just that, tales. He had never heard of anyone actually being attacked, let alone killed. His grandmother had once told him the story of how a wolf had carried off a child from the village where she grew up, but Eadwig had never believed it to be true. Eventually, however, Eadwig's curiosity was to be satisfied a little more that he might have wished.

It was not intended that anyone other than the more senior men of the village should see what his grandfather and Swein had carried back with them to the village that night. However, Eadwig had been awakened by his grandfather's return, and had got up out of bed to investigate. What could be happening at so late an hour? He heard voices outside. Although they were lowered, Eadwig easily recognized one as that of his grandfather. Oddly, instead of bringing his companions into the hall to get warm, as Eadwig had expected he would, his grandfather seemed to be leading them around the side of the building. A blanket around his shoulders, Eadwig had crept out, wincing a little as his bare feet sank into the cold snow. He could see from the light of the torches that something had been placed on a table in one of the small storage buildings at the rear of the great hall. It was wrapped, and was now being packed with salt from the meat store. Eadwig could not make out what it was at first. It was not shaped like a man, after all. Then, when a pale grey foot slipped out from beneath the wrappings, he was in no doubt about what the men had brought back with them.

All of a sudden he was no longer enjoying his little adventure, and was anxious to get back to the safety and warmth of his bed. He crept back inside before he was observed, but the next morning his grandfather stopped him.

"I tracked an animal last night, young Eadwig. A small one, to judge by the look of the tracks. And a foolish one."

"What do you mean, Grandfather?"

"Oh, I think you understand me very well."

"No, I…"

"Let me stop you before you tell me any lies. Footprints in the snow, boy! You should be more careful if you are going to spy on people. You left your tracks. What did you see? Tell me, boy."

"I'm sorry, I came out to greet you, that's all…Then I saw you had gone around to the back."

"You followed us?"

"Yes, only then I got cold and went inside again."

"Before that…did you see anything you should not have done?"

"No. Nothing. You were there. Swein too, I think. And some other men. I don't know what you were all doing. I don't think I really want to know."

His grandfather looked him up and down for a moment. Then he nodded.

"The first wise thing you've said so far. Now, get out of my sight."

Now the riders were back. Fewer this time. He'd counted only five. Still led by the tall man, Orderic. Also still among their number, Eadwig noted, was Walter. The one everyone had told such tales about. The one everyone was fearful of. The Bear. The one with whom he, Eadwig, had spoken. He had bragged about this to his friends, although never within the hearing of his grandfather who would not, he knew, approve of such talk.

******

"This is it?"

"It is, yes."

Orderic stepped forward and lifted the covering. It took him a few moments to trace the contours of the twisted form, and to fully appreciate that he was indeed looking at the body of a man. Careful to conceal the revulsion he felt from those watching, he leaned over and turned the head so the face was visible. Although the salt and the coldness of the weather had helped preserve the man's remains, death and the beginning of decay had still distorted the features sufficiently to make identification difficult. Orderic turned to Walter.

"Could this be Guy?" Orderic asked. "Too small to be Turold."

"Too small to be anyone now," replied Walter.

"He's wearing mail. What's left of him is, at any rate. And that hair there…it's Guy's colour, isn't it?"

Walter cocked his head, studied the dead features. "True, the hair and whiskers do have about them some of his redness," he said. There was a pause while Walter took a closer look. "Ah…now… wait a moment…if this is…" He reached forward and tugged at what looked to be a length of leather belt. There was a nauseating sucking as the leather ripped free of something it must have been caught around. Walter held it up, pointed to something hanging from it. "You see that? The remains of the scabbard there. The fancy pattern is familiar, is it not? Yes, that thing belonged to Guy alright. Without doubt. Personally, I always hated the damn thing. So, yes then, it's him. It's Guy. Has to be. There cannot have been *two* scabbards quite as ugly as that in the world."

Walter turned to Eadred and Swein. "Who did this?" He stepped towards the two Saxons, his hand wrapping around the hilt of his sword. "You *will* tell me!"

Despite the attempt at intimidation, both men stood their ground.

"We know no more than we have already told you," said Eadred firmly. "It was found by one of my servants on the way back from delivering a message to Aelfrith of Gyrtun. Up by the ford on the path there. Cut me down if you must. I cannot tell you what I do not know."

"No need for that just yet," said Orderic, putting a restraining hand on Walter's arm. "No need at all if you can convince me you speak the truth. For the present, at least, I shall assume you do. In which case, I would ask this. Why was the body not found sooner?"

"Yes," agreed Walter. "I rode that path myself after Guy and Turold did not return. If it was at the ford as you claim, surely I could not have failed to see it. We searched all along that route and found nothing. Nothing. Now you tell me, Saxon, how is that possible?"

"We believe it was placed there later," said Eadred.

"*Placed* there?" scoffed Walter.

"We too had searched and travelled that route many times without discovering anything. It was not found until Penda, my servant, came across it on his return from Gyrtun. Even then, he did not see it as he passed by on the journey there. Only on his return did he find it."

"I would speak with this Penda," said Orderic.

"I regret to say that will not be possible. He is dead."

"Dead? How is that?"

"He suffered a fall. In this cold weather…He was an old man, no longer strong. By the time he was brought back he had caught a fever from which he did not recover. His death is…"

"Inconvenient," said Orderic.

"Or convenient, maybe? For these people, at any rate," added Walter.

"I was going to say his death is a great loss," said Eadred, struggling to control his anger. "Penda was an old friend."

"We do not make friends of our servants," said Walter.

"You say he fell," said Orderic. "So, it was not then he who brought the body back here?"

"No, he brought us the news of his discovery. He was able to tell us that much before he died. It was Swein and I who carried it back. We took the necessary assistance with us of course…In case there was hope, I mean. Alditha, she has the gift of healing. If there had been any hope for your man's survival…"

"Why in God's name would you think there might be? Look at him! This Penda, did he not describe to you what he found? I find it very difficult to believe that anyone discovering a body in a state such as this one is in could possibly have failed to mention its condition!"

"He did, of course. But…just the same… we thought it prudent. We did everything we could. That's all I am trying to tell you."

"For a dead man?"

Eadred did not reply.

"For a dead man," repeated Orderic. This time he sensed that something passed between the two Saxons. The faintest of looks.

"There is something else? Something you have not told me. You…Swein, is it? What is Eadred not telling me?" Again the two Saxons appeared to exchange glances. "Don't look at him. It is I who am asking you. What else is there I should know?"

Swein remained silent.

"When the captain asks you a question, you answer!" growled Walter.

Swein drew himself up, as if readying himself for a blow. He glared defiance.

"You should know I always look forward to adding another to the number of Saxons I have killed," said Walter.

"Much as would I to adding to my number of Normans," replied Swein.

"It was a Norman who left you a cripple, was it not? On that great day. The day we broke your precious shield wall."

"Stop this! It is not called for. I will speak," said Eadred, stepping between them. "Orderic, I ask that you forgive Swein. He is a proud warrior. You of all people must understand that. He did not speak because I had forbidden him to do so. He was obeying my instruction. You understand that, I am sure."

Orderic thought for a moment.

"Very well. Nonetheless *he* must be the one to speak, not you. I wish *him* to tell me. So, Swein..."

Eadred nodded. "Tell him. You must."

Swein drew a breath, exchanged angry glances with Walter, then turned and addressed Orderic.

"He told us...Penda, that is...He told us that your man was alive when he found him."

"Alive?"

"He said the man opened his eyes. We had no reason to think Penda would lie about such a thing. Only when we saw the state of the body did we fully understand how absurd this claim was."

"Come now, it was his fever. The servant was confused. That is all," said Orderic.

"That was our conclusion," said Eadred. "We did not mention it, simply because it seemed unimportant."

"Unimportant."

"Yes."

"I can see that. I can understand that. What I don't understand is why then, when we asked, you were so anxious to avoid telling us. Why would that be? Particularly if it was, to use your own word again, *unimportant.* Why not simply tell us? Why hold back, even when we pressed you? Why not just... Ah, I have it. Because if he *were* alive, if he *were* able open his eyes, he could not, at the point Penda found him, possibly have sustained anything close to the degree of injuries he now displays. Which would suggest, would it not, a second set inflicted subsequently? He was in no state to defend himself, so advantage was taken, and this done to him."

"Not done by us," insisted Eadred. "He was like this when we found him. If our intention had been to finish him off, why bring along Alditha?"

"Ah yes, Alditha. Where is that young woman? Bring her to me. No, wait. Bring *me* to *her.* Let's not give you the opportunity to warn her. I want to hear her tell her story without the benefit of your instruction."

"Of course. Although, I cannot say with any certainty where she will be at this moment. However, she is often to be found in the church."

"She will not be gathered in the hall with the others?"

"No," sighed Eadred. "The girl will not be there."

"Despite having been warned of our approach?"

Eadred shrugged. "She does not feel the need… Alfred might serve your purpose in her place. He, I do know, will be in the hall."

"Alfred? I ask for Alditha. I am offered Alfred."

"The blacksmith. He also accompanied us. As I recall, it was Alfred who was first among us to see the body."

"This Alfred, he is also a healer?" Orderic asked, the sarcasm of the question obvious. "Tender work for the rough hands of a blacksmith."

"No, I merely thought he could answer your questions as easily as Alditha."

"We may yet come to this Alfred. It is Alditha I wish to question right now. She is in the village?"

"Naturally. Nobody can leave without my permission. She will be here somewhere. We will have to search, however."

"Then we search. Come Eadred. I believe you said the church was a likely place. Let us visit there first. Just you and I, mind you. The rest of you will remain here. No one is to move from this spot until I return. Oh, and Walter, Swein…if the pair of you could make an effort to avoid killing one another in my absence, I would be very grateful."

Walter laughed at Orderic's parting remark. Swein did not.

******

Alditha was in the church as Eadred had predicted. Since

the news that is was to be taken down and replaced, she found herself even more drawn to the building than she already had been. She was sitting on her usual bench, absent mindedly stroking a black and white cat resting in her lap when Orderic strode through the doorway, followed by Eadred. She rose to her feet, spilling the disgruntled animal to the floor. It ran off, keeping low to the ground and close to walls, avoiding the two men, eventually scurrying out through the door.

"Does that creature really belong in the house of God?" asked Orderic.

Alditha had known the Baron's men were in the village, and had hoped to avoid encountering them. She made no effort to disguise the bitterness and disappointment in her voice when she replied. "The cat? Why not? *She* is welcome here. *She* has a useful purpose here, after all."

"Useful?"

"It was God's will that she be a hunter. Matilda keeps the vermin out of His house....The smaller ones, at least..."

Orderic said nothing for a moment. His face remained expressionless. He would not allow this vexing woman to see how her constant foolhardiness puzzled him. The name of the cat was, without question, not Matilda. It was, however, the name of Duke William's beloved wife.

Behind Orderic, Eadred was anxiously shaking his head at Alditha. She ignored him.

"So, she keeps out the vermin, does she?" Orderic said at last. "Yes...well...we tolerate cats for that same reason where I come from... of course we do. Tolerate them. Not coddle them like infants. Or *name* them. I advise you against it in future. I find your affection for the animal a little unwholesome. Then again, I suppose it may be fitting for you and the creature to share a bond of affection for one another. I suggest that it is not the only thing you share."

Alditha raised her eyebrows inquiringly.

"What I suggest," Orderic continued, "is that you are little better than that cat when it comes to concealing your emotions. She was a little more direct, that is all. But you also do not enjoy my company. In fact, I think you may be even more anxious than that animal was to escape from my presence. Unfortunately, I cannot allow that just yet." He turned to Eadred. "You, however, may go."

"But…"

"Leave us."

When Eadred was gone, Orderic gestured for Alditha to resume her place on the bench. Then he himself sat down on a bench against the opposite wall, so they now faced each other across the floor of the church.

"Well now," said Orderic, "here we both are again. Although this must surely be an improvement on your having to pretend to clean the place like the last time we were both in here."

Alditha shrugged.

"I believe you would have wielded that broom like one of your English battle-axes that day were you to have had your way," said Orderic, a smile Alditha found infuriating playing across his lips. She shrugged again. "You go from saying too much, to saying nothing at all," said Orderic. "I do require some few words to be spoken out loud in order to answer some questions I will put to you. That done, you may be as silent or as outspoken as you please when I am gone. Silent prayers to the Lord that I fall from my horse and split my head, or curse me by name out loud. Just as it pleases you. Right now, though, I will have my answers."

"Very well," replied Alditha, her voice little more than a whisper.

"Good. You must speak up, however. I do not wish to strain my ears trying to catch your replies to my questions. Besides, if you continue to hiss in that fashion Eadred, who I'll wager is at this very moment stood just out of sight beyond the entrance there, will not be able to hear. Have some pity on the old man if not for me."

Alditha cleared her throat, lifted her head, and looked Orderic in the eye. "Very well. What would you have me tell you?"

"About your involvement in the discovery of my man Guy's body. And the events leading up to it."

"*Your* man? Surely he was Baron de Varaville's man if he was anybody's?" Alditha could see from Orderic's face that this remark had provoked the Norman more than anything she had said or done so far. She was unable to resist pressing her advantage. "Is that not so? The *Baron's* man."

Orderic's hands, until that moment resting at his sides on the bench, now came up and gripped his knees. He leaned towards her as if to say something then, seeming to think better of it, sat back.

"Now it is you who are silent," said Alditha, deliberately goading him.

"No, not silent. Restrained. A lesson you would do well to learn, Alditha. Whatever you may wish, brooms are not axes. My sword, on the other hand, is just that."

They stared at each other for a moment. Then the attention of both was caught by the slightest of movements outside. Eadred's shadow shifting on the ground beyond the open doorway.

"Very well, I will answer your questions," said Alditha. "It was late when they brought Penda to me. It was he who had found the body. But I am confident you have been told this already?"

"Never mind what I have or have not been told already. Continue."

"Penda was feverish, but he managed to tell us where the body lay."

"The *body*. Not the *man*. Dead then?" asked Orderic.

"Well, I cannot say. It was odd, but Penda was

adamant that the man was alive when he left him. He said his wounds were so severe that he should not be …But still he lived."

"How could he tell? How did it show?"

"The man…Guy, you say?"

"Guy."

"Well, Penda insisted he had opened his eyes. Looked right at him, he said. I would not have been asked to go with them…Eadred and the others…where it not for that. Penda seemed so sure, you see? I don't think any of us really believed it could be true…not as badly hurt as Penda said the man was. But Eadred said we must do all we can. We had to try. He said you would need to be assured that we had."

"Wise of him."

"That's why I went with them. From what Penda had described I couldn't imagine what I could possibly do to save your man. Still, Eadred said it was…." She paused, uncertain, glancing in the direction of the door.

"Was what? What did Eadred say?"

Before Alditha could answer, Eadred appeared at the doorway.

"I said it was not about saving your man, but saving us."

"Wise of you again," said Orderic.

"We did not do that to him," said Alditha. "You must believe that!"

Orderic ignored her, stood up.

"You heard all of that?" he asked Eadred.

"I heard enough. Not all of it, I can assure you."

"No, you cannot. You heard. It is well that you did. So, now…if I were to question this blacksmith…this Alfred, would he tell me anything I have not already been told?"

"He would not. I do not see what he could add."

"I thought as much."

"And so?"

"So, for the moment, let's assume I believe what I have heard. Even so, you must know what troubles me."

Eadred nodded.

"I do. It troubles me also. Even if we did not do that to your man, it was still done by someone. And it cannot go un-avenged. The Baron will desire that someone pay the price. So you look once more in the direction of Gyrtun."

"Blame must lie somewhere. Why not with Gyrtun?"

"They are guiltless in this matter, I assure you."

"Again you assure me. When will you understand a simple truth? *You* cannot assure *me* of anything, Eadred. If I cannot look to Elastun, I will look to Gyrtun."

"They are guiltless, nonetheless!"

"They can take no comfort from that. Or would you have me lay the blame at Elastun after all?"

"I am responsible for both villages. I would have you place the blame where it belongs!"

"Which is where? Hmm?"

Eadred shook his head. "You know I cannot tell you that."

"I don't know it for certain," said Orderic. "From my point of view it is still a possibility that you *can* tell me, and are merely choosing not to do so. I have to consider it. You see, the problem we both face, Eadred, is that neither one of us is a fool. Still, as I have said, I am choosing to believe you for the present. That is all. Either way, my men and I ride for Gyrtun."

"Then I request that you permit me to accompany you. They are my people at Gyrtun as much as they are here in Elastun."

"You may accompany us if you wish."

"I am grateful."

"Grateful? Are you? Well, just remember this one thing, Eadred. Whatever you may believe about your standing in this place or Gyrtun, whatever the arrangements once were, and even if you and these people still cling misguidedly to those arrangements when the Norman back is turned, when my men and I are present, they are *not* your people. They never will be again. That is something you will all need to adjust to if any of you are to survive."

"No," said Alditha, "they are the Baron de Varaville's, are they not, Orderic?"

******

Open your eyes Turold and feel proud. You have done well. I am satisfied. You have shown yourself worthy, and you shall join us. The pain endured is like heat. Most weaken and burn. Some, a rare few, are tempered by it. Made stronger. And you feel stronger, do you not? Made new? Yes, I see that you do. And so, your rage to ours. Your strength to ours. Strength for the grief and havoc we bring.

Now a fresh task is at hand. Where your pain ends, so theirs must begin. No one there will be worthy, I think. No one need be put to the test this time. We shall draw strength even so. Simply make them suffer, and then slaughter them. We shall draw strength.

******

CHAPTER 6

Little Hare never carried her fair share of water from the river. Not for the first time, her older sister, Ealdgyth reflected upon this as she struggled back to the village burdened by the weight of two large pails, full to the brim. Yes, Little Hare also carried two buckets, but they were never full. Not much more than half full each, if the truth were told. She might just as well carry only one. But of course that way the pretense would be impossible, and the difference in their loads clear to see. As if it were not already? Their father knew her little sister always did less than her share of the chores. He just indulged her. And why? Because she was his favorite, that was why. His little Hare he called her. Swift as a hare when she ran, he said, but light as duck down when you picked her up. What use was either of those things when the chores came to be done? She didn't *run* to the river when they were sent to fetch water, did she? Or *run* to the wood stack when the fire burned low? The abundant supply of energy she so clearly had for games seemed to desert her when she was called upon for any type of work. Oh, but come now, Little Hare was young and small, her father would say if Ealdgyth ever complained. But then she, herself, was not that much older. And even when she was the age that Hare was now she had not got away with doing so little. Since she had been old enough to carry two buckets to the river, she had always carried them back as near full to the brim as she could manage without spilling any. Even though her arms ached with the weight of them. Just as she always returned from the wood stack with her arms as weighed down with as much wood as she could manage without dropping any. She prided herself on it, in fact. Not like work-shy Little Hare. If anything, it seemed to Ealdgyth, her sister prided herself on exactly the opposite, on doing as little as she could possibly get away with. Father's Little Hare, indeed. What use are hares except for eating? And you couldn't even eat this one!

Their father's special name for Ealdgyth was Little Pony. This epithet always stung her somehow, and she wished he would not use it. Her father maintained it was because she was strong despite her size, but she could not help associating the term with what she worried was a slightly stocky appearance. If she ever objected, he would laugh, give her a rough hug or tousle her hair, and say she was just being stubborn. He had once gone as far as suggesting he should call her 'mule' instead. Naturally, this only made things worse.

It was getting late. The light was already beginning to fail, and it would be dark soon. Ealdgyth glanced around at the forest surrounding the path up from the river. The shadows were beginning to stretch and merge, coalescing among the undergrowth and pooling in the hollows. Soon everything would be in shadow. Nevertheless, if they had not returned from this trip to the river with sufficient water, another would have to be made. Little Hare would not be sent out again, though. Not into the dark. No, there would be no question of her having to make a second trip if it was dark. Even though it was her fault they were late fetching the water in the first place. Even though it was because she had been out playing in the woods - despite recent warnings against it - that her mother had not been able to send them sooner. Well, at least their mother had waited until Hare was found before sending them *both* to the river. Given his way, their father would probably have just sent her, Ealdgyth, alone. He might not even have scolded Hare the way their mother had for playing out in the woods. And it would, unquestionably, be Ealdgyth on her own if a second trip were needed.

She turned to her sister.

"Come on, hurry up. Not very fast for a hare are you."

The little girl looked up.

"I can't go fast. Not carrying these. My arms ache!"

"You say that every time!"

"But it's true, Pony."

"Call me that again and I'll thump you!"

"Father calls you it. You don't say you'll thump him!"

"That doesn't change anything. *You* still can't call me it. I don't like it."

"I'm sorry, Ealdgyth."

"Good. Fine. But hurry up, won't you."

Their house, and the rest of the hamlet of Gyrtun were just around a bend in the path, about two hundred yards up ahead, when the noise began. At first indistinct, high-pitched. Both girls stopped.

"What's that sound?" asked Hare.

"I don't know," said Ealdgyth. "It's coming from up at the village."

"Are they slaughtering the pigs?"

"Don't be silly. At this time of the day."

"Well, what *is* making that noise, then?"

"Shhh! There's something else now. Like growling or shouting or something."

A deep roaring had begun beneath the higher sound. As the noise level increased, both girls dropped their buckets and covered their ears. Hare began to cry.

"I don't like it!" she wailed.

"You stay here," barked Ealdgyth above the noise.

"No, Ealdgyth. I'm scared to stay here on my own. I want to go home. I want Father," protested Hare.

"It's coming from home. Just wait here. I will go and have a look. Just to see what it is, that's all. Then I'll come and get you. Look, I promise I'll be as quick as I can."

Before her sister could protest again, Ealdgyth grabbed her by the shoulders and guided her off the path and into the bushes.

"Stay hidden here until I get back," she shouted into her

younger sister's ear.

"What?"

This time Ealdgyth did not bother to shout. She simply gestured for her sister to get down and stay where she was. The noise had reached a level where simply taking her hands from her ears long enough to do that was uncomfortable. The little girl was sobbing now, and shaking her head. She made to stand up, but her older sister held her down. "No! You stay! *Stay!*"

Finally, Little Hare yielded, and stayed put. "Bring father!" she cried.

Ealdgyth nodded that she would, then stepped back onto the path. After checking that her sister was not visible from there, she began to move off in the direction of the village in a semi-crouching jog. After she had gone a few yards something occurred to her, and she returned to the spot where they had dropped their buckets. She picked them up and tossed them into the undergrowth. After checking again that Little Hare could not be seen from the path, she ran back towards her village.

There was a bright light visible through the branches up ahead. It could be one of the villagers having lit a torch now that it was growing dark, but it seemed too high, as if it were up in the trees. And it seemed to Ealdgyth to be swaying from side to side. It occurred to her that one of the houses or huts in their village might be ablaze. But that still would not explain the noise.

Finally, rounding the corner of the path into Gyrtun, the place where she had lived all of her short life, Ealdgyth saw what was happening to people of her village. Saw, but could not fully understand. She put her hands over her mouth, bit down on her fingers. The moving light she had seen was, as she had thought, coming from the trees. Human bodies hung there, burning. Although there was no strong wind, and nothing else visible to cause it, the bodies were swinging violently back and forth. They, at least, were dead now, and their torments at an end. This was not true for the others. The flickering light cast by the flames as the human torches shifted position illuminated scenes below them that made Ealdgyth think of the descriptions of demons administering the torments of hell to the damned that she had sometimes heard given by the priest from the Abbey at Menlac. From their open mouths, and from the expressions she had glimpsed upon their faces before she had shut her eyes and turned away, Ealdgyth knew the people of her village must be screaming. Just as she knew she herself must be, but the roaring noise vibrating inside her head was all she could hear. Before that moment, Ealdgyth could not have imagined wanting any of the people she cared about to die. Now, as the dark figures moved from one member of the village to another, slashing, tearing and even, it had seemed to her, biting, she prayed desperately that, for those of them that still lived, it would end soon.

Something reached for her arm. She leapt away from its touch, but panic made her clumsy and she stumbled backwards, tripped, and rolled over into a tangle of nettles and brambles. Desperate to escape, she thrashed about, unable to escape the pull of the thorns and the stings of the nettles, more maddening than painful. Whatever it was reached forward again. This time, however, Ealdgyth recognised the touch of her sister's small hand, and allowed it to close about her own. With her little sister's help, she tore herself free of the brambles.

Back on her feet, she grabbed Little Hare and hugged her as closely and as tightly as she could. But it was already too late. She knew from the little girl's trembling that she had already seen the waking nightmare that was taking place only yards away. The realisation that, in the midst of all that fear and confusion, the little girl had still found the necessary courage and composure to help her escape from the brambles made Ealdgyth's heart tighten with affection. Little Hare suddenly became all that was important in her world. All that was left. In that brief vision of the village she had witnessed the fate of the rest of their family. She must get her sister away from this place of bloodshed. She lifted Little Hare's face so she could look into her eyes.

"Demons have come. We must get away from here," she shouted. "We have to run!"

Whether she actually heard or not, the little girl understood, and nodded vehemently. Both girls now turned and ran back down the path. Little Hare, living up to her name, was the faster of the two, and quickly gained ground on her sister. Realising this, she began to slow down and look over her shoulder. Ealdgyth shook her head.

"No! No, you go on!" she shouted. Then, understanding that Hare could not possibly hear her above the noise, she gestured for her sister to keep going.

Even as she did this Ealdgyth was becoming aware that the ordinarily very familiar path was beginning to seem strange to her. Unfamiliar. She experienced a sudden sense of panic that they might, in some way she could not understand, actually be heading back to the village. It was then she felt, rather than heard, heavy footfalls on the path behind them. She glanced back. The light from the village was behind them. This must then be the right direction. It had to be. And whatever it was that followed them was still out of sight beyond the bend, and might not yet have seen them clearly. Or at least, not clearly enough to know there were two of them. That was why she did what she did.

Little Hare was still reluctant to race ahead of her sister, so it was possible for Ealdgyth, summoning all the speed she could muster, to get alongside her just long enough to push her from the path. The little girl tumbled into some tall bushes, rolled over, tried to stand, but fell back dazed. She wailed in anguish and astonishment as she watched her older sister continue running off down the path away from her until she merged with the darkness of the forest.

******

As his second in command, and the only one apart from himself who spoke English, Orderic had left Walter, and another man, Hubert, behind to keep watch over the inhabitants of Elastun. He himself had then ridden out for Gyrtun accompanied by his two remaining men, Rollo and Mark. As agreed, Eadred accompanied them and, at Eadred's request, so did Swein. Orderic's first response had been to refuse this request, until Eadred had succeeded in changing his mind, convincing him of the wisdom of it. Orderic had believed Eadred correct when he explained his concerns over the potential consequences of the tension between Swein and Walter were they to be left unchecked in each other's company. Walter was easily the most experienced fighter under Orderic's command. However, according to Eadred, Swein, notwithstanding his lameness, was also an experienced and capable warrior. Orderic's instincts told him that the man had about him the manner of one who had found his calling in the violence of battle. More significantly, Swein also had about him that air of impetuousness, born of a wish for any opportunity to redress the balance, that Orderic had seen before in the defeated. It was not a match Orderic wished to put to the test. And he needed his men, particularly Walter, focused on uncovering the truth of what had killed Guy, and the present whereabouts of Turold.

When they reached the ford, Orderic had Eadred show him where Penda had found Guy's body. He agreed with Eadred's assertion that the killing could not have taken place on that spot without the spilling of a great deal of blood. Always assuming Eadred was telling the truth about the circumstances surrounding the discovery, that was. Seeming to sense this, Eadred had once again asked Orderic why he would fabricate such a needlessly strange story to explain the body. Orderic had merely shrugged, and ordered that they ride on.

******

It was late afternoon when they finally approached Gyrtun. The winter light had already faded to grey, and it was growing colder. The partially melted snow along the hedgerows was beginning to freeze over once more, and the earth beneath the horse's hooves was becoming hard.

As was the case for all the Saxon communities contained within the boundaries of the Baron's lands, Gyrtun was subject to the same regular round of visits by the men of Rylemont Castle. However, it was so small a settlement that usually only two or three men were sent - that number being considered sufficient to make the necessary show of force. Orderic himself had only visited on one previous occasion, nearly a year ago. His memory of the place was limited. Even so, as they drew near, his instincts were telling him something was wrong. He turned about in his saddle to face Eadred, riding close behind him.

"My memory is that there are children here, are there not?"

"Some," replied Eadred, guardedly. "Why do you ask?"

"Better if you just answer my question."

"Very well…let me think... There are Aelfrith's three… Dudda has four. All of them lads. But only one of those has yet to grow to manhood. Toki the potter has daughters…two of them…both sweet things. The youngest everyone calls Little Hare. Now what is the name of the older girl? Something like…"

"The names are of no interest to me. What age are they?"

"Before I answer, you must explain why you wish to know," said Eadred, growing more suspicious.

Orderic sighed. "Must I warn you against this kind of

boldness once more? It is wearisome to have to do. You would do well to avoid being insolent, old man. If I ask you a question, you respond with a reply, not a question. This is not a matter of choice for you. None of this is. However, you may be assured that I have no unnatural interest in the children here, if that is what concerns you. In fact, I find the idea abhorrent and your concerns on that subject offensive. What I wish to know is whether there are children young enough to play."

"To *play*?" Almost as he said this it occurred to Eadred what Orderic what getting at. "Oh…the noise…There is no noise of playing up ahead."

"There is no noise of *anything* up ahead," replied Orderic, doubtfully. Then added, "Except for what sounds to me like a great many crows. In my experience, their presence in such numbers is suggestive."

Until then Swein had been riding in silence at the rear. Now, having overheard this exchange, he spurred his horse to a gallop and raced past the line of riders, towards the village. Spotting that Rollo was about to give chase, Orderic shook his head, and gestured for him to stay back. "Let him go," he said, and saw then that Eadred was now looking to him. "You may go too," said Orderic. "We will follow."

A few moments later, when the two Saxons must by now have reached and entered the village up ahead, the three Normans riding more slowly behind them heard what sounded like a howl of despair. This was followed almost immediately by shouting, and the sky above was suddenly filled with scattering crows. By the time Orderic, Rollo and Mark arrived, Eadred was standing on a small square of grass at the centre of the little village, his hands held up to his head as he looked around, trying to take in what he saw. From the expression on the old man's face, Orderic knew that the howl had been his.

The dead were strewn all over. Everywhere the ground was stained with their blood - still bright red where it had splashed across the remaining patches of snow, darker where it had soaked into the earth and streaked the grass. There were sprays of it on the fences, on the wooden sides of the buildings, and even some in the thatch of the roofs.

Wherever you looked there were corpses, all of them showing signs of torture and mutilation. Several, Orderic observed, bore the same peculiarly precise marks of intense burning he had seen on Guy. Most of them lay on the ground, a couple of them cut into pieces so small they were barely recognisable. A few had been raised above it, impaled on tall wooden stakes. Two bodies that, from the traces of grey hair still discernable, Orderic guessed to be an elderly couple, had been stripped and posed in an obscene parody of love making.

The cold weather made estimating the time this carnage must have taken place much more difficult than it might otherwise have been. The dead, and the blood that spilled from them, freezing overnight, then thawing, and now beginning to freeze again meant the bodies stayed fresher for longer than they would have done if the temperatures were higher. The process of decay was retarded. No flies, no maggots. Nevertheless, even allowing for the preserving effects of the cold, Orderic guessed it had probably happened as recently as the previous day. Probably in the evening, because the remains of fires lit for warmth or cooking still smouldered in some of the buildings. Although, given how cold it had been lately, they might well have been lit earlier in the day.

Hearing a slight creaking from in the trees above, Orderic looked up. From a branch overhead hung a length of fire blackened chain, parts of a human foot, charred crisp and black, still caught in a loop at the end. The rest of the body formed a burnt and twisted heap on the ground below, near the base of the fire blackened trunk of the tree. Two more trees, similarly blackened, also had chains hanging from their branches, with burnt human remains heaped at their bases. The burns on these people were not precise like on the others. These three had been left to swing in their chains, roasting in the flames like meat on a spit, presumably while still alive. Somehow they had been cooked so intensely that the flesh on their bodies had fallen away, their bones disintegrated, most of the results ending heaped on the ground beneath. Orderic had never seen anything like it before.

Swein emerged from one of the smaller huts, the blood-soaked body of a young boy cradled in his arms. What Orderic had at first taken to be the remnants of a torn and blood stained tunic, he now saw was actually the child's skin, hanging from his flayed body.

Rollo brought his horse to a halt next to Orderic.

"Reeks like the aftermath of a battle… Metallic smell of the blood …Stench of the shit…," he observed.

Orderic, preoccupied, did not answer.

"Like after a battle," Rollo repeated.

This time Orderic turned and looked at him. "What? After a battle? No one *fought* here. This was not battle. This was butchery."

"We've seen worse," said Rollo. "The ends of some sieges have been …well…you know how it can be."

"Yes," said Orderic, curtly.

He did know how it could be. His whole life had been about violence. He was who he was because his father had made sure his illegitimate son trained hard to be better than most other men at the use of violence. As a bastard, his father had told him, it was doubly important that Orderic prove himself worthy of respect. And skill at violence, when channelled correctly, in battle, as it should be, was a good way to earn you that respect. That didn't only mean mastering the use of weapons, it also meant mastering your emotions. Fear must be overcome, of course. But there was also the problem of rage. His father had taught him that rage was unhelpful because it interfered with judgement and wasted energy. It happened sometimes, all the same. It was inevitable. Blood lust and anger could get the better of even the best of men, Duke William himself among them. And the results? Well, after a time, you got used them, learned to live with what you had seen done by others, and even with what you yourself might have done. You accepted these occasional extremes as the unfortunate, but natural, and sometimes unavoidable, consequences of war. Yet this village, and what had been done to the people here, did not seem to fit in with any of that. Something about what he saw here suggested it was anything but natural. Contrary to Rollo's dismissive observation, Orderic did not believe he had seen worse, and this was definitely *not* like battle.

Nor had it been a raid for spoils. At a glance you could tell the place had not been plundered. The most valuable thing people in a village of this size would have was their food, but even from here he could see sacks of what looked to be grain sitting untouched at the back of a small hut, and the livestock in the pens had not been taken. Chickens and a few pigs still roamed freely about the place, one or two of the latter rooting disturbingly around the dead. The other potentially valuable thing in the village would have been the people themselves. However, while the taking of captives for selling on as slaves might still take place in some parts of the country, it was rare, if not unheard of these days, in areas like this, where the Norman rule had been fully and firmly established. Duke, now King, William might have no real love for the people of England, but they were *his* people nonetheless. No one else's to do with as they pleased. Besides, these people needed to be alive to have any value. Dead, like this, they were worthless.

What had happened here was something he did not yet understand. It troubled him, and he began to feel uneasy. He would have to take care that he did not display that unease to his men, and particularly not to the Saxons.

"My God, look at that," said Rollo, interrupting

Orderic's thoughts. He was pointing towards Swein who, having rested the dead boy on the ground, appeared to be trying to tidy the remains, attempting to lay the flayed skin back in place. His efforts were awkward and clumsy, his hands shaking, his fingers sticky with blood.

Rollo shook his head.

"What on earth does the man think he's doing?"

Swein's face was streaked with blood. For a moment Orderic could not understand why. Then he realised it had come from Swein's hands as he wiped at his eyes.

"He's helping the boy," replied Orderic, his voice low.

"He's what?" said Rollo.

"He's helping the boy!" said Orderic, loudly this time.

"*Helping* him? But…?"

Orderic rode forward, away from Rollo. "I want a count of the dead," he said over his shoulder.

"What?"

"I want a count. See if any are missing. Any taken. There must be around twenty out here. There may be more inside. Dismount. Make sure you look in all the buildings. Count them. Now, Rollo!" He turned to Mark. "You, stay mounted. Keep watch. Both of you, draw your swords. Whoever is responsible for this may still be near."

Orderic dismounted. Leading Malleus by the reins, he walked over to Eadred, who was now sitting slumped upon the ground, his head in his hands. Suddenly aware of Orderic's approach, the old man looked up.

"Norman animals!" he shouted. "*Why*, in God's name? Why have you done this? What could possibly justify *this*? Tell me. I want to know!" He gestured towards the surrounding carnage. "Just look at them all. These people…mine…your damn Baron's…it doesn't matter which. They were innocent. That's what matters, surely? They did *not* do it. They could not have done it. There was not a warrior among them. They didn't possess the skill. They simply could not have killed your man. And still they have been punished for it. Not a warrior among them. Not one. Farmers... a potter...and their families...their *children*... And you do *this* to them...? The brutality of it. Why did you have me ride out with you? Tell me that. Was that part *my* punishment? You offer hope when you know full well there is none? You know full well that revenge has already been taken...And with such cruelty! What for? A lesson in Norman power, is that it? In Norman brutality? That is not a lesson anyone in England has not already learned. It was not necessary. *This* was not necessary. Damn you! What manner of monster are you?"

By now the other men had heard Eadred's raised voice. Mark, as instructed, had remained on guard, but Rollo was striding towards them, his sword held out at the ready, prepared to administer immediate correction to the old man if Orderic were to give the order. Swein was coming just as quickly from the other direction, no sword available to him, his hands were clenched around a length of firewood, equally ready to defend the old man he still considered his rightful master.

Orderic lifted his hand to halt Rollo. "Wait!"

Seeing Rollo stop, Swein also came to a halt. Now both men remained where they stood, watching, determined to play their respective parts in whatever came next, should the need arise.

Orderic turned back to Eadred.

"I cannot tell you, Eadred. For I do not think I know what manner of monster I may be. I can tell you..."

"God does!" shouted Eadred, staggering to his feet, knocking away the hand Orderic put out to help him up. "*He* knows it. He knows it now, and He will know it when Domesday comes."

"Will he? Perhaps."

"Oh, you can rely on it. He will. He has seen. You will burn for this, Orderic the Bastard. Along with those other wild beasts you call your men. Brutes, all of you. The Lord sees everything. *Everything!*"

"Then he sees that my men and I did not do this," replied Orderic as calmly as he could, angered to discover that his illegitimacy of birth had somehow become known to the Saxons. "If monster I be…and no doubt you will tell me that to the people of England all my kind are…then let me be punished for it… Only justly so. For what I *have* done, not for what you believe I have done. Think, old man. Why would I do this? Your very question to me. Why? Why would I go to such lengths? Have you known us do such as this before? No. The Baron has better use for his men than this kind of butchery. This is mayhem, not discipline. Take a better look at them. Go on. Look. Can't you see it? Whoever killed my man Guy did this too. It is the work of the same people."

Even as he said this, Orderic was struck with a sudden doubt. Was it possible his half-brother had acted without his knowledge? Had Bertrand sent out other men, with orders to slaughter the people of Gyrtun despite - or even because of - Orderic's objections? It was not impossible. But then again the Baron had no knowledge of the peculiar nature of Guy's wounds, particularly those strange patches of seared flesh. How would the men he sent know to replicate them? Besides, he was not sure his brother, malicious and cruel as he undoubtedly was, had it in him to order the carrying out of acts of quite this degree savagery. Nor had he the imagination.

Eadred's tear streaked face which had, until now, been glowering at Orderic, seemed suddenly to drain of the fury that had contorted its features. In its place was an expression of incomprehension, almost as if the old man were waking from a sleep, and had not known Orderic was there, was seeing him for the first time.

"You did not do this?" he asked.

Orderic shook his head.

"You did not do this," repeated Eadred. This time it

was not a question. Then something seemed to occur to him. "Nor any other of the Baron's men?"

"No, none of them. Think on it. Why would I not tell you if that were the case? If this were intended as a lesson, I would surely want you to know we were responsible, would I not? Where would the lesson be otherwise?"

Eadred looked about himself once more, supressed a sob, looked back at Orderic.

"Who then?"

"That I cannot say. It is what we must find out. It appears, for some reason, that we have a common enemy. Which raises a second question. *Why?* We know there is no love between our peoples, Eadred. That is understood. Norman killing Saxon, Saxon killing Norman." Orderic looked from Rollo to Swein, then back at Eadred. "Not a desirable outcome for one or other of those involved, but not in any way an unexpected confrontation. The mutual animosity there is understood. Without a doubt, it has been the story of this land recently, and must be for some time yet, I think. This, however …what happened here…this I cannot explain. It seems that another party has joined the fray. One with a hatred for Saxon and Norman alike."

"Could this be the work of Hardrada's people?" asked Rollo.

Swein did not need to understand Rollo's Norman French to recognise the name he had spoken.

"Hardrada is dead," he said. "Tell him. This is not him or the work of his followers".

As soon as Orderic had translated this for Rollo, Swein spoke again.

"I was there in the field of battle the day we slew him. Him and the traitor Tostig Godwinson. Slew them both, and most of their Viking army. Then we ran what little remained of them from this land. *Our* land."

"Your land no more," corrected Orderic. "It was lost to you when the Confessor died. The perjurer Harold

Godwinson had no more right to the throne of England than did his brother Tostig or the Viking Hardrada. Your blood is up, Swein. I can understand that. However, I caution you not to let it get the better of you."

Swein's measured nod in response made it clear that he agreed only with the advice to exercise restraint, not with anything else Orderic had said.

"That aside… for the present…" continued Orderic. "I agree it is not likely this has anything to do with the men from the north. If they had returned there would be news of it. The Vikings are not a subtle race. They do not melt away into the woods the way the agents of this slaughter have. Hardrada and his kind leave their mark, and mean to do so."

"I saw *his kind* run from the field," continued Swein. "They had not honour enough to stand and fight to the last. That kind will not return. If the cow whose milk they steal kicks them, they move on, try another."

"What does he say now?" asked Rollo, impatiently. "What further advice does the cripple have to give us?"

"Is that so?" said Rollo, once Orderic had finished translating. "They had not honour enough to stay and die, he says. Did he himself not take to the field against us? Were not his side defeated? And yet *he* still lives. He seems to have limped away from the field with his life. Where is *his* honour?"

Swein cocked his head and narrowed his eyes at Rollo, sensing the Norman's words contained an insult.

Orderic looked once more from Swein to Rollo, shook his head, and did not translate.

"Enough of this," he said. Then to Rollo, "How many did you find?"

"What, Captain?"

"I tire of repeating myself to you, Rollo!" Orderic barked. "What is the number of the dead? How many did you find?"

"Between nineteen and twenty one."

"Between?"

"It was not possible to be sure…the state they were in. Some of the remains are incomplete. Some are heaped…mingled together. It's difficult. I cannot be entirely certain."

Orderic turned to Eadred.

"We find evidence of twenty one bodies. Twenty one at most. That being so, are all in the village accounted for? Is that the number you would expect?"

"No. No, it is not enough. That is not enough. Twenty three. There should be twenty three. That is how many lived here."

A second count was made. This time, at Orderic's insistence, with Eadred taking part. Once again the number reached was twenty one. Eadred, pale with shock at what he saw, still maintained this was not a full count of the villagers.

"Toki's girls. He had two young daughters. Where are they? I don't see any sign of them here. Swein…Toki's daughters…can I have missed them…? Do you see them?"

"No, Eadred. I see no sign of them either," replied Swein.

"It's possible they may have been taken as slaves," said Orderic. "I have to say, however, that this does not have the look of an attack where taking captives was ever the object. No, I think it more likely they were simply dragged out of sight to be raped before they were killed. Tell me, were these very young girls, or would you say were they old enough for that to be probable?"

"*Old enough*?" exclaimed Eadred. "What is *old enough*? What would you say is a decent age for *that* to happen to them? Perhaps you could explain to me how you Normans decide when something like that becomes acceptable. They were children for God's sake! Even the oldest one, Ealdgyth, was only... I don't know...ten. Her little sister…

about eight. Does that make it probable in your opinion?"

"I simply give voice to possibilities you yourself will have already considered, Eadred," said Orderic. "Do not say you have not. Similarly, do not tell me a Saxon never did such a thing either. Let me give you the same advice I gave to Swein. Do not let emotion get the better of you. I have shown restraint enough lately, it seems to me. Perhaps more than I should. At every turn it seems you cursed Saxons test me. Enough. Let there be an end to it. I urge you for the last time to test me no more. My patience has reached its limit. You are no longer the masters here. Accept that fact, and perhaps we can work together to resolve this. Refuse to accept it, and I do not need to tell you what follows. Surely your people have already endured sufficient bloodshed? Or would you have more of it?"

Nobody spoke for a moment. The only sounds were the wind in the trees and the crows overhead. Finally, Orderic sighed, and said, "So, Eadred. As we must look for signs of the attackers, we may as well search for your missing children at the same time. Before it gets too dark. We will make our search wider. Spread out into the trees, the forest, the undergrowth, all of it. Check along the tracks, in the fields. Look for anything that may give us a clue as to who these people were, how many there were, how they approached, where they went to. There has to be something."

It was approaching dusk by the time the search was complete. Despite the size of the area covered having been increased, still nothing was found that gave any clue to the identity of the attackers. The only new discovery was that of a young girl's body. Mark came across it lying on the narrow path to the river. The others having come in response to his shouts, all five men now stood around the girl's remains. She had been cut in two, split evenly from the top of her head, down through her chest, abdomen, and pelvis. The two halves lay side by side on the track, her spilled insides strewn between them.

"Is this one of the girls?" asked Orderic.

Eadred nodded. "It is," he said softly, his voice almost lost on the chill breeze. "Ealdgyth," he added a moment later. He said it almost as if the word were new to him, as if he were saying it for the first time, trying it out. "Her name was Ealdgyth. She has a sister. The one they call Little Hare. Where is she?"

"In the morning, perhaps," said Orderic.

Just then, Rollo held out his sword. For a moment Orderic thought with dismay that he was going to use it to jab at the body or lift the entrails. To his surprise, Rollo stepped away, held the weapon above his head, and then made a slow downward slashing motion, as if practicing some technique. Then he shook his head, and put his sword away. "Not possible," he said.

"What?" asked Mark.

"The blow…how was it done?"

"Head to groin? It's possible. I've seen it done before," said Mark.

"As have I," replied Rollo. "Only never quite as perfectly as this was, though. No, I don't think so. And on the run too. If she was running away from him, it would have to have been done to her on the run… catching up with her, and cutting down. She was not going to just stand there waiting while he came up to her and did it."

"Why not from a horse?" asked Mark. "More speed, and more height for the blow that way."

"No sign of a horse having come through here," said Orderic, joining in the discussion.

"That doesn't mean there wasn't one. There are no signs of footprints from the girl either, see?" said Mark.

"There wouldn't be. This ground's too hard for that. But a horse is heavier. It would have at least scuffed at the earth in places, and broken some of this bracken here. No, there was no horse. So it had to be done on foot, then. And running." Orderic rubbed thoughtfully at his cheek. "Through the shoulder and diagonally, maybe. I can imagine that. Not straight down through the top of the head as evenly and precisely as this. Rollo's right. That would be a miracle."

"And why not just take the head off?" added Rollo. "Sideways swipe. Much surer that way."

"Perhaps she *did* just stand there? Fear can freeze people," suggested Mark. "I've seen that too."

"Even supposing that were true, the blow was still so damned accurate," said Rollo. "Look at it."

"Just what manner of men are these?" mused Orderic. "To carry out a raid like this, and leave not the slightest trace of themselves. And to cleave a person in half so exactly it's as if she were no more than a rabbit on the butcher's block."

Swein must have guessed at least some of what was being discussed. He tugged at Orderic's sleeve.

"An axe," he said. "Tell them. With a battle-axe it might just be possible. Far better than a sword for such a thing. It would require great skill, even so."

Orderic was not surprised to note that Eadred was looking at Swein with obvious alarm. The battle-axe was the preferred weapon of the Housecarls, and if the killer was a Housecarl trained in the use of the battle-axe, he was also a Saxon.

"Swein! Think what you are saying!" said Eadred.

"If you mean that what I am saying implies that this poor child may have died at the hands of one of us, then so be it," replied Swein. "Whoever did this has to be stopped, whatever race they are from."

"And if they are a Housecarl," observed Orderic. "Then they bring dishonour to men like you, Swein, who was once one yourself."

"I am one still," replied Swein.

"Really?" replied Orderic, at first with what felt to Swein

like a suggestion of scorn. Then Orderic seemed to reconsider. "Yes, indeed you are," he added more sincerely.

Orderic turned to Eadred. "I imagine you will be wanting to arrange for the performance of whatever burial rites are your custom for this unfortunate child and the rest of her people. Regrettably, all that must wait. There is need for discretion at present. When we return to Elastun, you may tell the people there only the unhappy news that these people are dead. Nothing whatsoever about the manner of their deaths. All you may say is that they are dead. No more than that. Understood?"

"Of course it is," said Eadred. "I too would not have every aspect of what has happened here made known if it does not have to be. That said, if it does become necessary, if I deem it fit, I *will* tell them. I will tell them all of it, if need be. If in my judgement that is what is required for them to remain safe. I have a duty. You should understand that."

"We shall see when the time comes. For the moment, when we get back, you will select whichever of the men of your village you consider most suitable to assist my own in a more thorough search of this area when we return in the morning. Not many men, mind you. No more than three or four. And, of course, they must be instructed to remain silent on what they see here. They too may say only that the people of this place are dead. Nothing else. Not until I myself know more. Knowledge of this bloody business must remain limited. So, above all, you need to be sure they are people you can trust. For their own sake as much as anyone else's. They will pay a high price if it is discovered they are not. We will ride out at first light. Search again. Although, in truth, I suspect there is nothing more we can learn from this damned place now. One more search in better light to be sure of it, that is all." Then, as an afterthought, he asked "How well do you know this area? I take it that is the river I can hear beyond those trees?"

"It is," replied Eadred

"How far would you say?"

"Not more than a few minutes walk from here. But if it is water for the horses you are thinking of, why not simply water them in the village?"

"The ice in those troughs back there is made red with blood. I would not have the horses drink from the water beneath. It would not be fitting."

"I had not seen. If so, your consideration is appreciated," said Eadred.

"Well," said Orderic, "they would more than likely refuse it anyway. Besides, if they did drink, they would make themselves thirstier than they were already."

"Yes, that is true," said Eadred. "So…the path to the river…it will be single file most of the way, you understand?"

"As long as there is sufficient space at the water's edge for them to drink, we will have no problem."

"There is space for it. The way opens out a little at the far end. We should hurry, though. We are losing the light. It will be more of a challenge to make our way back up if we lose it completely."

The atmosphere was sombre as the five men mounted their horses and began to walk them down the narrow path, steering them carefully around the body of the girl when they came to it. As Eadred had predicted, it took only a matter of minutes to reach the river. The path there opened out into a small clearing, but the gap between the trees at the water's edge was narrow. There was room for no more than two horses at a time to drink without risk of jostling one another. This meant that, after the other four had taken their turns in pairs, Rollo was left to take his alone. The others sat silently in the failing light, watching as he walked his horse to the edge. When at last he turned his horse from the water, Rollo chanced to glance back up into the gloom of the narrow path behind the other riders. As he did so, it seemed to him that a patch of the darker shadow, beyond the grey of the leaves and branches, shifted very slightly. Without explanation to the others, he drew his sword for the second time that day, and spurred his horse past them, into the undergrowth beneath the trees lining the path. Catching sight of the movement again, and convinced now it was that of a human figure, he drove his horse forward, deeper still, the beast rearing and kicking its way through a mesh of shrubs and bracken. With Rollo in pursuit, the shadowy figure darted about recklessly, eventually stumbling backwards into the trunk of a tree, rebounding off it, twisting sideways into a tangle of brambles, and becoming ensnared there, flailing hopelessly until it appeared to trip over itself and fall. Rollo raised his arm to strike, deaf to the shouts from the men on the path that he should stop. Only when the figure beneath him screamed did he lower his sword. It was the scream of a child. By now the others had dismounted, and were making their way over.

Little Hare screamed, rolling over onto her hands and knees, and scrabbling away from them as they crashed and climbed after her into the gloom beneath the trees. She was so cold and tired from her time hiding alone in the forest that she found rapid movement difficult. Her usually agile limbs felt heavy and unresponsive. It had taken almost all the strength and speed she could muster to evade the one on the horse. Exhausted now, and with more of them coming after her, she knew the small reserve of energy that remained to her would soon be drained. She was moving far too slowly to hope she might get away from them, so they would surely be on her in a matter of moments. With the hope of escape gone, she prayed instead for death to come swiftly when it came. Please let it be for her as it had been for her sister. Please God, not like it was for the others. Even though Ealdgyth's end had been savagely dealt out, it had at least been quick, painless. Please God, let it be painless for her too. Not like what she had seen happening in the village. Please, please, not like that.

Little Hare screamed again as she felt a huge hand catch hold of the thin belt at her waist. She clutched and clawed at the frozen ground in her efforts to get out from the hand's grasp, but her own, much smaller hands, finding no purchase, simply filled with twigs and dead leaves as she was dragged backwards. Then she was effortlessly hoisted up, and out from the brambles, although she could feel a few obstinate creepers still clung to her. Whatever it was that had hold of her swung her around and gripped her by her sides now, lifting her in the air. Eyes screwed tight, face turned away, she beat and kicked weakly and ineffectually at what she imagined to be the monster's chest. Only when she heard it say her name did she stop.

"Little Hare? Yes. Yes, it is you. Little Hare. I know you. And you know me. Don't be afraid now. It's me, Swein," the voice said. "Don't be afraid. Open your eyes. Look at me. We are not going to harm you." But she *was* afraid. Afraid and confused. She couldn't bring herself to open her eyes. "Swein," the voice said again. It did seem to her that she had heard this voice, and this name, before somewhere. "You know me," it went on. "I know your father, Toki. He's the potter. A good potter too. He made me a pot with a dragon on. You remember that, don't you?"

She nodded. She did remember him. Swein, the big man from Elastun. Her father said Swein was a Housecarl. She had never fully understood what that meant, she only knew he had always scared her a little. But now he seemed like someone safe. Perhaps.

She still would not open her eyes. Not yet, not until she was sure.

A different voice said something now. It spoke softly, and a little further off. It did not seem to be talking to her, and she could not hear what it said.

"Eadred is with me," said Swein. "I know you know

who Eadred is. He wishes to talk with you. Will you not open your eyes for him?"

She felt herself carried through the air for a few paces, then lifted higher still, before being taken up into someone's arms. Whoever he was, he was on a horse. She could smell it, hear its occasional, huffing breaths, the shuffle of its hooves, felt the slight swaying as it shifted position beneath them.

"The child is freezing," said Swein. "Here, take this."

She felt herself being wrapped up in what she guessed was a cloak. There was something almost familiar about it. The scents it carried and the warmth of its owner still held within the wool made her think of her father.

"There now. Let's get you warm," said the second voice. Much nearer now. Leaning in close. She felt the gentlest brush of his beard, smelled a faint sourness on his breath. "Swein's right, isn't he? You *are* Little Hare. I know you. And you know who I am, don't you?" he asked. This voice she definitely recognised. Everyone knew this voice. Very old. Deep, but somehow strained and thin, as much breath as voice. It was serious and it was worried. But it was kind.

"Eadred," she whispered. Eyes still shut.

"That's right. I'm Eadred. I'm here with Swein and..." He hesitated, then said, "Some other men. You won't know them. They did not mean to frighten you. They are here to help us keep you safe. We looked very hard for you, and I'm very glad we found you. Won't you look at me, child?"

She felt a rough hand brush her hair from her face, touch her cheek.

"My God, girl, you're like ice!" He pulled the cloak even more tightly around her. "There, that's better. Now, I really would like you to open those eyes and look at me," he said again. "Just for a moment." It was both a command and a request. She was suddenly anxious to see him, make sure he really was there. She opened her eyes. It was now too dark to make him out clearly, but she knew him anyway. The long grey hair and beard, the contrasting darkness of the bushy black eyebrows at the base of his broad forehead - all these were known to her.

"That's right. Good girl. You see? You've seen me now. You know it's me, and you can be sure that you really are safe. All the same, I think you would do best now to close them again."

"Yes, I'm tired," she said.

"I know you are," he replied. There was a sadness in his voice when he said it that touched something within her, released it, causing her to sob uncontrollably, clutching to the chest of man who, although she had known him all her short life, until now, had always been someone she thought of as far too remote and imposing to even talk to.

"We'll take you back now," Eadred told her.

"No! No!" she protested, pulling herself even tighter against the old man's chest. "I don't want to go back there."

"No, not back to Gyrtun. Back to Elastun. I meant back to Elastun, child. You will stay there with me to begin with. With my family. Would you like that? Be a guest of my hall for while? Until you are strong again. Then, when you are ready, we will look to find someone in Elastun to take you in permanently. Get you settled with a new family." He had said the last part without thinking, and worried now the girl would ask why he had, why her own family were not part of her future in the way he had described it. But she said nothing, merely nodded. She knew why already. Eadred looked up into the darkness beyond the tree tops, and sighed.

"As long as I don't ever have to go back to Gyrtun," the girl whispered.

"You know our way back takes us through there. It must. Only for a few moments, though. We will be with you, and there is no one there to harm you now anyway. You will be safe. I can promise you that. But you must promise me something in return. You must promise me that you will not open your eyes until we have passed through that place. Will you promise me that?"

She nodded. Once again, she did not need to ask why.

As they rode, Little Hare began to hear other men talking around them. None of them sounded like Swein. They must be the others Eadred had spoken about. She did not lift her head to see them, she was too weary. It was odd though. Perhaps it was just her tiredness, but their voices sounded strange to her, the accents unfamiliar, and she could not seem to understand anything they said to each other.

"You should sleep now," Eadred told her.

She did not lift her head from his chest for the rest of the ride home through the darkness, or release her grip on his tunic until she fell asleep.

******

CHAPTER 7

It was the second time in less than a week that she had been disturbed in the night to tend to someone, but the truth was she was glad to have something to occupy her. Even so, Alditha had cried on and off throughout that long night for the people of Gyrtun, as she watched over the sleeping child. The only survivor of that village. At Alditha's insistence, Little Hare was to stay with her until she was well again, and there was every hope that she, at least, would make a full recovery - physically at any rate. The girl was exhausted, had a slight fever, and was covered in scratches and nettle stings, but Alditha could see no reason why good rest and the application of the right salves should not be enough to get her over the worst of it in only a few days. How much time would need to pass before she would be free of the nightmares that were even now making her writhe and cry out in her sleep was a different matter, and could not be predicted. From the little Eadred had been prepared to share with Alditha about what they had found in Gyrtun - and from what his guarded manner suggested about what he was not sharing - she sensed it might well be that Little Hare never fully recovered.

All the men who had ridden out for Gyrtun the previous day had returned from there grave and preoccupied. Even that brute of a man, Orderic, had not radiated his usual arrogance and self-assurance when he had ridden back in with the others the previous night. When Alditha caught sight of him early the following morning as he talked with the one they called Walter the Bear, she had watched the two men from a distance for a moment. Orderic was without doubt relating the events of the previous night to his second in command. There were none of the usual smiles, no casual laughter. At times Orderic had even seemed to her to be glancing about himself, and then leaning into the other man as if to be sure they were not overheard. Shortly after that, he and a shattered looking Eadred had ridden back out to Gyrtun, along with Swein, and Orderic's man Mark. They also took with them a small group of men from Elastun. Alfred the blacksmith, Cynric who kept the tavern, and Harold, one of the farmers, and his adult son Malo. All senior men of the village and, more importantly, men Eadred trusted. Much later, when they returned, all four of the village men were drawn and pale. All shook their heads and waved away the questions of family and neighbours.

Alditha looked down at the girl. Droplets of sweat shone on her forehead. The cloth Alditha was using to sooth her fever had become warm. She reached down and dipped it into a bowl of cool water next to the bed - a bowl, she realised with sadness, that had been made by the child's father.

"Excuse me, my lady."

"Yes. What is it, Hitta?" said Alditha, looking up to see her servant's anxious face appear around the side of curtain hanging over the entrance to the small inner chamber where Alditha had had Eadred carry the sleeping girl the previous night.

"Swein is outside. He asks about the child."

"Show him through."

Hitta nodded and went off. A few moments later Swein's voice came from beyond the curtain.

"Alditha. How is she? How is Toki's girl?"

"Come through, Swein. See for yourself."

The Housecarl stepped inside and stood there, obviously a little embarrassed. He would prefer the rage and fear of battle to the emotions of the sick room, thought Alditha. He was absently rubbing at his injured leg. In cold weather it pained him even more than it usually did. She must remember to give him something for it before he left. She watched as he quickly scanned the chamber, his gaze settling finally on the sleeping girl. He cleared his throat.

"So?" he asked at last, gesturing towards the child.

"She has a fever, Swein. It is not so great. It will break, I am convinced of it. She is young and healthy. It will pass. As for the rest…"

"Yes." Swein cleared his throat again. "A child should not have witnessed something like that."

"No one should."

Alditha knew Swein of all people understood about the long term effects of traumatic events. It was never discussed - he was too well liked and respected in Elastun - but Swein had changed more than physically when he returned from the terrible battle near Hastings. Even now he still came to her from time to time for herbs and powders to help him sleep. For the pain in his leg, he always said, and she went along with the pretence. If he understood that she sometimes included things more specifically aimed at calming the nerves than easing pain in what she mixed for him, he never acknowledged it, and she would never tell him.

She cared very much for Swein. When, as a young girl, she and her mother had left Menlac and come back to live at Elastun after the death of Alditha's father, Swein had acted as their protector. He had always maintained he was charged with the responsibility by Eadred. However, although she had never thought it her place to enquire, Alditha had often suspected that there might have been more to it where Swein and her mother had been concerned. When her mother had died a few years back, Swein, obviously grief stricken, had carried on in the role of protector to the young woman. Back then his duties as Housecarl to the Earl of Menlac kept him away much of the time, but he came back as often as they would allow. Only when she had married Hakon, did Swein seem to consider she no longer needed his protection.

Like many of the men of his rank, the Earl of Menlac

had died in the battle with Duke William, and his lands had been confiscated. They now made up much of the territory under the control of Baron de Varaville - his reward for having helped the Duke to victory against the English. So Swein, who had no Earl to serve these days, now lived full time at Elastun in Eadred's hall.

"What *did* she witness, Swein?" asked Alditha. "What did this child see?"

"Eadred has not told you?"

"Some. Not all of it. Very little, I think."

"Then it is not for me to do so."

"Was it like it was with that Norman soldier?" prompted Alditha. "The one Penda found."

"My lady, as I have said, I cannot…"

Little Hare cried out in her sleep.

"Do you hear that, Swein?" said Alditha. "I cannot help her if I do not understand. The fever, the cuts and scratches, I can sooth. I can provide warmth, comfort. All of that. But her wits may be a different matter. She has the resources to fight the fever. I do not know about her strength for the fight she will face after that. She goes into battle, Swein. A child. Alone. What is it she dreams of, right now, as we speak? What is she seeing? Anything that might help her…"

Swein looked from Alditha to the girl on the bed. Eyes still on the child he said "Yes. Like the Norman." He paused, and then added, "Worse."

"Worse? Swein, what does that mean?"

"I can say no more, Alditha. I'm sorry. If it is Eadred's wish that you learn nothing further of what took place there, then that is how it must be. I believe I have already said more than he would want me to have done as it is."

"I simply ask to know…"

Swein would not look her in the eye. His hand was still rubbing at his injury, more vigorously now.

"This much I will add. You ask what is worse. You have

imagination, use it. Imagine the worst, and that will take you close enough to the things we found. Press me no more on this. And I urge you, do not press the child when she wakes. It does no good to relive such things. Only harm comes of it. Trust me on that point if nothing else."

"Oh, Swein. You know that is unfair. You of all people must know I would not force the child to tell what she did not wish to tell," protested Alditha.

Swein turned to look at her again. When he spoke now his voice was softer.

"Of course I do. Please forgive me, Alditha. I should not have suggested you would do that. Nor should I have raised my voice."

"It has been a difficult time for all of us. For the little one most of all. I give thanks to God you found her when you did. She could have died alone out there. Would have, I am sure."

"Your praise is misplaced, Alditha. It was not me who found her, it was one of the Normans."

"Yes, I know that. The one they call Rollo. But Eadred told me it was you, Swein, who first saw it was a child, and you who stopped that beast Rollo from doing her any harm. As Eadred tells it, the Norman had his sword raised ready to strike when you grabbed his arm. The man was only a moment away from cutting her down. She is alive and safe thanks to your swift action to stop him."

Swein shook his head, unconvinced. "Safe?"

"Yes. Why would she not be, Swein?"

"It is nothing."

Alditha waited. From the look of Swein, she wondered if he might add more. If he were going to say something else, he was interrupted by the noise of a cry from Hitta the maid, coming from somewhere towards the front of the building. She sounded both angry and afraid at the same time. When Alditha rose to go to her, Swein put a restraining hand on her shoulder, shook his head. She struggled against him for a moment, then gave up.

"Wait," cautioned Swein in a whisper, years of habit sending his hand his to side, searching for the sword that he was no longer permitted to carry. He gave a low growl of frustration, and began looking around the small chamber, searching for an alternative weapon. He quickly settled for the stool upon which Alditha had been sitting. Taking it by a leg and lifting it up above his head, ready to strike, he stepped up to the curtain. Alditha came across, and stood next to him. He waved her away.

"No. You stay back. Stay with the girl. And be silent," he whispered, before turning back to the curtain and moving it aside just a fraction. He frowned, and then, to Alditha's puzzlement, lowered the stool and stepped back.

"I understand your caution, Master Housecarl," said a voice Alditha recognised, from the other side of the curtain. She searched for the usual contempt in Orderic's tone, and was surprised to discover that she did not hear it. She was even more surprised when, Orderic having pulled aside the curtain and stepped into the chamber, Swein and he appeared to exchange nods, if not of greeting, of recognition at any rate.

"My servant?" she asked straightaway. "What have you done with her? Have you hurt her?"

"If by that you mean that wailing woman out there, she is fine, believe me," Orderic replied, the customary note of derision in his voice returning. "Knocked aside, that's all. No real harm. A little bruised perhaps, no more than that. Although, for her sake, I suggest you find time to provide her with better instruction on the importance of obeying commands issued by me or by any of my men. Or teach her how to use a sword." His voice trailed off, and the haughty smile – the one Alditha so despised – left his face as he caught sight of the sleeping girl. "How is she?" he asked, echoing Swein's earlier question. Alditha gave him the same answer she had given Swein, once more stressing that it would help her if she understood more of the girl's ordeal. At this request, the two men exchanged a glance.

"Eadred has not told her all. That being so, I cannot either," explained Swein.

"I understand," said Orderic. "You cannot. Yet I can. I appreciate Eadred's restraint, in fact I ordered it. However, if this lady will promise to tell no other, I think it can do no harm, and may, as she says, do some good for this child. Leave us now, Swein. You need have no part of it. Eadred will not be able to hold you accountable for what I tell her. Take care there is no one listening on your way out. No one who might overhear. That wailing servant woman in particular."

"And why would someone like you, Orderic, care so much about the child of a Saxon?" asked Alditha when Swein had left. The contempt, this time, in *her* voice. Ignoring this remark, Orderic told her to sit down, and immediately began to tell her, in the bluntest of terms, the details of what had been found in Gyrtun, concluding by saying it was only possible to speculate about what aspects of it Little Hare might have witnessed.

If Alditha thought she had shed all the tears she was going to for the people of Gyrtun, she was wrong. By the time Orderic had finished, she was crying once more, one hand over her mouth to stifle her sobs, the other on the arm of the sleeping child at her side. She was not ashamed of her tears, but she waited until she was sure Orderic had gone before she ran out of the room and vomited.

Little Hare continued her troubled sleep for the rest of that day, and through into the middle of the night, when she woke at last, screaming from a nightmare. Alditha, who had made her own bed next to the girl, did her best to comfort her and explain where she was. Eadred had said the girl seemed to know that the rest of her family where dead. Even so, her first cries on waking had been for her parents. Alditha's heart sank at the thought that she must at some point soon learn she would never again see them.

"They are not here at the moment," she told her, holding the crying child to her breast. "Right now, you are safe in my home."

The child wiped her eyes with her sleeve and looked up. "Alditha?"

"Yes, that's right. And you are Little Hare."

"My father says you are a very handsome woman."

Alditha forced a smile. "Does he? That's very kind of him."

By the light of the single candle in the chamber Alditha saw Little Hare's expression become suddenly distant, flat and emotionless. She stared into the flame as she talked.

"He's dead now, my father. So is my mother," she said, so matter-of-factly that Alditha found it disconcerting. "And Pony, too," she added.

"Pony?"

"My big sister, Ealdgyth. Oh, I shouldn't call her Pony, she doesn't like it. She is dead as well. Did you know her too?"

"Yes, I did. I liked her."

"I did too. Most of the time. You won't tell her I called her Pony, will you?"

"No, I won't."

"One of the metal demons chopped her in half."

Orderic had told Alditha about the body of the girl they found on the path to the river. His conjecture had been that she had been attempting to escape into the woods with her little sister before she had been caught up with and killed. Little Hare had either been too fast for them to catch or she had escaped unseen. Either way, it was to be hoped that the child had not witnessed the fate of her sister. Unfortunately, it seemed she had.

"Metal demons?" Alditha asked, then cursed herself. She had not intended to question the girl about any of it. Not for a long while yet. Not until she was recovered enough to talk of it without reawakening the accompanying anxiety. If that was ever possible.

"Yes. From Hell. Demons from Hell. Like the priest says about, you know? When you have been bad, and they get you. He never said they would be metal, though, or anything about the thin grey man," the girl continued in the same unnervingly detached way. "He was horrid. He looked like he was made of twigs, and he was all twitchy and jerky when he moved." Little Hare shivered, but she continued to speak in the same unnervingly dispassionate way. "She saved me from them. Ealdgyth did. She pushed me away. I thought she was angry because I hadn't carried enough water. That made her very cross sometimes. It wasn't that, though. She pushed me into the bushes so they wouldn't see me. Then they saw her instead, and they chopped her in half." She looked up at Alditha questioningly. "But she hadn't been bad. I don't think father and mother were bad either. So that's not fair, is it?"

Alditha shook her head. "No. No it's not fair. But I wonder ...could it be that perhaps they were not really demons, Little Hare? Might you not be mistaken?"

"Don't be so silly," the child said. "What else could they be?"

******

"She spoke of metal demons, led by a thin grey man. *Metal* demons. I think that can only mean men outfitted as you are. Men of violence. Soldiers in steel helmets and mail," said Alditha, pushing against Orderic's chest to prevent him from entering the chamber in her house where the girl lay. "I will not have her wake to find you there, dressed in that way. Or will you push me aside too. Hitta still carries the bruises from your previous visit."

Orderic had arrived together with Eadred to once again ask after Little Hare's progress and, Alditha suspected, interrogate the child about what she had witnessed. She knew Eadred's intentions would be for the best, and could not feel anger towards him. As for Orderic, his intentions remained a mystery. She was not certain what use he might make of any information the girl could provide.

To Alditha's relief, Orderic stepped back.

Little Hare had no relatives among the residents of Elastun, but the majority of the pottery in their homes had been created by the girl's father. She and her family had been frequent visitors, and they were well known and liked. Consequently, the villagers were concerned for the girl, and many of them had already called to enquire after her. Alditha had instructed Hitta on what to tell these visitors, and the maid was becoming practised at politely turning them away. However, when Eadred and Orderic had appeared at the door of Alditha's house, Hitta was not confident enough to turn these two men away. One due to fear, the other out of respect. Alditha agreed to talk to them herself, telling them Little Hare was asleep and should not be disturbed. This was more than likely true. Even if it were not, she did not want them bothering the girl with questions. She certainly did not want Orderic, dressed as he was, to appear at her bedside.

"A metal demon?" he said. "It is an original insult."

"They were not *my* words, and were not intended to offend," replied Alditha.

"Men of violence?"

"I merely have the child's welfare in mind. You must understand my intentions?"

"You make them very clear. But you are correct, of course. Clearly the men who did this were fighting men of some variety. So my appearance would indeed be disturbing to her should she see me unexpectedly. Unannounced, so to speak. I will still wish to see her in the near future, however. But I am prepared, for the moment, to trust in your judgement about her readiness for it. When the time arrives,

I promise I will soften my warlike look as best I can."

"And smile?"

"Like a favourite uncle? It will not come easily."

"But you will try?"

"I will."

"Thank you."

"You are welcome. This thin grey man…I suppose she must mean he was old. She seemed to believe he was the leader, you say?"

"That is what she said. However, you must remember she is still very confused. We cannot believe with complete certainty any of what she tells us. Even though she herself clearly does."

"I fully understand. Unfortunately, these are the only details we have to go on at present. These metal demons she speaks of… as I said, it makes sense that they were fighting men of some sort. As such, they will have worn things similar to what my men and I wear. There is some truth in that, there must be." He hesitated for a moment before adding, "You will appreciate any similarity between them and us is superficial. So I hope you will not group us in with them any more than you would your own man, Swein? Or Eadred here, for that matter. Both are men who have also worn the armour of a warrior in their time. Like us they will have done what they considered to be their duty, and done so with honour. Whereas, whoever it was attacked the people of Gyrtun, these were men without honour. If they had possessed any at all, they could not have done what they did. Not in the manner that it was carried out."

Alditha looked at the ground. She was momentarily dumbfounded by this Norman knight's apparent need for her acknowledgment of the difference between his kind and the murderers of Saxon villagers in Gyrtun. This was a man she abhorred, and yet, inwardly, she found she did not believe him capable of quite so barbaric an act.

Nonetheless, he and his kind had been responsible for what she considered unforgivable atrocities of their own. It was only a matter of degree. His final qualification regarding the manner of the act hinted that he himself knew that. Also, she did not like his aligning his understanding of how a warrior should behave with that of Eadred and Swein. And, by association, with that of Hakon.

When she looked up, she found Orderic was still looking at her. She struggled for the appropriate words with which to respond. Before she could, Eadred had spoken.

"Without honour?" said Eadred. "They were savages."

"That may be," replied Orderic, turning to Eadred, obviously irriated that the old man had spoken before Alditha herself had had time to respond. "The difficulty is that they were savages with some training behind their actions. There was evidence of real ability. You have been a warrior yourself. I know you will have observed it too. There was skill in how they used the weapons they had. The reason for it all remains a mystery, and I agree with you that what they carried out was, as you say, savage in its nature. I ask you though, would actual savages be capable of such elaborate tortures? Those curious burns, the precision of the flaying, the accuracy of some of the blows. The girl on the path for example."

"I do not need convincing of this," insisted Eadred. "I share your view of the matter. You need say no more." He looked uncomfortably towards Alditha. "I'm sorry, Alditha. I had not wanted to..."

"Do not concern yourself Eadred, please," Alditha reassured him. "Orderic has already told me more of what was found. You were not prepared to provide them, so I confess I pressed him for the details. I asked only for the sake of the child. So I might better understand. Please be assured I have shared it with no one, and discussed it with no one who did not already know. But you must realise there is already plenty of speculation among the people of

Elastun. You know that such talk was inevitable."

"You mean gossip."

"No, Eadred! It is not so! That is unkind. There is a genuine need to understand. Particularly among those who had family or friends in Gyrtun. There is much grief here. They grieve for those they have lost, and want only to know what happened to them. Before long they will be asking when they can attend to them in the proper way. Will it not be soon?"

"It is not so simple," said Orderic.

******

The original intention, that the worst of the mutilation sustained by the dead at Gyrtun be somehow disguised, so that the full extent of the injuries the people there had suffered would remain a secret from the people of Elastun, proved impossible to accomplish. Even with Alditha's reluctant assistance, nothing done was sufficient to disguise the savagery of the attack and the terrible injuries inflicted. Some bodies were so hacked about that they would have required reassembling like some dreadful parody of a child's toy. Eventually, at Alditha's suggestion, Orderic had Eadred announce that the people of Gyrtun had been carried off by some unknown pestilence. As a consequence, they were to be buried as quickly as possible to limit the possibility of it spreading. Regrettably, this meant the bodies would not, therefore, be brought back to Elastun for burial in the consecrated ground of the cemetery adjacent to the church as was the usual custom. Instead, they would be buried in graves at Gyrtun, in a new cemetery to be freshly consecrated by a priest from the Abbey. Though relatives and friends might wish to visit to pay their respects, for the time being it was not safe, and was therefore forbidden. Only those men of Elastun already exposed, would be permitted to go out there.

In the event, the frozen ground was so hard that individual graves were not dug. It still took Alfred, Cynric, Harold, and Malo most of a day to create a single pit, pile the dead, and cover them over. Despite the promises, a priest from the Abbey had not yet been sent for. Nor would one be, until Orderic knew the truth behind the death of his man Guy, and those of the people of Gyrtun. So the ground was not yet consecrated, and many of the usual rites were hastily carried out, or omitted entirely. The Saxons made their dissatisfaction with this known, but Walter, who had been sent with them to oversee the work, made it clear that anyone who made this known to the rest of their people back at Elastun would soon find themselves joining the bodies of the dead in the very pit they themselves had just been digging.

******

CHAPTER 8

It was about an hour before dawn when Swein limped silently past the sleeping figures gathered around the dying embers of the fire in Eadred's hall, and out into the cold air outside. He took with him the battle-axe he kept hidden at the rear of his chest of belongings. It was not the fine weapon he had once owned. He had lost that the day he was injured, and doubted he would ever own its like again. The one he carried now was the one Alfred, against his better judgement, had agreed to forge for Swein, on the understanding that he never told anyone how he came to have it. He had also made Swein swear never to use it unless he believed he absolutely must. It was Swein's belief that such a time had come.

Careful to ensure he was not observed by any of the lookouts Eadred now had guarding the village day and night, or Hubert, the Norman soldier Orderic had posted near the gate, Swein walked to the rear of a nearby building that was close to the wall. He stood for a moment in the darkness, the axe held in both hands, familiarising himself with the weight and the feel of it. Then, having adjusted the position of his feet, and bent his knees just a little, he swung the axe slowly through the night air. The weapon was not as finely balanced as it could be, and the steel not as pure. But neither was it as poor as it might be. Alfred had listened carefully to Swein's requirements, and done his best to meet them. He swung again, a little faster this time, in the figure of eight pattern that marked him out as an expert in the use of the weapon. He swung again, full speed this time, cursing under his breath as he lost his balance slightly, and the arc made by the sweep of the blade faltered and dipped before he rectified it. He would have to learn to compensate for the weakness in his leg. If he lived through all this, he would have Alfred add weight to the haft to help with the adjustment. He took a few more practise swings, each one better and more confident than the previous.

To his surprise, Swein found himself smiling slightly - an expression at odds with the gravity of the situation. But he had missed this - the feel of a weapon in his hands. After a few more swings, he grunted in satisfaction, and slipped the axe into the leather sling he wore over his back. Then he checked the dagger in his belt - another of Alfred's creations - and heaved himself awkwardly over the wall, bracing himself in readiness for the inevitable pain that would shoot through his thigh when he landed on the other side.

Earlier that day, Swein had saddled his horse, and ridden out through the main gate, which opened onto the track through the forest. Once he was a good five hundred yards clear of the village, and sure he was unobserved, he had dismounted, led the horse off the track, and tethered it there, out of sight. He had then walked back through the forest, around the outside of the village, and into the open fields skirted by the river on the far side, re-entering the village by the gate at that end. Now, he made his way back to the spot where he had left the horse, untied it, led it back up onto the track through the forest, mounted, and rode off into the dawn.

Swein did not look forward to returning to Gyrtun yet again, he simply had no choice. Not if he wanted to examine what he had seen there more closely, without anyone else looking on. One particular aspect had been uncomfortably familiar to him, and he felt he must look it over once more. Seeing it again after all this time had unsettled him. He could not believe its being there was of no significance. He did not know what he expected to find, or what looking again might reveal to him, and he had not yet settled in his mind what he would do with the information were he to discover anything. He would definitely not share it with those damn Normans. Perhaps not anyone yet. If it was anything in the nature of what he thought it might be, he must have absolute proof if he were to be believed. The worse thing he could do would be to return with a tale of dark powers and evil spirits that perhaps the credulous Alfred might believe, but at which Eadred and Orderic would simply scoff.

Dark powers? He shook his head in disbelief. Was he *really* considering these as a possibility? Was he becoming like Alfred? Attributing anything he could not explain to black magic or the devil. He was a Housecarl for God's sake! A warrior. A man whose profession had always been the least otherworldly one that existed. A battle was as firmly rooted in this world as it was possible to be. Only those who died during one had any business with other realms. It was men who made war. That had always been what Swein believed. Like many he prayed before a battle, and thanked God afterwards for the victories He bestowed. That was if God did bestow them. Perhaps He merely allowed them? Either way, during the fight itself, metal, mud, and blood were all there was to know. That's what Swein had always believed.

He brought his horse to a stop, suddenly uncertain about what course of action he should take. He could still turn back. Maybe even get back to Elastun before he was missed. There was still time if he hurried. Eadred and, more importantly, Orderic and his men need never know. The problem was that there was something that maybe they *should* know. Eadred, at least. Possibly even Orderic. There *was* some connection between something Swein had seen at Gyrtun and something he had seen once before. Coincidence would not do as an explanation. The resemblance was too exact for that. He sat back in his saddle, looked around at the early morning light starting to brighten the gloom of the forest, the sky above the treetops beginning to lighten. He took a deep breath of the cold, fresh air. Why had he allowed himself to even consider the possibility that dark forces might have been involved? How had that idea even entered his mind? Because of something he had once heard an addle-witted old crone say after a battle? That was madness! Simply because *she* had believed in that sort of nonsense, it did not follow that he must. What she had hinted at was absurd. Blasphemous even. What was wrong with him? True, coincidence would not do as an explanation. That did not mean that one did not exist that did not involve gods and monsters. It was that explanation - the metal, mud, and blood one - that he must discover. He shook his head again, forced a smile at his own foolishness, and then spurred the animal forward, and faster now he could see better where he was going.

If any of the others had also noticed what Swein spotted, they said nothing of it. Then why would they? It would probably not have seemed worth remarking upon even if they had, given everything else that they saw in that village, full as it was of the imagery of violent and agonising death. It would probably appear as little more than an accident of chance in all that bloody chaos and, as such, barely worth a mention. Even Swein, who had seen its like it before, had not noticed at first. It was not until they visited the next morning that he saw it - the shock of recognition sending him staggering behind one of the wooden buildings to regain his composure. No one had thought his behaviour strange given where they were, surrounded by what they were. His companions had been retching and vomiting throughout the morning. But they were wrong in their assumption that it was seeing the dead once more, now in the cold clear light of morning, that had so thrown Swein. It was the burnt trees. All of them oak. All marked by fire in the exact same way he had seen others marked on the afternoon of the worst day of his life. The same day he had received the injury that left him lame.

Swein had never told anyone everything he knew about Hakon's death. When pressed he had simply explained that all he knew for certain was that Hakon and his father, Wulfstan, had not returned from the field of battle when King Harold lost to Duke William of Normandy. That, and Swein's assurances that his son and his grandson had fought with courage and honour, had been enough for Eadred. Perhaps because he had seen battle for himself, the old man had never asked for more. Alditha, however, was different. She had wanted to know all Swein could tell her. He had not liked lying to her, particularly when her need for any detail that would help her make sense of her loss was so clear from the expression on her face and the note of desperation in her voice. Nonetheless, Swein did not believe what he knew would have been of any comfort to her. He would have considered inventing a better end for her husband if he had been more gifted at stories. Unfortunately, Swein knew that imagination and storytelling were not among his strong points. If Alditha were to see through any tale he told her, it could only make matters worse. She would know for certain then that he was keeping things back from her, and he would be compelled to tell her or let her own imagination torture her even more than it was already.

As a Housecarl Swein had been at the very front of the Saxon shield wall as it braced against the charges of the Norman knights, occasionally using his skill with the battle-axe to bring down a rider. Wulfstan and Hakon were not professionals, they were members of the militia, Fyrdmen. So they had been further back in the great throng of men, clammy hands clenched around sword handles and spears as they waited for the call to come forward and replace the fallen at the front of the line.

They were good men, the men of the Fyrd. Many had already demonstrated their worth only weeks earlier against Hardrada in the north. As long as they kept their courage and stood their ground there was every chance king Harold would be victorious against Duke William. But something had happened to cause the shield wall to collapse at one end. Not because the Normans had broken through, but because the men on the Saxon right flank appeared to have mistakenly believed the day was won when the Normans at their end of the line of battle began to retreat en masse back down the hillside. Against every instruction they had been given, the Saxons on the right of the shield wall had broken ranks, and streamed down the hill after what they had wrongly supposed to be an enemy in flight. Instead of fleeing from the field, however, the Normans had, in what could only have been a planned manoeuvre, turned about, come back up the hill, surrounded the men who had left the security of the shield wall, and slain every one of them. Swein and the other men watching from the crest of the hill could do nothing to help. They had been forced to look on as the Normans overwhelmed and slew their comrades below without mercy.

Despite the remaining Saxons regrouping and closing ranks, their numbers had been depleted, and the wall irrevocably weakened. More significantly, the ensuing confusion and the sight of so many Saxon dead below them had significantly damaged the confidence of many of the less experienced militia men who remained. This, perhaps more than anything else, was what eventually won the battle for the Normans. By late afternoon the shield wall had completely disintegrated. Saxon and Norman were now mixed in a brutal and bloody hand to hand struggle. Swein knew that the end had arrived when news reached him that King Harold was dead. There were rumours of an arrow having pierced his eye, felling him on the spot. Others said he had been targeted by a group of Normans knights who had surrounded him, cut him down, and shamefully mutilated his body. Whatever the truth of it, Swein and the Housecarls who still stood had resolved to die alongside their king. They would fight to the last, as was their duty, even as many of the remaining members of the Fyrd fled the field. It was at some point during this final stage of the fighting that Swein had been caught in the thigh by the lance of a Norman knight. The momentum of the horse's charge lifted him from the ground and carried him backwards for several feet before his weight pulled the lance's end downward, its tip sticking in the earth, and lodging there. It tore itself free of the muscle tissue of Swein's leg, splintered in two, and then snapped back under the legs of the horse, caused it to trip, fall, and unseat its rider, who then landed on top of Swein. The fall must have broken the man's neck because he simply lay there, unmoving, sprawled across Swein, who had to crawl out from beneath his dead weight, his hands struggling for purchase in the blood and mud, all the while trying to avoid the stamping feet of the men and horses fighting around him. But adrenaline could carry Swein only so far. Soon after that he had blacked out, coming around shortly afterwards as he was being dragged to the rear of the battle, away from the carnage. Though he protested that he must stay and die with the others, weakened through loss of blood he lacked the energy to pull himself free of his rescuers, and he passed out once more.

When he came to again, Swein had opened his eyes to see Eadred's son looking down at him. He too had been injured and carried from the field. But Wulfstan's injury had not been as severe as Swein's. In spite of a smashed shoulder, he could still wield his sword with his undamaged arm, and he announced his intention to return once more to the fight. Swein had gripped at his wrist, insisting that Wulfstan help him to his feet, so that he might join him. Despite several attempts, Swein was unable to stand. Eventually, he had lain back down dejectedly. As Wulfstan turned to go, Swein had called after him that as a Fyrdman there was no dishonour in him leaving, perhaps even to fight another day. Wulfstan, however, had replied that he could not live with himself if he did not go back to avenge the man he fought alongside. Swein, misunderstanding, had shouted after him that it was not required of men of the Fyrd. It was only for the Housecarls to die alongside the king. Wulfstan turned back and explained that he fully understood that. It was not King Harold he was avenging. It was Hakon, his own son. Hakon had been in the crush at the front just before the final collapse of the shield wall. Distracted by an arrow that had grazed his face, Hakon had not seen the approach of the rider who had driven his sword into Hakon's mouth. Wulfstan said his son had not died straight away. Borne up by the crush of the men around him, he had been swept back and forth on the tide of the fighting, howling and gurgling, choking on his own blood, until at last he died, his body for a time still held up by the pressure of those around him. Even now, Wulfstan said, he could not shake the noise of his son's anguished cries from his ears.

It had been as he was preoccupied watching Hakon's final moments that Wulfstan had received the blow to his shoulder. This wound would not have been enough to kill him, had he chosen to leave. Instead he returned to the thick of the fight and Swein had never seen his friend again.

The few injured that had been successfully pulled from the battle were carried to a spot of relative safety in a clearing in the woods on an adjacent hill. Once there, what little could be done to the alleviate the suffering of the wounded and the dying was being attended to by a small number of the men and women who had followed the army, most of the others having already fled when they sensed the battle was lost. Among those that remained was a priest. He had tended to Swein's leg, stemming the flow of blood and, so Alditha told Swein later, probably saving his life. Swein remembered someone asking the priest if the defeat of King Harold and his army was God's judgement on the people of England. The priest had said it was a possibility. It was certainly what many of his brothers in the church would claim. Yet, be that as it may, he himself found it hard to imagine the God he worshipped and had served all his life would want any part of such a terrible waste of life. He thought it just as likely, the priest said, that the Lord looked on in anguish at what men were capable of doing to one another in the name of what they considered to be a just cause. Then someone else asked why did God not intervene? Why did he not simply put a stop to it? Overhearing this, someone Swein could not see, but from her voice he took to be an old woman, had said that God had done nothing because he was not present in England that day. The Lord had turned his back on both armies. To the astonishment of all there, she had gone on to ask which side God should have taken if he had been present? When she was rebuked by many who overheard this remark - Swein among them - telling her that Harold had the rightful claim, she had merely laughed. There were times, she said, when the powers of darkness were exalted. Something else was now guiding the hand of man. Most present had then turned their back on her, presumably considering her treacherous talk to be nothing more than the ranting of the mad woman she so clearly was. She had been lucky not to be beaten or even killed for her words, but few there had the strength left or the inclination. That would probably have been an end to it had not the priest, either intrigued or disturbed, taken her to one side and enquired in a whisper if by this she had meant the Devil was at play that day? From where he lay, Swein had managed to overhear her harshly whispered reply which, at the time, had made no sense to him. "Yes, he is," she had said. "Only *which* devil? Or did you believe yours was the only one? Have yourself a look at what has been done to the trees hereabouts, why don't you. All these oaks surrounding us…they are not here by chance. They were planted here…and for good reason…To keep something in. But now, do you not see how they are marked…burnt? The God you worship gave you eyes, did he not? Well, use them now, priest. See the mark. And see how it is only them that are marked. Not any of the others. Not the elm, nor the beech. But then why would they have been, eh? The oak trees alone have been chosen for it. Singled out for the burning. That suggest anything, eh? Does it mean nothing to you, man of God? No? Well, then your learning has not shown you as much as you and your kind imagine it does. It has not helped you to understand what even some among the beasts in these woods will know. Mainly the hunters among them. The ones that kill, that is. They will know what you do not, it seems."

Swein remembered now how the old woman had spat at the ground in front of the priest in disgust and walked off. At the time, he, like everyone else present, had dismissed her words as the ranting of a mind enfeebled either by extreme old age or by the strain of the day's terrible events. Nonetheless, following her suggestion to the priest, Swein had glanced around at the surrounding trees, and discovered that all the oaks he could see bore the marks of fire, and that those marks were identical to each other, and remarkably precise. However, given all that took place on that day, this had seemed of little consequence either then or later. So, someone must have marked the trees. What of it? It was more than likely just some local acting on an old superstition. Maybe the mad old crone had done it herself or, if not her, then someone she knew.

Swein had put the old woman and her ranting from his mind until recently, when he had observed what he believed were those exact same markings again at Gyrtun, more than a year since he had first encountered them.

Eadred, Orderic and the others, doubtless distracted by the more striking, and grotesque sight of the heaps of roasted human flesh and bone at the foot of each trunk, did not seem to have noticed, or did not think it significant, that the burning of the trees had happened in such a way that it formed an almost perfect representation of the wings of huge black bird wrapping themselves around each trunk. Each tree marked in exactly the same way.

******

Eadwig's fear of his grandfather's rage, and the whipping with his belt the old man had sworn to give the boy were he to be once more caught sneaking out of the village without his permission, had not lasted long. If anything, now that Eadwig was out among the trees beyond the confines of the wooden palisade, it made the whole business a little bit more exhilarating. After all, what was an adventure without at least some element of danger? Besides, if he were caught, it would not be the first whipping he had received. He would survive. And the adults never stayed cross with him for long, anyway. It was part of a young boy's life in Elastun to be scolded by the women and cuffed by the men. A whipping with a belt was not much worse, and never that severely administered. In fact, it was strange how he almost missed being reprimanded by his father. Although his grandfather was far from being soft, Eadwig felt he never quite punished him with the same zeal as his father had. Perhaps for the very reason that his father was not there to do it.

It had been dull being confined to the village. Eadwig understood that he should do his fair share of chores, and the need for the training in various skills he received. He actually enjoyed some of the weapons training he had recently begun to receive from Swein now that he was considered of age. But he was used to spending much of his spare time beyond the village borders, in the forest. The trees had been tempting him for days now, and he had finally given in to that temptation this morning, climbing the wall before it was light, and before he thought anyone else would be awake. Even so, he had not taken Gra this time, just the hunting bow. Gra had been twitchy of late, and he did not think the dog could be trusted not to bark.

It was still too dark to move safely through the trees, let alone see to hunt, when he had dropped down on the other side of the wall. He considered skirting around, and going out into the fields that spread out beyond the other side of the village where there would be rabbits and hare, but the farmers were early risers, so time out there before he was discovered would be limited. Besides, it was deer he was after - his father's bow was designed for that - and they were more likely to be in the woods this time of day. So he decided he would stay put, just a few yards from the wall, until he judged there was sufficient light to hunt. He sat back against the trunk of a tree just a few yards from the wall, and closed his eyes for a moment. He had stayed awake so he could get away before sunrise, and he was a little tired. It would not hurt to get a bit of rest.

Eadwig sat up, gasped. He could not have been asleep for very long. Probably just for a few minutes, because it was still dark. Something had woken him. What was it, though? It might have been a noise, perhaps. But he did not have the half-echoed memory of it that one has when awoken by a sound. Instinct, then? Some subconscious warning that he was not alone out here. He crouched low, scanning the surrounding patches of grey and black for signs of movement. He remembered now how frightened he had been previously, when the Norman riders had discovered him hiding in the woods. The big man, Walter, had warned him not to hide from them next time. Some of them were staying at Elastun at the moment, in his grandfather's hall, so it could well be them out here now. If it was, he would show himself straightaway. Whatever the possible consequences, they would not be as bad as those should he be caught hiding from them again.

For a while nothing moved. Then, over on the path, beyond the trees, the figure came into view, walking away from the village. Until then, Eadwig had been holding his breath. Now he relaxed, breathed out. Even in silhouette, he had recognized who it was immediately. The man's shape and height, combined with the way he limped, were unmistakable. It was Swein. Not any of Orderic's men, thank God. But what on earth was the Housecarl doing out on the track at this hour? He could not be leaving early for a long journey. He was on foot. A sickening thought struck Eadwig. Was Swein out looking for him? Had Eadred somehow discovered his grandson was not in his bed, and sent Swein out into the darkness to bring him back? Eadwig was about to stand up and make himself known, when it occurred to him that Swein was not calling his name, as he undoubtedly would be. And why send only Swein? Could this possibly be something to do with all the increased security around Elastun at the moment instead? Not to do with Eadwig at all. Some pre-dawn patrol, maybe? Yet something in the way Swein's head moved suggested he was not looking for intruders, he was looking to see if he himself was observed. Eadwig ducked back down into the undergrowth, and watched Swein walk off around a bend in the track. He could not be certain, but after a while, he thought he heard the sound of distant horse hooves on the frozen forest floor, their volume lessening as horse and rider drew further away.

The whole idea of the dawn hunting adventure no longer seemed such a good one, so the boy retraced his steps to the wall of the village, and began to climb back over, eager to make it back to his bed before he was missed. He was straddling the top, with a leg on either side, about to swing himself around, and drop back down into the village when a hand wrapped around his ankle and began pulling him back into the forest, the grip so tight it tore at his flesh.

******

CHAPTER 9

The boy was not by habit a liar, but Eadred found it very difficult to believe his grandson's story. Mainly because it simply did not seem like the Swein he knew, whatever the boy might claim. Eadwig himself confessed he had not actually seen the face of his attacker. If there had in fact been one, that was. Only because he had seen him in the woods moments beforehand was Eadwig apparently so convinced it had to be Swein. The lookouts that had run to the boy's aid had not seen anything of the man either. Or anybody at all, for that matter. There was only the boy's story to go on. It was more likely he had simply fallen from the wall and hurt himself, and had invented the whole story about receiving his injuries at the hand of some imaginary attacker to deflect attention from the fact that he should not have been out there in the first place. If it were not for the fact that Swein had been missing since the attack, Eadred would not have paid it any attention at all. Even so, why would Swein have done that to the boy's ankle? And once he had him, if he had meant to discipline him, why let go so suddenly? It made no sense. If nothing else, it was far too ill-disciplined an act for the Housecarl. If Swein had spotted the boy on the village walls where he knew he had no business being, he would surely have just let him drop back down inside, and told Eadred what he knew later, not lunged for the boy in such a clumsy fashion. Swein was not the kind of man to waste his time sneaking around after mischievous children, and certainly not the kind of man to deliberately injure them, albeit not very seriously. Alditha had wrapped Eadwig's cuts, and said that, although there was a possibility of faint scarring, it was nothing more serious than a few relatively minor flesh wounds. As long as infection did not set in, there was nothing to worry about. No, the more Eadred thought about it, the more he supposed the boy must be mistaken if he thought Swein would do such a thing. At worst, it was an accident. An uncharacteristic error of Swein's usually very sound judgment. If the Housecarl had actually intended to hurt him, Eadwig would be in a lot more pain than he was in right now, that much was certain.

The whereabouts of Swein remained a matter of concern, nonetheless. His best horse was missing from the stable, and no one, with the possible exception of Eadwig, if his tale were to be given any credence, had seen him since the previous evening. The man's absence could not be kept from the Normans for long. He was a prominent figure in Elastun, and one of the few Saxons Orderic appeared to, if not trust entirely, at least be prepared to engage with. Eadred knew it would not be long before he was asked to explain why Swein was not in the village. In the event it was less than a day.

That afternoon Orderic had called Eadred and his own man Walter together for a council. It still vexed Eadred that the Norman had the power to issue such orders to him in his own village, in front of his own people, but he had no choice in the matter, and must comply. It infuriated him further that, now Orderic and four of his men were temporarily lodged at Elastun and staying in Eadred's own hall, Orderic felt he had the right to call for such a meeting to take place in Eadred's family rooms at the rear of that building without first seeking his consent. Two years ago only an Earl or the King himself would have assumed such a right, and it was hard not think that even they would have been more gracious in how they went about doing so if they had chosen to exercise it. To Eadred's mind, Orderic did not have that right, he only possessed the power. That was not the same thing, and never would be. Either way, Eadred now found himself sitting at a table in one of his own rooms - the one he used when he feasted with guests in private - with these two damned Normans. Men who were not his guests by choice. It was bad enough that Walter sat in what was usually Eadred's own chair. More painful still, Orderic had chosen to sit in the thick oak chair Eadred's son Wulfstan always used to prefer when he was alive. Orderic was tall and broad-shouldered, much as his son had been. A man of similar shape and size to Wulfstan - although somewhat younger - sitting in his place was hard to see without calling up sad recollections of happier times.

To Eadred's surprise, at the last moment, Orderic had also called for Alditha to attend. A woman at such a council was rare, if not unheard of. Aware of this herself, Alditha, usually quite bold in the presence of these men, stood in the corner of the room. Eadred was gratified when it occurred to him that it was not out of respect for Orderic, but for him that she was behaving in such a fashion.

"Will you not sit, woman?" Orderic barked. "I will get a stiff neck if I must look around at you there. Come into the light, and sit yourself down."

"It would not be my place."

"Your place? You worry about that do you? This is a new attitude from you, my lady. To my mind, you have not known your place since first we met. Yet now I find you are all deference, back there in the shadows like a servant girl. What has happened to cause such a change, I wonder?"

"I am merely being respectful of the customs of my people, and of this hall," Alditha replied. She looked to Eadred, who nodded in gratitude. Turning back to Orderic she continued, "In the past, I would not have attended such an assembly, and I do not know why I am called upon to do so now."

"It is hardly an assembly with only four of us met around a table. I merely wish to confer with those gathered regarding recent events in this forest. To discuss what might best be done next. You can *discuss* can you not? You are capable of that? I know from recent experience that you can talk. I am in no doubt about that. But it does not necessarily amount to the same thing."

"I can, yes."

"Which?"

"Yes, I can discuss."

"Good. And can you sit?"

"It is for Eadred to give permission..."

Orderic sighed.

"I am losing patience with this nonsense."

"As am I," replied Alditha.

"Ah, she bites back at last. The woman I recognize has shown herself once more. Very well. Eadred, may the lady sit at this table?"

Eadred nodded and gestured for Alditha to take a seat.

"Thank you, Eadred. I am honoured," she said.

"She is honoured. Good. I am sure we are all very gratified to hear it," said Orderic. He mimicked Eadred's gesture that she should take a seat. "So...sit." There was a moment of uncomfortable silence while they waited for her to take a seat. Orderic put his hands on the table top, drummed his fingers on the surface. He still did not speak, even after she had sat down. This man uses silence as a weapon, thought Alditha. It is one of his devices. Always just long enough to make others around him uncomfortable.

"Will you not speak?" she asked, peremptorily.

Orderic looked at her, and nodded, slowly and respectfully, as he would in greeting to a high born Norman lady. Alditha let out a breath, not quite loud enough to be taken for a sigh. Not quite. Orderic's eyes narrowed very slightly, he waited a few moments more, then addressed everyone at the table.

"This is an unusual state of affairs we find ourselves in, you will all agree? And so far, we make no progress in addressing it whatsoever. Nothing we have found points to who killed my man or the whereabouts of my other man. Or, before one of you Saxons insists on reminding me, who slaughtered your people at Gyrtun. We know nothing. That is not acceptable to me, and it will not be acceptable to the Baron. Trust me when I tell you that you will not enjoy *his* likely approach to addressing this business if he should decide he must become further involved. It will be swift, and it will be ruthless. Above all, as far as you people are concerned, it will not be evenhanded. He wants someone punished. He has made that much plain to me already. It will be a punishment based only on the need for a demonstration of Norman power. Not on guilt. I can promise you that much. There will be none of the justice you Saxons claim to so revere. I leave it to you to imagine where his hand will fall."

"Justice? What would you understand of that?" asked Alditha.

Orderic suddenly leaned over and grabbed her by the wrist, pulling her forward across the table, so his face was close to hers. Alditha gritted her teeth and met his stare, trying not to wince at the force of his grip. Eadred rose from his chair, but was gestured back down by Walter. When Orderic spoke it was not in a growl or even an angry whisper, as Alditha had expected. His tone was calm, almost reasonable, which was somehow much worse.

"Alditha, you do not much like me. And I understand that. I do. You think me a brutal man. You think all of us brutal men. Walter here. My men outside. Would it surprise you to learn that, up to a point, I agree with you? Meting out death is what a warrior does. Brutality, force. These things are as much a part of our profession as the hammer and the forge are part of that of your blacksmith. Alfred, I believe his name is. What you need to understand, however, is that, brutal as we are…as *I* am…The Baron, I can assure you, is far worse. Better you co-operate with me, than have to submit to that man's approach. The problem is I can prevent that happening only if you co-operate with me. I do not ask that you like it. I only ask that you do it. That is all I require from you, your co-operation."

His grip relaxed, allowing Alditha to sit back. Her wrist ached, but she resisted the urge to rub at it. However, much to her chagrin, she felt tears forming in her eyes. More of rage than pain, but they might not be read as such by these men. She attempted without success to blink them away, refusing to acknowledge them by wiping her eyes. She felt one spill over, and run down her cheek, and was dismayed to see Orderic's gaze trace its path as it fell.

"You make your point," she said, giving in and wiping her hands across her eyes and cheeks before more tears could fall from them.

"I have your co-operation then?" asked Orderic.

"You do. I must. However, I still do not understand why I am called here."

"Have you considered the possibility that it might simply be because I find you pleasing to look at?" said Orderic, finding to his surprise that he regretted the suggestion immediately it was made.

Alditha sneered. Rising from her chair, she said, "If that really is your only reason, then I would ask that you allow me to leave. You have looked enough, and I have things I must do."

"It is not. The remark was ..." Orderic looked away, ill at ease. Angry to discover himself searching for words. This exasperating woman. She *was* pleasing to look at, but what had led him to make such an imprudent comment? If his intention had been to gain some advantage by making her feel uncomfortable, he had badly miscalculated, and it had rebounded back upon him. He caught sight of the expression on Walter's face. Amusement or consternation? Maybe a mixture of both. Whatever it was, it was sufficient to remind Orderic that he must take care. "I have told you it is not the reason," he said, more firmly this time, and looking directly at her once more. "Now, you will be seated again. If you would but listen for a moment, I will explain why you are here."

Alditha sat back down as instructed, and raised her eyebrows expectantly. Orderic found her contemptuous expression to be even more exasperating than Walter's one of poorly concealed amusement.

"So?" she asked. "Your explanation. Why am I here?"

Irritated, Orderic cleared his throat.

"I am, as you so frankly put it only recently, a man of violence. With the exception of you, Alditha, we all of us are, around this table. Apart from you, each of us has killed at one time or another. I know this is true of myself, and I know it to be true for Walter here. I believe it to be true of you also, Eadred? You have been a warrior in your time, I know that much." Eadred nodded in confirmation. "And you have killed other men in battle?" Eadred nodded again, more slowly. "As I thought," continued Orderic. He turned back to Alditha. "Now, I'm sure it will come as no great revelation to you when I tell you that the act of killing, of taking another man's life, changes a man. It is well known, is it not? And it is a necessary change for those in my profession. Only the ruthless survive the battlefield. There is rarely occasion for mercy. Nevertheless, I hope I am not capable of what was done at Gyrtun."

"You *hope*?" asked Alditha, genuinely surprised.

"Yes, of course, I hope it. But I can never be sure. That is the point I am attempting to make. Gyrtun...that was cruelty for no purpose. It goes against everything I was taught. That said, whilst I cannot foresee a time when, or imagine any justifiable reasons why, such as that would be carried out by me, or by any of the men serving under my command, I cannot be certain it would not. Even though it would be a source of the utmost shame and dishonor if it were to occur, I can still never be certain. No matter how unlikely, no matter how remote, it is a possibility. I remember my father once telling me that once a man has another man's blood on his hands, he also has a little of it in his eyes.

Alditha's expression was now one of deliberately exaggerated bafflement. Orderic resisted the urge to grab her by the wrist again. He took a deep breath before he spoke.

"His meaning was that such a man sees the world differently. Necessary for a soldier, as I have said. The difficulty is that the boundary between extreme, but necessary acts of violence and violence for its own sake… such as the merciless depravity of what was done to your people at Gyrtun… is a narrow one. There are borderlands into which a man may stray. I have witnessed them for myself."

Alditha's face had changed. She had become serious, no longer mocking.

"So, what you are saying is that I can see just how terrible all of this is in a way in which you yourself are no longer capable? It is for that reason my opinion is useful to you? My God! Can you really be so corrupted, all of you? You have my pity if that is truly so."

"Your pity or you contempt? Either way, you may keep it to yourself. The one is not asked for, the other not justified. However, yes, I believe that is something of what I am saying. Your different outlook may prove helpful if we encounter the like of the attack on Gyrtun again. And it is conceivable that we shall. So, yes, any view…anything that anyone can see that I cannot see myself, might prove of use. That is all. You make too much of it."

Encounter it again? Alditha felt a tinge of alarm, but made sure to keep any suggestion of it from her voice. "I understand you only in part. You claim that I may recognize what is wicked more readily than you are able? Possibly so, but I am not numbered among the saints myself. I am not without weakness or sin. And what if I have seen somewhat less of the violence of the world? Might that not, in fact, make it harder for me to judge what crosses those boundaries of which you speak? After all, you speak merely of degrees. It is all of it terrible. I think you are mistaken if you think I can tell what is evil and what is only the everyday brutality of men like yourself. If you must have someone for it, why must it be me? Why not one of the others? Why not Alfred, or Cynric?"

Eadred spoke now.

"Alfred is a blacksmith. Cynric farms and keeps a tavern. They are good men both, but their outlook is simple. Yours, my daughter, is far from it. Orderic is simply saying that he recognizes that. Forgive me, Orderic, if I place words in your mouth."

"No. You put it better than I have done, Eadred," said Orderic. "Alditha, it is not just the lack of blood on your hands that makes your counsel of value. Perhaps I make too much of that part myself. You have... abilities. The information you gleaned from the girl, for example. And was it not at your suggestion that we disguised what we had discovered as the work of a pestilence? That was shrewd. Impressive. You understood these people. It was an account of events that would both satisfy and frighten them in the right measure. Would your tavern keeper or blacksmith have come up with such a thing?"

Alditha agreed the logic of what Orderic had said. She did understand her own people in a way that these men never would. Be that as it may, the guilt she already felt for having deceived them about the events at Gyrtun was not improved by praise received from this man for whom she had no fondness.

Orderic leaned towards her. Instinctively she pulled back the arm which she had been resting on the table.

"It is only your opinion I would seek to know," he said. "Your interpretation of things, should I think it helpful. It may well be that you are able to add nothing, who can say? Either way, it would be better if you would give it freely, rather than my having to persuade you as we both know has been the case up until now."

"Intimidate me," she corrected, showing her bruised wrist.

"You made it necessary."

"Did I?"

"If your reluctance is because you are afraid…"

"Of you?"

"Of whoever is out there in the forest," Orderic corrected.

Alditha shrugged as casually as she could, hating the thought that Orderic might somehow have seen her fear at the mention of more such attacks.

"Be assured you will be protected," he said. "You will not be in danger. The evil which you fear is only the evil of men. Nothing more."

"I do not see how that lessens the danger. However, if you are asking for my help…my cooperation… I will not refuse it."

"For that I am grateful. We all of us wish an end to this business, do we not? I do not deny that my reasons for wishing it are somewhat different from your own. It is in all of our interests, nonetheless. Whatever you may think of me, I am not in the habit of killing my own men, nor butchering villages for no reason. There is someone else out there doing this, and they must be stopped. Now, I understand why a Saxon might wish a Norman dead. That much would explain Guy and, I suspect Turold. What I do not understand is why a Saxon would want the people of Gyrtun dead also. Although I am aware of the emphasis you people put on the blood feud, I cannot imagine what a few farmers and, what was it?…a potter and his family?...could have done to bring down such a violent vengeance upon themselves. These were people with no experience of weapons. To attack them as part of some feud would be an act without honour. It does not serve as an explanation. Farmers and potters. So, if there is anything you, Eadred, or you, Alditha can suggest…Anything that my men and I, as Normans, might miss or might not understand, or anything you have thought prudent to keep back… I ask you to share it with me now."

Both Eadred and Alditha shook their heads.

"There is nothing," said Eadred. "I would tell you if there was anything that would help. Like you, I fear this may happen again. Perhaps here, in Elastun."

"My men and I are here," said Orderic.

"Our safety is not their concern, though. Is it?" said Alditha.

"You are wrong about that."

"Am I? Why?"

"Because I act for the Baron. Eadred understands, I think," said Orderic.

"I believe I do," said Eadred. "This country was conquered by your kind to be occupied and ruled, was it not, Orderic? Not plundered and abandoned. It is a kingdom of the Normans now. William's kingdom. And he has entrusted this part of that kingdom to the Baron. That being so, unfortunately… perhaps almost as much for the Baron as for us… we are the Baron's people now. His and, through him, the King's. Keeping us safe is as much an aspect of the Baron's maintaining his rule over us on behalf of the King as is keeping us subjugated by that same rule. We may not be enslaved, but we are part of the land that is the King's property. As much as are the animals, the fields and this forest. His property. Now ask yourself this, Alditha: How much respect does a lord deserve who cannot keep safe his own property? Or that of his king."

"So, I am to be offered the same protection as might be a horse?" said Alditha.

"Ah, but my horse still lives, does he not?" replied Orderic. "So," he continued, "you can offer me nothing more? There is no one you can suggest who might?"

"The heads of the other villages?" suggested Eadred.

"Yes, that was my next step. When we are done here,

two of my men, including Walter here, will ride out to the nearest villages. Firstly to warn them to be on their guard. Also, in to order to question the head men. I would hear their views. They may even know something of this already. I've chosen Walter to go because he speaks your language, of course." He turned to Walter. "The other should be Mark, I think."

Walter nodded. "Good."

Orderic pushed his chair back, as if preparing to stand. "Oh, Eadred, I propose that your man Swein ride with Walter to the villages. Swein will be believed, if Walter is not. His word will be trusted. He can make it known that I am sincere, that this is no Norman deception. He is respected hereabouts is he not?"

Eadred frowned.

"There is some difficulty?" asked Orderic.

"There is."

"You think he will object? Walter here will be on his best behavior, will you not, Walter? I will order him to be. Just as you must instruct Swein to do likewise."

"I regret, Swein is not in the village," said Eadred.

"Then where is he? When will he return?"

"I also regret that I cannot answer either question. He was seen on the track early this morning. Before dawn. Not since."

"Seen by whom?"

"Eadwig."

"The lad?" asked Walter. "He was out there again?"

Orderic looked questioningly at his second in command.

"I had warned him to avoid the forest. No more hunting trips," explained Walter.

"I am sorry to say he respects neither your counsel or that of his own grandfather," said Eadred. "Young fool paid the price this time."

"Paid the price? How so?" asked Orderic.

"He claims he was grabbed by someone. Not badly hurt.

Seems they let go of him almost as soon as they had him. It gave him a fright, though."

"Claims? Well, was he or not?"

Eadred shrugged. "His ankle does look like it would if it were grabbed by someone, but he might have got it caught when he fell from the fence. He is just a boy. I don't think he really knows what happened himself."

"Why was I not told?" demanded Orderic, turning again to Walter. "Where is Hubert? He had the guard at that time. Why did he not inform me?" He paused. "Oh… now wait. Let me guess. He did not tell me because he did not know himself." He looked to Eadred. "You contrived to hide it, old man. God in heaven!" In his anger, Orderic raised a hand as if to bang it on the table top. Catching sight of the way Alditha had once again flinched back as he did so, he stopped himself, lowered the hand slowly, and clasped it in his other. Alditha gave a very slight nod in gratitude.

Orderic drew in a long breath, then said, "So, Eadred. My man Hubert was not told. No doubt you wish to offer me an explanation?"

"You are correct. Will you hear it if I do?"

Orderic nodded.

"Your man on guard duty…Hubert... *was* told. But only that the lad had attempted to climb the wall to go hunting. The rest, I do confess, was kept from him. However, before you object, let me give you that explanation. We thought the lad was telling tales. Truly we did. We thought he'd hurt his leg trying to climb down, and was making things up to distract from the trouble he knew he would be in. Only later did we discover Swein was missing."

"God in heaven!" Orderic said again. "Do you see now why I have had such difficulty with you people? Why I have had to…what was your word? Intimidate? You will simply not co-operate. This already looked badly for Swein, and you knew that. Now it looks worse because you attempted to hide his absence. Can you not understand that? Let this be an end to this sort of behavior. No more concealing things. I'll have no more of it. So, you will tell me then, where do you think the Housecarl will have taken himself?"

"I have no idea. Wherever it is, whatever has taken him away, Swein is an honourable man. He can have nothing to do with…"

"Of that much, at least, you do not need to convince me. Still, when he returns, I want to know. Meanwhile, we are left with the question of who should ride with my men to visit the other villages. It must be someone they will know and trust. Your blacksmith, perhaps."

"No. Not Alfred. He is known, true. Unfortunately, he is…erm… confused by all this."

"Confused is he? Not any more than the rest of us, surely?"

"Alfred is a superstitious man, and as ready to attribute this to black magic or fiends that live in the forest as to the work of any mortal man's hand. He would not be the right person. I would go myself, were I not required here."

"Why not Harold?" suggested Alditha. "He was among those who helped bury the dead. He knows enough of what took place."

Walter frowned. "Will he be levelheaded? If the man is to ride along with me to the other villages, I need to know he can be trusted not to tell them tales about sprites or fairies of the forest?" He danced his hands about in derisive imitation of the movements of supernatural beings. "I don't want him with me if he can't stick to what we actually know."

"He will," said Eadred. "Harold may have a king's name, but he is a simple farmer, and as such he may have some beliefs you and I would not understand. But, for all that, he is no fool. More significantly, he is a man that I trust. It was for that very reason he and his son were among those I chose to help deal with the dead at Gyrtun. In the absence of Swein, he is the best choice. Alditha is right about that.

You should take Harold. Oh, and do not concern yourself, I will instruct him on what, and how much, he is to tell."

Once they were alone outside the hall, Orderic turned to Walter.

"I also intend to send Rollo back to Rylemont with news of these events, and a request that the Baron send me more men."

"You will send Rollo alone?" asked Walter.

Orderic shrugged. "I have no choice in the matter. I need Hubert here with me."

"Let Mark go along with Rollo."

"No, you will need Mark. You will be stopping at the villages you visit, and I would not have you lingering alone among these people. Not with things as they are. Mark must go with you and this Harold. Rollo will be moving swiftly. When he stops, he can do so in the forest, out of sight. I do not like this any more than you, my friend. Dividing what small force I have this way. Still, it is as it is."

"Can you trust him? He has been brooding a little of late."

"He has been a sullen arse of late. The man is unhappy with how I conduct affairs. I know this."

"It will colour how he relates what is happening out here to the Baron."

"Of course it will. But he knows better than to lie. He will not go as far as that. As long as he sticks to facts, he can add as many of his ill-informed opinions about them as he likes for all I care. They will not be listened to unless they serve my brother's purpose. Bertrand will want to condemn my actions for his own reasons, you know that. Not for those of one of his men whose name, assuming he has ever heard it to begin with, he will definitely not remember. Go now, inform Mark and Hubert. And send Rollo here to me."

As Walter walked off, Orderic saw Alditha leaving the

hall and crossing to her own house. She was rubbing at her wrist. He looked away, considered for a moment, then turned back and called to her.

"Your wrist…it still pains you?"

Alditha looked up, startled, glanced down at her wrist, but did not stop. She continued walking in the direction of her house as she spoke.

"It does, a little."

"I regret…" Orderic began to say, then faltered before continuing. "It was wrong of me. I should not have…"

Taken aback, Alditha stopped, looked at him.

"No, you should not have," she said, then made as if to continue walking, but stopped again. To her surprise, the expression of slight shame she saw on the face of this unpleasant man struck her as genuine. Rather than taking pleasure in his discomfort, against her better judgment, to ease his awkwardness she found herself adding, "The pain fades even now."

"Good…That is good."

"Perhaps in the future you might be a little less quick to action?"

Orderic nodded.

"Of course. This business…you can understand that it is difficult for me. I am not accustomed to …that is to say… I am used to being obeyed by…"

"Saxons?"

"Most people."

"If it is difficult for you, imagine how much more so it is for us. For Eadred in particular. You cannot expect him, or any of us, to have any love for the Norman."

"I do not. I am sure that in his position I would be the same. Still…as I said earlier, while this business still tasks us, I hope you can find it in yourself to be…"

"Co-operative?"

"Yes."

"If the situation calls for it, I will be."

CHAPTER 10

In some ways it resembled a man. Legs, arms, head, torso. But it was much taller – Siward estimated it could have been eight feet – and thinner, with the limbs disproportionately long. And it didn't move like a man, either. It convulsed. The limbs jerked and shuddered violently as if the joints were being pulled and pushed into each new position by some unseen external force, rather than by the work of muscles from within. Something about these movements was disturbing, almost sickening. They made the prospect of touching it, or worse, being touched *by* it utterly appalling. In the same way the snakes you sometimes came across warming themselves out on the heathland in the summer could make you flinch on sight - even those ones whose bite was known to be free of venom and therefore harmless. It appeared grey, although silhouetted against the fires it was hard to be certain. And its skin seemed to writhe as if beneath it squirmed thousands of restless worms or maggots that might burst through at any moment.

Siward tried to get up, go towards the cries of the others, but found he was still unable to make his body respond the way he needed it to. He could not understand. No one held him down that he could see, but he could not rise, no matter how hard he struggled. Always it seemed something was forcing him back. He pushed once more against the unseen hands with all his strength, and only managed to make himself topple on to one side, where he lay, trembling from fear and exhaustion. The thing came closer, bent down, and lowered its face into his. Siward screamed. There were no distinct features, and yet the face held an expression so intense he screwed up his eyes against it in the way he might have had it been an intense light. The expression was one of absolute rage and utter hatred, all of it at that moment, it seemed to Siward, directed towards him. In that expression he had seen something of what it intended to do to him. A weight of darkness and despair that foreshadowed the agonies and humiliations to come. He felt his thoughts beginning to lose any sense of shape, his reason collapsing in on itself, rather than allow him to fully comprehend what lay ahead for him. His desire to escape spiralled into a kind of madness. But he fought against the panic. He must escape, get himself and the people of his village as far away from this creature of insanity and torture as he could.

Your village? Your thoughts are for them, even now? There is some sort of strength in that, I suppose. What your kind would call goodness? Love? How unfortunate for us both that it is not strength of the kind that is of any use to me. From you, as from them, I have use only for your capacity to suffer. Only that, nothing more. However, I believe I will make theirs a part of yours. You understand me? No? I shall explain. You, Siward, shall be last. Until your own turn arrives, you shall see and hear all we do to the others. Ah, I see you do understand. Good. So then, shall we make a start? Who's to be first? Oh, I failed to explain that part of it. I do apologise. The thing is, you, Siward, must choose who it is to be. We can't have it all chaos, can we? We need an order in which we do things. So, what about this one? No, not her? Very well, this one then? Oh, I know, I know. It's so very hard. All the same, you must choose. This will not end for any of them until you do. The pain will just go on and on and on. So, this one? Or this one? Him, perhaps? Or her? I require an answer.

******

Swein knelt down carefully, and studied the pattern on the tree. It was just as he thought it would be. A few feet up on the trunk the bark was burnt and blackened, forming the shape of huge wings that wrapped themselves around the base of the tree. It reminded him a little of the Landwaster, the raven banner carried into battle by the army of

Hardrada in the fight up north. But Hardrada's was not the only army ever to have rallied around the Landwaster. Besides, the man was dead, as was most of his army of cowards. But *someone* had done this. It was no mere chance of the flames. This was deliberate, each wing an exact mirror image of the other. The ends did not fade out into the fainter grey of areas less touched by the flames as would be usual. They finished abruptly. The line where burnt black met undamaged bark was crisp and precise. Almost impossibly perfect, in fact. He leaned forward intending to run his ran his hands along it, and then almost immediately pulled his hand back. There was still heat coming from the tree. This was the oak on the track to Gyrtun. It had been damaged even before the ones in the village. Since then there had been frost, snow, and even freezing rain, and yet, despite all of that, the tree still seemed to be giving off warmth. Very carefully, avoiding touching the tree with his bare flesh, he held the side of his dagger to it. When he pulled it back and put his fingers to the blade it was warm. Conceivably the fire was somehow still burning inside the tree, but there was no trace of smoke escaping to suggest that. Leaning in again, he sniffed at the area, and picked up no smell of burning. Very gingerly, he touched the area of bark about two feet above where it was black. It was cool. Now, slowly and cautiously, he began to run his hand down towards the black. It was cool all the way down, only hot where the bark was black. Using his dagger he traced the outline, and discovered that it dropped inward very slightly, suggesting the tree had been stamped, branded. He sat back, perplexed, and uneasy in his mind. The strangeness of all this was beyond his range of experience. He would have preferred something he could swing his axe at. Something he could kill. He had a momentary inclination to chop down this tree, and then go do the same to ones at Gyrtun. He shook the thought off as ridiculous. Was he doing battle with trees these days?

All the same, he knew, before he even got there, that the trees in Gyrtun would be exactly the same as this one. A thought struck him, and he looked up to see if, like them, any chain hung down where some poor unfortunate soul had been roasted alive, but saw nothing. He had not really expected to. There was no blackened corpse at the foot of this trunk.

Swein struggled to his feet, grimaced, rubbed at his thigh, and cursed his own foolishness. Kneeling had been unwise. As he walked back to his horse, his limp was more pronounced than usual. Fortunately, he was still strong, and could haul himself up into the saddle easily enough using the other leg.

Once up, he looked about to see if he had been observed. He did not expect it, out here in the middle of the forest. He felt uneasy, just the same, as if there were eyes on him all the while.

"Show yourself!" he bellowed, and then felt immediately ashamed at his nervousness. For the second time in a matter of minutes, he cursed himself for the foolishness of own actions. If there were anybody in the vicinity they might not yet have seen him, so why make it possible for them to hear him instead? There was a time, no so long ago, when he would not have made that mistake. Still, he must not let that make him doubt himself further. He still retained some of the edge that made him the warrior he had once been. He had known that Wulfstan's lad was watching him from the trees that morning, hadn't he?

Swein rode on for Gyrtun, already reasonably certain of what he would find there. What he was less certain of was what the significance might be of his discovery, or what use could be made of it. It might only add to the already mystifying collection of facts, while adding nothing of use. And with whom should he share it? Eadred, of course, if it led to anything. Perhaps Alditha first? She struck him as the person most likely to have something of value to say about it. For all her devotion to God, and the scrupulous care she took of the church building, some knowledge of the older traditions was implied by her understanding of the flowers, roots, and remedies that she used to treat the sick. The girl was no sorceress, however. No one could believe that, and he would strike down the first man to accuse her. She was probably the most genuinely devout person Swein had met. Much more so, in fact, than the priests from the Abbey who visited far less frequently than their exaggerated godliness and concern for the spiritual wellbeing of the humble villagers suggested on the rare occasions when they actually did. But Swein had sometimes wondered if Alditha's devoutness, although unquestionably born mainly of a simple belief in, and love of, God, might also be associated at some level with a desire to protect herself from what she feared might exist outside the realm of Christianity. Dark powers, again?

It did not take long to reach the village. Once there he dismounted, walked over to the oak trees, and confirmed that they were indeed marked in the same way as the one back on the track had been. They were identical, in fact. And, from his recollection of them, the same as the ones he had seen towards the end of the day of the disastrous defeat the previous year. He checked the area for further signs. Finding nothing after searching for nearly an hour, he decided to leave. By now the unease he had felt earlier was growing, and he did not wish to stay in this place any longer than necessary. He was crossing back to his horse when he came across the site of the single large and shallow grave where the villagers had been so hurriedly and unceremoniously laid to rest. Swein's own faith had always been the straightforward faith of the battlefield. God was either on your side, or he was not. It was, therefore, more out of respect, than any complete understanding of the act, that he paused at one end of the grave, crossed himself, and said a quick prayer for the peaceful rest of the souls of those buried there. Peace that they must surely deserve after what they had been put through. He closed his eyes, remembering the body of the boy he had held, his skin ripped away from his flesh like rags. When he opened them again the first of the wolves padded into view, at the far end of the grave.

It was a medium sized grey male. Swein, although no expert, knew enough to know this was probably not the pack leader. He would be somewhere close by, watching from the trees. Swein also knew enough to know that this was unusual. No matter what the grandmothers told the children, wolves were no threat to man unless provoked. They avoided people, in fact. So what was this one doing in front of him now? They had been drawn by the smell of the bodies, of course. Harold, Alfred, and the others should have buried them more deeply. So what if the ground was hard? They should have kept at it until the job was done properly. That bloody Walter should have made sure of it. Even so, why had the wolves not waited until Swein was gone? The winter was proving to be a hard one, but surely not so hard they would take a risk like this? The animal did not look especially thin. It was clearly not starving.

Swein stamped his foot, and shouted for the beast to go away.

This was a mistake. To Swein's surprise, the wolf only shrank back a little. It did not leave. Instead, it lowered its head and began to growl, white fangs showing. What was wrong with it? Did it have the madness sickness like the stray dogs he had heard stories about? The ones that had to be chased from the villages and towns? It looked too healthy for that. There was no froth about its jaws, and it did not seem to have lost its wits. Far from it, in fact. This animal seemed to know exactly what it was doing. A fact borne out by the arrival of two of its companions, who padded in and sidled up next to it, adopting the same aggressive posture. The breeze was blowing from behind

Swein so, although he could not see them, he caught the scent of the other pack members approaching from behind him, even before he heard their low growls.

Adrenalin caused Swein's heart to beat much faster, and a slight tremor in his muscles as blood flow to them was increased, but he had trained all his life to master and channel these feelings. Careful to ensure his movements were not sudden or jerky, he set his feet in the same way he had when practising in the darkness that morning, and reached over his shoulder, undid the cord, and slowly pulled his battle-axe from its sling. He told himself he must remember to adjust for the weakness in his leg, lean back a little more, compensate for it. Very slowly, he turned in a circle. He counted five of them. The three in front, and now two behind. There would be more. He still didn't see one that struck him as the leader. Just how many he could hope to finish before they brought him down depended on how they chose to attack. All at once, and he would be lucky to get two. One at a time, and the odds would be better, but they would surely learn quickly and soon attack as a group. So, this was to be how he would meet his end, and join the other Housecarls. Not the battle he had expected, but it was a battle nonetheless. He adjusted his grip on the axe, then raised it ready to strike.

"So, who among you is to be the first?" he asked. "Do you have a champion for me, or do I just wait and see who comes at me? Yes, you know I do believe that is what I will do. So, who will oblige me? You do look brave to me, my friends."

And they were brave, these animals. He found, in spite of the situation in which he found himself, that he could not hate them. He would have preferred to be fighting Normans. For them, he had plenty of hate. Better even than Normans, would be to fight whoever it was had murdered the people in the shallow grave at his feet. That was not these creatures. He knew that much, even if he did not know what had made them so intent on attacking him now. What was happening went against their nature. These beasts should not be doing this. Then neither, Swein thought, should he. A fight to the death with these animals would be a death without purpose. It might be possible for him to fight his way to his horse instead. If he could do that, and he could manage to mount it, he might out run them. His horse. It was helpless, tethered to a post nearby, whinnying and rearing in fear. Why had the wolves not attacked it? And, he remembered now, there had still been a number of chickens left clucking and scratching around the place, so why not them? The majority of the livestock that had belonged to the villagers of Gyrtun, far too valuable to waste, had been carted back to Elastun where Eadred had distributed it among the poorer residents there. Some of the animals had been missed, and doubtless these wolves had already picked off most of what had been left behind. Why not continue doing that? Why risk attacking a man when there were much less risky alternatives they might prey upon?

As if in response to Swein's question, the three wolves in front of him stepped aside, and into the gap they left strode a dark grey male - much taller at the shoulders, and heavier in build than the others. This, without question, was the pack leader. Unlike his fellows, he did not have his head down, or his teeth bared. You, my friend, are calm, thought Swein. Like the leader of some opposing army riding into the center of a field to discuss terms before battle commenced. The animal stopped less than six feet from him. Close enough to leap up and tear out Swein's throat, and close enough for Swein's axe to split it in two. It would be a matter of who was the swifter should one of them try. Something about the animal's manner made Swein stay his hand. It would have to be the wolf's choice. The animal's head tilted to and fro, and Swein could hear the swift streams of air through its leathery nostrils as it studied his scent. After a few moments the beast simply turned around and trotted back out of the village towards the treeline, followed immediately by its companions. In a matter of seconds, all of them had disappeared back into the forest from where they had come. The last to go was the first wolf he had seen.

Swein remained standing where he was with his axe raised, unsure if this was some kind of trick, a pretense at retreat to make him drop his guard long enough for them to race back in and take him to the ground. Were these creatures even capable of that sort of strategy? It was surely ridiculous to imagine they could be. Even so, he remained where he was for several minutes more, finally lowering his axe only when he heard them calling to each other in the distance, the noise echoing through the forest, too far off now to mount any kind of surprise attack.

What had the wolves been after? Had they considered him a possible source of food, then simply thought better of it, or had something else more complex than that taken place? The leader had undeniably studied him, as if looking for someone or something. The question was who or what? Was he hoping that Swein was that someone, or satisfying himself that he wasn't? What was it the old woman had said? *Some among the beasts will know. The ones that kill.*

As he was riding away from the village, Swein heard the noise of the wolves drawing closer again. They crashed out onto the path up ahead of him, and turned in his direction, coming at such speed that his horse panicked, and threw him before he could bring it under control. He was lucky, and managed to land well enough to prevent serious injury, but still yelled at the bolt of pain that shot threw his bad thigh. The wolves came so fast there was not enough time for him to get up from where he lay on the track, let alone reach for his axe. He had raised his arms ready to defend himself when the first of them sped past, closely followed by the rest. Confused, Swein rolled over and watched as they continued past him down the track. They re-entered the village and, from the sound of things, were making short work of the last of the chickens there. He breathed a sigh of relief, and had managed to struggle to his feet when the large male, the leader, came out from the bushes close by. It paused briefly, close enough to touch if Swein had wanted to. It did not look up, although it seemed to Swein that it inclined its head very slightly towards his bad leg, and sniffed faintly. It stood for a moment longer before padding off slowly to join the rest of its pack in the village.

******

Alditha was content that Eadwig's ankle was healing well. There were none of the signs of infection that could be so dangerous. When she had finished applying a fresh dressing she turned to his mother, Godgifu, and asked, deliberately so Eadwig would overhear, if she believed her son's story about Swein grabbing at him as he tried to climb back into the village over the wooden wall.

"No, I do not," Godgifu replied with conviction.

"Nor would anyone who knows Swein for the man he is," added Alditha, turning back to Eadwig. "Why not tell us the truth now, hmm? Please. I have known you all your life, Eadwig. We've been friends all that time, haven't we? When I married your brother, I became your sister. So, I know you. This is not like you. If you are afraid of what your grandfather is going to do if he finds out you are lying, I shouldn't worry. It's gone beyond that now. He is concerned about you. As we all are. Besides, he already believes you are not telling the truth. He will forgive you more easily if you tell it now. Can you not understand that?"

Eadwig groaned in frustration. "So, I'm already in trouble whatever I say. It's not fair! I tell you the truth and you think I'm making it up. What am I supposed to do now? Make up a lie you will believe instead of telling the truth which you won't? How did my leg get like this, then? If someone didn't grab me, how did it get hurt?"

Alditha reached forward and touched the boy's arm, trying to calm him. "I can't say with any certainty. I think, perhaps, when you fell from the wall it got caught. That is what really happened to it, isn't it? Just tell the truth now. It is important that you do. There are things happening at the moment that you don't know about."

"Tell me, then."

"We cannot. But you should understand that this may be more significant than you might think."

"You must tell us the truth, right now!" said Godgifu.

"I am!"

"If his father were here, he would get it from him," said Godgifu, a little tearfully.

Alditha took Godgifu's hand in her own and squeezed. Between the boy and his mother, Alditha was not sure who was the more distressed.

"But it *had* to be Swein," the boy protested, upset by his mother's tears, and fighting back his own. "Can't you see? He was on the track. There was nobody else. Then, when I was climbing back, a hand grabbed at me. I didn't get it caught. I didn't slip. I was grabbed. I'm telling you."

Alditha thought for a moment.

"Very well. Let's suppose we believe you were grabbed. Let's say that much, at least, is true. Was it *Swein's* hand, or just *a* hand? Did you actually see him? It was still dark, wasn't it? Yet you say you saw him…clearly?"

"Yes…No…"

"Well...?"

"I saw his shape. A big man wearing the helmet of a warrior…Exactly the same as Swein was wearing when I saw him just before…out on the track. Look, I told all this to Grandfather."

"Tell it again. Maybe you got a bit confused."

"No, I didn't. Swein was wearing the same things he went to fight in when he rode off with Hakon and Father that last time." He glanced briefly at his mother, saw the look of pain on her face, and wished he hadn't called upon that particular memory to make his point.

"You haven't answered my question. Did you actually see his face?" Alditha persisted.

"No, I didn't. That doesn't mean…"

"Oh, Eadwig," his mother cried. "That's enough! You must stop this nonsense right now! You should be absolutely sure before you decide to accuse someone of something. You can't simply invent things to conceal your own guilt. Nobody believes you were grabbed. Don't you understand that? Nobody! Why should we? The truth is you fell when you were climbing back over. Maybe you thought better of it because you knew you shouldn't be out there, and wanted to get back inside quickly. Or maybe you thought Swein had seen you, is that it? You know I really don't care. For whatever reason, you were in a hurry to get back inside. You were in a hurry, it was dark, you were clumsy, and you slipped."

"No! It's because you all want it to be a lie because you all like Swein, isn't it?" Eadwig's expression changed abruptly from one of frustration to one of sadness. "I like him too. I thought he liked me. I only know what he did. I don't know why he did it."

The boy was crying now. His mother sighed, sat down next to him, and put her arm around him.

Alditha supressed a yawn, stretched. She was tired. She did not sleep well any more.

"Look, Eadwig," she said, "If you were grabbed…"

"I was, I was, I was!"

Ignoring the boy's protest, Alditha went on in a tone as reasonable and friendly as she could manage. "If you *were* grabbed, as you claim. I suppose it is just possible it was

Swein. You don't know it for certain, though. There is a difference. You said yourself he likes you. Personally, I think it would be very out of character for him to do what you say he did. Have you ever known him do something like this before? I know I haven't. Swein is a disciplined man. He doesn't act thoughtlessly or hastily. He would have spoken to you first." She smiled. "Probably given you the good telling off that you deserve. I really think he would have said something rather than just pull at you so fiercely that he hurt you."

"It's because he was father's friend that you won't believe me."

"Nonsense," protested Godgifu, shaking her head.

Alditha shook her head too, but had to acknowledge to herself that what the boy said was true, at least in part. If someone really had tried to pull the boy down from the wall, she did want it to be someone other than Swein. Even though the facts as they stood pointed to him being the most likely party, she could not believe it of him. Could not or would not, she wondered.

"I think it was him, mother, I don't care what the rest of you say."

"You see," said Alditha, "that's the problem. It's only what you *think* he did. It's not the same thing as knowing. It's not proof of anything."

Eadwig hit the bed in frustration.

"I saw him on the track, wearing his battle outfit. And then someone wearing the same thing took hold of me. It wasn't even dawn. Who else could it have been? There was only him out there. Why are you all being so stubborn? Everyone is taking his side against mine!"

"It's not a matter of sides. Listen, Orderic's men wear the same sort of thing. Could it have been one of them, I wonder?"

"No. Apart from the one on guard, they were all in Grandfather's hall. You know that, Alditha. Grandfather says so. Or is he a liar too?"

"Eadwig!" warned Godgifu.

"The one on guard, then?" suggested Alditha, then immediately corrected herself. "No. We know it couldn't have been him. He was seen coming across from the other side of the village when they were helping you down. He was mounted. It's not possible he could have got back there like that in the time without being seen."

"There! So who was it then, if it wasn't Swein?" demanded Eadwig, getting to his feet, and stomping angrily out into the daylight to find his friends.

"Well," said Alditha, "obviously it's not hurting him much at the moment. That ankle of his will be absolutely fine in a few days."

"It's his backside that will hurt, if he is proved to be lying," replied his mother, with a long-suffering sigh.

When Godgifu had gone, Alditha decided to visit the church. She was on her way there when Orderic walked up alongside her.

"May I join you?"

"If you desire it. After all, could I stop you?"

Orderic smiled. "No, you could not. Nonetheless, it would be better if you agreed. Even if you yourself don't desire it."

"Better?"

"More agreeable."

Alditha nodded. "Come, then, if you wish. You do not need my permission to talk with God in his house."

"It is not God but you I need to talk with. I saw the lad, Eadred's grandson, leave your house just now. He is well? His leg, it is better than it was? He did not appear lame to me."

"It was his ankle. Yes, it will be fine. It will not trouble him much beyond a day or two more."

"The boy claimed it was your missing man Swein, did he not?"

"He did."

Orderic studied her as they walked.

"But you think he is lying."

"I think he is mistaken."

"I see. Why should that be? Because it is not the sort of thing a man like Swein would do?"

"Yes."

"Hmm. From what I have seen of Swein, I would agree."

Alditha glanced up at him. "I'm glad of it. Glad you can see as much."

"And the little one? The girl we found… with the odd name. She is still in your care. Tell me, how does she do? Would it do harm if I were to talk with her now?"

"Little Hare? I'm sorry, it would not be possible. It will require much longer I'm afraid. In truth, I do not know when, if ever, she will be ready for that. I wish I could tell you, but I cannot. Something like that…it is more than her body that is injured."

"Her mind is sick also."

"Yes, that. That, and her soul… I wonder if you can you appreciate that? "

Orderic shook his head.

"I confess, you will have to bear with me. I do not think I would recognize where one ends and the other begins. Such things are not usually my concern. They are a mystery to me."

Alditha was not sure herself. She knew she would struggle to describe what she meant, and almost wished she had not said it.

"I think they are intended to be. Perhaps if I explain that the child believes she has seen something of Hell. Or something she believes to have originated from that place."

Orderic frowned.

"You are not suggesting her own soul is in torment?" asked Orderic. "That small child? What possible sin...?"

"No, not that. Perhaps it's something like the heat you feel when coming too close to a flame. It does not necessarily burn you if you do not actually touch it, but the heat can still be unpleasant. I'm sorry, I don't think I know precisely what I mean myself. Ah, we are here…"

They had reached the church. Alditha pushed open the doors. Immediately she caught the scent of the fresh holly she had recently placed inside. The smell comforted her. She doubted it had any effect on Orderic.

"I'm sorry, was there more you wanted to discuss?" she asked.

"No, that is all for now. I will let you be about your business inside. Please inform me when the times comes that you think it would be safe for me to talk with the girl. Oh, Alditha…"

"Yes?"

"Thank you."

Alditha closed the door behind her, stood for a while as her eyes grew accustomed to the gloom. The black and white cat appeared from the shadows, a dead mouse clenched between her teeth. Alditha opened the doors. "Take it outside, Friddy! Go on!"

As she chased the cat out, Alditha caught sight of Orderic, still standing close by. He had stopped only a dozen or so yards away and, with his back to her, was looking up at the sky above where the forest opened out into the fields that ran down towards the river. He turned when he heard her. "Looks like more snow may be on the way," he said. Then, indicating the cat, which had scuttled off beneath a pile of wood next to a nearby hut with her catch still in her mouth, he said, "So, she does keep down the vermin, then." After a pause, he added, "Most of them."

Alditha nodded, uncertain to what extent she trusted the seemingly humorous tone of his voice. "Friddy? Yes, she does."

"So, she's called Friddy, then? Not Matilda, eh?" asked Orderic.

Alditha, still a little cautious, nodded. "Yes, well, Elfrida, actually." At that a curious expression, one Alditha could not read, crossed Orderic's face. "This time I truly meant no harm," she explained, confused. "Elfrida is honestly what I call her. Or Friddy…I meant no…"

Orderic smiled - the smile seemed genuine - and lifted his hand, palm outwards, and shook his head to indicate he was not offended. "It is a good name. A very good name, in fact," he said, enjoying her confusion. The woman was disconcertingly clever, there was no denying it, but even she could not have known the significance that name held for Orderic.

******

His horse having deserted him, frightened away by the re-appearance of the wolves, Swein had had no choice but to walk back to Elastun on foot. Ironically, its flight to safety had been the animal's undoing. Only a short time after it ran off, Swein had heard its cries of pain and distress echoing through the forest as, somewhere in the distance, the very wolves it had so desperately sought to escape had cornered it and brought it down. Swein shook his head, reflecting that if the beast had come back to him, it would have lived to see another day. It was his best horse and would not be easy, or cheap, to replace.

He had not even arrived at the fork in the way where the path from Gyrtun joined the wider track back to Elastun by the time full darkness descended. Thankfully, the sky above the treetops was clear, and there was enough moonlight falling on the ground for him to make out the way relatively easily. But his leg throbbed as he walked, and worse, what food and drink he had brought with him had been carried off by the horse. Eventually, thirst drove him to pick up handfuls of old snow from the patches of it that still remained along the edge of the track, and put it into his mouth to melt. Still, it was relatively clean, and he had tasted worse in his time.

Swein had no fear of the wolves on the walk back. His encounters with them so far had suggested they meant him no harm. They would not attack him simply for the sake of it, and he did not seem to have entered any territory they felt the need to defend. Also, if hunger were a factor, even after their finishing off the remaining livestock at Gyrtun, his horse had surely taken care of that for a while. But the unease which he had initially felt on recognizing the black marks on the trees had taken root, and grew with every painful step. By the time his route took him alongside the blackened oak on the edge of the forest he had examined earlier, it was only pride that had made him continue down the centre of the track. He had to resist a strong urge to cross to the other side, as far away from that disfigured trunk as possible. Maybe it was fatigue, or maybe it was the surrounding darkness. Whatever the cause, Swein now found it much easier to believe that something evil, and outside his understanding, had made those marks. And whatever that thing was, it also lay behind the recent deaths. The sooner he got back to the relative safety of Elastun the better. He knew fear itself was not something to be ashamed of. It was as natural as pain. But like pain, the test of a man was his ability to rise above it. Swein held his head high, made a point of looking directly into the darkness beyond the trees, facing down his fear of what it might conceal. All the same, he kept the leather tie of his axe sling unfastened.

It was near dawn the following day when he neared the gates of Elastun. From a distance he saw one of the villagers was manning the gates. Beyond him, in the centre of the village, Swein could make out a figure on horseback - one of Orderic's men by the look of him. Swein made no attempt to get back into the village unobserved. There was no reason to, given that his absence would almost certainly have been noticed by now. He called to the man at the gate, one of Eadred's servants, and was disgusted to discover the man was asleep. By the time he had roused the fool, the horseman had also become aware of Swein's arrival and had ridden over. It was the one they called Hubert. The same man who had been on guard when Swein had slipped out the previous morning. Hubert spoke harshly in French to the man at the gate, saying something that neither the man nor Swein could understand. Swein did not need to know Hubert's language, however, to recognise the anger in his voice, and guessed he was reprimanding the gatekeeper for having fallen asleep - probably saying more or less the same things as Swein himself intended to say to the fellow later. Now, while the man hastily opened the gates for Swein to enter, Hubert turned his attention to the Housecarl. The anger in his voice was more restrained, a whispered hiss of irritation, but it was there to be heard nonetheless. Swein's leg was throbbing with pain, and he was close to collapsing with exhaustion, but he raised a smiling face to the enraged horseman and nodded a deliberately over-friendly greeting, purposefully ignoring his tirade.

A little later that morning, shortly after Alditha awoke from her usual restless sleep, her maid came to her and said that she had discovered Swein sitting against the wall next to the door of the house, and that, as far she could make out, he was fast asleep.

******

Riding back to the castle, Rollo was glad to have left Elastun behind him. For some time now he had not been at all comfortable with how things there were going. He did not approve of the growing spirit of co-operation that was developing between Orderic and those pitiful Saxons. Rollo had no use for it, and he couldn't see why Orderic should either. The situation was not so difficult to assess. Guy had been murdered and, most likely, so had Turold, or he would have shown up by now. So someone needed to be punished, and that was all there was to it. Simple really, when you thought about it. The Baron had said as much himself, and he had been correct. He had also been correct when he made it clear it didn't much matter to him who was actually guilty when it came to choosing who it was should receive the punishment. Just so long as some unlucky Saxon or Saxons were punished, and the example duly made. That was all that really mattered here, wasn't it? That the example was made. The message being that killing Normans would never go unpunished. What of it if they punished the wrong people? Quite frankly, who but the Saxons themselves would really give a damn about that? Orderic claimed there was a danger that those who were genuinely responsible might be discovered subsequently. He seemed concerned that it would make the Normans appear disorganized to these people or something of that nature. Disorganized? Hadn't the Normans just conquered their country? Besides, the answer, as always, was simple. If the true culprits were discovered, punish them too. There would be no harm in that. These people could use all the lessons on the perils of killing Normans they could get. If the selection for punishment seemed indiscriminate, well so be it. There was nothing even-handed about the business of conquering a people.

And as for that other business....Well, as far as Rollo was concerned, what had taken place at that dung heap of a village, Gyrtun, was no concern of his, or of any of theirs, for that matter. So someone had got a little carried away out there. It happened, didn't it? Yes, even he was prepared to concede that he had never seen anything quite as out of control as that, but it didn't alter the basic fact that the victims were Saxon, not Norman. So not anything that the captain should be worrying about. Who knew why those people had been killed, or who had done it? More to the point, who cared? It didn't matter, did it? Those people were about as insignificant as it was possible to be, living out there in the middle of nowhere. Not much better than the pigs that rooted around their houses. All that fuss that had been made over the unpleasant little child he had spotted still alive in the bushes down by the river. Scurrying about like an animal with the hounds on its tail. A pity, really, that they had stopped him killing her when they did. An orphan now, she was just another mouth to feed. Another Saxon to cause trouble when she grew up. Unless she grew up pretty, of course. She might have a use then. But, my God, anyone would think it was their job to protect these uncultured Saxons, not keep them subdued under Norman rule. The Baron would agree with him about that, even if Orderic didn't.

The more he turned it over in his mind, the gladder Rollo was that Orderic had selected him to ride back to Rylemont to report on events. He might even make use of Orderic's absence to request that he be put under Richard's command. Best to make a decision on that when he saw how the Baron viewed Orderic's conduct in all this nonsense so far. Better not to declare a lack of allegiance to his captain before he knew which way the wind was actually blowing. He didn't want to be seen as the disloyal type. Orderic and the Baron shared a father, after all. That had never seemed to count for much thus far it was true, but you never could tell when it might.

Talking of the truth - that Guy was dead did not bother Rollo very much. That was one man he had never been able to get on with. Turold he had liked. But then everyone had. It would be a shame if Turold were dead, as it was suspected. As for Guy, though, that really was one man Rollo had never liked. The man was an exhibitionist and a braggart. He was one of best men with a sword Rollo had ever seen, and Rollo was not too proud to admit that, but there was more to fighting than needlessly elaborate movements and posturing. So, he was the most gifted with his sword among them - what of it? That was all very well in the practice yard, but had he done better service than the others when it came to actually fighting? That ridiculously decorated scabbard said it all really. Very fancy, but at the end of the day, no better than the plainest of its kind. And a lot of good his skill did him in the end. He was dead, and that scabbard twisted and broken. Both of them now useless to anybody.

Rollo cursed. He would not reach the castle until tomorrow afternoon at the earliest and, from the look of the sky, it seemed there would be no let-up in this cold weather. There would probably be another hard frost overnight. Perhaps more snow. Really, when it came down to it, the Saxons could keep this country of theirs as far as he was concerned.

******

Alditha had been preparing a salve for Swein's aching leg while he told her about where he had been, and what he had discovered there. By the time he had finished his story the salve was ready to be applied. He sat back, flinched, made uncomfortable by the intimacy of having his leg touched as she knelt down before him to massage it in and apply a dressing. Alditha glanced up. Her face, serious until that moment, broke into a brief smile.

"Oh really, Swein!"

"I could do that myself, if you would only let me," he protested.

"And have you waste my labours by simply slapping it on like one of your battlefield remedies, then knotting the dressing around it like a fat priest's belt? I think not. This has to be rubbed in properly and wrapped up tightly… and *carefully*. Can you do that with those big hands of yours? No, you can't. So, for heaven's sake, Swein, will you let me get on with this? The sooner I'm done, the sooner you can cover up. Really! How many years have you known me?"

Swein grunted in acknowledgment that the girl was right. Then, after a minute, asked her, "So what do you think about what I've told you? Do you think me mad? Ranting like poor old Penda was when his end came?"

Alditha looked up from binding Swein's thigh. It seemed as if she were about to say something, then she closed her mouth again. She looked down, but did not continue with her work.

Swein breathed in through his nose, grunted. "Hmm, so you do think I've lost my reason," observed the Housecarl. "I swear to you, I have not. I'll even swear to it on your dear mother's grave, if you so wish it."

Alditha lifted a finger to silence him.

"No. Don't! You don't have to do that."

Alditha did not think Swein mad. Nothing in his manner suggested he had lost his wits or was running a fever, as had been the case with the unfortunate Penda. The old servant's claim that the Norman soldier he found at the ford had still been alive was quickly, and easily, dismissed as impossible by all those who had subsequently seen the body. It was commonly agreed upon as the product of the old man's confused mind. But Swein was very wrong if he thought Alditha's difficulty in replying to his question was due to reluctance on her part to tell him she now believed the same to be true of his own claims. If Swein said it was the truth, then that was enough for her to accept it as such. She did not think the man had told her an outright lie in all the years she had known him. Unless, that was, she were to include his avoidance of admitting he and Alditha's mother had been lovers at one time. Even that, he had never actually denied. He had simply gone out of his way to avoid discussing the subject. If she were to ask him now, he would probably confess to it.

What made Alditha reluctant to answer him was a disinclination to give voice to her belief in what he had told her. Once said, it could not be un-said. She knew it made no difference really whether she spoke the words aloud or not, it just seemed so terrible because of what it might mean. "I believe you," she made herself say at last.

"You believe *I* think it is true, or you yourself also believe it to be so?"

"In some ways I wish I *could* think you were mad. Unfortunately, there is something in what you say that suggests otherwise. The oak, you see… It was once said of it that…" she hesitated. "There are things about it. Stories from the past. My mother, she was no witch…"

"Of course not."

"But she knew things. You, of all people, must remember how she was? She told me things sometimes. Things that came from the old beliefs. Handed down through generations, for years and years. Blasphemous things some of them, I used to think. I didn't like hearing about them. Mother said I was wrong to call them that. She said the people who had worshipped those things were misguided, that's all. Not necessarily evil. When it came to it, much of it was true, she said. What she meant was that a lot of what they had handed down to us about which plants could heal what particular ailments, and things like that, was correct. So, I should respect them for that, and learn what they knew. Not condemn them for what they didn't. The fact that back then they did not understand that it was God who had created these things was not their fault. And I understood that, I really did. But the other things… I could not accept them…How they put their faith in the wrong things…it was so…"

"Alditha, what is it you are telling me? How does this apply to…?"

"The oaks. You said it was only the oaks."

"Well?"

"The oak tree has long been considered powerful. Before they knew of the one true God, some people even worshipped it. Faith in the wrong things, as I said. The oak tree was at the centre of much that was believed. It was seen as imbued with a great deal of power."

"Dark powers," said Swein. He gave a hollow laugh that took Alditha by surprise.

"What is it?" she asked, bemused.

"Dark powers. So, it is dark powers after all. You're telling me the fools worshipped the oak tree because the Devil was in it? Now someone is using that power again in our valley?"

"Not necessarily the Devil. That's not what I said. The power that they think they are using was supposed to have been neither good nor bad. Only powerful." Alditha thought for a moment. "Like your axe there. It is neither a weapon for good or evil. It depends entirely upon whose hands it is in… which master it serves. It can be made to work in the service of either." Then she added, "Oh, and may I say…about that axe of yours… you know you really should not have that thing. You must hide it as soon as you are able. Heaven knows what Orderic will do if he learns of its existence. Better still, get rid of it entirely. Please."

"I will not," said Swein, offhandedly, and grunted. "I will not waste Alfred's work so easily."

"Alfred? You involved poor Alfred…?"

"What if I did? He was glad to do it. Anyway, we have strayed from our subject. So, you believe whoever marked those trees might have been invoking this power of which you speak. Summoning it up?"

"Exactly. Unfortunately, I think we can say without question it was for evil on this occasion."

"What of the wings?"

"The wings?"

"The shape of the marks…like a crow's or a raven."

"Crows, I can't think of anything particularly significant. They eat the dead, but so do so many things. I'm sure there was nothing special about them. Ravens, though..." Her frown deepened. "Mother told me there were various things once believed about them. Not one of them good, that I can recall."

"War? Like the Landwaster banners carried by the Vikings?" suggested Swein. "That nonsense is well known."

"War, yes. Death too, along with ill omen, and disease. None of it nonsense. All of it bad, unwelcome things." She put her face in her hands, so that when she spoke it was muffled. "I never wanted to talk about such things again. To do so always frightened me back then. Even now..."

"I know, and I'm sorry I had to come to you with this. If there had been anyone else...I regret I have one more favour still to ask of you. I understand you find the subject distressing, but I need you to come with me when I talk to Eadred about all this. Will you do it? He will trust in your knowledge as I do."

"I will if I must," said Alditha. Then a thought struck her. "What will you tell Orderic about it?"

"That man? Nothing if I had my way. Still, I suppose we will have to, in due course. Hard as it is to admit, we may need his help. Yet, I would tell him only when we must. Not before that. I will counsel Eadred against telling him until we know more, and ask that you do the same. Being a Norman, Orderic will not share our understanding of the world. Apart from their own, it seems to me the only power those people will concede is that of God Almighty. And that only if it serves their purpose." Swein glanced at Alditha, saw the worry on her face. "That salve," he said, to change the subject. "It smells like the dogs have been..."

"Never mind what it smells like," she admonished good-humouredly, pulling the dressing tight enough to make him grimace a little as she did so. But the smile she gave him was only a fleeting one. She stood up. "There, that's done for now. You will need to take it off in about two days."

"You trust me to do it properly?"

"That part, yes." Alditha looked up at him, asked, "What happened with Eadwig?"

Obviously surprised by the sudden change of subject, Swein looked blank for a moment.

"Eadwig? What has the little pup been up to now?"

"He was hurt."

"Hurt? Badly? What happened?"

"No, not badly. I think he was more upset than he was injured. He's already on the mend. It's only that…"

Something seemed to occur to Swein. "Oh, don't tell me..."

"What?"

"Last time I saw the boy he was where he shouldn't be. Beyond the wall, on one of his forbidden hunting adventures was my guess. It happened then, I suppose?"

Alditha was making a show of cleaning the utensils and clay pots she had used to make the salve, trying appear as casual as possible. "So you did see him?" she asked, keeping her tone as relaxed and conversational as she could manage, and not looking up from what she was doing.

"Oh, yes, I saw him alright. Hiding there in the bushes like that. It wasn't difficult, despite the fact that I was yards away from him on the path, and it was still dark." Swein, chuckled. "Heard him, too. Crashing around like that. No wonder he never catches anything. I've known plough oxen move with more grace. Listen, don't tell him I said that. If he doesn't know I saw him, let it stay that way. I'm sure Eadred will have seen to any punishment he saw fit."

Alditha breathed out, relieved. So, Swein was not the person who had grabbed the boy. This was enough to convince her. She had never thought Eadwig's story was entirely true, but had thought there might have been some misunderstanding. From what Swein was saying, however, he hadn't even approached the boy, let alone grabbed for him as he tried to escape back over the wall. As she had expected, Swein was not pleased when she told him what Eadwig had claimed, and it took some persuading on her part to stop him storming out to confront the boy about the lies he was spreading.

"Tell me, what does Eadred think?" Swein asked her, calming down a little.

"The same as I did. That even if there had been some sort of confrontation between you and his grandson, the boy was confused about what actually took place. He would never have believed you attacked the boy. And, if you must know, nor did Orderic when he found out. Nobody thinks you are that sort of man."

"Well, that is good to hear. Although I care not what the Norman thinks. The question remains though, doesn't it? Why would the lad say such a thing? He's always been mischievous, disobedient, much like his father was as a lad, but I never thought he was a liar. Someone hurt him, you say? It couldn't have been an accident climbing the wall?"

"Maybe. I thought it possible, but I don't know. I don't think so. It did look like grab marks…the shape of them…like fingers had made them." She lifted her hand, fingers spread, and raked it down through the air. "Strong fingers. And Eadwig seems so insistent."

"Yes, well, he also insists it was me! That nonsense aside, if there were somebody else out there, why didn't I see them? Why hurt the boy? Then why stop when they did?"

Alditha had folded her arms tightly about herself as if suddenly cold or anxious.

"What is it, Alditha?"

"All this. All that has been happening. And now we are discussing the old ways. Mother used to think they were…I don't know…amusing, almost appealing...exciting. She would tell me about them as if they were like any other fireside tale. The truth was I never enjoyed hearing about them. I hated them, and never wanted to know. I complained once and she said I was being ridiculous. Her mother had told her, and hers before that, and now I should be told. I understood why that was so when it came to what roots and plants held the power to soothe and heal…the things that could do good. It seems to me such things were put in the world by God for us to find and use. But the old beliefs were misguided, maybe worse. There may be things we are not supposed to find. Or if we do, maybe it is a test, and we fail it if we make use of them. Maybe we are damned." She paused, looked Swein in the eye. "Perhaps we fail simply by believing in them?"

******

When Walter, Harold and Mark rode back into Elastun all who saw their faces knew immediately that the news they carried with them would be bad. Eadred and Orderic, who had both been told of the riders' approach, were waiting, along with Swein and Alditha, at the entrance to the great hall to meet them.

Alditha glanced up at Orderic, and contemplated how strange it was that, more often than not these days, it was him, or men like him, that the villagers had gathered anxiously in front of the great hall to receive. Now here he was himself, not only standing at its entrance but, for the time being, actually lodging in it along with his men. Perhaps he had sensed her gaze, because he turned in her direction, and gave the slightest of nods. She returned the nod, but quickly looked away. Swein was standing only a little behind her, and she knew he must have seen this exchange, and that he would not approve if he mistook the civility between herself and Orderic for friendliness.

She had already spoken to both Eadred and Orderic separately about the accusation that Swein had injured Eadwig. Neither man had taken much persuasion to accept that the Housecarl was entirely innocent. And Swein, at Alditha's suggestion, had explained to Orderic that his recent absence from the village was due to an ill-advised and unsuccessful hunting trip. If Orderic had noticed Swein's best horse was still missing from the stable, he had not seen fit to comment upon it.

When Walter and the others drew level with the small group standing outside the hall, they halted. All three riders then dismounted, handed their horses over to the care of Eadred's servants, and followed Eadred and the others into the hall. They were led to the same room in Eadred's private chambers where, less than a week ago, the decision to send them out on the very errand from which they had just now returned had been reached.

Up until this point, apart from a few murmured greetings, no one had spoken. So, when Orderic and Walter simply pulled chairs out from the table and sat down, without having been invited to do so by Eadred, whose private guest table it was, the dismay Harold felt at this lack of respect for his village head man was obvious. He hovered, embarrassed and uncertain what to do next. The expression on Swein's face in reaction to this outrage was less of dismay, more one of unconcealed anger. Alditha prodded him with her elbow and shook her head, surprised to find herself in the role of pacifier for a change. The tension was relieved when Eadred gestured that Swein, Harold, and Alditha should also be seated. However, Swein's expression remained sullen, and he cast angry glances at the two Normans, who either did not notice or chose to ignore him. Eadred then took a seat himself, only then realising that Mark remained standing by the door. Eadred leant over to Orderic.

"You may tell your man Mark he need not stand guard. We will not be interrupted, nor will we be overheard."

"You have power over your servants' ears?" asked Orderic.

"I trust them."

"You will understand when I tell you that I do not share your trust. You, these villagers follow. Me, they only obey. And that is because they must. There is a great difference between the two things, as I am sure you appreciate. Mark will remain where he is. So then, Walter, what is your news?"

"They are dead, Eadred! My sister…All of them," cried Harold, before Walter could answer his captain's question.

Orderic glared at him. "So will you be, if you do not keep your damned voice down, man! My question was directed to Walter."

"He knows as much as I," said Walter with a shrug. "Let him tell it if he wishes."

"Very well," said Orderic, a little surprised at Walter's new-found tolerance for this Saxon farmer. He supposed it was the result of their having ridden together for some days.

Walter nodded, turned, and spoke to Harold.

"Tell them, if you will. Slowly, though. Maintain your calm. And for God's sake keep your voice down".

So Harold, with occasional interjections from Walter, began to relate what they had discovered on their journey to the neighbouring villages. Most, it seemed, remained unharmed, and were completely unaware of the danger that had found its way into their valley. Only after Walter had agreed to Harold's suggestion that they extend the range of their trip to take in Tunleah, a small village, only slightly bigger in size than Gyrtun, that stood at the centre of the heathlands on top of the furthermost of the surrounding hills, on the western edge of the valley - and was not, strictly speaking, *in* the valley, and therefore not among the villages they had been tasked with visiting - did they find evidence of a similar attack to the one sustained by Gyrtun.

Harold, clearly struggling at times with his emotions, explained that the first sign was at the foot of the hill, on a track leading up out of the forest, and towards Tunleah. There, they found what looked to have been the deserted camp of a charcoal burner in a clearing among the trees. From the size of the hut, and the belongings they found, it looked as if a man, a woman, and at least one child had lived there until very recently. Harold had guessed it to have been the camp of Wilfred, who had often supplied charcoal to Alfred for his forge. There was no sign of life in the place now, however, but nor were there any bodies, or even blood stains. In fact, there had been no indication of violence or any kind of struggle at all. It seemed the place had been deserted as it stood. The burner's wood stack, left unattended, had simply burnt itself out, or had been extinguished by the dampness of the weather being allowed to get through to it. Either way, it seemed as if Wilfred and his family had quite suddenly decided to break off from whatever they were doing, and just walk away into the forest. Concerned by the strangeness of what they had discovered, the three men had re-mounted and ridden their horses at the gallop to the top of the hill, and over the heath towards Tunleah. All of them slowed their horses to a steady, unhurried walk when they drew near, and could see something of what lay ahead.

At this point Harold broke down and could not continue. He slumped forward, his face buried in his hands. Walter took up the story in his place, explaining what Eadred, Swein and Alditha already knew, and what Orderic had guessed. Harold's suggestion of also visiting Tunleah was prompted by the fact that he had relatives living out there. His sister and her family. He had wanted to reassure himself that they were unharmed, and to warn them about the danger that roamed the valley.

Sadly for Harold, he was too late. His sister, her husband, and her children, like everyone else in the village, had already met similar violent and painful deaths to those dealt out to the inhabitants of Gyrtun.

"Did no one survive? None of Siward's people?" asked Eadred, reaching across, and putting a comforting hand on Harold's shoulder.

"No one this time," Walter replied. "We searched…rode all over the heath… we found no one out there. No one still alive. All we found beyond the huts was more dead villagers." He looked suddenly uncertain, as if he could not quite believe what he was about to say. "There was a stack of wood smouldering out there on the heath. Two, maybe three, hundred yards off. I rode out to take a closer look. It was just like the charcoal stack down the hill. Arranged the same way. *Exactly* the same way. Only this one had the remains of people burnt alive inside."

"The charcoal burner?" asked Eadred, already knowing the answer.

Walter nodded. "Harold thinks it was him… and his family"

"They made a jest of the manner of their deaths?" said Alditha, dismayed.

"It would have taken time and effort to do it," said Walter. "That's what is so strange. To have gone to all that trouble."

Eadred stood, and began pacing the room. "It is an ill thing. So many dead, once again. Siward, the head man…he was a good man. My son fought alongside him years ago. Now he, too, is dead. Walter, tell me, please… Siward… What was the manner of his end? What did they do to him?"

"Why ask, Eadred. What good does it do to know?" protested Alditha.

"It matters not," said Walter. "I cannot tell you. Mark and I would not know which was him. As for Harold here, he was in no state by then…His sister… her death…it was not a decent one."

"I did not see him," said Harold, lifting his face from his hands.

"What?" asked Orderic.

"I know Siward...what he looks like anyway. I did not see him there. See his body, I mean. I can't be sure, though. The bodies were all...It was a terrible thing. Terrible."

"If he did survive, there is no one there for him to return to," said Walter, his bluntness making Alditha wince.

"True," agreed Eadred, and punched the wall in frustration.

"That gets us nowhere," cautioned Orderic.

Eadred turned, looked back at them all, embarrassed. "Forgive me. Siward was a good man. Brave in battle. Always strong in support of his people there. He did not deserve this."

"Nor did my sister!" protested Harold, looking up at him, his eyes red with tears. "She was a good woman, was she not? She did not deserve such an end."

"She was, Harold. And, no, she did not," agreed Eadred, his hand once more on Harold's shoulder.

There was a brief silence, broken eventually by Orderic. "When did it happen? What is your estimate?" he asked Walter.

"Difficult in this weather to tell. By the look of the bodies, the freshness of the blood, not long before we got there, was my guess. Without question, more recently than Gyrtun."

"And the injuries?" ask Swein, who had sat silently until now. "You would say these people met their deaths at the same hands?"

"Yes," replied Walter. "I would."

"You are certain?" asked Orderic.

"Had to have been. Everything points to it. The similarity was too great for it not to be. Those strange burns, the accuracy of the blows...like the girl we found on the path. Precise, perfect. We searched again for signs of who had done it, of course, but there was nothing to be found. No footprints, nothing."

"And the trees?" asked Swein.

"The trees? What about them?" Walter turned to Orderic to see if he could explain the reason for question, but saw immediately from his expression that he too was mystified. Orderic, himself, had noticed a look he could not interpret exchanged between Eadred and Alditha when the question was asked.

"There is something I should know?" Orderic demanded, glancing around at the Saxons sitting at the table. Eadred looked uncomfortable, Alditha looked down at her hands, but Swein met his gaze, so it was to him Orderic directed the question. "Swein. The trees. What of them?"

"You may as well answer him, Swein," said Eadred. "It was your discovery, and you should be the one to tell of it." He turned to Orderic. "Before he does, know this. We are none of us comfortable with it. And we are far from believing it is what it seems to be. However, it may still mean something. Only, what that is, we cannot yet say. So, before you ask, that is why you were not told."

"Not told? What is this?" demanded Orderic.

"Listen to me, please, Orderic. When Swein and Alditha came to me with what Swein had found, I was as sceptical then as I know you will be now when he tells you. Only after I had had time to think on it did it strike me that it might actually be significant."

Orderic's eyes narrowed. "Why do I sense that I am about to hear more talk of forest sprites and fairies? I had thought only your blacksmith held such notions. Yet you tell me it is significant."

"That is precisely why I was waiting until I judged the time was right before I talked of these things with you. The important point to remember is that it does not have to be *real* to be significant. Its significance may lie in the fact that whoever is behind all this are the kind of people who believe it to be real. Whatever kind of people that may be. I only ask that you keep that in mind."

Swein did not look forward to the prospect of telling his story yet again. Alditha had been open to what he said. Eadred, as Swein had expected, was sceptical. This Norman's reaction was likely to be more sceptical still. Perhaps not unreasonably, given that Swein himself was not certain how much he believed. As he spoke, he made sure to hold his head up, and make himself look directly at Orderic and Walter the whole time. He refused to look away, despite the occasional derisive smirk he saw register on Walter's face, and refused to be unnerved by Orderic's total lack of expression. He knew the latter to be deliberate and designed to have that very effect.

When he was finished he fell silent, but still he did not look away.

"What am I to make of this, Eadred?" said Orderic, brushing a hand across his face, dismissively breaking his eye contact with Swein. "More to the point, what would you have me do because of it?"

"It is as I explained," replied Eadred. "You need not accept the beliefs behind it as true. I do not give them much credence myself. The marks are there on the trees, nonetheless. Someone believes. Or would have us think they do."

"Much?"

"What?"

"Much. You said you do not give them *much* credence? That leaves room for *some*, then, does it not? You tell me you do not believe, and then you say there is room for it. What's it to be?"

Eadred shrugged. "These things go back a long time. Who can say if there was not once something that the world no longer knows? If, like on the battlefield, you would have me choose a side, then I do not believe. Does that satisfy?"

"It is the Devil's work! It must be!" yelled Harold. "The

Devil has done this to my sister and her sons!"

"You were warned!" hissed Orderic. He then issued a command in French to Mark, who immediately stepped forward, grabbed Harold by the hair, pulled his head back so violently the Saxon nearly fell off his chair, and put a sword blade to his throat.

Alditha put a hand to her mouth, too late to stifle a cry of shock. Despite all that had happened, the violence that came so easily to these men still distressed her.

"I've told him to bleed you out like a butchered pig, Harold, if you say another word louder than a whisper," said Orderic, speaking in little more than a whisper himself. However, no sooner had Orderic said this than he seemed to relent. He spoke to Mark once more, and Mark immediately released his grip on Harold, who slumped forward with a gasp. Although Harold now seemed to know better than to give voice to any kind of protest himself, he looked immediately to Eadred in the hope that Eadred would protest on his behalf. Eadred's only response was a shake of his head, and a gesture that Harold should leave them. Dismayed, almost as much by what he felt was Eadred's failure to stand up for him as he was by his treatment at the hands of the Normans, Harold stood up, knocking his chair over, glanced angrily around the table, and stormed out. As he did so, he raised a hand and ran it around his neck, then checked his palm for any signs of blood. He was clearly relieved to have found none.

Watching Harold go, Alditha was grateful for Orderic's unexpected restraint, however she was troubled by the notion that it might, in fact, have been for her benefit rather than Harold's. Orderic had glanced in her direction when she cried out, and for a brief moment something in his expression suggested that it had made him uncomfortable, possibly even a little ashamed. She studied him now as he turned to address Walter. There was no sign of shame now, although there was no mistaking the fact that he was ill at ease with his subject matter. "Shall we turn our attention back to this extraordinary question about the trees? Well...? Did you notice anything of that sort?"

"No, nothing like that. But then it is all heathland up there. Few trees to speak of, and no oaks that I can recall seeing. Besides, I was not looking for them. But then neither had I taken a fisherman's net to catch fairies in."

"The charcoal burner's camp, then. That was down in the forest, was in not? Surrounded by trees, presumably. You saw nothing there?" asked Orderic, throwing Walter somewhat by failing to smile at his last remark and, apparently, taking what these Saxons were talking about seriously.

"No, there was nothing like that there either. Then again, I was not looking for...that sort of thing. Why would I have been? It is possible there were marks, I suppose. The only burning I recall was the charcoal stack, and that definitely had no unusual markings on it."

"What about the fire up on the heath? Was there anything out of the ordinary about it?"

Walter was becoming exasperated by this constant questioning. "You mean apart from the fact that it resembled a charcoal stack fuelled by the charcoal burner himself and his family?"

In French, Orderic said. "Walter, if you also begin to try my patience, what hope is there for us to get sense from these people? Come now, my friend. I look to you to set the example. You know very well what it is I'm asking you."

"But this is madness. Are we looking to hunt down a witch now? Or is it the Devil himself, perhaps? I have neither the skill nor the stomach for that. Consider this, Orderic. Might not the real devilry here be closer at hand? Might this not be something this Housecarl himself has devised to mislead us? It could be something he has come up with to divert us in order to shield his own actions. After all, it is only he who has even seen these strange markings of which he speaks. Not a single other soul has, Saxon or Norman."

"We can look for ourselves."

"That proves nothing. Even if we ride out right now and find them, he has had time create them. Nobody else saw them when we were there. Think on it! All of us that have been to Gyrtun, and not one of us but him sees them? Then he disappears for a day and a half, returning with this old woman's tale of the black arts. What are we to make of that?"

"My God man, do you seriously imagine I have not considered that the man may be deceitful. But what has he to gain by it? He was not especially suspected before this. Such a fanciful tale as he has told, what purpose could it possibly have when it only serves to draw attention to him if he is guilty of something? Surely it would be the least of his wishes if that were so."

"Perhaps it was not Swein alone. Perhaps they are all of them part of it?"

Orderic glanced around at the watching Saxons, aware that they would have no difficulty guessing what was being discussed.

"Do not use names," he cautioned, "that much they will understand. Listen, I ask you again, my friend, what purpose could it serve? It seems like madness, I know. Nonetheless, I need you to think back. Was there anything that resembled what the Housecarl has described? Were there any of those wing-like marks, or any odd marking of any kind?"

"It *is* madness. But no, there were not. Then again, there were no oaks near at hand."

Orderic now turned to Mark. Although he still spoke in Norman-French, Mark's perplexed look, followed by the shaking of his head, made it clear to the Saxons present what had been asked, and what the response had been. Orderic nodded, unsurprised by his man's answer, then turned back to face the rest of them. They all watched him as he looked down at the table, itself made from oak, and studied its surface for a moment, running his finger along it, tracing the path of the grain. Finally, he rapped it with his knuckles, and looked up at them again. Speaking in English once more he said, "This is good wood. We have…" He corrected himself. "*Had*, once, similar beliefs about the supposed power of the oak tree where I come from. Although I do not know much of what was believed. Alditha, you have shown some knowledge. Can you tell me any more about it? What might such things mean to whoever is behind this? Why would they draw attention to themselves in this way when they go out of their way to leave no other trace? We find nothing else…not even a footprint…yet they mark their presence like wild animals?"

"I'm sorry," said Alditha. "I regret not. I have told you all that I can, and that is only what my mother passed on to me. It was old back then, when she told me. Stories of ancient beliefs handed down that will have changed much through the years with the telling."

"Yes of course, my mother also…" here he stopped, changed the subject. "This is outside my knowledge. We need someone versed in such things."

"There are no witches we can consult around here," protested Swein.

"No, and I had not suggested there were. Though you could not find fault with me if I were to begin to wonder. Still, you have a priest visits your church, do you not?"

"Yes, of sorts. Brother Theodric," said Eadred. "I cannot say when next he will visit."

"In this cold weather? I would not look to see him here in the valley any time soon," scoffed Alditha. "That round-bellied man much prefers the warmth of the Abbey, and the comforts offered by the refectory there to the cold of our church and the humble fare we serve. Besides I am not so sure how well versed he is in his own faith, let alone the superstitions of times long out of memory."

"I do not think our fare so very humble," said Eadred. "But Alditha is right. He is not so devoted a man when travelling is involved. His arrival at our gates in the near future is unlikely."

"Very well, you will send to Abbot Robert at Menlac, requesting he arrange for this Brother Theodric's presence here as soon as possible," said Orderic. "You will explain something of the nature of the problem, and the knowledge it requires. If this Theodric is not the right man, perhaps Robert will have someone who is. Someone better suited. The Abbot need not know all of it, just enough for him to judge who is the best man to send. Swein, will you carry the message? In such dangerous times it requires someone with the ability to take care of themselves, and look to the safe conduct of any man of God whom they might have in their charge upon their return journey. I want my men here from now on. You, I know, have the necessary experience."

"I will," said Swein. "If it is…"

"Swein, your leg is not yet fully recovered," interrupted Alditha. "The Abbey is far beyond our valley. Such a journey will not be good for it. There is more snow in the air, too. You know only too well how the cold and damp can affect that injury of yours."

"If it is what is agreed upon here, I shall ride out today," said Swein, ignoring Alditha's protests.

"But Swein…"

"Alditha, please! I am not quite as ruined as you make out. If it is needed, I am more than capable of the journey."

"Good," said Orderic. "Oh, and Swein…" he added, with a knowing smile, "why not take that axe of yours along with you for protection, hmm?"

"I will. Thank you," said Swein, careful to conceal his surprise and irritation at Orderic's awareness of the weapon's existence.

"And perhaps Eadred can offer you the loan of a good

horse, as I see you seem to have somehow mislaid your best animal?"

"I have others up to the task," replied Swein, bluntly.

Eadred gave a hollow laugh. "Forgive me. Send to the Abbot? He will not respond favourably to such a request from a village such as this as a matter of principle. That is if he responds at all."

"Such holy men have a sacred duty, do they not?"

"Yes, but we are Saxons. Abbot Robert is not."

Orderic's expression grew hard. "Then I will send Swein on my behalf. And so, through me, on the behalf of the Baron. Menlac will respond to that. It will not be a request."

******

CHAPTER 11

As Alditha had predicted, the snow had come later that day. It was a particularly heavy fall - the heaviest so far that winter - covering everything in a deep blanket that did not look set to thaw for some time, and driving the majority of the adult inhabitants of Elastun inside, only venturing out for the essential tasks. The children, in contrast, were much less downcast about the heaviness of the snowfall, and groups of them could usually be found chasing about in it, and throwing snowballs. However, they were frustrated at not being permitted to venture out beyond the village walls, and into the forest where there was a seemingly unending carpet of deep, fresh snow in which to play. Additional men from the village, armed with an assortment of improvised weapons - knives, tools, and farm implements - had been posted as lookouts at intervals on a new, hastily erected walkway that ran around the entire inside of the wall, so climbing over unnoticed, as Eadwig - whose ankle was almost fully healed - continually boasted he had done, now seemed to be an impossibility.

If the guards drawn from the villagers alone were not sufficient to deter their children from attempting escape, one of Orderic's men was also always to be found seated on his horse at the centre of the village, or riding it slowly along the perimeter, following the line of the wall, checking the Saxons had not fallen asleep and were maintaining a constant lookout. This afternoon it was the turn of Hubert to sit his horse on guard. As he neared the gate at the far end of the village, leading out towards the fields and the river, he heard the soft thud of a snowball as it landed on the wood of the wall only feet from him, followed by the laughter of the children as they ran away. Had this been

Normandy he might have indulged in a playful exchange of snowballs, providing, of course, that Walter or Orderic were not around to witness it. Today, however, in this grey and forbidding forest, knowing what he knew about the nature of whoever was out there, he did not even turn around, but ignored the snowball entirely and maintained his watch. He also knew that, unlike a similar snowball thrown by the children of his homeland, this one was not necessarily good natured. These people feared and hated him in equal measure, and these sentiments were shared by their children. He himself was only guarding them out of duty to the Baron, not out of any fondness or concern for their safety.

Another snowball hit. More accurate this time, it found its mark, and burst against his helmet. He could not afford this distraction any longer. Instead of ignoring it, this time he spun around, scowling, only to discover Walter heading towards him, brushing the remains of the snow from his palms. Despite knowing that this particular snowball had been a good natured one, Hubert still felt a flush of anger which he struggled to supress as the big man approached him, still grinning, pleased with the success of his throw. It was possible Walter had seen something of it in his face because his first words when he reached him were placatory.

"Don't take it to heart, man. You could not have expected an attack from within the walls. No shame in it. Had those children managed to land a successful blow…now that might have been a different matter. I, on the other hand, am light of foot when I need to be, and possess a fine throwing arm. So, like I say, no shame."

Hubert huffed in disbelief. "Light of foot? *You*, Walter the Bear? I think not. You forget, I've been hunting with you. I know how you crash about through the bushes. It was the wind in the trees muffled your approach, that's all."

"There is no wind. Not even a breeze."

"The noise of the children making their escape, then. Or the two things combined."

"You protest because I have got the better of you. Now, there *is* shame in that. Admit it man. Show some good grace."

Hubert's expression turned sour.

"I tell you, Walter. I am short on grace of late." Walter made a reproachful face. "No, not the children, nor your lucky snowball," continued Hubert. "You know of what I speak. This place…I begin to lose all patience. If I had my way I would…" Hubert did not finish. Instead, he suddenly stood in his stirrups, craning his neck to see over the wall.

"What is it?" asked Walter. "You hear something?"

"There was no sound to speak of, only…it is more that I can feel something….in the air itself."

"You feel it, indeed. You grow fanciful, man! Lord save us, you are not turning Saxon on me are you? Letting your imagination get the better of you like these simple souls? I feel nothing. And that is because there is nothing to *be* felt. Nothing at all."

"Well, they can, if you cannot," said Hubert indicating the men at the wall. "These Saxons feel it…simple souls or not. Look at them! I tell you, something *is* out there. And it gets nearer."

The men on guard at the wall had begun to shout and gesture towards the forest. One had jumped down and was slowly backing away from the wall. Walter scooped up snow, formed another snowball which he aimed at the back of the man's head, at the same time shouting that he should go back to his place on the wall. The snowball missed its mark, breaking on the man's shoulder instead. He did not even look around, so Walter shouted at him to get back to his post, but still he did not respond. Seeing that some of the others were close to following their companion's example, Walter drew his sword and shouted a warning that he would have the next man that left his position killed. He turned to Hubert. "Hold your position here. I'll take a look. If another man gets down from the wall, you ride him down, you hear me."

As Walter stepped up onto the makeshift ramparts, he at last began to understand what the men at the wall were reacting to. There was indeed a strange tremor in the air. It was as if a great many horns were being blown together. Only for some reason, they were making no actual sound, just causing vibration in the air. The sensation grew steadily stronger, and still no definite sound was audible. Looking out, it appeared to Walter that it had begun to snow again, until he understood that the vibration, whatever it was, was shaking the snow free from where it had settled on the branches of the trees. Glancing around, he saw that snow was also slipping down from the sloping thatched roofs of the huts and houses. At the same time, he saw villagers beginning to emerge from within them. He caught sight of Orderic running from the hall, headed in his direction, closely followed by Mark. Eadred appeared from the same doorway a moment later, his wife at his side. From his gestures, it looked to Walter like he was giving her some urgent instruction. The young woman, Alditha, then appeared, having run from the direction of the church.

"What in the name of God is it, Walter?" called Orderic, still on his way over to him.

"I don't know. It's coming from out there, beyond the wall somewhere. I can't see anybody, though. It seems to be all around us, whatever it is. "

Orderic stopped running, raised his hand in the air, attempting to feel the direction from which the vibration was coming. He was forced to agree with Walter that it did seem to be coming from every direction. He turned to Mark.

"Get over to the far gate. Make sure they keep it closed. And watch the fields. Anything shows up, you send for me."

Instead of continuing towards Walter, Orderic now ran towards a villager standing on the walkway at a different part of the wall, intending to ask him what he saw. Before he reached him, however, the man had shaken his head, anticipating the question. Orderic spun around, looked to the others. All shook their heads, so, without bothering to reach the nearest steps, he hauled himself up onto the walkway of the closest section of wall to look for himself. Walter ran over and joined him there. Side by side, both men scanned the treeline.

"Nothing," said Orderic. "There is nothing to see. They would seem to have skill in the art of concealment."

"Do we risk sending someone out there to take a better look?" asked Walter. "See if they can see something more than we can from here."

"I think we must."

"Then how about sending one of the younger men from the village? One of these farm boys…One who can run."

By now they had been joined by Eadred who had been delayed while he ordered his wife and Alditha to take charge of gathering the rest of the villagers at the hall. "And what if they meet someone?" he asked. "As you say yourself, these are only farm boys."

Orderic signed. "Eadred is right, of course. It has to be one of us." Anticipating Walter's objection, he added. "Because if there is someone out there, and they do run into them, they will not stand the same chance as one of us would when it came to fighting their way back."

Walter looked irritated. "Why must all the risk fall always upon our shoulders? Is it not *their* village, hmm? Besides, if they die, they die," he shrugged. "That is the way of things."

"Yes, and if they die, so does the knowledge they gain by going out there in the first place," replied Orderic. "They are no damn use to anyone bleeding what they discover into the snow. We need it brought back to us."

"Or maybe then you die too!" snapped Eadred, looking pointedly at Walter. "*That* will be the way of things. All the same," he continued, addressing his words to Orderic now, "can we not wait? Let whoever it is show themselves? How much difference can knowing what is out there ahead of that really make? They will bring the fight to us in time."

Orderic considered this. "Can we be sure of that? What if it has never been their intention to meet us head on? What do we learn? This may be an enemy that does not intend to face us out in the open. We may have to run them to ground like a wild animal. If that is so, I wish to know the nature of the animal we must hunt. If they do not intend to make themselves known to us, we may learn nothing of them if we do not take advantage of this opportunity now presented."

"I think they will show themselves soon enough."

"Better that we know them first," replied Orderic, becoming impatient. He looked about himself, spotted Hubert, and called him over. "Hubert, you are already mounted, so the luck is not on your side, my friend." Hubert nodded his understanding.

When Hubert was in place, sitting on his horse before the gate, Orderic walked over to him, and looked up. "Remember what I told you. You're to ride straight down the track. That way you can travel fast, unobstructed by the trees, and we can still see you. The problem is, of course, they can see you too. It's a gamble. We trade the advantage of cover for the advantage of speed. You can't go anywhere near as fast among the trees, but keeping to the track will put you out in the open, exposed. That said, at present, there doesn't look to be anyone close by, so there should be no surprises. But you keep your eyes open from the moment you clear the gate. Only leave the track if you feel you must. Unless that happens, just see what you can from it. Understood? Good. Go swiftly. Ride like the Devil himself is at your heels. I need you back here alive. No fighting unless you must. Even if you think you can bring them down. We want information. Anything you can see. Go out as far as where the way bends out of sight. If there is still nothing to see when you reach there, take a look round the corner. Maybe twenty five, maybe fifty yards if you consider it safe to do so. No more than that, though. Then straight back, you hear me? Very well…"

Hubert nodded, and Orderic stepped back. "Open the gate!"

At the same moment the gate was opened, the noise began - a wave of it that rushed in at them. A high, ear-piercing whine above a sickening, low reverberation. Hubert's horse whinnied, took a few paces back, reared up. When he had finally managed to get it under control, he looked down questioningly towards Orderic. Orderic raised his arm as if in readiness to wave Hubert on, but before he could, Walter had seized it, and leaned in to shout something Hubert could not hear above the noise into Orderic's ear. Orderic, turned and nodded grimly at his second in command, then beckoned for Hubert to lean down. Orderic had to shout to be heard, but even above the noise, Hubert heard the graveness in his tone.

"If it looks like you will be captured…We've seen what these people do… I wouldn't choose to let that happen to me." He tapped the dagger hanging from Hubert's belt. "Do not relinquish that if it looks like you will be caught… use it on yourself first…Better for it than the sword. You will not be thought a coward if you do."

Hubert nodded his understanding. Wrestling down his fear, he turned back, and looked out the gate, down the snowy track between the trees. He took slow, deep breaths, focused on the task, not the possible outcome. Only another enemy like so many in the past, he told himself. Only another fight. A thought then occurred to him, and he called Orderic back.

"Will you have someone ready with a bow? In case I am

prevented from doing what is necessary myself should such a time come. Perhaps there is a good shot among these people. Otherwise, I judge Walter is our best."

"I will," replied Orderic. "But if you ride fast…do as I have instructed…you should be back here among us in no time. Take a look, nothing more. That is your task. I want to know what it is we are dealing with here. What is behind this horrendous noise, if nothing else. And remember, no engaging with this dishonourable scum unless you absolutely must. Good luck, man."

Orderic stepped back, looked up at Hubert, meeting his gaze directly for a brief moment before waving him out of the gate.

Not waiting for the gate to be secured behind him, Hubert immediately launched into a gallop, grateful for the obedience of his horse, despite the animal's very evident fear. The ground rushed past beneath him, and the cold air whipped at his face. For a few seconds, Hubert forgot the purpose of his ride. Remembering at last, he began to glance into the surrounding forest. Orderic had said he was to keep moving, and moving fast. The difficulty with riding at such speed was that everything about him raced by so fast that he could not make it out clearly. Certainly not clearly enough to spot if there were anyone attempting to conceal themselves out there among the undergrowth in the shadows and half-light beneath the trees. They could be standing up in plain view and he still might not see them. He came to a decision. It was a risk, and he would have to explain it to Orderic later, but he reined in, slowing his horse to a brisk trot. Now he could study his surroundings more easily, and he turned his head about to look into the gloom of the forest on either side of the track. As far as he could make out, there was nothing there, other than an endless succession of trees above a deep carpet of snow, all of it merging into a dark grey haze in the distance. There was nobody there, and nothing to account for the noise, which was strange, given that it seemed to be louder, and all around him now. Was it possible he could have drawn that much nearer the source, be at its very centre, and still not have seen it? What was it, anyway? What was he expecting to see? What were these people using to make the sounds that combined to create such an oppressive and uncomfortable sensation in the air? Wild animals of some kind, bound and beaten so they howled and roared in protest? Or could it be man-made? Drums and horns, perhaps? Maybe some dreadful combination of all of those things? Whatever the cause, it was beginning to make it difficult for him to think clearly. Orderic had said to keep going to the bend up ahead, but his horse grew ever more skittish by the moment. Soon the beast would be impossible to control, and he did not fancy being thrown off in the midst of whatever it was that was happening out here. He turned in the saddle, looked back down between the avenue of trees, towards the wooden wall of the village, its gate now firmly closed. On either side he could make out the shapes of the men standing there watching him – Orderic and Walter among them – no doubt wondering why he had stopped and what he thought he was doing. He had a sudden vision of Orderic's face, and the anger and disappointment stamped upon it at Hubert's failure to complete this simple task. He uttered a curse, but could not hear his own voice above the noise. Surely they would understand why he could go on no further? The terrible noise. Worse now. Making him grimace at the thrumming in his head, disrupting his thoughts. And there was the panic it was causing his horse. That alone was reason enough to turn back. He would not be able to control the beast much longer. Now was his last opportunity if he wanted it to carry him back to safety. Uttering another curse he could not hear, he turned the animal about and began to gallop back towards the gate, and the relative safety of the village.

"What is the man doing?" said Orderic, watching from the wall. "Why is he coming back so soon? There's been nothing so far? Is it possible that already he sees something out there that we cannot from here? Have you got the bow we talked about?"

"I have," replied Walter. "Belonged to Eadred's son, he tells me. Looks up to the job."

"I don't give damn where it came from, so long as you keep it ready. If Hubert's returning because he's lost his nerve, I've a mind to have you shoot him for it. Be ready."

Walter gave a grim smile, but did not lift the bow. "I will if I must. Though he's never shown himself a coward before. No, it will not be that." He chuckled to himself. "Either way, I think we should at least wait to hear what he has to say. Give the man a chance to explain himself before we waste a perfectly good arrow on him."

Orderic grunted his agreement. "True enough."

"And at least we will be able to hear him now," said Walter.

"Huh? Oh, you mean all that noise has stopped?"

"I do, thank God. I have never heard its like before. Made my head ache it did," said Walter. He thought for a moment, then added, "Strange, was it not… how it coincided with our opening the gate, and ended the moment we closed it?"

"That it was."

"You know, I can only think it was done to inform us that someone is out there. Timing it to our actions like that was their way of signalling their presence to us. Letting us know that we are being watched, and trying to make us nervous by it. They saw the gate opened, and they saw it closed."

Orderic looked doubtful. "That would be a great amount of trouble to go to, would it not? Just to play on our nerves? Waiting all the while for it to happen simply to let us know they were watching. Particularly if you consider they have already achieved as much with this perplexing throbbing in the air." Orderic paused, cocked his head. "The noise may be gone, but that is still there. Irritating. How is it done, I wonder? These people like to play games, God damn them! Tricks and…What now?"

Less than a hundred yards from them, Hubert had stopped, and dismounted, making no effort to catch his horse as it bolted away.

"Does he *want* to die? Why is the fool just standing there?" asked Walter. "His horse has more sense than he does."

"Move man!" shouted Orderic.

"It doesn't look as if he heard you," observed Walter.

"Of course he heard me. That's no distance at all."

"Look at him, Orderic. It almost as if he doesn't see us either. What's he looking at? He's saying something, too. Can't be to us. Who in hell is he talking to? It cannot be us, he would have raised his voice. Why does he not return?"

As they watched, Hubert got to his knees.

"Is he *praying* now?" asked Walter.

"Much good it will do him if he does not get out from the open. At least find some cover in the trees." Orderic put both hands on the wall, and leaned out to call to Hubert again.

The noise hit him immediately. This time so intense it was as if he had leaned into the rushing waters of a waterfall. He staggered backwards, and would have fallen from the walkway had Walter not grabbed him in time.

"Are you well? What is it?" asked Walter.

Orderic frowned. "What do you mean?" He saw the others on the wall. None of them ruffled as he was. "You did not hear that?"

"Hear what?"

Walter, Eadred, and the others all stared at him.

"What is wrong, Orderic?" Walter asked in hushed tones.

"The noise, it came again, I would swear to it! Did you truly hear nothing?"

"Not a thing."

"Argh, my mind must be playing me false. It would seem Hubert may not be alone in losing his reason. It is strange. I could swear I…" Orderic saw Eadred and the other Saxons on the walkway still staring at him. "Never mind what I thought," he said, more firmly, and looked out again to where Hubert was now curled up in foetal position in the snow. "We need to get that fool back here."

It was Walter who now leaned forward to call out. And he, too, staggered back.

"My God! What is that?" he asked.

"A noise like a thousand hell hounds howling and charging at the same time?"

"Yes, but *what is it?*"

"I did not hear it this time, Walter. Only you did," said Orderic. His voice was steady, but the tension in it was unmistakable.

"What do you mean? How then can you know? I don't understand…"

"Nor do I." Orderic held up a hand. "Wait." Mystified by what he now suspected, and surprised by his own willingness to even consider it, he leaned forward beyond the wall, and once again the sound crashed about him. When he pulled back, it was gone. Walter stared at him, his mouth hanging open in confusion. Orderic said nothing, but gestured for him to lean forward beyond the wall again. Having done so, Walter stepped back, his eyes wide with astonishment.

"We are bewitched! We must be," he whispered, as much to himself as to his captain.

Behind them, Eadred, who had been observing them, now leaned out, with the same result.

"God save us!" he cried "It *is* devilry! It has to be!"

As Eadred spoke, he was interrupted by a scream of

agony and terror that came from the track up ahead. It rose in pitch, then was abruptly cut off. At first it looked as if Hubert had risen to his feet and was walking - his gait peculiarly straight and upright - back towards them. Only when he drew nearer did the men on the wall see to their utter bewilderment that what movement there was from his legs was not the result of him walking, but from his feet skidding and bumping against the ground as he struggled against whatever it was that was lifting him, and dragging him along against his will by some means they could not see. There was nobody with him, and no visible means for it, but he was being lifted nonetheless, in some crushing embrace. His arms were clamped to his sides, his head was thrown back, and his face had upon it an expression of sheer agony, as if he were being suffocated, his jaw opening and closing as he fought for air. He was close enough now for them to see the blood spraying from his mouth. Then, whatever was holding him must have released its grip because he slumped to the ground. Able to breathe again, Hubert struggled over onto his back, gasped in air, then screamed.

By now, many of the villagers had climbed or jumped off the walkway, and run from the wall. Only a few remained, watching, alongside Orderic, Walter, and Eadred.

Hubert, only yards from the gate now, staggered to his feet, raised his arms, imploring them to come to his aid.

"What do we do?" asked Walter.

"Nothing. We wait," replied Orderic.

"How can you say that?" The question came from Alditha, who had joined them on the wall. "We must help him!"

"If we go out to him, we share his fate."

Alditha knew Orderic was right, but still she protested. "There must be something…some way…"

"There is something," said Orderic, his voice flat. "Walter…the bow. End this. Now."

Walter closed his eyes for a moment, mustering the resolve for what he had been ordered to do. Although this would not be the first time he had killed an injured comrade in an act of mercy, it never came easily. Especially when that comrade was also an old friend.

"Now!" commanded Orderic. "Do it!"

Walter raised the bow, aimed, and released the arrow. It was a short distance, and he was a good shot. It should have been over for Hubert in an instant. Instead, the arrow flew from the bow, then froze in the air, just inches from him, hovered there a moment, rose up a few feet, then shattered in the air.

"What the…?" mumbled Walter.

"Again!" shouted Orderic. "Shoot again!"

Once more an arrow left the bow only to halt and shatter before it could deliver the mercy it was intended to bring. Alditha screamed. Walter dropped the bow and put his hands to his head.

Below them, Hubert was once more lifted from the ground. This time he was high enough to be on eye level with the people watching from the wall. The heads from the two broken arrows had risen with him, and now began to circle like insects around his head, jabbing and cutting at his face. He howled in pain as one gouged at an eye, and the second arrow darted into his mouth, ripping at his tongue. As if in order for them to see more clearly, Hubert's struggling form had drifted forward, towards the onlookers on the wall. For some moments they did nothing, merely looked on, dumbfounded.

Orderic was the first to take action. By now, only Alditha, Eadred, Walter, and a villager whose name Orderic could not remember remained on the walkway. "Help me pull him in!" Orderic shouted at them. "Reach for him!"

They all joined with him as he leaned out to reach Hubert who, despite his obvious pain, was himself reaching forward in order that they might take his hands.

Once again the noise roared in their ears as they leaned out beyond the wooden wall. But it was what they saw, rather than what they heard, that most astounded them. Where, beforehand, Hubert had seemed to be floating in the air, now the figures holding him there could be seen. On either side, lifting him high above themselves with what would have required tremendous strength, were what seemed to be two men, both clad in the outfit of a warrior. Despite their deathly grey skin, their sunken cheeks and eye sockets, their faces, surrounded by chain mail, beneath their steel helmets, were still recognisably those of the men they once must have been.

In front of Hubert, facing away from the wall, was a far less distinct figure, the like of which none there had ever seen before. He was tall – a good ten feet – so that, even with his feet on the ground, the back of his head was level with them. He was naked. His completely hairless body was thin, sinewy, and his skin, a paler grey than the others, appeared to ripple with the movement of tiny, maggot-like creatures writhing just below the surface, occasionally wriggling out through his flesh, crawling across, then burrowing back beneath again.

He reeked of blood, death, and decay. The smell making the onlookers at the wall retch and cough. Worse still, he radiated such a powerful sense of hostility that it made it difficult to look upon him for more than a few seconds at a time, for fear he would turn his face and direct that ill will directly upon you. The mere thought of it alone was like experiencing a nightmare. In his hands were the arrow heads that were the source of Hubert's torment. After a moment he dropped one of them and reached forward, almost tenderly, placing his hand on the top of Hubert's head in a gesture that parodied a blessing. The instant his bony palm and thin fingers made contact with the chain mail Hubert wore it sizzled, glowed, and melted onto his head. Hubert screamed.

Alditha screamed too, stepped back, was caught and steadied by Orderic who had already stepped away. When he released her, she fell onto her hands and knees, sobbing and vomiting.

Walter leaned back inside the wall, then leaned out again, repeating these movements over and over, as if testing the truth of what he was seeing.

In contrast, Eadred had not moved. He remained rigidly in position, bent forward, tears running down his face, and emitting a low moan of despair. Orderic took one more look himself, swallowed down the bile that had risen to the back of his throat, then turned towards Eadred and tried to pull the old man back. Eadred fought against him, his hands gripping more tightly at the wood beneath them. Orderic then saw the other villager, pale and shaken by what he had witnessed, step up to Eadred and take his arm.

"He is right," Alfred, shouted. "You must come away, Eadred. He cannot be helped. He is beyond us now. Darker powers have him."

"Your man speaks the truth," said Orderic. "Hubert cannot be saved. The risk is too great."

To Orderic's surprise, Eadred released his grip on the wall, spun round and glared at him. "I give not a shit for the sufferings of your man. It is my son whose torment I would end!"

"Your *son*? I do not understand. What in God's name do you mean, man?"

From beyond the wall Hubert screamed again. Strips of skin were now peeling away from his flesh, torn from him by the long hands they had all seen only moments before, but could not see now. As they watched, Hubert was suddenly swept back down the track, and away into the woods, his blood spraying the snow beneath him as he went, and his screams echoing back through the trees.

"Did you not recognise him, Orderic?" asked Walter appearing at his side.

"What? How could I? I don't know what his son looked like."

Walter shook his head, took Orderic by the shoulders. "Turold! The other was Turold! Where were your eyes, man?"

"What?" Orderic had not studied the other faces well enough to have seen what Walter now claimed he had seen. His own gaze had been drawn to the central figure, the one from whom all the evil they must now confront had seemed to emanate. "No. No. This is madness!" he said, and pulled himself free from Walter's grasp.

"It *was* him, Orderic!"

"Madness, I tell you!"

"All that we have witnessed, and still you think it impossible it was your man?" asked Alditha, pulling herself up from the walkway, and brushing the tears from her face with her sleeve as she spoke.

Orderic took a deep breath and leaned back out over the wall. Walter did the same. The noise had ceased, and there were no figures to be seen now, only the blood stains in the snow churned by Hubert's struggles. There was nothing to show that there had been anyone or anything else out there with him. Orderic banged the wall with his fist. "I do not know what I have seen. Can you tell me, Alditha? Can any of you tell me? Can any one of you explain it? I think not. What we saw and what we imagine we saw are not necessarily the same thing. It may not have been there at all. None of it. All of it may be a trick of some kind we have yet to discover."

Orderic began to make for the steps down from the wall, but Walter hurried forward and stood in his path.

"Don't be a fool. Let me pass!" hissed Orderic.

"Wait, Orderic," insisted Walter. "That *was* real. You know it was. You know this was no trickery. None of it. How could such a thing be arranged by mortal man? How could we be made to see that which was not there?"

"I don't know…Some concoction…a potion of some kind to confuse the mind might do it. A brew of particular plants and roots. I have heard it said that in the right mix such things can make a man see all manner of monsters and sprites. You know about such things, Alditha. It could be done, could it not? Tell him."

"Something like this? No, I do not believe so," replied Alditha. "We all saw the *same* thing, Orderic. An individual mind can be fogged with the right mixture if it is brewed and administered in the right way, it's true. But all of us made to see the same thing…I do not see how that could have been done. No, that cannot be done. It cannot be done. What just took place…I believe to have been real."

"She is right," said Walter. "It *was* real. Truly there. All of us saw it. Hubert is dead. That blood is no trick. You can see how it has sprayed the ground from high in the air where we saw Hubert held. I saw it happen. And you saw it too. Something lifted him up and butchered him like an animal. Up there, in the air in front of us."

Orderic, glanced down at the blood.

"You see," continued Walter. "There it is. You saw what caused it. And if you saw that, you must also have sensed the evil that came from it."

Orderic grunted. "Possibly…"

"*Possibly?* That thing was there. You cannot think me, of all people, a fanciful man. I know what I saw. That thing…it has bewitched Turold. It was him. I saw his face, if you did not. If Eadred says the other was his son, then I have to believe him."

"Wulfstan," said Eadred softly, behind them. "My eyes are not what they once were, it is true. Yet I would know my own son, and it was him I saw out there. My son…or his spirit…something of him was there.

"Ghosts now!" said Orderic. "Must I do battle with ghosts?"

Alditha had stepped across to Eadred's side. "Perhaps

you must," she said, turning to embrace Eadred. The old man drew back slightly, embarrassed at such a display of intimacy in front of the Normans, but Alditha was insistent, and he relented, returning her embrace. For a moment nobody spoke, then Alditha lifted her head from Eadred's chest and looked back at Orderic. "It *was* my dead husband's father, Wulfstan. There is no doubt. The only question is how. In what form does he appear to us? What realm has he travelled from?" As she said this, Alditha shivered. If Wulfstan was bewitched, could not Hakon be also?

Orderic looked around at their faces. It was clear that all of them, Walter included, believed what they had seen. Perhaps, Orderic thought, even he himself did. "Forms, realms. What am I to make of this? Black magic? Ghosts? The Devil himself? I am a soldier, not a priest. This is far beyond what I know."

"It is beyond all of us," said Alditha. "That makes it no less real. There is much we do not…"

Orderic raised a hand. "Enough!" He sighed, then spoke more gently. "Enough… please. You need not continue. I know what you would say, and it is not necessary. Although I cannot explain what I saw, I must accept what my eyes have shown me, or consider the possibility that I am either intoxicated or have entirely lost my reason. But then, as you have already asked, how is it that you all saw the same? Besides, if either one of those is the case, then we are already lost. So, I will go with the evidence of my eyes instead. However, if I am to believe it… as I begin to think I must…answer this. Why only out there? If this truly is some form of black magic we face, why then not cast the spell over us all, and be done with it? Why claim only Hubert, Turold, and this Wulfstan?"

"I do not know," said Alditha.

Frustrated, Orderic banged his fist against the wall again. "I cannot fight what I cannot understand… cannot even see half the time."

"The wall!" exclaimed Alditha.

"The wall? What of if it?" asked Orderic, perplexed.

"I don't know... It's just that...I think it may have been the wall that sheltered us. *Shielded* us..."

"What? The *wall*? It protected us? Perhaps you *are* intoxicated."

"Why not listen to her, Orderic?" said Walter. "Only a moment ago you claimed she understood these things."

"Potions yes, but..."

"*Please*, Orderic, just listen to me a moment. Will you do that?" asked Alditha. Despite looking sceptical, Orderic nodded, so Alditha continued. "Our wall is oak. Look at it. You see? Oak. It's always built and repaired entirely with the wood of oak trees. We choose it for its durability. Of all the trees hereabouts it has the greatest strength and longest life. I think there may be more strength in it than we realised. If it *is* the old magic, then it cannot pass beyond the power of the oak. Think. That terrible sound...what we all saw ...none of it could reach beyond the wall. It stopped right there. Only when we leaned out...only when we crossed from its protection did we see and hear those things. I told you before, remember, the oak has always been thought of as special."

Orderic looked doubtful. "No, it is too simple an explanation."

"Why? You believe the cross wards off the evil eye, do you not? It is not for us to say where God places His power."

"Only a moment ago you said this is old magic...before God...pagan."

Alditha looked shocked. "Before He chose to reveal himself. Before Christ brought us the word. God has always been."

"And you believe He has provided *oak* as our shield?"

"I don't know. Yes. He may have done. There is always

a war being fought between good and evil. There must be weapons with which to fight it."

"An ordinary wood has protected us?"

"Yes." Alditha was far from certain, but put as much certainty into her voice as she could manage. "I do."

Orderic studied her for a moment. "And what of the oaks burnt in Gyrtun?"

"Marked like that to put an end to their power, perhaps. Contain it or destroy it somehow. What if they were not *claimed* by evil as we thought? What if they were *attacked* by it?"

"Why, then, did this thing…this evil… not simply mark the wall?"

Alditha shook her head. "I don't know, I don't know. I'm only guessing at this."

"Possibly there is just too much of it?" suggested Walter. "All of it acting together, making it stronger."

"Too much?" asked Orderic, looking at Walter, then back to Alditha.

Alditha nodded. "Yes, that could be it. Why not? Look, I told you, I am only guessing at all this. I make no claim to know for certain. Walter could be right, though."

"It might be like a wall of archers," suggested Walter.

"Archers?" asked Orderic.

"Yes. You know what it's like with them. You can easily kill one or two if they are out in the open, and on their own. But put a hundred of them in a line, then it's you that gets killed. You can't even get close. And they don't need to."

"What of the vibration? We felt that inside the wall."

Alditha glanced around as if looking for inspiration. "The noise out there shaking the trees?" she suggested after a moment. "You saw how the snow fell from the branches. We could feel that although we might be deaf to the noise itself. Like an axe handle when you chop wood."

Orderic shook his head. "Archers…The handle of an axe...What next?"

"Have you got any better suggestions?" asked Alditha.

Walter stepped in close, pulled Orderic to one side. "I know your difficulty with this, but what choice do we have? The girl is clever. We should heed her words. Once I would have thought it madness too. Now? Now I have only what my eyes and ears tell me. I must believe them."

"And if they deceive you?"

"I ask again, what choice do we have?"

"Wait! Do you feel that?" asked Alfred.

The vibration had returned. They all turned to look out at the track beyond the gates.

"Stay back!" commanded Orderic, sensing that his companions were contemplating leaning out beyond the wall. "I alone will look."

With a mixture of fascination and dread, Orderic leaned forward into the space beyond the oak wall.

The tall grey figure was standing there again, less than ten yards away. It was facing towards the wall this time, and he sensed that it was looking directly at him. Sensed, not saw. Unlike the rest of its body, which was horribly clear and definite, where the figure's face should have been was only a hazy greyness, darker patches where the eyes and mouth would have been on a human face. Despite this, it still seemed to be capable of conveying the utter hatred it felt for Orderic. It was hatred so intense it drove him back beyond the wall.

"What is it?" asked Eadred. "Is my son…?"

Orderic shook his head. Even so, the old man leaned out, and Alditha, Walter, and Alfred all looked as if they were about to do the same thing.

"Don't!" said Orderic. This time it was more a warning than a command.

Eadred, still leaning out, shouted his son's name. The next moment, he began to howl.

"Get him in," said Orderic.

When Alfred and Walter had pulled him back in, Eadred

slumped down against the wall. He turned and looked up at Alditha and the others. His face was pale. "Orderic is right. Don't. Don't *ever*!" He buried his head in his hands. "I asked about my son. I wish to God I had not. It shows you things if you let it. I saw him at Gyrtun. Wulfstan. *My son.* Doing those terrible things."

"Hakon?" asked Alditha, anxiously.

"Hakon? No. I did not see him there. But I think your man Turold was there, Orderic. Hurting people…doing dreadful things." Eadred paused, looked up at Orderic. "It wants to talk with you."

"It told you that? It spoke?"

"It didn't speak…it…I don't know how it told me. I just know it wants to talk with you."

"No! No, Orderic, you mustn't," pleaded Alditha. "You don't know what it will say. How it will play with your mind."

Despite her protests, Orderic leaned forward. But he did not lean forward far enough to cross the wall.

"What would you say to me?" he shouted defiantly at the empty air in front of him. "Whatever it is, I promise I am ready to listen. Only you must come here to me. I grow very weary and have not the energy to lean out. So it follows, does it not, that you must lean in? Whisper to me, if you will. Lean in, speak in my ear. You can do that, can you not? You need only cross this wall…"

The vibration grew much stronger for a few seconds, before fading away completely.

Orderic looked around at the wall surrounding the village, and then back down at the section next to him. This time, when he brought his hand down, it was not in a fist. He brought it down more slowly, pushed against one of the posts, gauging its strength. He turned to Alditha.

"It is all of it oak…the gates…all of it? And it is always repaired with oak?"

"Yes. It is Eadred's instruction that it always be so."

"It is the best wood for a wall," added Alfred. "Strong, and long lasting. It is not so common in the forest, but it is better for the job than the wood of the other trees. They perish much sooner."

Orderic nodded, satisfied. "Then we have our first advantage."

A scream rang out from somewhere among the trees, followed almost immediately by another.

"How can he still live? When will his suffering be over?" asked Alditha, shuddering and raising her hands to cover her ears.

Orderic looked in the direction of the screams, frowned when another one rang out. "Only when Hubert's strength leaves him. Not before. I think this creature enjoys it too much to end it fast. The oak doesn't block any sounds Hubert himself makes. The creature must know that, and it will know that hearing him plays on our nerves. The end for my man will not come swiftly. Certainly not while he still has breath enough in him to scream."

******

Orderic sat opposite Walter at a table in the great hall, both men eating the food placed in front of them by Eadred's servants. They understood the need for the energy it would provide, so they ate, despite having no real appetite. To one side of them, at the far end of the table, sat Eadred. Unlike them, he ate none of his food, just stared down at it without really seeing it. His mind was still too occupied with the image of his son - a revenant of some kind, back from the world of the dead, a slave of something evil, and doing its bidding, no matter how obscene or sinful. He had not told his wife. He could hardly bear the horror of what he knew himself, he would not ask her to endure it too. And what could he really tell her anyway? How much of it did he himself really understand? She had heard what he had eventually chosen to tell the rest of the village when they had gathered in the hall, that was enough. That was all he would burden her with. There was nothing to be gained by her knowing of their son's – their *dead* son's – part in it. He would spare her that pain if he could.

It had been difficult to know what to tell the villagers about what had happened out there beyond the wall, and what dangers now faced them. Some of them had witnessed the Norman soldier's ordeal for themselves, and those who had not seen it would still have heard Hubert's screams – screams that, almost impossibly, went on for over an hour after he had been swept back out of sight among the trees.

As his people stood there in front of him, with their fear and bewilderment plain to see on their faces, his usual confidence - a confidence that these people depended upon - had deserted Eadred. For the first time ever he had experienced an urge to turn away, to abandon them, tell them they were on their own and would have to think for themselves for once. It was not because he despised their apparent inability to function without him, the way any difficult decision about their future always fell to him, but because, this time, he worried that he was not any more up to the task than any one of them would have been themselves. Who was he to tell them what to do in the face of something like this? What did he know or understand of such things?

The burden of leading them had been heavy in the past, especially with the changes brought about by the coming of the Normans. That they had survived so far sometimes seemed to him something of a miracle. It was a source of pride to Eadred that he had shepherded them through it all, and he had sometimes to remind himself that, if they had survived, it was God's doing, not his own, and he should curb his pride. Despite all that had happened, all the grief and destruction wrought by the ruthless new king and his brutal kind, by God's grace, Elastun had looked set to endure. The Lord, it seemed, had guided him in his choice of actions. But then Eadred had been born to the role. Raised by his father to take his place as the head man of the village when the time came. The problem was his father had never foreseen anything like this. Orderic and his kind, no matter how hard-hearted or cruel they had seemed, were, if nothing else, human. They ate, slept, felt pain, happiness, perhaps even love. These were motivations that could be anticipated, and allowed for when dealing with them. What was out there now, somewhere among the trees, had no such qualities. The only feelings it seemed to possess were those of rage and hatred - an almost palpable sense of ill-will. How did you face up to that? What action could you take against it? Kill it? Could such a being even *be* killed the way an ordinary man could? Was Elastun's fate inevitably going to be the same as that of Gyrtun, just as that thing out there had shown him it would be? Perhaps God had abandoned Elastun after all?

So, as Eadred had gazed out at the frightened faces of the villagers, all looking to him for guidance, and a reassurance he had not known how to give, he had struggled for what to say. Earlier, the thing out there had shown him images of a future with many of those same faces contorted by agony and terror. If that fate was a certainty, as the thing had told him it was, there were no words of hope he could offer these people. But what would they gain by knowing that? How much should he even tell them of what lay beyond the protection of the oak walls? Always assuming that protection was real. He prayed to God that Alditha's theory was correct. Right now, it was all they had.

In the end, he had told his people as much of the truth as he thought they could cope with. He told them there were some manner of murderous outlaws abroad in the forest, and they were using witchcraft to aid them in their deeds. Fortunately, their witchcraft did not seem effective inside the village boundaries, so the villagers must pray that these evil men chose to move on, leave them alone. The harvests complete, and the winter stores having been gathered, there was food enough for some time to come, so they must sit tight and trust in the Lord. Swein had been sent to fetch help from the Holy Brothers at Menlac and, in the meantime, Orderic and his men were on hand to lead them in a defence of the village should it prove necessary. Eadred had no real faith in any of what he said, including the last part. It was his firm belief that, should the evil gain entry to the village, Orderic and his men would mount their horses and ride away. There had been little attempt in the past to conceal the shared enmity between the Norman invaders and the people of England, and there was no reason for the members of either group to expect the loyalty of the other now.

The same thoughts were troubling Walter at that very moment. He looked up from his food, and asked, in a whisper only Orderic could hear, "If it comes to it, will we stay…die for these people?"

Orderic looked irritated by the question. His response was blunt. "What do you think?"

"I think we should not."

"Well, then," replied Orderic. It was clear he would say no more on the subject. He looked up the table towards Eadred. "You should eat, old man."

Eadred looked up, his thoughts disturbed by the interruption. "What? Oh…No, I have no appetite for it."

"You have need of the nourishment, all the same. You are no good to me weakened by hunger." Eadred looked at him blankly. "No good to your villagers, then? Eat that you may do better service to them," offered Orderic. Eadred nodded, placed a small piece of salted meat in his mouth and forced himself to chew and, eventually, even to swallow. When he looked up from his food, he saw that Orderic was watching him.

"How long can we expect this to last…The food, I mean…How much of it have you in store?" asked Orderic.

"Would you have me eat or speak," protested Eadred, through a second mouthful of the meat.

"I would have you do both. So, how long?"

"If we are careful, to the spring, if we must. We have provisioned for the winter months as we always do. And there is the stream to provide water. It runs through the village on its route to the river, as I'm sure you know."

"To the spring! Save us, I will have run mad by then," said Walter.

Orderic smiled slightly. "Let us hope it does not come to that."

"God forbid." said Walter.

"You have never been on the receiving end of a siege?" asked Eadred.

"Once, briefly," said Walter. "Didn't care for it. Laid a few in my time, though. The Duke…the King, I should say now…he was never a man to be trifled with. I remember the siege of Alencon. He took a harsh revenge on them there."

"*Did he?*" asked Eadred. Although Orderic had picked up on the deliberately exaggerated surprise in Eadred's voice, Walter, it seemed, had not.

"Hands and feet cut off," said Walter, making a chopping motion with one hand, towards the wrist of the other. "A harsh reckoning. Too much, some said. Not to his face though. If you ask me, the fools brought it upon themselves. They should never have risen in support of the Count of Anjou. More to the point, they should never have mocked the Duke for being a bastard. That's what did it. He might have forgiven their support for Anjou…eventually. He never would have forgiven the mocking of his bastardy. The Duke has always been more than a little prickly about that particular subject. He was never one to…" Suddenly remembering Orderic's own background, Walter decided it would be wise to change the subject. "The point is…as I said…a long siege is not something I care to endure. You never win. You either survive or you don't. I don't care for the prospect. Not one bit."

"You may trust that none of my people care for it either," said Eadred, his voice now free from irony. He managed to eat only a small amount more of his food before he pushed back his chair, and rose. "You will excuse me."

When he had gone, Orderic met Walter's eye, shook his head, then continued eating. Walter shrugged, reached across the table, took what remained of Eadred's food and, to the disgust of a servant who had remained in the room with them, divided it between himself and Orderic.

******

CHAPTER 12

Swein had disliked having to use the name of the Baron to get the necessary cooperation from the Abbot. Less than two years ago, if a request from Eadred, the head man of a village, had not been sufficient to motivate the brothers at Menlac, a request for their aid made in the name of the Earl would have been enough. Now these holy men seemed more interested in their how their actions would be viewed by the Baron and by King William than their responsibility for the spiritual well-being of the people of the countryside about them.

At first, Swein had been told at the Abbey gates that Abbot Robert would not even grant him an audience. It had not been necessary for the lay brother acting as gatekeeper to add that this was because Swein was a mere Saxon. Only when Swein had explained that he came at the behest of Orderic de Varaville had the man relented. It had not even been necessary to mention the Baron. The mention of Orderic alone – a Norman with whom the man was clearly familiar – was enough. No proof of Swein's claim was requested. What Saxon would risk claiming to act on behalf of a Norman if he were not really doing so? Only a fool would risk the punishments that would follow were his lie to be discovered.

Abbot Robert, a Norman himself, had been more difficult. He spoke in French at first, and looked exasperated when Swein indicated that he did not understand, even though it could not have come as a surprise to the Abbot. Even when he consented to speak in English, his accent was particularly thick, and Swein had to listen carefully in order to be sure he understood.

The Abbot, it seemed, knew Orderic and - presumably for similar reasons to the gatekeeper - never seemed to doubt the truth of Swein's assertion that he was acting on his behalf. However, the Abbot's evident dislike of Orderic seemed to make him reluctant to lend him any assistance if he could possibly avoid it. Only when Swein, as respectfully as he could manage, reminded him that, just as Swein himself was acting as a representative of Orderic, so Orderic was, in his turn, a representative of the Baron, did the Abbot seem more inclined to assist.

The Abbot had frowned. "I have been told there is no love lost between the Baron and his bastard half-brother. Yet I doubt that would be any hindrance to Bertrand de Varaville choosing to take uncalled-for offence at my not aiding his representative. So, you see, I have no choice but to agree to send someone back with you to look into the problems of your commonplace little settlement, Master Saxon."

"Elastun may seem commonplace to you, my lord Abbot. You may be assured, however, that our problems are far from being so," said Swein, his voice tight with supressed anger. "Ask yourself, would Orderic, a Norman like you, have sent me if they were? He is greatly concerned that something be done to address them."

"So it seems," said the Abbot, and then surprised Swein by adding, "Yet, I cannot help but wonder if Orderic's mother has anything to do with this interest in your people and their affairs? What do you think, Master Saxon? Perhaps you might ask him when you return, hmm?"

"His *mother*?" asked Swein.

"Wait…Can it be that you do not already know? Oh, how truly splendid! You Saxons, I thought you knew everything there was to know about your new rulers? It's said you chatter to one another like sparrows in the hedgerows." Then something seemed to occur to him, and the Abbot looked suddenly anxious. "Ah, now…I do not believe I shall be the one to tell you. You will not learn it here. Not from me." More to himself than to Swein, he added, "Orderic dislikes me more than he does his powerful brother." Then, looking back at Swein, he said, "Take it from me, my hobbling Saxon friend, do not ask him. One ruined limb is enough, eh? Now, leave me. Wait at the gatehouse. I will think on this unusual request of yours, and your *not commonplace* problems. When I have decided who to send, they will join you. Mind you have them back here at Menlac within the week. Now, get out."

There was no offer of shelter for the night, or even of food and drink. Swein was escorted to the gatehouse, where he waited for over an hour before a thin, bony looking monk leading an equally bony looking horse joined him.

"You are the one who asks for my help?" asked the monk who, on closer examination, seemed to Swein to be little more than a boy. "I am Brother Edmund. And you are…?"

Swein studied the young man for a moment. His large, hooked nose looked red and damp, and he sounded congested when he spoke. His accent, at least, was that of a Saxon.

"I simply wish to know your name," said Edmund, following this up with a sneeze, and wiping the sleeve of his habit across his face.

"I know what it is you ask, boy. You think me a fool because I have not taken your vows?"

"You think me proud because I have?"

Swein grunted. "I think you are very young. That is what I think. And I think you are unwell, that you appear sickly. Elastun calls for help, and the Abbot sends an ailing child."

"It is only a slight cold of the head. I am not feverish. This winter weather has affected me. A cold of the head. It is nothing more than that."

"The winter weather affects you? Here? In this house of privilege?" Swein nodded towards the Abbey building.

"It is the house of *God*," corrected the young monk.

"That may be. It doesn't alter the fact that you monks

do not know what discomfort is."

"The life of a monk is not all about comfort, I can assure you. You do not know of what you speak. And I am no child. I would remind you, it is *you* needs *my* help, not the other way around. I have shown manners, and told you my name. Will you not do me the same courtesy? Show me some of the same respect I have shown to you."

Swein grunted again. "My respect you will have to earn. Courtesy? I suppose you deserve that much, at least."

"At the *very* least." Edmund sneezed again, and made use of his sleeve once more.

"My name is Swein. It is not me who asks for you assistance, it is my village. Have you the kind of knowledge to do so?"

"Abbot Robert has told me something of your request. I believe I am as well suited as any here. You think me too young, but I have studied what texts there are that may have a bearing on your problem."

"I think you cannot have studied for very long."

"Not as long as I intend, I grant you. Nevertheless, I am the Abbot's choice. The matter must be of some urgency, for he has allowed me to take a horse rather than a mule."

"It is. Can you ride?"

"I can, of course. What use would a horse be otherwise? Tell me, is it far?"

"Some distance. If we ride through the night, we can be there noontime tomorrow. Assuming that beast of yours can go the distance."

"Hildy? Of course she can. You must not doubt her. Tell me, must it really be through the night?" When Swein did not reply, the young monk continued, "Ah well, if such a hurried journey is necessary, so be it. Who am I to complain? Indeed, it is my hope one day to be among those chosen to bring the word to villages such as yours on a more regular basis. To pay visits. Much as some of the other brothers here already do. I look forward to that time. So, as I am sure you can imagine, I am very grateful for this opportunity. I shall look upon it as a chance to..."

Swein had already ridden out through the Abbey gate.

******

Rollo's satisfaction with the Baron's response to his news had been short-lived.

On reaching Rylemont Castle, he had reported immediately to the captain of the guard. As he relayed his report, exactly as Orderic had instructed, partially melted snow still clung to Rollo's boots and dripped from his cloak. After that, he had been permitted to retire for the night, having beforehand eaten what had been his first decent meal in several days, and the drunk his first decent wine in several weeks. To his surprise, early the next morning, his head still cloudy from having drunk a little too much of the wine, he had been ordered to report in person to the Baron. This was something men of his rank were very rarely required to do, and something Rollo himself had never been required to do. As he climbed the steps leading to the inner keep, Rollo glanced up and thought he saw the Baron watching him from high above in the great wooden tower.

To Rollo's relief the Baron had shared his views about the inappropriateness of Orderic's recent conduct. Of course, on both occasions when it had been necessary for him to do so - first to the officer of the guard, and then to Baron de Varaville himself - Rollo had been careful to deliver his report exactly as Orderic had laid it out, and had not risked even the briefest of comments. Nor had he allowed any tone of disapproval to enter his voice, or expression of such to show on his face. He was merely the messenger and, as such, he knew his place. Only when he had finished speaking, and the Baron stood up from his chair, angrily pacing the room, rehearsing what he would have said to Orderic were he there in person, did Rollo allow the slightest trace of a smile to play across his face. Even then, only when the Baron's back was turned. Why should he not? He felt no guilt. He had not betrayed Orderic. Orderic had betrayed himself with his own report. Rollo had merely been his instrument. If the Baron had reached the conclusions Rollo had hoped he would, it was solely because they were the correct conclusions. The *only* conclusions that could be reached by anyone of sound judgement, in fact. The sort of judgement that Orderic's recent actions demonstrated he lacked.

In the Baron's view - and Rollo's - Orderic should have taken swift and bloody retribution against the local Saxon community the moment he had been presented with Guy's body. All this nonsense about finding the genuine perpetrator was all very well, but it had become a luxury that could no longer be afforded - not now it was known beyond any doubt that a Norman had been murdered by a Saxon. Yes, it was true that, at the start of this business, the Baron had agreed it would be preferable that they were seen to have full knowledge of what had befallen the two missing men before any punitive action was taken. Preferable, not essential. There was a difference. Besides, that was when the men were simply missing, and it was not known for certain they were dead. The Baron's view now was that, given that it had been established the man Guy was dead, it was extraordinary that Orderic had not taken instant, and severe, steps to avenge him - particularly given the extremely brutal nature of his death. Had not the Baron made it clear that someone must pay? More than anything else, that was what mattered. Someone must always pay whenever a Norman was killed. It should never, *never* go unpunished. As for the other business at the hamlet - this Gyrtun place - well, yes, it was undeniably out of the ordinary, and perhaps even a little troubling. And yes, it would be good to track down whoever was responsible. People should not be able to do that sort of thing to King William's subjects. But the subjects in question were only Saxons, were they not? There was a limit to how much time and effort should be put into tracking their killers down. For all Orderic knew, whoever was responsible could be the other side of the realm by now. His focus should be on avenging the Norman death. A hundred, a thousand, Saxons could be murdered, and it would not outweigh the death of a single Norman. That was the balance of things in this country.

All this had pleased Rollo. It was exactly what he wanted to hear. The more the Baron had railed at the failures of his half-brother, the more satisfied Rollo had felt, the more justified in his own opinions of Orderic's conduct. He imagined Walter and some of the others might accuse him of being disloyal. The thing was, loyalty was like respect. It had to be earned. And it could more easily be lost than gained.

It was only when the Baron finished his tirade and addressed him directly that Rollo realised his mistake.

"Your name again?"

"Rollo, my lord."

"Tell me, *Rollo*, what was your part in all this?"

"*My* part, my lord?"

"You were there. What did *you* do? What was *your* role? Presumably you witnessed all of this?"

"I did."

"Yet you did nothing."

"I…I did as I was ordered."

"As you were ordered. I see."

Rollo wondered what else he could say. He had been ordered. To have disobeyed would have been out of the question, perhaps even suicidal when you considered the punishments handed out to the mutinous. Discipline was everything in Duke William's army. The Baron knew that as well as anyone. What else would have induced them to have charged again and again, uphill, into those damned Saxon shields?

"Ordered? Do you tell me you are blaming Orderic? *My* brother. You think he has acted unwisely? Shown poor judgement? Someone with whom I am tied by blood, and you dare to criticize, to judge. If I did not know better, I might say it seemed to me you enjoyed relating this sorry tale."

"No, my lord."

Rollo's chest and neck tightened with a combination of anxiety and anger. Brothers. He should have known the Baron would side with his own. A man to whom the Baron was related only through illegitimate bonds, and a man whom the Baron was known to detest, could still not be permitted to be ground into the mud of dishonour because of the risk of some of it splashing up onto his noble born brother.

"That is just as well. Does it not occur to you that my brother is not himself? Did none of you wonder *why* a man so trusted, a man considered by my father…by *me*… to be fit to command you had gone so astray in his thinking?"

"No, my lord. How could we? What could cause such a…?"

"Damn it man, he is surely unwell in some way! Can you not see that? Some fever….some disorder of the mind is clouding his judgement. I do not for a moment approve of what he has done. Of course I do not. But what is behind it, hmm? What is the cause? He has to be suffering a disorder of the mind… Has to be." Then a thought occurred to the Baron. "Or wait now, is he perhaps bewitched? Ah, now there is something to consider. Tell me, man, is there anyone out there in the valley… a woman...it would be a woman … who could have accomplished such a thing? Some pagan sorceress. Think. She would be wily, cunning. She may well be as comely as she is clever and sly. It was ever Lucifer's way. She'll have used her beauty of face and form to gain Orderic's trust. Anyone like that in this village, hmm?"

Rollo did not hesitate. The Baron was providing a means for him to escape censure, and for the Baron himself to limit the damage to his family's reputation.

"There is Alditha. Yes. Alditha. She fits that description. She fits it perfectly!"

"Well, there it is then. This devil's bitch of whom you speak has surely bewitched my brother. He has shown weakness, I grant you, but it is a weakness common to a great many men. Women are never to be fully trusted. They are sly, evil. This Alditha proves it once again. She is a witch. That is it, is it not? You agree? You *do* agree?"

Again, Rollo spoke without hesitation. "I do. That is surely it. What fools we were not to have known her for what she is…Not to have seen it straight away as you have been able to, my lord."

"Ah, but then you and your fellows may also have fallen a little under her spell. It's quite likely with such a woman. But you are free of it now." The Baron's face wore a smile of satisfaction. "You know, I do believe we have answered two questions with this one explanation."

"How so, my lord?"

"If this woman can bewitch a man as strong willed as my brother, what else can she do? Might she not also be capable of murder? First a Norman soldier, and then a village of her own people. Now, that being so, is she not the very embodiment of evil?"

Rollo nodded emphatically.

"You agree. Of course you do. I would in your position. You understand me?"

Rollo continued to nod.

"What action to take, I wonder?" mused the Baron. He moved to the doorway, spoke to one of the guards standing there. "Whose men have the guard at present? Whose man are you?"

"I am with Bohemond."

"Not him then. Richard. Bring Richard to me. Quickly now!" When the man had gone, the Baron turned back to Rollo. "Your time at Elastun is not done. You will accompany Richard when he rides out there with a small body of men. First light tomorrow. We will bring Orderic back that he may be healed of this malady, and no longer held under this woman's sway. I think Abbot Robert may have his keeping for a time. But before we do even that, we will put an end to this woman's works. The whole valley should be purged of her influence. Only one way to achieve that. It will not be quick, however. I fancy she will face the torments of the next life only after she has faced her just punishment in this. Another task for the good Abbot, perhaps."

Rollo did not really believe Alditha was a witch any more than he imagined the Baron himself did. That was not the point. The point was to end this business as conveniently as possible with an explanation that satisfied the need for reprisal while, at the same time, explained why they - more specifically, Orderic - had not acted sooner in the matter. However, if accusations of unstable minds were to be made, Orderic's was not the first that suggested itself. As far as Rollo could see, the Baron's own mind danced from one point of view to another more often than a minstrel's tale. One minute he condemned his brother's poor handling of the business, the next he was finding any excuse, no matter how far-fetched, to defend him. He and Orderic shared no bonds of affection, but clearly blood was blood for all that. Nonetheless, Rollo was relieved to have had any share of the blame shifted from him. It was far better that Alditha should suffer for it, guilty or not.

Relieved as he was, Rollo still cursed the fact that he had to travel back out to that godforsaken village once again.

******

Of the forty two adult males in Elastun, there were just about enough who were not yet too old or infirm to make up the number required to mount a full time guard to cover every part of the wall. Some of these men had served in the Fyrd, the part-time army called upon to fight for the Saxon kings in times of danger. Some had even fought at the battle near Hastings. But they were all only part-time soldiers, with limited knowledge of the use of weapons and hand to hand fighting. Their leaders in the Fyrd might have had training in sword, axe and spear, but most of these men were inexperienced fighters, and possessed no such weapons, let alone the knowledge of how to wield them effectively. Their weapons were the club, the scythe, and the haymaking fork. The axes they carried were designed for felling trees, not enemy soldiers like the axes of Housecarls like Swein.

It was Eadred who suggested that the villagers would therefore be better used defensively, as part of a shield wall, than as any sort of attacking force. With shields made from oak, his people could be taught to band together and form a movable oak wall that might be used to repel anything that found its way into the village. If necessary, they could be used to surround or corner the enemy while the experienced fighters - Eadred, Swein, Orderic, and his men - went in and used their skills to attack and kill whatever it was while it was held at bay. If things went badly, the men would retreat, and join the women and children who would gather inside the hall. It was the largest of the buildings, and made mainly from oak – those parts of it that were not were being replaced or reinforced with oak. Of course, all of this was still reliant on the wood possessing the power to ward off whatever it was out there, but it was a gamble they had no choice but to take.

Orderic had agreed to this suggestion, with the single

revision that Eadred should command the shield wall, and not be part of the group that entered and fought. As Orderic fully expected, Eadred had objected to this change, finally consenting only when Orderic pointed out that Eadred's people needed to be co-ordinated and commanded by someone they completely trusted, and from whom they were used to taking orders. Once this was settled, Orderic had left the task of organizing the villagers, and the making of the shields to Eadred. The shield wall was, after all, a Saxon fighting technique, not a Norman one.

"A shield wall. Is that all these people know? It failed against us at Hastings," Walter commented later.

"Not before a great many of us were killed coming up against it, or had you forgotten what a close run thing that was?" Orderic replied. "Either way, these people will be better employed in Eadred's wall than swinging those makeshift weapons of theirs."

"And us? Suppose something does get in, hmm? Suppose they do manage to corner it with those planks of wood of theirs. Are we really going to climb inside their temporary barricade and try kill what it may not be possible to kill? I think I would rather hide behind a shield with the villagers."

"If it comes to that, what choice will there be? If whatever we face truly cannot be killed, what difference does it make where you stand, my friend? We are already lost."

"If that is what happens, then we must ride away... leave these Saxons to their fate. It would not be our fight, Orderic. Not our fight."

"I know that, man! Have I not already made it clear? If this thing looks set to overrun us, and if we can still find a way to leave, then we will. If it is an option still open to us, then we ride. All I am saying is that we may not get to choose. Tell me, my friend, would you venture out there right now? At this very moment. Simply get on your horse and go. Ride away. You think you would be safe? Would you care to attempt it, knowing what befell Hubert?"

"No, I would not."

"So, the fight may be just as much for ourselves as these villagers. You understand now what I'm telling you?"

"You know I do. I simply meant…"

"I only hope Bertrand sees fit to send Rollo back with enough reinforcements to make a difference when the time comes. We need sufficient men to get through to us. If they can make it in here, perhaps we can make it out. Too few and it may be as disastrous for them as us."

"If he doesn't, or they can't get through?"

"In that case, if we can't ride away, we make some sort of stand. With these people if needs be. On our own if that looks the better option. I don't know, maybe we risk riding away from here anyway."

"And the woman?" asked Walter.

"Alditha? What of her?"

Walter shrugged. "I have eyes. I see you take an interest. Or do you tell me you do not?"

Orderic did not answer.

******

Rollo was growing concerned. The route back to Elastun from the castle should have been simple to remember. He had ridden it often enough - particularly of late - but somehow he was having difficulty. He had done his best to hide his concerns from Richard and the other men riding with him. He did not relish the idea of admitting he was at all uncertain of the way, let alone that they might be completely lost. So, when the light started to fade, he had suggested they make camp for the night, hoping that in the morning he would remember the way. Richard had questioned this suggestion. He had not been to Elastun for some time he said, but if memory served, they should be there by now. When Rollo had made the excuse that the wintery weather conditions were making the way far slower than it would be in the spring or summer, Richard had not look very convinced. Whilst poor weather conditions could add hours to such a journey, for them to cost a whole day seemed unlikely.

Eventually, the fading light convinced Richard to agree to Rollo's proposal that they camp. The Baron had said the matter was important, not urgent. Nonetheless, Richard had remarked, pointedly, that Rollo had better have his wits about him the next morning. Any further delays would not be tolerated.

When Rollo awoke later that night, the wine he had drunk earlier, combined with the chilly air, meant the pressure on his bladder could not be ignored. With a groan of frustration, he threw aside the cloak he was using as a blanket, and stood up. The nearest fire was burning low, so he tossed on another of the logs piled next to it, and then, nodding to the man on watch, he stepped in among the trees at the edge of the clearing where the troop had made camp. He walked several paces, then relieved himself up one of them, groaning again, only this time with relief. It was as he was returning to the camp that the noise began, high and unnatural. Confused, he hurried forward, then halted, still concealed among the trees. In the light of the fire that only moments ago he himself had refuelled, he had seen something appear from the trees on the other side of the clearing. Something unholy. He dropped into a crouch behind the cover of some dead bracken. The men in the camp had been taken completely by surprise. Very few of them had even had time to reach for a weapon before the things fell upon them.

As he watched what was happening to Richard and the other men, Rollo knew without question that these were the things responsible for the carnage he had seen in Gyrtun.

He stayed where he was, unable to look away, unwilling to run in case he was seen, biting down upon his fist for fear he might cry out involuntarily.

It was when one of the creatures came close enough to the light from the fire for Rollo to see its face that he did finally let out small cry of alarm. The face, though grey and hollow, still retained enough of the features it had had in life for Rollo to recognise Turold.

Turold looked over. If he recognised Rollo there was no sign of it in his expression. He had, however, seen him. Rollo tried to stand. A combination of fear and of having squatted for so long made his legs weak and awkward. They slipped on the damp earth, buckling under him. With every steady pace Turold took in his direction, Rollo's scrabbling grew more frantic, and more clumsy. Unable to stand, he scrabbled further into the undergrowth, sobbing with panic and fear. When he felt a cold hand take him by the neck, he cried out, clawing at the earth and roots as he was pulled backwards.

Turold lifted Rollo, who must have weighed more than he did, with only one arm, holding him up by the neck like a puppy. He swung him about, turning him to so he could look into his face.

"No, please, Turold, please. It's me, Rollo. You see? I know it's dark, but look closer. You know me." For a brief moment Rollo considered suggesting that Turold carry him nearer to the fire so that he could see his face more clearly in the light of the flames then, just as quickly, he thought better of it. "We are friends, remember? Good friends."

What little still remained in Rollo's bladder now trickled, steaming, down his legs, droplets flicking from his kicking feet onto the frozen ground.

"Whatever it is you are thinking of doing, please, don't!" he pleaded.

Turold's face remained blank, not even curious. Rollo whimpered as Turold reached up with his free hand. The fingers explored his face for a second or two, painfully prodding at an eye, then clamped around Rollo's cheeks, squeezing so hard his jawbone creaked. "No…Nuh… Nnnn…! pleaded Rollo. The bone creaked again, gave, then shattered completely. Rollo shrieked. The hand came up again. This time it reached inside the splintered, sagging mouth, took hold of the tongue, and pulled.

******

CHAPTER 13

Brother Edmund was holding on as tightly as he could. It had been a long time since he had ridden a horse at a gallop, and he prayed to God he would not fall off. He also prayed the horse would be fast enough to put a safe distance between him and what he had seen. He couldn't make sense of it. He only knew it was evil, and he must get away from it. His mind raced. Everything he had been taught at Menlac, everything he had learned from the brothers there about the never-ending struggle between good and evil had not prepared him for this moment. Today he had seen evil with his own eyes. Not the sordid, dissipated, and degenerate evil that weak mankind participated in, but something absolute. It must have risen up from Hell itself, because surely the tall one, the one at the centre of it all, had been a demon from that region. Not Lucifer himself - for what man could gaze upon him and not go mad – but, without question, a demon of some sort.

He must get to the village. Swein had said it was just up ahead - less than half a mile. Edmund didn't know if he would really be any safer there, but where else was there to go? What else could he do? He felt sure whatever they were back there would catch up to him eventually if he did not find somewhere to shelter.

Only a matter of minutes ago Edmund had been so tired he was close to falling asleep in the saddle after riding at such a forced paced through the night. That pace was nothing to the speed he was riding at now, and the weariness he had felt was swept aside by adrenaline occasioned by fear like he had never before known. But the horse had done most of the work. Please God let the animal's fatigue after such a long journey not rob it of the energy it needed to carry him to safety now, and please let it not lose its footing on the frozen mud and snow of the track. *Please.*

Edmund heard the sound of another horse coming up behind him. It was gaining. He prayed again. Please Lord let it be Swein. He wanted to turn his head, take a look, reassure himself it was only the Housecarl, but fear of what else he might see prevented him.

"Ride, boy, ride!" Swein shouted behind him. The relief seemed to free Edmund's movements, allowing him to glance back in time to catch sight of the big man as he raced up alongside him.

"Straight ahead!" shouted Swein. "Follow me!"

"No…Wait…!"

"I must get them to open the gate. They will know me. Keep riding, boy!"

Edmund sobbed in despair as Swein overtook him, and rode ahead. He knew in his heart that Swein was not abandoning him, that it was just a matter of the man having a stronger horse, and yet the sense of being left behind was almost unbearable. He had never felt more exposed and vulnerable in his life. There was now nothing and no one between him and those terrible deathly men and their demon leader.

They were within a hundred yards of the gates when a noise roared up from behind them. It grew in volume, swelling up from behind like it was being carried forward on the breeze. Swein bellowed at the top of his voice to the men watching from the gate.

******

"It's Swein, can't you see that? Open up, let him in!" shouted Alfred from his place on the wall, just along from the gates.

The men at the gates hesitated, looked afraid.

"We were told to let no one in without Eadred or one

of the Normans agreeing to it!" protested one of them.

"He is right, we must have their permission," added another.

"There is no time for that. Are you blind? Look how they ride. They are fleeing from something. You must open up."

"And let whatever it is chasing them in with them?"

Alfred took a deep breath, leaned out beyond the wall.

"It's not near to them. There will be time to close the gates behind them, I swear to you."

When the men at the gates still refused to move, Alfred jumped from the wall, ran over, and removed the wooden bar that held the gates in place. A little way off, Walter, whose turn it was to sit his horse on guard, called over. "What's happening there? What are you doing?"

"The blacksmith is opening the gates," cried one of the men at the wall.

"We'll see about that!" shouted Walter. He galloped over, and used his horse to barge Alfred away from the gates. Alfred fell, struggled up, and immediately began to pull at one of the gates again.

"Next time I'll knock you down so hard you won't be able to get up, if you don't stop that," warned Walter.

"It's Swein! There's someone with him, a monk, I think. They ride as if they are being chased, but nothing is close to them. There is time."

"You looked?"

"Yes."

"You're telling me you leaned out beyond the wall?"

"Yes."

"Very well." Walter took hold of one of the gates and rode his horse back a little so the gate opened up just enough for a horse and rider to enter. "You leave the other one shut. And be ready to close this one the instant they are inside, understand?"

"It's open," Swein shouted back to Edmund. "Don't you slow down now, boy! Don't you slow down. Straight on through, now. Straight on through." The young monk could not hear him above the noise, but he nodded his understanding.

******

They were gathered in Alditha's house. She had insisted that Edmund be taken there straight away when she saw him staggering, clearly exhausted, towards the hall, in the company of Walter and an almost as exhausted looking Swein. At first, Walter had objected, saying the monk was not injured, but Alditha said it was plain to see the young man was worn out and in a great deal of distress. The symptoms of such a state could be serious if they were not attended to, and there was a draft she could prepare that would help calm them. It should not be too strong, Walter had warned her, because they urgently needed to hear whatever the monk had to tell them. But Swein had assured Walter there was nothing the lad could tell them that he himself could not. If Alditha thought it best for the monk to be taken to her house, then so be it.

Looking at him, Alditha had thought Swein might also benefit from a little of the draft she had prepared for Edmund. She knew he would not accept it if it were offered so, without his knowledge, she simply added a little to the drink she gave him. She explained that, if it tasted odd, it was because she had added something to ease the pain in Swein's leg because she could see from his gait that it was bothering him more than usual. Alditha pretended not to notice how Swein's hand shook when he took the cup she offered.

By the time Orderic and Eadred had joined them, Edmund was asleep. Swein looked across at him. Alditha followed his gaze.

"He's so very young," said Alditha. "Barely a man. I'm not surprised he's exhausted."

"That he is. Don't let it fool you, though. We spoke on the way here. He has his ways…a bit odd, I will not deny it, but he is clever, I think. And he kept his head...more or less. I've seen bigger men than him turn into whimpering babes when their nerves failed them. Can't be predicted, can't be helped." He looked round at the others. "Something from your faces…not to mention the extra guards at the gate, and on the wall…tells me that when I tell you what I've seen, it will not be entirely new to you? I am right, am I not?"

"We cannot know unless you tell it," said Walter, a little impatiently.

"Continue," said Orderic, his tone carefully judged to be neither request nor order.

"Please," added Eadred.

"Very well," Swein replied. "You saw how we were running from something. Well, *you* did Walter. I wasn't sure you would open that gate. For that much I'm grateful."

Walter shook his head. "Don't be. We need every able fighter we can get. If the lad here had been on his own…" He left the implication hanging.

"That would have been a mistake. You may find him useful yet," replied Swein. "As I said, we were running. I think you may know what from."

"Tell us anyway. We must be certain," said Orderic.

Swein took a moment to gather his thoughts. "We were on our way back from Menlac. I had told Abbot Robert of our problems. He was not enthusiastic about sending anyone to assist. Still, that is a tale for another time. In the event, he sent this lad, and he and I rode through the night to get back to you. We were nearly here when it happened. Just back along the track there, near the clearing, the old charcoal burner's copse from years back. You know where I mean? The lad, Edmund here, began to mewl that he needed to empty his bladder. I said he could hold it, that the village was up ahead. When his griping looked set to carry on, I told him to get down and relieve himself in the hedgerow. He got off, but did not seem willing to get on with it. I grew impatient."

"I know the feeling," said Walter.

"I am telling you how we came to be where we were. If you do not wish to hear it you are always free to leave!"

"Continue," said Orderic, then scowled at Walter, who merely shrugged in return.

"As I was saying, I grew impatient with the poor lad. When I pressed for haste he confessed the urge was in his bowels, that the sickness had perhaps affected him there, and it was now a matter of some urgency. Even so, he wanted privacy for it, so I said he should leave the track, but should not go far. That is how he came to be at the old copse." Swein looked pointedly at Walter. "That is how he came upon the scene he did."

"Which was?" asked Orderic.

"Something like we found in Gyrtun. Only these were soldiers. Normans," said Swein, stressing the last word a little.

Orderic raised an eyebrow. "Normans? Really? How do you know this?"

"I know a Norman when I see one. Besides… your man…the sullen one…He was among them. Among the dead."

"He must mean Rollo," said Walter.

Orderic said nothing.

"Rollo, then," said Swein. "If that is his name, I never learned it. The sullen one. They had all of them been torn about…You understand me...? Like those at Gyrtun? Blood and filth all over the place. It did not look to me like they had been able to put up much of fight."

"How could you tell?" asked Orderic.

"Swords still in scabbards, shields left leaning against

trees, that sort of thing."

Orderic frowned. "I see. And how many?"

"Dead? I don't know. Ten? Perhaps a few more. A dozen maybe. Hard to say. There was no time to count them. The lad came hurrying back when he saw it. He had been sick down himself …there were tears in his eyes and streaming down his face. I thought at first it was just the illness getting the better of him. But when he spoke his words were all over the place, confused. He said he had seen the work of demons. Naturally, I got down and tried to shake him to his senses. When I finally understood, I went with him. Of course, I had some idea of what to expect. I'm more ready to believe such things these days. I wish I were not. And there they were. Strange thing was, they looked to have made camp there. Looked to me as if they had spent the night. I couldn't make it out. Why do that when they were already so close to Elastun? They must have been confused in some way. Your man, Rollo, if he was leading them back to Elastun, he must have misjudged the distance. Always struck me as a fool, that one."

"Well, he's a dead fool now," said Walter. "Died bringing help back to this place."

"Not so. He died bringing help back to *you*. Normans helping Normans. Nothing more."

Orderic banged his fist against a low roof beam, shaking dust from above. "Enough, both of you! Walter, you will remain silent. Go on, Swein."

Walter scowled, but did as he was ordered.

Satisfied, Swein continued with his story. "The lad insisted we must help them. I said they were beyond our help, every one of them. He still maintained that we should check if any yet breathed. It was our Christian duty, he said. He could not look God in the eye when the time came if he had not at least reassured himself that there was not a man there who could be saved. I said a child could see not one of them still lived. Nobody could live through that. I told him he could take my word for it." Swein gave a slight smirk. "I said I was happy for him to blame it on me when the time came to answer to God. The lad insisted anyway. So, I told him, 'help yourself'. He gave me a look, and walked in among them. Brave, really. Only, within seconds, he was throwing up again. It was plain to see he was not up to the task. He came back, begged me to look instead. Said he would not move from the spot until I had. So I agreed. I had no choice. He stood back while I walked in among them. A waste of time it seemed to me. He wanted it though. So, there I was, stood in the middle of all that slaughter, the monk there hovering in the bushes like a shy maiden caught bathing. That's when I heard it. A sort of whispering. Voices. Although, not voices like I've ever heard before. Raspy. Strained. Distant even when they were near. Hard to explain. It was coming from the other side of the clearing, so I ran back and pulled the lad down, gestured for him to be silent. As we watched, something stepped out from the trees. Something evil. I have never seen its like before. It may have been like a man in shape, but it was no man, I can tell you that much. An abomination masquerading as a man is what it was. Huge, grey,…a thing of evil." Swein's eyes were fixed on the empty space in front of him, focused on what he had seen in the forest earlier, not on the people listening. "Now, the other two that followed it in from the trees…they *were* men…or had once been, I don't know. The thing is… one of them…I might almost swear he …" Swein fell silent, thought for a moment, and then came to some decision. "No, not that. I must have been mistaken about that," he said to himself.

"Mistaken about *what*?" asked Eadred.

Swein looked uncomfortable, did not look at the old man. Ignoring Eadred's question, he went on with his story.

"It seemed to me then the lad was right about demons after all. I tell you, the thought of that creature coming near… of him seeing us…it made my blood run cold. Like a serpent. Like the feeling you get when you come across one of the diamond patterned snakes that sleep in hedgerows in the summer. That feeling of utter revulsion. Worse, though. Much, much worse." Swein shivered. He looked embarrassed, defensive. "You'll think me raving. Foolish. It's hard to explain unless..." He frowned suddenly. "Wait now..." He looked around, studied their faces. "You know I did not know if you would believe me about all this. I thought you might think me raving. The same as we all thought old Penda to be. I see now from your faces that you *do* believe. More than that, you require no persuasion at all. Why is that? You've seen him too?"

"We have," said Alditha softly.

"When was this?" asked Swein.

"While you were gone. He took one of Orderic's men. It was terrible. They killed him in front of us. The grey man... and the others with him."

Swein looked away, rubbed at his leg. "Killed him you say? Well...possibly." He looked back. "Possibly not. Some of those that were dead. And they *were* dead, I would swear an oath upon it. There was no question about it. And I know what death looks like. But what we saw next, I can't explain it. They were dead. Not possible they were not. But when that thing appeared, some began to move. Not all. Some. Just a few of them. Small movements to begin with. Twitches, flicks. There on the ground, and that thing leaning over them. The closer he drew to them, the more they writhed about until...and I still can't believe it....they stood up." Swein narrowed his eyes, gazing into the space in front of him again, at things only he could see, checking his memory. He nodded to himself. "They did. They stood up. Hacked to pieces some of them, and then they stood right back up again as if it had never happened. They came together. I can't explain how. It was as if they had been sewn back up." He paused, looked down again at his hand as he continued to rub his bad leg, studied it in silence for a few seconds, and continued to look down at it when spoke. "Ruined bodies made whole again. All the smashed and splintered bone, torn flesh…the pieces joined and mended. All the strewn entrails gathered, the spilled blood soaked up again. I saw it happen. It should not be possible, I know that. It isn't possible. And still I saw all this happen in front of me. You have to believe it. Some of them got up. I don't say they weren't different. They were not as they had been, not as they were. Monstrous versions of their previous selves. Them and not them. Recalled from death by whatever devilry was at work in that place among the trees. I don't know what they are now. Is there even a word for it? A name for it? Ghosts? I've never really understood what was meant by that word. Is that what those men have become? I can't say. Whatever they now are, I know they are something that is not meant to be. The dead should stay that way. They should not walk again, enslaved by that abomination." Swein looked into their faces. "More of the world has revealed itself. Some of what lives in the shadows has stepped into the light and shown itself. You understand what I'm telling you?"

"We do. We've seen them too, remember," said Alditha.

"Yes. Oh, but then you have seen… Ah…" Swein fell silent again, uncertain how to continue with an aspect of his story he knew would be so painful to his old friend.

"You can tell me," said Eadred. "Tell me what you are holding back."

Swein looked up at the old man with an expression that was both quizzical and concerned. His mouth opened as if he might speak, then closed again.

"I ask about one who was among their number. You have not looked me in the eye throughout your tale, my friend. Please say it," pleaded Eadred. "If you do not, I will be forced to ask it, to say his name myself. Out loud, and in connection to these events. To do so would pain me more than you can imagine. We too have seen the things of which you speak, Swein. I would hear you say it, nonetheless. Say the name of the one who was among them that I know you thought you recognized."

Swein looked to Alditha for guidance. She inclined her head, the movement barely perceptible, just enough to indicate that Swein should continue.

"Wulfstan," said Swein, flatly, as if he would not risk showing any emotion in connection with the name.

Eadred sat down heavily on a chair opposite the Housecarl, closed his eyes, and shuddered.

"You know, I thought I might have been mistaken. Hoped I was. But you spoke as if you knew," said Swein, worried by Eadred's reaction.

Eadred looked up, waved away a concerned looking Alditha who had approached him with a cup of water. "I did, Swein, I knew. It still pains me to hear it from you," he said. "I saw my son when they took Orderic's man. What I witnessed Wulfstan do... it was wicked. What they put that poor man through was appalling. He may have been a Norman, but that was wicked…sinful."

Swein leaned over, gripped Eadred's arm. "It was not your son. Not my old friend. Not as he was. It was not him. I cannot explain it. The monk had been crossing himself over and over, and I had to cover his mouth to muffle the sound of his constant praying. I confess I nearly cried out myself when I saw Wulfstan's shape emerge from the trees. He walked behind the grey creature like a servant. Took me a bit of time to master my own nerves after that. Eventually, I pulled Edmund back and we crawled away through the bushes on our bellies. The lad was behaving as if he were half in a dream by then." Swein gave a humourless smile. "A nightmare. Anyway, I got him back to the track, and onto that scrawny horse of his, and gestured that we should ride away as quietly as possible. Stupidly, I thought he was fine…thought he understood. Then the fool sneezed. Would you believe it? *Sneezed,* as if we were children playing hide and seek in the woods, and there were no more danger in it than that. Fear, I suppose. He forgot himself. Anyway, there was no doubt that they would have heard, so a quiet escape was out of the question. Nothing for it then. I slapped his horse and shouted that he should ride as fast as he could. That, at least, he managed to do as instructed. I followed and, by the grace of God, here we are."

******

A little while later, when Alditha judged Brother Edmund sufficiently recovered, he was summoned to the hall for a discussion attended by Orderic, Eadred, Swein, and Alditha, where he was questioned as to whether there was any additional course of action he, as a member of the church, could recommend. The young monk was disappointed to read from the expressions on the drawn and anxious faces that looked at him, that they were not particularly hopeful he would be able to suggest anything. He was even more disappointed to have to admit the same thing to himself. There really was nothing he could think of to suggest.

"All this…what you tell me, and what I have witnessed for myself…it is beyond my understanding."

"Who among the brothers *would* have an understanding?" asked Orderic. "Who, then, is the right man for such a task? More to the point, why is *he* not here with us in your place? Menlac sends us a mere boy. I swear, should I survive this business, I will ensure Abbot Robert is made to pay for this display of slight regard."

"It is not so simple," said Edmund.

"It would seem with you Menlac brothers it never is," said Swein.

"Please…you misunderstand me," said Edmund.

"Oh, I do not think I misunderstand you or your Abbot, boy. On the contrary, I understand him very well," said Orderic.

"Be patient, I beg of you. I do not explain myself as well as I would wish to."

"Yes, a little patience, both of you," said Alditha frowning at Swein and Orderic. "Between you both, you fluster him. Please allow *me* to explain, for I believe I understand what our young friend is trying to tell us," said Alditha.

"Good. Please do," said Orderic.

"I believe what the brother is saying is that this is outside *anyone's* knowledge. That there is no one at Menlac who would be better placed to help."

"Nor worse," said Edmund despondently. "However, what Alditha says is correct. Though you think I fail you in this matter, there is nobody who would not. Do not allow my lack of years to mislead you, for I am as good a scholar as any in Menlac, and better than most."

"Is not pride a sin?" asked Eadred.

"It is. You admonition is justified. Forgive me," replied Edmund, his face flushing with embarrassment. "I mean to say that I know enough…have studied enough…. to be sure there is nothing written on this matter. Nothing that would be of help."

"That is something you would be prepared to swear to?" asked Orderic. "Even if your life were to depend on it?"

"There is nothing in the writings held at Menlac. If the knowledge rests elsewhere, I do not know who holds it. I cannot swear to it not existing somewhere, but, with respect, I suggest my life already lies in the balance simply by being here. I did not ask to come. I was sent…at your request."

Orderic sighed. "You are sure that in all your learning, all your books, there is nothing like this? This is not discussed anywhere?"

"It grieves me to say it, but no. That is, not specifically. There is much of demons. Of the Devil. A great deal, in fact. There are writings on the ways of witches, also."

"Is not this the work of those very things?" asked Eadred.

"Not exactly. I fear it is of all of those things… and none of them…at the same time, if you understand me."

"I do not. You talk in riddles, boy," complained Orderic.

"*Brother,* please. I would prefer it. I am of age, you see. I am a brother, not a boy."

Orderic frowned. "Hmm. We shall judge that in time. Continue with what you were saying."

"Ah, well…yes…Please forgive me, I do not mean to talk in riddles. It is certainly not my intention…The thing is, it is extremely difficult to explain…"

"So it seems," muttered Orderic.

Edmund paused for a moment, gathering his thoughts, then began again. "I mean to suggest that, while there is the work of the Devil and… perhaps… magic in this, I think it is an aspect of such things never before recorded. What there is that is written does not deal with the form the Devil…or one of his demons, at least…has taken here. All that I can suggest is that we combat it in the way we are told to combat other such things."

"Which *is*?" asked Orderic.

"With prayer, with the power of the cross and, where it is required, with the sword. I think too, that what you have told me about the power of oak is possibly of importance. I confess my first instinct was to say such a claim was blasphemous. After all, it was thought to be powerful before we knew better. Or maybe we simply thought we knew better. God may work his will in ways we cannot understand. It may be that he has put the power in the oak that we might use it on His behalf. It may be that we ignore its power at our peril. It may be that not to use what you have discovered would be the profane thing to do."

Orderic could not disguise his frustration. "Damn it, boy! There is nothing in what you have said that has not been considered by us already. We are using the oak…profane or not…as we have already guessed this to be an ancient evil. I do not see what it is that you add? You, or your kind."

Edmund looked close to tears. "I offer what I can. This is ungodly. It is evil. I would have it destroyed, and I will help in its destruction in any way I can. Am I to blame for what I have not been schooled in? Particularly when I strongly believe no man has. Such a thing would be spoken of in all of Christendom if it had been encountered before. Any man of God who met with such a thing and discovered the means to destroy it would ensure all his fellows were told. It would be recorded, and the writing disseminated widely. That it has not been tells me it cannot have been encountered before now. Menlac would have knowledge of it if it had. *I* would have knowledge of it. Unless…" The monk stopped, his hand going to the crucifix about his neck.

"Unless what, Brother?" asked Alditha.

"What is it, lad? Unless what? Answer us…" said Swein.

"Unless all those who have encountered this…whatever it is…unless they all perished. Then we would not know. If none live to tell of it, it can never be recorded."

"This gets us nowhere," said Orderic, leaving the room without a further word.

"Don't mind him, lad. He's a Norman, and naturally rude," said Swein.

"He is also very concerned," added Alditha. Swein gave her a look, which she interpreted as his questioning her defence of such a man. She did not look at Eadred, but suspected he too had a similar expression on his face. "All I mean to say is that his reaction is natural under the circumstances, and Brother Edmund here should not take it as in any way personal if Orderic, or any of us, seem strained or abrupt in manner. That is all. Really, Swein, I should not have to explain myself to you. Nor to you

Eadred."

Swein grunted.

Edmund managed a weak smile. "Thank you. I am well used to the arrogance of Normans. Abbot Robert, after all, is a Norman himself...Oh, perhaps I should not say such things."

"About the Normans? You will find none of us here quick to *their* defence. Say what you will about them," Swein reassured him.

"Thank you."

"Only take care you don't let them hear it, hmm?" added Eadred.

"Yes, obviously, that is good advice. I will endeavour not to."

"In fact, better to keep all such thoughts to yourself," suggested Alditha. "Just in case."

"I think I shall," agreed Edmund. "Now, I wonder, could someone possibly tell me, how are things with Hildy?" When no one answered him, Edmund smiled self-consciously, then added, "My horse. She is my horse. Will someone show me to where Hildy is kept? I must check upon her. Poor Hildy, she will be worn out after such a gallop. She is not actually *my* horse, obviously. She belongs to the Abbey. But I am fond of her. And she was entrusted to my care. I would not have the Abbot accuse me of not looking after her properly. Her welfare must be my concern."

Swein smiled. "That bag of bones?"

"She saved my life."

"She ran because I slapped her."

"Hush, Swein," said Eadred. "She is in my stable, Brother. Under the care of my people. You need not trouble yourself on her behalf."

"I would still like to..."

"Come on, then. Follow me," said Swein.

******

Despite their repeated questions, cajoling, and even a degree of bullying, Alfred had resisted all attempts by his fellow villagers to make him reveal exactly what he had seen beyond the wall when Orderic's man, Hubert, had been taken and killed. Eadred had not wanted to alarm the villagers with too many details so, with Orderic's agreement, had instructed those who had witnessed Hubert's end about how much they could reveal. It was sufficient, Eadred told them, that the villagers knew there was danger and witchcraft beyond the protection of the oak, and that they should on no account venture out into the forest. They should not even lean out beyond the edge of the wall if they valued their lives.

Inevitably, it was this last instruction that puzzled the inhabitants of Elastun the most. That some of them would, sooner or later, be driven to test it was to be expected. Some probably had already, but had been fortunate enough not to have done so when the danger they had been warned about was present, and so had learned nothing from the terrible risk they had taken. Of course, any that had leaned out were unlikely to reveal it. If word got back to Eadred of such a thing he had promised them there would be a harsh reckoning.

Now, in Cyrnric's tavern, two farmers, Leofric and Tosti, were once again attempting to get more detail from the blacksmith. To their frustration, Alfred continued to refuse to divulge any more than they had already heard from Eadred.

"Why will you not tell us?" demanded Tosti. "What right have you to withhold what you know, Alfred blacksmith? Who are you to decide? If there is danger, we should be told."

"Don't be in such a hurry. You will see it all when the time comes. Then you will understand," Alfred told them.

Although no sooner had he said this than he inwardly questioned the truth of it. They would not understand it even then. Nobody did. If these people imagined he was holding a lot of information back from them, they were wrong. In reality, he had not much more of an understanding of exactly what it was moved out there beyond the village boundaries than they did. He knew nothing of its origins, or what it actually was. The only additional detail he could have supplied was something of what form the danger took - about the appearance of the grey man, and of what he was capable of doing.

Should Eadred insist those facts were kept from them? Did he even have the right, Alfred wondered? Perhaps knowing the worst might help them. After all, it had helped him. When the first body – that of the Norman – had been discovered, Alfred had been more frightened than he could remember being at any time in his life previously. He still felt ashamed of how he had behaved. Oddly, now, with the fact that this was the work of a dark sorcery of some kind beyond any doubt, although he remained frightened, he had been able to master his fear. He looked down at his hands. They had been shaking on an off for some time. They were steady now.

"Take it up with Eadred, not me. You know all Eadred thinks you need to know for now. It is not for me to say more. Take my advice, and pray you never need to know more than you already do. If you knew what lay out there..." Alfred paused, drained the last of his drink. "You would hope it leaves us, and soon. You should hope it goes away and you never have to know. That way, you can return to your fields when the better weather returns, and be about your business. Now leave me to be about my own."

"Right now, this is our business," insisted Leofric. "As much ours as it is yours! Our lives are at risk too. We have a right to know what you saw. Perhaps then we would be able to do something about it."

"All that can be done is being done. You are part of the guard, aren't you?"

"Guard, indeed. We should be hunting whatever it is down, not hiding from it behind the wall. I don't wait for the fox to come to my chickens, I search for it…seek it out… kill it in its den. This danger we are told of, why wait for it to come to us?"

"It already has! Why is it you fools can't understand that?" asked Alfred.

"Has it? There is nothing out there now!"

"Oh, and how is it you are so certain? Can it be that you have looked, Leofric? Shall I explain to Eadred that he is mistaken? Shall I tell him that Leofric the farmer knows better than he? Problem is, he may ask how it is you come to be so sure? What I mean to say is you can't have looked, now can you? You can't have seen for yourself because that would mean you have leaned out, wouldn't it? And that would have been against what has been ordered, wouldn't it? Hmm?"

The farmer, previously red in the face with anger, now grew pale.

"Now wait a moment, Alfred. I didn't mean… I only meant …"

Alfred waved him away. "I'll not say anything. Not *this* time. But you run a risk." He glanced towards the doorway. "Look, there now, the sun fades. We should all go take our places on the wall. Our turn has arrived. We should relieve the others. Come on, you damn fools!"

As the two farmers stood to leave, a thought occurred to Alfred. "Wait," he said, holding up a hand. "How much have you two had of Cynric's brew? Not so much you are unable to stay awake and keep a clear head, I hope?"

Cynric, on hearing this last question, called over.

"No need to concern yourself about that, Alfred. Eadred has given me strict instructions to limit how much a man may drink if he is shortly due to take up his place at the wall. Those two will be fine, don't you worry. They have not had so very much. Eadred's rule is costing me dearly, if you must know."

Both Leofric and Tosti nodded smugly at Alfred, as if to confirm Cynric's claim.

"It is true what Cynric says," said Tosti, drawing himself up and puffing out his chest as if this somehow illustrated his sobriety. "No need to concern yourself."

"Alfred, the new village elder," said Leofric contemptuously. "You need not go running to Eadred with any tales on our account."

"Get going," said Alfred dismissively, and waved them on their way. All the same, as he followed them out, he could not help wondering if perhaps some secret bargain had been struck. Had they made it worth the tavern keeper's while to part with more drink than they were otherwise permitted?

A few minutes later, as Tosti and Leofric mounted the steps to the walkway along the part of the wall it was their duty to watch for the night, Tosti asked his companion, "Have you, Leofric? Have you leaned out? Despite what we were told?"

Reaching the top of the steps, Leofric turned and pulled Tosti close.

"Quiet, you oaf!" He pointed to the retreating backs of the men they had only a moment before relieved. "Do you want them to hear?"

Whispering now, Tosti asked again, "Have you, though?"

Leofric made an exaggerated show of looking about himself, even though it was plain there was now no one close enough to hear, as long as they whispered.

"Alright, yes, I have," he whispered, then added, "And so, Tosti, have you." Tosti looked as if he were about to protest, but Leofric spoke first. "If you ask me, every man in this village will have done. Some of the women too, when their husbands' backs were turned. There is no shame in it that I can see. Eadred cannot have expected otherwise. Have you ever heard such nonsense?"

"Well I…"

Again Leofric spoke before Tosti could fully respond. "What did you see? Nothing, that's what. You saw nothing, the same as I did, because there is nothing out there to be seen. Well, nothing that cannot be seen as easily from behind the so-called protection of the wall as beyond it."

"There have been deaths… Gyrtun…"

"I don't deny there is danger. I never said that. There have been evil deeds done. I won't deny it. It may well be that witchcraft is afoot. I trust Eadred about that. He would not lie to us on that score. It is just this business about not leaning out. Come on now, how could that really be true? How could it? I don't doubt there is a reason, but it is not what Eadred hints at. There is no danger in simply leaning out. There is something we are not being told. Something we are not supposed to know."

"What is it though?"

"If I knew that, I would have said. What I do know is this witchcraft affecting the wall story is a distraction. It's to keep us from noticing something else. Like shaking the food trough when you're taking the piglets from the sow. The point is, it isn't true. There is danger, but not unseen the way they claim."

"Alfred said there was."

"Alfred has always been Eadred's man. There is nothing we can see by leaning out that cannot be seen from where we stand. I've looked, you've looked. No one has seen this mysterious danger."

"We were told it is not always there."

"That's because it *never* is. Trust me, it doesn't matter when you lean out, you'll never see it."

To illustrate, Leofric did just that.

He did not lean back as quickly as Tosti expected.

Something, it seemed, had caught his attention.

"What is it? Is something there? Do you see something?"

Leofric did not respond. In the fading light, Tosti could see his friend had begun to tremble all over. Had he really seen something that frightened him that badly? But what? There was nothing out there that Tosti could see. Even in the poor light, anything moving below would show grey against the white of the snow. Surely Leofric was playing a joke. Yes, that was it. It would be like him to play a joke. That must be it.

Leofric had started a low murmuring. Was he praying? He should not joke about such things.

"Leofric? …Leofric! Stop it. That's enough. Stop acting the fool. Get back in now, come on."

Leofric began to scream and his body began to spasm. Tosti's heart raced, and his hands shook as he hovered them close to, but not actually touching, his friend, uncertain what to do. He peered once more into the gloom beyond the wall, but saw nothing apart from his friend's grey outline, rocking and twisting as if in the grip of something he could not escape. Tosti knew then beyond any doubt that if he were to lean forward he would see what that thing was, but he could not bring himself to look for fear that he too might be taken hold of and pulled to the same fate as Leofric. He took a deep breath, stepped forward, reached out a trembling hand, and grabbed his friend by the collar of his tunic in order to pull him back inside, beyond the wall.

At first he was aware only of feeling the coarseness of the cloth beneath his fingers. Then, in an instant, the warmth, which he had at first taken to be Leofric's own body heat transferred into the fabric, grew rapidly in intensity, and the fabric in his fist began to smoulder, then burn. A searing heat scorched Tosti's hand, shrivelling the skin and roasting the flesh on his palm and the pads of his fingers. He howled in pain and tried to pull away, but his fingers were locked around the now flaming cloth and would not let go. In panic he pulled again. This time the cloth tore, then gave way. Released, Tosti stumbled back, and with a cry, fell from the walkway. Hitting the mud and snow below, he yelped and rolled over. Then, moaning, he thrust his hand into a puddle of icy water to ease the burning.

For a few moments his own pain and distress had taken Tosti's mind from the fate of his friend. Now, as he looked back up at the wall, he could see the orange glow of the flames that engulfed the man who, only minutes before had been sharing a drink with him in Cynric's tavern. Leofric's screams were like no sound Tosti had ever heard another person make. Only the noise of the squealing pigs on slaughter days came close. He got to his knees, began crawling towards the ladder. He must help his friend. He could hear the sounds of others running to help, but knew that they, like himself, would be too late.

For the men on the more distant parts of the wall it was difficult to fully understand what they were witnessing. In the fading winter light they saw the orange glow of the fireball that was Leofric. They heard his tormented screams. What they could not understand, however - what utterly bewildered them - was how that ball of flames rose in the air, a good ten or fifteen feet higher than the wall. It hovered there for a time before it drifted slowly away into the treetops, igniting some of the twigs and the few remaining brown leaves as it went, burning scraps of which fell to the ground below, and were soon extinguished in the blanket of damp earth, mulch, and snow covering the forest floor. For Leofric there was no such release. The flames tormenting him continued to rage.

Tosti, having struggled painfully back up the ladder, now stood gazing out at the distant glow of flames through the trees, praying that the noises coming from his friend would come to an end. It seemed impossible to him that Leofric could continue to suffer for much longer. It must end soon. Instead of this hoped for mercy, however, the flames rose up again, propelled through the air at great speed this time, reminding Tosti of the comet that had risen above England the previous year, greeted by many - correctly as it turned out - as an ill omen. This new shooting star sped through the rapidly darkening sky, back towards Elastun. Its trajectory carrying it over the wall and down into the open space at the very heart of the village.

By the time Tosti reached the spot where Leofric had landed, the dark shapes of a few other villagers were already standing there, looking down in shock and dismay at what Tosti imagined would be the dead body, and other figures were racing up to join them. But Leofric was not yet dead. The rise and fall of his chest, and the gasp and hiss of his laboured breathing told Tosti that, despite the work of the flames and the impact of the fall, unbelievably, Leofric's suffering continued. Tosti crouched down at his friend's side. Ignoring, as best he could, the pain in his own hand, he reached forward with the other as if he might offer Leofric some comfort, but quickly withdrew it, unable to find anywhere he could place it that would not cause his friend more pain.

"Leofric?" he said, "it's Tosti. Can you hear me? It's Tosti."

Leofric's eyes moved beneath their lids, but did not open. Then his lips parted.

"It hurts…" he whispered, then, more loudly, "Hurts!…Hurts so much…"

Tosti looked up at the others. "What do we do?" he asked.

"Fetch his wife?" suggested one.

"What about Alditha?" said another. "Better to fetch her. She may be able to help…She may be able to…"

"To what?" asked Swein who had at that moment

joined the group, along with Brother Edmund. "Look at him, man! He is beyond anything but suffering. There is only one thing you can do for him now."

"No!" said Tosti. "He may yet live."

"Don't be a damned fool," said Orderic, who had also now joined them. "What he needs is the mercy of a blade. Here, let me attend to it," he said, unsheathing his sword.

"No! Not you," said Tosti.

Orderic considered using the sword on Tosti in punishment for the Saxon's insolence, instead he turned to Swein. "Swein, will you do what must be done?"

Swein nodded. "I will."

"I'll fetch his wife," said one of the villagers. But Swein grabbed him, and held him back. "You are to tell her he is already dead, you hear me. He is *dead*. This…" He gestured towards the dying man. "This never happened. He was dead when he fell. Understand? All of you. She does not need to know. If I hear of her learning any different from any of you…you will answer to me for it."

"Shouldn't we wait for her?" suggested Edmund.

"Why?" asked Swein.

"She may want to be with him…at his passing I mean…"

Perhaps Leofric had heard, perhaps it was only coincidence, but at that moment he reached up and grabbed Tosti's wrist. "Hurts. My God how it hurts," he gasped.

"You heard him, monk," said Orderic. "How much more must he endure before you are satisfied?"

"That is unfair!" protested Edmund.

"Unfair? Unfair is letting him suffer to ease your own conscience. If he were a horse, we'd do what was necessary. I tell you now, if he were one of my men…"

"He is not one of your men!" snapped Swein.

"What difference does that make? Pain is pain. Suffering is suffering. What difference is there?"

"None," Swein conceded. He released his hold on the

villager, but the man hesitated. "Go on then," said Swein. "Remember what I told you, though." The man ran off. "Only the wife," Swein shouted after him. "Not the children. They should not see this." Swein knelt down beside Tosti. "Give me some room here." He bent down and whispered in the ear of the dying farmer. "Not long now, my friend. Not long now. All over soon."

"Wait! Wait, please. You would not send him to his maker unshriven?" protested Edmund. "You must not!"

"What would you have him confess that he cannot have paid for with this?" demanded Swein.

"It is not so simple," replied Edmund. "He must be in a state of grace."

"*Grace*? Like *this*? Oh, very well, quickly then."

"Alas, I am not permitted… I'm merely a brother, not yet ordained a priest…not yet…I hope to be, but…"

"Who more fit for the task is there among us right now, eh? At this moment?" asked Swein. "It must be you, boy. There is only you. If you know the damn words, then you say them."

"I think I know them. I have been in attendance at …"

"Just say what you can. Whatever you can remember of it will be good enough. God will forgive any omissions. Do it. Quickly, lad."

Edmund nodded. "Yes, I will." But no sooner had he said this than doubt overtook him once more. "I hope you are right. Yes, yes, God will surely forgive. He will understand, will he not? If I could only fetch my bible…"

Swein sighed in exasperation. "Damn it, Brother, there is no time for that! Look at the poor man, he is in pain. *I* understand, *you* understand. Even this damned *Norman* understands. If we can, God surely can. He sees everything, does he not? Get on with it."

Orderic chose to let Swein's 'damned Norman' remark pass. If there were to be a reckoning it would come at another time. "He is right, boy," he said. "Do what you can.

Then the Housecarl will do what he must."

Edmund looked up into the dark sky, crossed himself, said a brief, silent prayer to God for guidance, then squatted down next to Leofric, and began to administer the last rights as well as he could remember them. All the while he ignored the distraction of the dying man's sobs and whimpers as best he could. However, when Leofric, in his distress, began to scream, Swein pushed the monk aside. "Enough of this!"

"But I am not done!"

"He is. God will forgive," said Orderic.

"You cannot know that? I thought so, but I do not know if I have done enough. There is more to say and do."

"You wish to save him from Hell…" asked Orderic.

"I do…very much…yes."

"The wretched man lingers there with every moment we delay what must be done."

Even as Orderic and Edmund were arguing, Swein squatted down and lifted Leofric into his lap. Leofric cried out at the movement.

"Sorry, my friend. Only a moment more and it will be over." Swein's voice was calm, matter of fact. As he spoke, in a series of swift movements, so precise and practised that all who saw them knew that this was not the first time the Housecarl had performed them, Swein drew his dagger from his belt, lifted Leofric's left arm, and drove the long blade firmly home through the armpit, piercing the heart. Just as swiftly he withdrew the blade, then laid the body gently back down onto the ground.

As he attempted to stand up, Swein's bad leg gave slightly, and he staggered a little before being steadied by Orderic. When he had regained his balance, Leofric lay still and silent at his feet.

"Misericordia," whispered Brother Edmund.

******

CHAPTER 14

After Leofric's death, the villagers no longer questioned Eadred's order not to lean out from the wall. They no longer had to take it on trust that danger lurked beyond its protection. If anyone in the tavern had been inclined to question this, a drunken Tosti was frequently on hand to put them straight on the matter. Lean out at your peril, he advised them, because the Devil himself waited beyond the wall. He did not know what sin his good friend Leofric had committed. That did not matter. What mattered was, whatever sin it had been, the Devil had known, and he had come to claim Leofric for it. Tosti would then raise his bound hand, and declare himself to have felt the touch of the very fires of Hell itself. Word of this soon reached Eadred's ears, and Tosti was summoned before him, and warned that the already terrified villagers needed no more of his particular brand of counsel.

Brother Edmund was asked to say some words for the dead man in the church. At Eadred's request, he also took the opportunity to reassure the villagers of Elastun that, no matter what some might say, God had not abandoned them. He, Edmund, was here in demonstration of that very fact. It had been Abbot Robert himself, Edmund told them, who, upon hearing of their troubles, had insisted that a brother from Menlac be dispatched immediately to show the Abbey's faith in their worthiness, and offer whatever spiritual guidance he could.

A small number of the congregation – those close enough – might have heard Swein's contemptuous grunt when Edmund made his claim about the Abbot's concern for their welfare. Most simply mistook it for Swein clearing his throat. Orderic did not, having himself had to suppress a similar grunt.

When Edmund's address came to an abrupt end, there followed a minute or so of awkward silence, with the villagers not knowing what they should do next, only relieved when Eadred stepped up next to the monk and told them to go about their business. At this, the majority of the villagers shuffled out - most silently, some muttering to themselves or whispering to their neighbour - but a few remained where they were. One of those that remained, a middle aged woman, rushed over to the monk and threw herself at his feet, pulling on his habit, and pleading incoherently. Edmund, clearly uncertain how to deal with the situation, looked around, hopeful that Eadred might once more come to his aid. Eadred, however, had already left, so it fell to Alditha to rescue the monk. She hurried over, bent down, and whispered something into the woman's ear. The woman looked up at Alditha. For a moment she appeared not to recognise her, but then she nodded and stood up, allowing Alditha to lead her by the shoulders to a bench. Once there, she sat, and stared into nothing.

It was as Alditha turned from the woman, about to begin the task of tidying the church, that she noticed Orderic, still standing at the back of the building, half hidden in the shadows behind the door. She considered ignoring him, but curiosity got the better of her, and she crossed over to him.

"Still here," she observed. "I had not expected you to attend at all, if I am to be honest."

Orderic, ignoring this remark, asked, "That woman on the bench there, what ails her?"

"She was Leofric's wife. She is grieving, and she is afraid. As we all are."

"Why do they remain?" asked Orderic, pointing to the small group who had not left the church with the other villagers. "How is it they feel safer in here? I would have thought the hall, with its oak walls, a better place to shelter from what threatens them."

"As you know, many do go there. Eadred has opened his doors to everyone for that very reason. As for these people… It is not so difficult to understand, is it? They seek comfort more than they seek safety. Many spend nearly all their time here. Some sleep here."

"Comfort?"

"In the presence of God."

"I know what it is you meant, but…"

"But what..?" Alditha looked up, directly into Orderic's eyes. Despite a strong inclination to look away, he met her gaze.

"Can God not comfort them wherever they call upon him? I know you will tell me this is His house, that His presence is stronger here. I, myself, I cannot…."

It was Alditha who broke eye contact first. Shocked, she thought she understood now. She looked about the building she had loved and cared for all these years. Then, turning back to Orderic, before she could stop herself, she said, "You cannot feel it," her hand coming to her mouth immediately she had said it. Orderic looked surprised, then, just as suddenly, he seemed angry. For an instant she thought he might even strike her, and she flinched, but the impression vanished as quickly as it had arrived. In its wake, he seemed to her ill at ease. She had seen him this way before, and nearly always caused, it now occurred to her, by words or actions of hers. But then it was no surprise he should react this way after these particular words. The implications of what she had said were profoundly dangerous. Not only for him, but for both of them.

For Orderic the danger was obvious. If there were any truth in what Alditha had said, he would be open to accusations of heresy, and the punishments for that could often be terrible. For her the danger lay in him, and what he might do. If he feared that she would make his secret known – always assuming she was correct – he might think it best to silence her, and that was something a man like him could easily accomplish. If he chose to, a Norman warrior could end the life of a Saxon woman as easily as he might end that of any animal that displeased him. The space between her and Orderic was so small he could, if he wished, do it at that very moment. It would not even require him drawing his sword. He could strike with his dagger, ending her life as quickly as Swein had ended that of Leofric. Maybe even with his bare hands. She was sure he was capable of it. And yet the fear she had of him striking her had been brief. It had already passed. She knew now this man would not hurt her. The certainty of this caused her some embarrassment, as well as some comfort.

All these thoughts had passed very quickly through Alditha's mind, and the shock of them made her slightly dizzy. When she had steadied herself, she raised her eyes. Orderic was still looking at her. When he spoke it was slow and deliberate.

"I assure you I *do* feel the presence of God. What I think is that I do not feel it as *strongly* as you. I think I am not so blessed by God in that way. Cannot feel what it is you feel. However, I think what I meant to say just now…what I expressed rather poorly… was that I do not feel the presence of God *any less* in other buildings. He is…after all…all around us, is he not?"

Alditha inclined her head very slightly, a gesture of collusion as much as it was of agreement. "Yes. Yes, he is," she said. She looked about her again. "Well, I must sweep the floor. Unless you have lingered here because you intend to help with that, I suggest that you leave us. Be about whatever you intend to be about." She caught sight of Brother Edmund who, until then had been kneeling at the altar in private prayer, and had now risen to leave. "Ah, the young brother," she said so he could hear. "Now there is a pair of hands more suitable to assist in the neatening of the house of God. Come Brother, lend your assistance and the task will be done in no time. I cannot ask Orderic here, for he will surely break more than he straightens." She gave Orderic a more obvious nod of her head, which he acknowledged with a slight bow, then she took Edmund by the arm and attempted to steer him towards a broom that was leaning in one corner. Surprised, and a little irritated, Edmund pulled himself free as good naturedly as he could manage.

"Not one for woman's work?" asked Alditha. "Surely you brothers take it upon yourselves to keep the Abbey at Menlac swept and orderly?"

"I will gladly lend a hand presently. May I first say something to the captain?"

Orderic, who had begun to walk away, heard this and paused. "What is it, boy?"

"I am no boy, nor am I a novice. I am a brother, and due the respect of being addressed as such," protested Edmund, the pitch of his voice rising higher than he intended, much to his chagrin.

"Respect? Unfortunately for you, if that's what you seek from Orderic, I suspect you will receive it only when he believes you to have earned it," said Alditha, leaning in to Edmund's ear in a parody of a confidential whisper that Orderic could clearly hear. "I also suspect, the more you demand it of him, the less likely you are to receive it. His is the sin of pride."

"What would you say to me, *Brother*," said Orderic, surprising both Alditha and Edmund by smiling slightly as he emphasised the last word.

"Ah, I am made a liar," said Alditha.

Edmund hesitated, uncertain if Orderic's unexpected affability was genuine.

Orderic studied the monk in front of him. "I am listening."

Edmund stepped in closer. He might protest that he was no longer a boy but, when it came to size, he might as well have been, compared to the tall warrior in front of him. It made him nervous, and his nervousness was apparent when he spoke.

"I thought…that is to say…I have a suggestion…and I believe it may be of some merit. I don't know for certain. Unquestionably, that is for you to judge, not me. It can do no harm, however, and if it may do some good then…. I merely offer what I hope to be a…"

"Enough of this, boy!" growled Orderic, his smile gone, replaced by a grimace - almost as if he were experiencing an unpleasant smell - as he leaned over the smaller man.

Alditha felt a brief wave of anxiety that Orderic might be about to strike Edmund, similar to that which she had experienced only moments before about the possibility of Orderic striking her. Even though it passed just as quickly, there was something about these men from across the channel - this one in particular - that made them difficult to read, and the possibility of violence was always something you felt you must consider in any dealings with them.

"Brother Edmund," said Orderic. "I cannot judge what I have not been told. Make your suggestion, or leave me in peace. Which will it be?"

"My suggestion… I will make my suggestion, if I may," said Edmund. He glanced at Alditha for support.

"Tell me, not her," said Orderic.

"Oak crosses," Edmund blurted out at last.

"What's that?" asked Orderic.

"Oak crosses. Crosses of oak."

Orderic looked interested. "Continue."

"You say…and I do not doubt…I believe you, naturally…"

"Stop babbling, boy!" growled Orderic.

Giving Orderic a reproachful look, Alditha took Edmund's hands in her own. Unaccustomed to the touch of a woman, the monk attempted to pull free, but Alditha was insistent.

"No, Brother, it's alright. You will listen to me?"

"I think I must."

"Good. Now, take a deep breath, and calm down. Take another if you need to. Then say what it is you have to say. Say it slowly, and Orderic will listen. I promise you."

Edmund did as he was advised, and took a breath. Calmer now, he addressed Orderic. "The only proven defence against our adversary so far is oak, is it not?"

"So far. Am I to understand you have a different idea?" asked Orderic.

"Well, I do not doubt the power of the oak. It seems to have been proven thus far. The wall, after all.... From what I'm told it has been effective. No, not for a moment do I doubt it. And, after all, it makes sense. I mean, as we have previously discussed, the oak has long been held to have special properties. I think its use is wise."

"I'm so pleased," said Orderic, his impatience beginning to return. "What is your point? You mentioned oak crosses."

"The crucifix. The cross upon which our lord sacrificed himself is well known to be a protection against the evil eye. My suggestion is we combine the two. The power of the oak *and* the power of the holy cross. Oak crosses."

Orderic studied Edmund, who stepped back a little. "You would do what with them, exactly?"

"Mount them on the walls. Large ones, that is. After that, if there is wood enough for it, smaller could also be made. They might be worn about the necks of all the villagers, in the same way I wear mine. As does the lady Alditha there, I notice." Edmund reached up and gripped the crucifix he wore about his neck. "It has long been part of my protection against that which might seek to do me harm."

"I know why they are worn, brother. As for myself, I have long put my trust in chain mail and a strong shield for my protection."

"And in prayer also, I trust?" asked Edmund.

Orderic felt Alditha's eyes upon him. "That goes without saying, does it not?" he snapped. "Still, there may be something in what you suggest about the crosses."

"They can do no harm, and may bring some good," said Alditha.

"As you say, what harm?" agreed Orderic. "There is a carpenter in the village?"

"You know there is," said Alditha. "You will have seen him and his sons leading the work to build the walkway around the wall, and to shore up any weakness."

"Yes, of course. The man's name?"

"Dunstan."

"Like the saint," said Edmund. "He hath made a remembrance of his wonderful works, being a merciful and gracious Lord."

"What's that?" asked Orderic.

"His last words...Dunstan..."

"Hmm. You have done well with your suggestion. I was beginning to think you useful, despite appearances. Do not lose the benefit of that."

"Shall I fetch him? Dunstan, I mean," offered Alditha, quickly.

"No, Brother Edmund will go. It should not be difficult for a monk to pick out a saint among sinners. Failing that, you might ask one of the sinners to point him out, eh?"

"What am I to say to him?"

"I'm coming to that. Tell Dunstan that he…No, wait, Dunstan must keep at his work on the wall. Tell him he is to get one of his sons to make these crosses you describe. That is if Dunstan is sure there is wood enough for them. If so, you are to instruct him in how they should look. Tell him it is my order, and he will not give you any trouble. Go... Now."

When Edmund had left them to go find Dunstan, Orderic looked about the church once more. The villagers who remained had gathered together a in huddle before the simple wooden altar, and were kneeling together in prayer. He studied them, as he had studied those around him in countless other chapels and churches in the past.

At the same time, Orderic himself was also being studied. Alditha, standing to one side, saw his eyes narrow, and wondered at the thoughts that were troubling him. She considered asking him. It would be safe to do so, she knew that now. This man would never raise his sword against her, no matter what the provocation. What troubled her now was that, for the few seconds earlier when she believed he might, her fear of death had not been as great as it once would have been. With all that she had had to live with recently – first grief over Hakon, and now this almost intolerable, unending sense of dread – it might come as a blessed relief. But it would not be blessed, would it? To welcome death was a sin, wasn't it? Only she had not truly welcomed it. She had still been afraid, only perhaps not as much as she might once have been. Or was she just afraid of the pain she might be forced to endure before death came, not death itself?

Orderic must have become aware of her scrutiny because he looked over in her direction. He pointed at the group before the altar. "Comfort, you say?"

"Yes," replied Alditha. "Some."

Orderic frowned. "In times like these?"

"In what comes after."

"It is not promised."

"Hoped for, then. Earned."

"Aught I to envy them?" Orderic asked.

"Do you?"

Orderic considered this.

"No, I do not. I cannot."

Alditha would have told Orderic she pitied him this, only she knew it to be a bad idea. He would not welcome her pity. Still, she did pity this man the lack of faith she suspected in him. If she was correct in her suspicions, what must it be like for him to travel through this vale of tears expecting nothing at its end but silence and darkness? Or, at least, to have doubts about what was to come. What must it be like to be unable to voice that doubt? She stepped forward and stood next to him, both of them now watching the group kneeling before the altar. Her mind travelled back to a conversation she had had with Orderic on this same spot only a few weeks before, although it seemed much longer. She had hated him then.

"It will not comfort them any better when the walls are stone in place of wood."

"What?" asked Orderic.

"Stone in place of wood. That is the intention, is it not?"

"What?"

"Stone in place of wood. The Baron, that is his wish, or so you told us. We should be rid of this…what was the phrase you used? S*hit heap*? And we should replace it with one of stone."

Orderic frowned a little on hearing his own words spoken back to him.

"Please accept my apology for that. Although, I must tell you, it sounds far worse when you say it."

"No, it was worse coming from you. It carried weight."

"The poor choice of words was my own, but I cannot, I suppose, persuade you that the decision was not mine to make?"

"Your brother's then?" When Orderic did not reply, Alditha prompted him. "The Baron, he is your brother, is he not?"

Orderic nodded. "He is. I do not hide the fact, nor do I announce it. I certainly do not rejoice in it. How is it you come to know?"

"Eadred told me." Anticipating his next question, Alditha said, "Before you ask, no, I do not know how he came to know. There is much about you and your kind that has become known to us since you took this land from us. It bothers you that I know your relationship to the Baron? Your bond of blood."

"Half blood. We do not share the same mother. My birth was not blessed in the same way his was. I am only a..."

Alditha did not wait to hear if Orderic would complete the statement that would surely cause him further embarrassment. "Nevertheless, I would have thought there were some advantages..."

"Advantages? Huh! There would be if I were fully his brother, not merely his father's bastard! Perhaps then I too would be warming my backside against a fire in the keep of my own castle somewhere at this very moment. I too might be looking ahead to the day its walls were of stone in place of wood. I might even be planning the same for the church buildings in my lands, and sending a half-brother of my own out on a fool's errand to inform the villages thereabouts. Although, I confess, I can't imagine the latter being of such concern to me as it is to Bertrand. He shares your love for the buildings where God is worshipped."

"Oh, I think he does not. I think the nature of our devotion will be very different from each other's, our concerns entirely different. As for love, I think he does not know it. Perhaps though, his choice of words in condemning the state of this particular building might have been less crude than those you chose to use."

"You have already had my apology for that. If my words were ill chosen, I can only say I did not know you so well then."

"It should not have made a difference. Must respect always be earned with you? Cannot it sometimes simply be due? Lost only when it is discovered to be underserved?"

"That has not been my experience. Take Abbot Robert, a man of God, who loves me not. Can you tell me it is not because I am not honourably born? Where is his respect for me?"

"He responds to a request for help when it comes from you, where he would not if it were from us."

"He responds because he must. Because of who my father was, and who my brother is. Yet he sends a boy. Why is that, do you think? Could it be because of who my mother was?"

Alditha wondered where this was going. "I cannot tell you. Please, I beg you, do not tell me now something you may regret revealing to one of my kind later. If you tell me something that will advantage us, and disadvantage you, I would have to tell Eadred and the others, even if, morally, it were against my better judgement. They are my kind, you are not. I owe them a loyalty."

Orderic laughed. "Your kind. I am not your kind, you say? Perhaps so. My mother though… I wonder if you would say the same of her? What would you say if I were to tell you she was raised in London, hmm? What do you say now?"

"I don't understand, I'm sorry."

"It is not a riddle. It is very simple. She was raised in London for the simple reason that she was born there. She grew up as part of the household of the Confessor, and so, when he fled to Normandy, she accompanied him. It was there she met my father. I believe you would consider theirs a union of love. He was not yet the Baron, of course, but he was already betrothed. A longstanding arrangement that could not easily be broken without much harm. So, I was born a bastard. A bastard, and with half the blood running in my veins that of a Saxon mother."

"It was from her you learned the English tongue?"

"There was time enough for that before I was taken away into my father's household to be raised. Do not misunderstand me, it is the choice I would have made." Orderic met Alditha's eyes, did not like what he saw there. "Do not you dare pity me, woman. I am, as you say, advantaged. Better a warrior than some Saxon serving boy. Do not be sad for me. ”

Alditha sat down on a nearby bench. “It is not for you that I am sad.”

Orderic studied her for moment. “So, this is not already known to you? Any of you?” he asked.

Alditha shook her head. “It is not. Nor will it come to be. At least, not through me.”

“There is nothing to be gained by the knowledge, I assure you.”

“Who would gain? You are Norman. You made that choice years ago. Or had it made for you. Either way, there is nothing to tell.” She looked down. “I should really get on with sweeping this floor.”

“Yes. The monk was no help to you.”

“How about you, then?” Alditha proffered the brush to Orderic, who looked a little startled at her jest, but not unamused.

“Regrettably, I must go and observe the practise with the shields.”

“You do not trust Walter to do it correctly?”

“I trust Walter with my life. I have had cause to do so before now. But he is used to drilling men with more experience, so it is to Eadred I have entrusted the task of leading the shield practise. I believe him better suited to it. If nothing else, he will be able to instruct them without losing his temper at their lack of discipline quite as quickly as I know Walter would. More importantly, Eadred has more experience with the shield wall. It is a Saxon way of making war, after all. It will be under his command when the time comes, and it is right that it should be.”

“It may be true what you say about their discipline. Remember, they were only part-time warriors at best. They do not lack for courage, however.”

“Unfortunately, there are times when discipline is the more important of the two. When courage fails a man - or even encourages him to take the wrong course of action - it is the other that may hold him where he is needed."

******

Orderic found Walter in an open space at the far end of the village, standing to one side of a row of nine villagers, each man holding before him a rectangular shield comprised of three short planks of oak. The carpenter, whose name Orderic had already forgotten, had done a good job. The joins were firm, and the shields strong. But there had been wood enough to make only fourteen good shields in total. There were the nine these men were carrying, plus another two for Eadred and Swein, who would also fight as part of the wall. The remaining three shields would be carried by Orderic, Walter, and Mark, who would do their fighting independently of the wall, and on horseback, if there were sufficient time for them to mount up.

In front of the line of men stood Eadred, who appeared to be in the process of explaining some important point, using his own shield to demonstrate.

"Why can't...?" one of the men began to ask. It was Cynric, the tavern keeper. Before he could finish his question, however, Walter had stepped across, pulled the shield from his grasp, and used it to knock him to the ground.

Cynric sat up, ran his hand over his lip, and studied the small amount of blood there. Then he looked to Eadred, expectantly.

If he hoped that Eadred would speak out on his behalf he was mistaken.

"Why do you look at me like that, Welshman?" Eadred asked. "You would have me remonstrate with the Norman for knocking you down, would you? Well, hear me. It was only because Walter was closer to you than I was that it was he, and not me, who put you on your behind! If I want advice on running a tavern, I seek you out. When it comes to how to make war, *you* listen to *me.* And you do not question, unless you are offered the opportunity. The lives of everyone here may depend on you knowing your part. You cannot be sure of knowing it if you do not listen. The wall reacts to commands as one. So you need to know what those commands are and what they mean. Most of all, you need to know that, while you are a part of the wall, you belong to me, or whoever else commands you. Lives depend upon it. Now get up." Eadred offered his hand to Cynric, who took it, and got to his feet. Walter stepped forward and returned the shield to him. His pallor betrayed the fact that Cynric was still shocked and angry, but he took the shield from Walter with a nod of thanks, and quickly resumed his place in the line.

"Now," continued Eadred. "Keeping the wall locked tight is the most important thing to remember. I can't say that too often or too strongly. You men were picked for two reasons. Because you are strong, and because you have served with the Fyrd. When you were with the Fyrd, I know you will have seen the shield wall in action. You saw how the Housecarls stood with it at the front of the army. Now you must act as they did. Their shields were locked tight. *Tight!* When one fell, the wall closed the gap immediately. *Immediately*, you hear me? Maintain the integrity of the wall. That must always come first. Before you do anything else. You do not help the fallen man. It sounds harsh, I know, but he must look to himself. You cannot help him. That is not your role here. Not your duty. Your only concern is to close the gap, hold the wall. Do your duty. Your *duty*." Eadred waited, allowing time for his words to be absorbed. "Now, here is what is new. What will be different. The wall as it was used against our enemies in the past was just that… a wall. A vast line of defence that stood its ground if we were not to fail. That alone is difficult enough. Unfortunately, I must ask something more of you. Ours is not a vast wall. We are few in number. As you know, these few shields are all there was oak enough remaining to make. So they must be made to count. We cannot protect the size of area we might wish. So we must also be mobile. Our wall has to be like a swarm of bees. Or the starlings when they gather over the fields in autumn. We should move as one. Reposition as one. The wall may need to bend, enclose, shift position and re-form elsewhere. This last is the most dangerous. We may be forced to splinter the wall if we are to get it to a new position as quickly as necessary and re-form it there. It is asking a great deal of you, I know that. But these actions and commands must be learned so you can act without thought, and without question. So, let us go over them again."

Orderic held up his hand. "One moment, Eadred. Before you continue, I have something to add."

He walked over and stood in front of the row of men, next to Eadred, facing them.

"For the moment, Norman and Saxon must put aside our mutual hatred, and fight alongside one another if we are to survive. That is how it has to be. It cannot be avoided. Still, I know it does not alter the fact that you men do not like me, nor do you like Walter here, or any of us Normans. So, think on this. When I fought in the army of Duke William against you and the man you considered your king, Harold, I came up against your shield wall. And I can tell you this. It was a formidable thing. Countless times Walter and I rode against that wall, and each time it was a daunting prospect. Yes, it broke in the end, but our charges alone did not break it. A failure of discipline is what broke it. The will of the men was strong, but communication and discipline were weak. The wall collapsed because discipline collapsed within it. It was not broken from without, but from within. The point I am making is that, had things been otherwise, you might never have seen my kind in your valley. Think on that, eh. The wall works… if you do as you are commanded."

From where he watched, Walter sighed inwardly when he saw Cynric's mouth begin to open as if he would ask yet another question, but it closed again very quickly. The lesson was learned. The necessary example made.

******

CHAPTER 15

Following Alditha's advice, Edmund had skirted the perimeter wall in search of the carpenter, Dunstan. Finally, after no success, he was informed that Dunstan could be found at work making sure that the oak walls of the hall were also free from gaps, so it could serve as a final place of safety should the perimeter be breached. Dunstan's manner when Edmund first approached him made it clear that the carpenter resented any interruption to his work. Only when Edmund told him he carried instructions on behalf of Orderic did the man give him his full attention. Even then, he was abrupt to the point of rudeness. Scratching his head, as if the very idea of anyone being foolish enough to ask the question posed by Edmund mystified him, he explained that, if more oak was required to make the crosses he suggested, the monk was free to go off into the woods and cut it down himself - he would even lend him an axe with which to do it. He, Dunstan, in the meantime, would remain safely behind the walls and await news of his return - if it ever came, that was. Although the fact that Dunstan's gruff manner was quite likely a way of concealing his fear was not lost on him, this did not alter that fact that Edmund was offended. Dismayed at the ease with which the man could use the subject of anyone's death - let alone that of Edmund himself - as a source of levity, Edmund remained determined to stand his ground. Should he, Edmund asked, convey the same message to Orderic, or did the carpenter wish to revise his response? This seemed to be enough for Dunstan to alter his attitude. The thing was, he said, that all the oak, save for a very small amount, had already been used. Parts of other buildings, and some furniture had had to be sacrificed to ensure that even the slightest of gaps in the wall was plugged. And then there were the oak shields that had been made. There were now no pieces left of sufficient size to manufacture a single cross big enough to be mounted on the walls. What little remained were only scraps and off-cuts. These might serve to make some of the crosses to be worn, but not enough for the entire village, only a handful, and they would have to be very small. Well, then, a handful should be made, Edmund told him firmly.

Leaving Dunstan to set one of his sons about the task of making the crosses, Edmund walked from the hall, intending to find Orderic and let him know the situation. His route took him across the open ground at the village centre where, up ahead, a group of the village children were using what remained of the snow for a game of snowballs. Most of the snow inside the village walls had already been trampled into mud and slush, so the majority of their time was spent running off in search of the few remaining patches, returning to the village centre, and hurling the ball, however small, at the first of the other children who came into view. Seeing him coming, one of them, a young girl, shouted to the others that they should stop until he had passed, which all of them did, albeit very reluctantly. One boy, a young lad who had been introduced to Edmund as Eadred's grandson, looked down at the snow in his hand, and gave the impression that he was giving serious thought to throwing it at the monk. He had even raised his arm. However, before he could muster the courage to actually throw it, Edmund had raised a hand. "I am a man of God, boy!" he said, in as serious a voice as he could manage. "Come here."

Eadwig, head bowed, walked slowly over.

"Now, give me that," commanded, Edmund. "Go on, hand it over."

Eadwig looked down at the snow in his hand, passed it to Edmund.

"Run!" said Edmund.

"What?"

"Run!" said Edmund, smiling.

"You mean…?"

"Run is what I mean. You can do that, can't you? I know I would if I were you and someone were about to throw a snowball at me. Run!"

Surprised, Eadwig turned and ran. Before he had covered ten yards, the snowball burst on the back of his head. This was much to the amusement of the other children, who all cheered. It had been a well-aimed throw. But Edmund's triumph was short-lived. As he brushed the remaining snow from his hands, a similar missile burst against his own shoulder. He turned to see a young girl – the same one who only a minute or so before had cautioned her playfellows to hold their fire until the monk had passed – grinning in pleasure at the success of her throw.

The Norman, Orderic, could wait a while longer for news about the crosses, decided Edmund. He had known nothing but fear and confusion for some time. It would be good to find distraction in a brief exchange of snowballs with these children, who must themselves be afraid. Even if the details of their situation had been kept from them, these youngsters could not fail to sense the fear in the adults that surrounded them.

For the next ten minutes or so, as Edmund played with the village children, he did his utmost to forget the danger that might be only yards away beyond the protection of the oak. He saw the expressions on some of the adults who observed him. Some were too wrapped up in their own fears to show any sign of even registering what was happening. Others shook their heads disapprovingly. Just as many smiled.

If the Abbot were here, thought Edmund, he would not be among those who smiled. The dignity of the church, he would say, should not be sacrificed merely in order to entertain these children, most of whom were of low birth.

He would most assuredly disapprove. Then of what *did* he approve? Nothing beyond the stone walls of Menlac as far as Edmund was aware. Stone walls, mused Edmund, what good would they be here?

Out of the corner of his eye he saw one girl sitting alone on a barrel, watching. Ducking a snowball, he crossed over to her.

"Will you not join us?" he asked.

The girl did not seem to hear him at first. "Child?" he said again, "Will not join us? It is cold on the fingers I admit, yet it is fun." He reached out to take her by the shoulder, but thought better of it. "Child?"

The girl finally became aware of him. "Ealdgyth is better at it."

"Ealdgyth?"

"My big sister. She is better at snowball games. I cannot make the balls hit the right place like she does. Anyway, she says I should not play. It is not safe to be outside. She lets me watch only as long as I stay near her."

"And which one is she?" asked Edmund, turning to look at the other children.

The girl raised a thin arm. Edmund, noticing that it seemed to be something of an effort for her to do so, guessed she must have been unwell, and was still recovering. It would explain her reluctance to join in the game.

"There," she said, "Pony is there. Oh, if you talk to her, don't tell her I called her Pony, will you. She doesn't like it much, and will be cross with me again."

"No, I will not. I can well imagine she would not like that," said Edmund, recalling for a moment the cruel names he himself had been called as young boy, due to his slightness of stature, and his unusually large nose. Presumably, the girl he was looking for would be larger than most. A strange contrast to her frail-looking sister.

Looking in the direction indicated, and seeing no child

there, large or small, he asked, "Is she hiding? Lying in wait in order to surprise one of her friends with a snowball? Behind that manger perhaps? Or that water trough? Very cunning of her. She must be very skilled in the art of concealment for, I confess it, I cannot see her. Where *is* she hiding?"

"She's not hiding."

"Then how is it I cannot see her?"

"You have to look very hard because she is dead, and being dead makes her harder to see than the other children," said the girl, in such a casual, matter-of-fact, manner that Edmund was not sure he had heard her correctly. Appearing to understand this, the girl said again, more firmly this time, "She is dead."

"Dead?" asked Edmund, struggling to sound unflustered.

"Yes. The thin grey man had her killed. Poor Pony. Oh, don't tell her I called her that again."

"No, no, I will not," said Edmund, taking an involuntary step backwards, completely ignoring a snowball that burst against his head. He was about to take another step away when shame overcame him, and he stopped, stepped back towards the girl. "Tell me, what is your name, child?"

"Little Hare."

"Your parents…are they nearby…which is your house?"

"The grey man killed them too. I live with Alditha now. Until I am better, anyway. Then, when I am, I will be a servant in the hall. Eadred says he will not let me go hungry. I have no one to look after me in my own village because the grey man came and took them all to Hell."

At last, Edmund understood. "You are from Gyrtun, then?" As soon as he had said it, he knew he should not have done. Little Hare's eyes widened, seeing something only she could see, and she began to sob violently, then to howl. Edmund put his arms about her. Holding the girl tightly, he called over to Eadwig who, like his companions, had stopped playing and was staring at Little Hare.

"You must run to the church and fetch Alditha."

Eadwig hesitated."That's Little Hare. She's mad," he said. "Ever since what happened…"

"Never mind that, child, fetch Alditha!"

Eadwig nodded, and ran off.

******

"I am to blame for it. I should not have talked of Gyrtun. I regret it very much if I have made things worse for her."

Alditha glanced up at the monk angrily. "*Worse*? How could you have made things worse? How could they possibly be worse for this child?" Alditha stopped herself. "Forgive me, Brother. I am tired. I meant no disrespect."

Looking down at Little Hare, who was sleeping now, Edmund crossed himself. "She spoke to me of her sister…as if she could see her…"

"I think in her way she does. Her sister died horribly, and she saw it happen. She sometimes pretends her sister is alive, nothing more. Pony… Ealdgyth, her sister, is not among the dead who walk again, if that is your concern. She walks only in the mind of this child, her sister. She would not be the first person who chooses to live with what is not real because reality is far too painful."

"Will she ever…?"

"Who can say?"

"You are a good woman to care for her as you do."

"Am I? You would not say so if you could hear my thoughts, or look into my soul. All you would see there would be hate and fear. I hate whatever is causing all this. I hate it for what is has done to my people. I hate it for making me afraid. And I fear it more than I have ever feared anything before in my life. My fear makes it hard for me to think sometimes. My head is so full of images of what I know has happened to others, and of what I fear may happen to me. I wonder how will I stand such pain when it comes."

"*If* it comes. We may yet be free of this monster. We may yet be spared."

"I pray you are correct."

"As do I."

"I pray a great deal."

"Does it help?"

"It does. There is always comfort there. But not as much as I want, Brother. Fear and hope are not an equal match in my head. Fear takes the field more often than it relinquishes it. So I busy myself with anything I can to take my mind…if only for a moment… off the things it keeps returning to…again and again, Brother. Again and again."

"As does my own. You clean and tidy your church to wrench it away from such thoughts, I play snowballs with the children. Not very becoming for a brother of Menlac Abbey."

"The Abbot would not approve."

"He would not."

"Only because he would not understand. If he were here he might feel differently." Alditha smiled. "Although, I cannot imagine, even then, he would play snowballs. Beneath his dignity."

Edmund smiled too. "He might if he were assured of winning, and never being hit. The children would have to be firmly instructed on how to behave."

The smiles lasted only for a moment.

"You spoke of hate. That is natural. I am a man of God. I should not accept hate into my heart any more than I should pride or greed. Yet it has found a home there despite my best attempts to shut it out. When I remember what I saw done to those men in the forest, when I hear of the harm done to villagers like this child's family, I cannot help but wish ill on the thing that inflicted it."

"I could live more easily with hate alone," said Alditha,

coldly.

Edmund raised his eyebrows. "Do not wish for such a thing. To live with only hate in your soul would be a curse unlike any I can imagine."

"I have done so already. The Normans… I have hated them for a long time now. They killed my husband. Is that not cause for hate, if ever there was one?"

"Yes, but not hate alone. There was grief too, surely? And grief is born of love, is it not? Hate alone… hate and nothing else… would be beyond redemption. It would be a pathway to Hell."

"Are we not already on that path?"

"This is not Hell we face, Alditha, and you know that. That thing out there, and the slaves it has made of the dead, they may be the instruments of Hell, but they are not a barrier to our salvation. The suffering they inflict may be unimaginable… I too fear it more than I think I can bear at times…but it is not everlasting. Little Hare's family is not in Hell now. Ealdgyth…she is gathered unto God as surely as I sit before you now. You know that, I know you do. She died without her soul overwhelmed by hate. As yours is not either. If you had only hate inside you, you would not be capable of caring for this child that sleeps here now."

"I know, Brother, truly I do. I spoke in haste. It is this fear again. I cannot put it aside. I remember once as a child, when the spring celebrations were at hand, I fell sick from eating something I should not have. I knew all about me were happy and enjoying the day. I knew that I too would also happy were it not for the churning of my stomach and the spinning of my head. If I could only ignore those feelings the day might still be enjoyed. Yet I could not. It is like that now, only far worse. Food tastes of nothing. The warmth of a fire is necessary, not enjoyable like it can be. Do you understand?"

"I do. There is not one soul here that does not wrestle with fear every moment of the day, and would not agree with everything you have said about it. It could not be otherwise with what threatens us."

"Oh, sometimes I think there are some. Some who the fear seems to torment far less than the rest of us."

"You speak of Orderic and his men?"

"Them, yes. Eadred and Swein also. They are all more afraid of showing their fear than of the thing that frightens them, it seems to me."

"Yet they *are* afraid, are they not?"

"I suppose so. They would be fools not to be. Although Orderic is many things I do not admire, a fool he is not. As for Swein, I have known him all my life, he is a good man. Eadred too."

"Alditha, all those men have that you and I do not is experience with coping with their fear. They have learned the skill of mastering it, that is all. They have lived their lives in preparation. They have stood their ground while enemies drew near. You and I have never known what it was like to have to do that. To stand in the middle of a battle. I myself doubt I could do it and still preserve my wits. It may be that even for them there is some doubt that they can do it again. Perhaps they must find their courage anew for each fight? Men can fail sometimes, it is in our nature, and part of the burden we are given to carry. Maybe they fear more than we do for that very reason. We can be sure they have never had to deal with such as this. In the face of this they cannot be certain of their nerve. To be used to finding courage in the face of one type of threat does not necessarily mean you can find it when the nature of the threat you now come up against is so very different from all you have known previously. My kind have been accused of hiding from the evils of this world behind the walls of the Abbey. There are, I believe, men who hide from them in the middle of battles. Let us be strong in our way, they in theirs."

When Edmund had gone, Alditha looked down at Little

Hare. She wanted the monk to be right. She wanted to believe she had the strength to face what was coming. If she found she did not possess it, let death, when it came, be swift and painless.

******

It had begun to snow again. Under different circumstance the villagers' talk would have been of almost nothing else. They would have said this had been the hardest winter they had known for many years. They would have expressed concern about how long it would last, yet would also have been pleased with themselves for setting aside sufficient food to see it through, as they always had. Eadred was a wise and careful leader, they would say, because he always ensured they were prepared for the worst the winter could throw at them. Unlike other villages they had heard of where the people had gone hungry, and some had even died. Today, however, as the snow fell through the last of the daylight, most did not even comment upon it at all, and those who did mentioned it only briefly. A very few whispered that this was part of the evil that beset Elastun. The heavy snow, they said, had been brought here by the malevolent presence that waited in the forest.

Outside, the men standing guard at the wall pulled their cloaks tighter around themselves, and pulled on caps and hoods. Among them was Swein, who glanced up at the falling flakes, cursed the additional trouble his leg would give him as a result of the cold and damp, then returned his gaze to the gloom beneath the trees.

After a while there came shouts from Swein's left, so he turned and looked along the wall in that direction, his hands tightening on the haft of his axe. He saw nothing, so called over to the next man along, who shrugged his shoulders and replied that he could not make out exactly what the trouble was, but there seemed to be some commotion at the far side, where the forest opened into the fields and the plain of the river. Swein told the man to stay put, maintain his watch, and let him know if he saw anything more. He also reminded him that, whatever happened, he was not to lean out beyond the wall. Before the man could reply, Swein saw movement beneath him – a group of grey shapes running in his direction through the snow covered space between the wall and the trees. Swein's grip on his axe relaxed; he knew the shapes for what they were. Wolves, a pack of perhaps a dozen or so. Ahead of them, a deer ran for its life. Without thinking, momentarily caught up in the thrill of the chase, Swein leaned forward to get a better look. Only at the last second did he realise what he was doing and pull back before he had moved his head out beyond the protection of the oak. His heart pounded in his chest and, to his shame, he found his hands were shaking.

When it was almost directly beneath him, the deer swerved into the trees. Careful now not to lean too far forward, Swein continued to watch, expecting the pack to follow it into the darkness. They did not. Instead, they halted, abruptly, as if all had come to the full length of invisible tethers that would allow them no further slack. Their heads lowered and, even in the fading light, Swein could see their backs bristle as their hackles rose. They began to back away, slowly at first, and then, suddenly, as one, they turned and ran back the way they had come, always keeping close to wall, and away from the trees. Only when they were out of sight, and he had turned back to watch the forest - curious about the fate of the deer - did Swein see that one wolf remained. A dark grey male, tall and heavy. He knew immediately that this was the same wolf he had encountered some days ago, on the track to Gyrtun. It padded up to the nearest tree, seemed to look into the forest beyond, then lifted its head and sniffed the air. After a few seconds it let out a low growl but, instead of backing away like its companions had, it turned about and began to pad away slowly, almost casually - if such a deliberate display were possible for a beast. After a few paces it stopped and looked up, directly at Swein.

"Hello, old friend," said Swein, meeting the animal's eyes. "Your courage has not deserted you, I see. You are an example to us all."

As they stood there, the falling snow settling on the shoulders of man and beast alike, Swein wondered whether the glimmer he observed in the eyes of the wolf was the light of understanding, or simply the dumb curiosity of a wild animal.

Behind the wolf, the bushes rustled. Swein lifted his axe. A second later the deer leapt out and ran off. The wolf did not react. He stood a moment longer before turning and walking off in the opposite direction - the direction taken by the rest of his pack.

"Good fortune to you," whispered Swein, and then glanced back at the space where the deer had emerged. The branches there were swaying and shaking, and the snow swirled as if in reaction to a wind that had risen in that spot alone. Everywhere else the flakes fell straight and silent into darkness, free of all but the lightest breeze.

"So, you want me to know you are there, is that it?" shouted Swein. The shaking of the branches ceased briefly, then began again much more violently. "Very well," Swein said with a sigh. He looked down at his hand. It was no longer trembling. He took a deep breath, filling his lungs, as if he were about to plunge his head underwater, raised his axe in readiness for any attack, and leaned out. From behind him he heard the cries of warning from some of the other men on guard further down the wall. Then the cries were swallowed up by the high-pitched shrieking.

******

CHAPTER 16

Orderic was in council with Eadred when Walter found him. The soldier burst into Eadred's inner chamber without announcing himself. There was anger on the faces of both men at the interruption, but it was only to Orderic that Walter addressed his apology and explanation.

"Forgive me, Orderic, but you should come. Now. You should come now. Swein. He is at the gate."

"What do you mean, *at the gate*? How is this possible? Where has he been? I swear I saw him earlier, on guard at the wall. Can the man never be trusted to stay where he is needed?" Orderic glanced at Eadred as if the old man might be able to offer some explanation, but saw straight away that Eadred was as confused as he himself was by Walter's news. "Very well. Take us to him."

By the time they reached the gate, a crowd of men, including Brother Edmund, were gathered on the walkway looking down at the track beyond. Orderic was about to order them back to their stations, but was beaten to it by Eadred. The men turned at the sound of Eadred's voice.

One, Wilfred, a farmer's son, and still not much more than a teenager, climbed down and said, "Eadred, it is Swein. He leaned out. We tried to stop him. It must have taken him. Then he came back. He came back. What do we do? What do we do?"

Eadred took him by the shoulders.

"Be calm now, lad. You do as I have told you, and get back on guard at the position allotted to you…*entrusted* to you." Eadred looked past the boy, and up at the others. "All of you. Listen to me. You should not have wavered. You should not have allowed yourselves to be distracted. Can you not see? Even as we stand here the evil out there may be taking advantage of your lack of steadfastness to gain entry. Did in not occur to you that this may be a diversion? Fools. Get back to your positions now. All of you. Right now! Brother Edmund, you should stay."

All but two of the other men left the gate, and returned to their positions on the walkway. One of the men who remained was Wilfred. The other was Alfred the blacksmith. "I tried to tell them, Eadred," he said.

"I'm sure you did, Alfred. Never mind that now. I take it you two were here on guard to begin with?" asked Eadred. "Where is Swein now?"

"He is below, on the other side of the wall."

"Why have you not let him in?" snapped Eadred.

"We would have…we nearly did when he first appeared at the gate… only…"

"Only *what*?"

"We did not know if it would be wise to do so."

"What do you mean?"

"He is not himself, Eadred. He is changed. Come see for yourself."

"It is true, said Walter. Look for yourself."

As he climbed the ladder to the walkway above the gate, Eadred's heart beat heavily in his chest. *Not Swein too* he prayed. Not Swein. Had his old friend been taken in the same way his beloved son had? Was Wulfstan also out there? He did not know if he could stand to see his son that way another time. Panic began to overtake him, he felt dizzy, felt himself sway back from the ladder. A large hand was placed on his back to steady him. "There now, careful." It was Walter. "Can't have you falling now, can we?"

Eadred turned, nodded his gratitude to the Norman. Even then, in his state of anxiety, the strangeness of this exchange was not lost on him. There was no mistaking that this big man was his enemy, was part of the army that had slain Eadred's own son and grandson, and taken over his country. At any other time that enmity would have been insurmountable.

Another hand appeared at his face. He took it, and Orderic pulled him up onto the walkway. Once up, Eadred waved aside any further offers of help, and went straight to the wall.

Below him he saw his old friend. The Housecarl was on his knees in the mud and snow of the track. For a moment Eadred thought Swein was pleading to be admitted, and he felt a twinge of pity mingled with shame on behalf of his old friend - a proud Housecarl reduced to pleading on his knees. Then he saw the blood that covered Swein's body and stained the muddy snow surrounding him. Swein was not begging, he was struggling to stay conscious. As Eadred watched, Swein swayed slightly. Simply maintaining that upright position on his knees was taking an act of great strength and willpower. Swein would never beg for anything.

Only when he found yet more hands upon him - Alfred's, this time, pulling him back - did Eadred realise he had leaned forward beyond the protection of the oak.

"There is only Swein out there," he told the others. "I saw nothing else. Why did you not let him in, Alfred? He is not changed like the others, he is injured, that is all."

"His face…his eyes, Eadred. Look again."

Eadred leaned out again and called down. "Swein, it is I, Eadred. What happened to you? How is it you find yourself out there? How badly are you hurt?"

Below them, Swein rocked slightly. He did not look up.

"Swein? Will you not talk to me?" Still Swein said nothing. Eadred turned to the others. "Damn you all, he is injured. If you will not open the gate, I will do it myself."

Before he could take a step, Alfred had grabbed his shoulder. "No, Eadred! No!"

"Can I not do anything without one of you manhandling me?" growled Eadred.

"Alfred is right," said Orderic. "We do not know how

he comes to be out there. Nor what has happened to him. You spoke of diversions and trickery yourself. This may be that very thing. We cannot let him in. Imagine if it were a pestilence that ravaged the land beyond your walls. You would not be so hasty to allow entry to one who might be suffering from it."

"Swein is my friend."

"You must not let him in!" cried Edmund.

"You should listen to them, old friend. You cannot let me in. I will not answer for myself if you do."

Eadred ceased to struggle. At the sound of his friend's voice all energy had left him. The hands that had held him released their grip. He looked back down at Swein. "How can that be true? How can you be a danger to us? I will not believe it. I cannot. I will not!"

"You must. Orderic is right. I do not know how much affected I am. It matters not, for I will shortly die, whether I am within the walls or not. I have been given enough life…enough time… to deliver a message…no more."

"I will not watch you bleed to death at my gates and do nothing about it," cried Eadred.

"I say again that you must. I will not enter inside, even if you open the gates."

"Then I will drag you, if that is what I must do."

"If you drag me, I will struggle against it. Look at me Eadred. *Look at me.*" Swein raised his head. For the first time Eadred was able to look directly into the Housecarl's eyes. In contrast to the deathly pallor of his skin, and the dark streaks of his blood, they shone with an unnatural light. The same light Eadred had seen in the eyes of his dead son. He stepped back, looked away.

"No, do not turn away. You must keep looking at me, for it helps hold on to the part of me that is still of this world. All of you, look at me. Listen, and mark what I have to tell you."

"How can we know it is safe?" demanded Edmund.

"You can see me without crossing the protection of the wall, can you not? Therefore it must follow that I am not fully changed."

"Must it?"

"If I were, you would not see me, Edmund. I am not one of his. Nor will I be while I still live. I am still the Swein who rode with you from Menlac. Those who serve him do not breathe the air of this world." Swein paused, sadness crossed his features. "Although I fear I am not as I was. And I will not last long." He fought to regain his composure. "See… there is no one and nothing with me right now, I swear it."

"A demon's oath!" cried Edmund.

"Hush boy!" hissed Walter.

"I understand your mistrust, Brother. So, I swear it again…on my immortal soul if I have to… I *am* alone. Will that not satisfy? Eadred has already seen that much. Lean out again now, Eadred… Tell them what you see. There will be nothing there. Trust me. I am not as Wulfstan, and he is not with me. I know that is what you fear."

Eadred's jaw clenched, and he gripped the wall with both hands.

"Wait," said Orderic.

Eadred ignored the warning, cleared his throat, and leaned over the wall again. "He speaks the truth. There is nothing to see out there other than Swein, and the blood that his courageous heart still pumps from his body."

"You understand now?" asked Swein. "As long as one of you keeps forward of the wall…keeps a constant watch… then nothing can come near without your knowledge."

Orderic tapped Walter on the shoulder, indicating that he should do as Swein had instructed. Walter looked doubtful for a second or two then, at a scowl from Orderic, and a second, much harder, tap on the shoulder, did as he was ordered.

"Good. Now, you must hear what I have to say," said Swein.

"First, tell us why is it that you are not dead like the rest, or become one of them?" asked Orderic.

"If you would listen, I will tell what I am permitted."

"*Permitted?*" asked Orderic.

"Please, let him talk," said Eadred.

As if prompted by Eadred's words, below them, Swein attempted to stand up and draw himself up to his full height. Instead, he swayed, falling back onto his knees once more, coughing as he did so, and spraying the snow in front of him with blood. Steadying himself with one hand, he used the other to wipe his sleeve across his blood-stained mouth and chin. "You will forgive me. I cannot stand. It seems I have little time. You must understand that it is against my will that I am sent here to talk with you. I would rather have died than serve that monster, even for the shortest of times. Once he has you, his will is too strong for you to resist. But listen to me… What you make of the message I bring is for you to decide." Swein paused, emphasizing this last point. "I have no choice in the matter. You do still have a choice. You could…" Before Swein could say more he was seized by some inner agony and fell forward, twisting and writhing on the ground. When the pain had passed, he pushed himself back up onto his knees. "He will not permit me to say what I would say. Only the message he wants me to bring to you. Nothing more."

"Then let us have that message," said Orderic.

The expression on Swein's face was one of sorrow despite the malevolence of the words he began to speak.

"He wants the strong among you to join him. Those warriors who pass his ordeal are granted the honour of becoming one of his servants. Those who do not…those who are not of the right kind…they are killed… their life drained from them. Every murder committed in his name adds to his strength. The more painful the victim's end, the better. He feeds on it. The villagers at Gyrtun…they were just the sort of weak scum upon whom he could feed. It was a shame that little bitch of a girl was able to escape. Never fear, he will have her life yet, when he takes Elastun. And he *will* take Elastun. That is his promise. Her kind…their only value to him is their capacity to suffer and die. Others, however…a very few…the strongest of the warriors among you…Wulfstan…Orderic's man Turold…they become his servants…are chosen to join him…kill in his name. And now he has more of them… "

"From among the men my brother sent. Is that not so?" interrupted Orderic.

"It is," replied Swein.

Orderic thought for a moment. "Well, the fact that he sends you tells me he is not yet so powerful he can take this place at will. Come now, why does he send you? Explain that, if you can."

"You resist him…" Swein spoke quickly, the words now his own. "The oak…He is vulnerable. He has weakness still…." Swein winced, as if saying this caused him pain, and coughed up more blood. "Damn it…I cannot say what I would, only what I must." He fell silent. His head dropped forward, and his body slumped over. To the onlookers at the wall he appeared dead. Only when a further cough wracked his body was it clear he was still alive. When he eventually looked back up at them, the unnatural light in his eyes was more intense. His voice when he spoke was no longer his own.

"*This wreck before you, it was once one of your strongest, was it not? A warrior. Proud, courageous. Then the work of an instant in battle snapped his leg like a twig. Left him lame, ruined, bitter. Such a waste. Still, it was from that very same battle that I derived my freedom to roam the world again. The energy and will that drives mankind to gather in vast numbers on the fields and plains of this earth in order that you might so clumsily hack and stab at one another until only the victors are left standing is what my kind once used to thrive upon. The violence, rage, and pain of the battlefield in those days…it was glorious… nourishing to us. But those days soon became yesterdays that eventually became 'once', ultimately became forgotten, and in time we faded from the ever failing memory of man. Yet now it seems I, at least, am summoned back. We may have been forgotten, but your taste for war it seems has never ceased, and what took place on the hillside near the place you call Hastings was so close to where I had been imprisoned it drew me out again, freed me, imbued me with vigour once more. Such hate there was that day, such anger, and oh, what violence! Glorious!*

Odd, both sides claiming your God's support. Neither deserving it. I don't believe your God was even there to see any of it. The only awesome or mystical presence there that day was mine.

Pure, bloody, greed for power was all I sensed when I walked among those who fought. Well, whatever it was, I am returned. It was there I met Wulfstan, and it was he who led me here. Now I need more such men of strength. I know there are some of those among you. I sense it, and I would have you serve me. You, Orderic, are one. I know your twisted bastard's soul. And you, Walter, let us not forget about you. And I believe there is another…Mark, is it? Where is he? On guard somewhere else at your thin, thin wall? Well, no matter. I would add all three of you to my ranks if you prove worthy. But you must prove worthy. Oh, and there is Eadred. Let us consider him. Too old, perhaps? Only the flesh. No, the problem with you, Eadred, is the heart. You have too much regard for your people to be of any use to me. It is your heart that is weak, not your old flesh. As for the others… your cherished villagers…their pain will be my nourishment, like so many of their weak kind. Swein is wrong. You do not have a choice. You have none. Then you already know that, don't you? I will take the village. It will happen. My only wish is to hasten things. This, then, is my message to you. If those who I have named join me now…step down from that foolish wall of yours…Well, things will be over sooner. I will make the deaths here swifter than I usually do. Better for everyone that way. Your response?"

"We say damn you back to Hell, Demon!" shouted Edmund.

"Quiet, proud priest! I have no interest in what you would say to me. I await only the responses of those whose answers matter. Those I have named. Those who have a chance to serve me. You, boy, are not numbered among them. Like the rest, you die whatever answer is given. You are a man of your God, so I suggest you pray they make the choice that brings you a rapid and pain-free death. An opportunity to stand before your God sooner than you could have expected. Discover if you are right about His mercy. See if He forgives you for letting Leofric burn in Hell because you, Edmund, failed him when he needed you most. Where was your calling then? It was not me you damned, boy. Oh...and perhaps you might also ask your God why he abandoned you to this fate."

The voice that was not Swein's fell silent, waited. For a time the only sound was the wind in the trees, and the agitated praying of Edmund who, resisting the temptation to run from the wall, stood his ground, defiantly holding before him his cross of oak.

Orderic glanced at the monk, then at the others. He then leaned out to address the thing speaking through Swein. "How is it that you know our names? Know so much about us? "

"Turold, Wulfstan, Swein here... Men in pain tell me much. They need not utter a word. I read them as the monk reads his peeling parchments."

"Well, as you know mine, tell me, have you a name?"

"A name? I have never had need of a name. They are a human device. Clumsy, sentimental."

"Then should I simply call you Demon?"

"Ha! I am no demon. At least, not what your frightened monk means by it. I never fell from grace. I have never met with Lucifer or God. Although I find I am risen. Perhaps I am Christ-like? You could call me..."

"Blasphemer!" screamed Edmund. "Monster!"

"Monster? To you I may seem so. But only as the fox is a monster to the hare."

"A fox is a natural thing. You are not that. You are

*un*natural," said Orderic.

"It is true. You do not belong in this world. God is appalled and nature is disordered by your presence," said Edmund, lifting his cross high.

"Tell me, monk who sees fit to speak on behalf of God, why do you provoke me? Could it be that you have spent too many hours with your books? Has your reading inspired you to you seek a martyr's death? They are always so drawn out, so agonising....It can be arranged. But I would like to know how it will be different from the millions of terrible deaths suffered by so many others before you. Your Christ was not the first to die on a cross. What makes him so special? Or any of your saints?"

"They die for faith!" shouted Edmund.

"They die to be witnessed. I promise you this, monk. No one will ever know the torments I put you *through.* Your *suffering will be wasted because it will be hidden from the world."*

"It will not be hidden from God!" replied Edmund.

"I will debate this no longer!"

"Because you fear God. Because you..."

"Enough, boy," cautioned Orderic.

Swein's body stiffened, his mouth opened unnaturally wide - the click of the dislocating jaw audible - and emitted a roar like that of a wild animal. *"Silence the monk. He offends me. I will speak to none but Orderic. And I will be treated with respect."*

Orderic forced a laugh. "Oh, now, if you knew me as you so claim, you would know that that will *never* happen. You are too obvious, Demon. Your bargain is no bargain at all. Die sooner rather than later. That is no more than a fool's trade. You show your weakness with it. If you were sure of overcoming our defences you would have no need of such a message or such a messenger. Swein would already be dead, or he would be among your ranks. No, it is clear to me that you fear that this will cost you. And yet you stay. Why is that? What am I to make of it? Could it be that you are not yet as strong as you claim? You need to feed on the people here just like any army of men needs the food it takes from the villages along its way. Without it, you fade, you starve. Why do you not just move on, hmm? Could it be that you cannot? That you have not the strength? Your boasts are empty, Demon. Do your worst, I say!"

"So you make your choice. You have condemned yourselves to torment. You and the weaklings you defend!" shouted the voice.

"How will that be avoided either way? If we open the gates you will simply do what you wish. You will not honour the pledge of merciful ends for the people here. Do you think me a fool? You will kill all before you in the same brutal manner as you did at Gyrtun and at Tunleah."

"This from a Norman? What do your kind know of mercy? And you, Orderic the Bastard, what have you ever known of God? I see into your black heart, remember."

Orderic became aware of the others on the wall looking at him. He saw Edmund take a step backwards.

He chose his words carefully.

"Perhaps I am not like the boy here…the monk…I have not his certainty. I have seen too much for faith not to be diminished. But flames that burn low are still burning, for all that. I place my faith in honour and courage."

"Even if it is misplaced?"

"Even then. That is why I have no faith in your promise to end the lives of the villagers painlessly. You will betray them the moment you are free to do so."

"Not if I allow you and your men to do it first. Kill them, Norman. Kill the Saxons, and gain immortality at my side."

"If it were only that easy. I regret you underestimate their resolve. These Saxons cling to life like rats, and there are only three of us here against their many. Numbers will tell against experience if the numbers are sufficient."

"You lack the courage to try."

"I lack the will to be your servant. I serve no one."

"An empty boast, I think. For that is not what I learned from Rollo. The Baron…your brother…there is no respect there, and yet

you serve him."

Orderic found himself unable to answer this. While he was struggling for a response, Walter came up next to him.

"I think what my captain is trying to say is that we serve no one, and no thing, that we consider of inferior status to us, as you most certainly are."

"What if you do not serve? What if I were to allow you to ride away?"

Walter huffed contemptuously. "*Allow* us?"

"There you have the problem," said Orderic. "Why do *you* not leave? Why not take the little monk's advice, and go back to Hell or wherever it is you crawled up from? Failing that, simply go somewhere other than this. There must be easier villages? Ones that do not bite back."

Swein's mouth opened wide again, and let out the same animal roar, before his body slumped forward onto the ground. His head turned to one side, his cheek pressed against the cold earth. In his own voice this time, he said, "Kill me. Before it returns. I will be a vessel for the monster no longer."

"No, there may yet be hope for you," protested Eadred.

Swein struggled over onto his back, so he could look up at them. "No, Eadred, old friend, there is none. Whatever happens now, my time is done. If I have any choice in it, I will not serve him! So, it is my wish that you end my life, and with it my usefulness to him. Now! It must be done now, while there is time for it. Before he can claim me. There is no hope for me otherwise."

"I will not believe it."

Swein lifted a hand towards the wall. "The cross, the wooden cross you have about your neck, Eadred. I see it is one of those the monk had made. Throw it to me."

"What?"

"Please, throw me the cross."

"I will if it will bring you comfort…but there may not be a need for it. Alditha may be able to help more…"

"I have need of it."

"The boy…the monk…can he not…?"

"It is not for *my* spiritual comfort that I ask this. It is for *yours*. So you understand, and can do what I ask with a clear conscience. Throw it, Eadred, please man. Throw it."

Bewildered, Eadred nonetheless did as his friend had asked, though his arm shook and his aim was off, so the cross fell short. With a grown, Swein began to crawl over to where it lay, half buried in the snow.

"No, wait, Swein. Have mine," shouted Alfred, and threw his cross.

Alfred's aim had been truer, and Swein was able to reach the cross with only a slight stretch of his arm. He grasped it in his palm, shook off the remaining snow, and lifted the arm so they all might see. Immediately, the skin of his hand began to split and curl. The flesh beneath it sizzled like meat on a spit, and fell in small, bloody gobbets that steamed on contact with the cold ground. Despite the obvious agony, Swein did not release his hold. "You see?" he cried through clenched teeth. "You see why you must put an end to me while it can still be done?"

Eadred fought back the urge to turn from his friend's suffering. "I see it, I see it. In the name of God, man, no more of this. Let it go, Swein. Release your hold!"

"Look how the cross rends his flesh," cried Edmund.

"Or the oak," said Orderic under his breath.

"Will you see to it, Eadred?" asked Swein. "Will you do what must be done?"

"I will, I swear it. Release your hold."

Swein let the cross fall from his grasp, and rolled onto his back.

"Keep watch for me," said Eadred. "Open the gate."

"I will not allow you to bring him in, if that is your intention," said Orderic.

Eadred drew his sword. "It is not. I will finish him out there. Listen, if anything appears while I am down there, you are to close the gate, you hear me. I insist."

"I will not open the gate."

"I swore to him!"

"I'm sorry, but it can be done just as surely from here." Orderic turned to Walter. "Make ready."

Walter raised the bow he had taken from Alfred. Seeing this, Swein rose to his knees. Then, slowly, and with great effort, he got to his feet, presenting Walter with a clearer target. "I would die standing up," he said. Walter acknowledged this with a brief incline of his head, and took aim.

"Get it done with," ordered Orderic.

Before Walter could shoot, Eadred pushed him back, and stepped in front of him, blocking his line of sight. "No, not one of you! It should not be one of your kind. He should not die at the hands of a Norman!" he cried.

"Again, you Saxons and your pride," said Orderic.

"Death is death, old man," said Walter.

"Give me the bow," pleaded Eadred.

"I will not. Your hand shakes too much," said Walter.

"Walter is right," said Orderic. "A moment ago you could not even throw the cross so it landed where you intended. Could you be certain of your aim with the bow? Would it be true? If it were not…"

"Alfred then…" suggested Eadred.

Alfred shook his head vehemently. "I am a blacksmith. Killing is not my trade. I have never taken a life. Swein is my friend. I could not do it."

"I must do it then. My hand will be steady," said Eadred.

Ignoring him Orderic turned back to Walter. "Have you an aim? A clear one?"

"I have."

"No, not one of you," cried Eadred again. "Not for Swein. He deserves better than that. It is not right for it to be one of you. It is not fitting."

"Do not trouble yourself, Eadred," said Swein. "It *is* fitting. Do I not face the enemy on my feet? What better way is there? It should be this way."

Before Eadred could reply, Orderic gave the order for Walter to shoot.

Swein met Walter's eye. He blinked slowly, with a slight nod of his head, to indicate his readiness.

Walter released the arrow.

The shot was well aimed. Swein grunted and fell back, his limbs twitching only briefly before he lay silent and still. As the onlookers at the wall watched, his last breath rose up into the air above his body, into the space where he had been standing only a moment before. It showed there for an instant as a pale cloud in the cold air before being swept away, melting on the breeze.

When Walter passed the bow back to Alfred, he shook his head, and refused to take it. Eadred, who had forced himself to watch his friend's death despite an almost overwhelming desire to look away, saw this. He took the bow from Walter, turned with it to Alfred. "You must take it. You may have need."

"Swein…"

"Swein would understand. He would want you to do your duty, as he did his."

Reluctantly, Alfred took the bow, and resumed his position on guard above the gate. As Eadred, Orderic, and the others climbed down from the wall, Alfred watched the track and surrounding trees. Despite his best efforts, his gaze occasionally strayed to the body of Swein below.

As they walked from the gate, Eadred increased his pace in order to catch up with Orderic. "I am grateful to you for the decision you have made to stand by Elastun," he said. "I know if I were in your position…"

Orderic kept walking, and did not turn to look at Eadred. "Well, you are not. And I am not deserving of your gratitude, believe me. I do not know what my response to that thing's offer would have been had I had more men at my disposal, and the odds, therefore, been different. I do know that if I were in your position I would not sell my life easily. That much I do know. Consider this, however. What if the beast out there does get in, hmm? Will your people not then wish they *had* allowed our blades to do their work? Would that not be preferable to the torments that are in store for them at the hands of your son, and Turold, and whoever else of the Baron's men is now with them? Death at our hands would at least have come quickly, with little time for suffering."

Eadred stopped, allowing Orderic and Walter to walk off ahead of him. At their backs he shouted. "You fear compassion as you fear weakness. They are not the same thing, Orderic. They are not the same thing."

******

Sometime later, shortly before they were due to be relieved of the guard, Alfred and Wilfred sensed movement among the trees closest to where Swein's body still lay in the snow. Wilfred gripped the scythe he carried more tightly, and Alfred raised his bow, as a large dark wolf emerged slowly from the tree line, and walked over to the body of the Housecarl.

Alfred was still taking aim in preparation for loosing an arrow to prevent the animal from desecrating the remains when, having circled Swein's body, occasionally sniffing at it, the wolf padded slowly back into the forest without looking back. Alfred relaxed the tension on the bowstring, let the arrow drop from the notch, and caught it with his other hand.

******

CHAPTER 17

Fear and bewilderment took an ever greater hold of the inhabitants of Elastun. An increasing number of them began to spend as much time as they possibly could in the church - often attending one of the regular prayer meetings held by Brother Edmund. Many other villagers could also be found huddled together inside the great hall, in the hope that, should the perimeter walls be breached, the oak walls of the hall would provide further protection against the Demon - for that was what it was now being called by most people, largely due to Edmund's frequently referring to it as that in his sermons and prayers.

Many theories as to why the Demon had chosen to come to Elastun were whispered among the villagers, and one in particular began to take hold, though no one could say where it began. The first Alditha heard of it was from Eadwig, one morning while he was helping her prepare the church. He was irritated at having to do so, especially when he heard the sound of other children playing outside - those few who still felt the urge to play, and were permitted to by their parents - but his grandfather had said if he was old enough to take unsanctioned hunting trips, he was old enough to make himself useful. Given that having the boy's assistance was often more trouble than it was actually worth, Alditha herself suspected that part of Eadred's intention had been to provide her with something more than just the upkeep of the church with which to occupy her time. Recent events weighed heavily upon her, so anything that helped take her mind off them - however briefly - must surely be a good thing. Eadwig was certainly that. She found herself spending almost as much time supervising the boy, and telling him off for slacking as she would have spent had she completed the tasks she set him herself. It was when he was handing the brush back to her after sweeping the floor that she heard him mumble something about Little Hare.

"What was that? What did you say?" she asked.

"Nothing. It doesn't matter," replied Eadwig, looking embarrassed, and clearly regretting whatever it was he had just said.

"No, it *does* matter... *very much.* You said something about Little Hare, and I want you to tell me what it was."

"It's not me who says it."

"Says *what?*" demanded Alditha. Eadwig looked at the ground. "No, you look at me, young Eadwig. Says *what?* What do they say? Whoever *they* may be. We'll come to that. First you will tell me what it was you said." Still Eadwig resisted. "Very well," said Alditha, "I'll simply have to take this to your grandfather. We'll see what Eadred has to say about it. You will tell *him*, I think, even if you refuse to tell me."

This was enough to break the boy's resistance. "If I tell you, you must not tell Grandfather. You have to promise me."

"No, I'm sorry Eadwig, but I cannot make that promise. If people are saying unkind things about Little Hare, I think your grandfather should know about it." She softened her tone. "Listen. If you tell me what is being said, I won't tell Eadred I heard it from you. How is that?" The boy nodded. "So, what is it you heard them say?" Even as she said this, Alditha had already guessed what was being said. The boy would only be confirming her suspicion. "Speak up," she urged.

Although he had raised his head, Eadwig would still not look directly at Alditha. He looked away to his side, as if addressing the wall. "They say that if Grandfather and the Normans had not brought Little Hare back, the Demon would not have followed them here. They say that it must have been something they did in Gyrtun that they were being punished for, not something Elastun did, and the

Demon only wants Little Hare for it. If we hand her over to it, the Demon will spare Elastun, so we should just let her get the punishment she deserves."

"*Deserves?*" said Alditha more loudly than she intended. She was so upset at the idea that for a moment she had wanted to slap the boy's face. She stamped her foot instead. "Ah, what nonsense. What foolish, foolish nonsense. Sin is punished by God, and God alone. What lurks out there is not of *God*. How could you believe something like that? It is as far from God as anything can be. You think it was *God* killed Swein? You think Swein deserved to be punished after all he had done for this village…for this country? A man who fought for his king and had to live with the consequences." To her frustration, Alditha found she had begun to cry. "Who is saying this? Tell me. Who?"

"I don't know." Eadwig shrugged defiantly, but in his eyes too, tears were beginning to form. "I didn't mean it. It's just what they said."

"I understand that. I still need you to tell me who it was said it. Where did you hear this foulness?"

"I don't know. I don't know!"

"You must."

Eadwig was crying openly now. "I heard it from some of the other children. Maybe their parents said it. Don't make me say which ones. Please, Alditha, please."

Alditha pulled the boy towards her, hugged him. "I won't. I will tell your grandfather I overheard it. I will not say it came from you. Now, go and join your friends. Go on. We're done here for today."

******

Alditha deliberately chose to tell Eadred what she had heard from Eadwig at a time when Orderic was also present. Authority in the village rested now with both men, and while the respect still rested with Eadred, the power to act was firmly with Orderic. Eadred might be inclined not to tell the Norman what was being said for fear he would dismiss it as unimportant, whereas Alditha felt she knew Orderic well enough now to know that he would react to the foolishness of the rumour if not the injustice of it, and would act to stamp it out more decisively than might Eadred. She felt a sense of shame at what might be considered her disloyalty to Eadred. All the same, her concern for the well-being of Little Hare outweighed any feelings of guilt.

Alditha also felt unease at the possibility that it might, in some way, be his regard for her that would prompt Orderic to act, but again there was Little Hare to think about. If she must exploit that regard for the sake of the child, then so be it.

******

It was not only the tall fires that blazed in the great hall, or the body heat from the mass of villagers crowded inside that was making Eadwig feel uncomfortably warm, and his cheeks flush pink. He knew why they had all been called in that morning. It was to end the talk about Little Hare. Talk that had come to Eadred's attention via Alditha, and which had come to hers via Eadwig. Alditha had promised him that she would not reveal to his grandfather where she had learned what was being said, but past experience had taught him that the promises made by adults to children were not as inviolable as those they made to one another. A hoped for gift was not given, a promised hunting trip not made. There was often some reason given that, it was claimed, the child would one day understand, only not for a while yet - perhaps when they were much older. Eadwig suspected the real reason was usually just the inconvenience honouring the promise would cause the adult when balanced against the temporary disappointment of the child. This time, however, the consequences of the promise being broken could be far worse than mere disappointment. He had been out of favour with his grandfather more than once in the last few weeks, and the old man's patience would be sorely tested by further misconduct on his grandson's part. Was it Eadwig's imagination, or did his grandfather's eyes keep straying in his direction. Eadwig felt his face burn with shame every time the old man caught his eye. But would Alditha really have broken her promise? She did not seem the type. She was not quite like the other adults. She always seemed kinder, more willing to make an effort to understand things from the other person's - specifically, Eadwig's - point of view. At the time it was made her promise of discretion had seemed perfectly genuine. Only as time passed had Eadwig's doubts about that set in. Much as he sought to avoid eye contact with Eadred, he tried just as hard to make it with Alditha, to see if he could read her thoughts. It was difficult, and Eadwig began to suspect she was avoiding him. She was standing behind his grandfather, on the dais at the far end of the hall. She was next to the Norman, Orderic, and there was no doubting *his* mood.

The anger in Orderic's eyes was unmistakable. They blazed with it, as if the fires that burned in the hall were a reflection of the flames in them, rather than the other way around. Despite the uncomfortable heat, Eadwig shivered involuntarily at the thought of that anger being directed at him. His grandfather's fury would be one thing, the Norman's something else entirely. So it was with dismay that Eadwig heard his grandfather announce that it was not he but Orderic that was about to address them.

"You will heed what he says," said Eadred. "And should any one of you feel aggrieved at his words, or ready to dismiss them because they come from…you will forgive me, Orderic, I know no better word…our enemy…" Orderic inclined his head to indicate his acceptance of the comment, and Eadred continued, "then you would do well to will remember this. I am in complete agreement with him on this issue. Those of you to whom what is said applies have no right to anger. In its place you would do better to feel shame. That said, I do not know who you are, and I do not wish to." At that, Eadred stepped back, and indicated that Orderic should step up.

Orderic did not speak straight away. Instead, he let his gaze wander over the rows of Saxon faces that looked up at him, giving them time to take in the way things were - although he would be surprised if they did not already know it. They should already understand that he was not here to answer questions or discuss anything. Their views were nothing to him. They were there to listen, and to obey. As his eyes crossed from face to face, now and then he deliberately paused on one of them, mostly at random, but sometimes if he thought there was any trace of defiance there. Without particularly intending to, he let his gaze rest for a moment on the boy he knew to be Eadred's grandson, skulking at the back. Perhaps it was because he was so clearly trying not to be seen that Orderic had picked him out. The lad seemed to wither under his inspection, looking almost as if he would cry. Still, it was not that surprising or unusual. Orderic had found most Saxons had a habit of looking afraid, guilty, or both in his presence. Why should the boy be any different? And, after all, there was guilt here in this room. It was possible the boy had a share in it. Orderic moved on, looked at other faces.

When, after some minutes had passed, Orderic decided to speak, he was careful not to be seen to take a deep breath as if in preparation for beginning a speech. Speeches were made to sway people. To persuade and influence them. There was an art to it. His brother was fond of explaining how it should be done, and fancied himself skilled in it. He never seemed able to recognize the quite obvious fact that, as a Baron, very few of the people he encountered in his life were equal in rank to him, and it was his higher social status, and the power that went with it, that influenced most people, not his choice of words. His over-elaborate speeches were superfluous at best and, more often than not, in Orderic's view, an embarrassment.

Here, in this hall, the power was with Orderic, and that gave him all the rank he needed. He had no need to persuade these Saxons of anything. He was simply here to tell them how things stood, what they could, and what they could not do. They had no choice but to obey. He need not, and would not, make any show of addressing them as if in order to convince them. No deep breath, no clever argument. When Orderic spoke to them, he did so calmly. He did not alter the volume or pitch of his voice to give emphasis to any aspects of what he said. He simply spoke. Loudly enough to be heard, slowly enough to be understood.

"All talk of appeasing the beast beyond your gates…what you have chosen to call the Demon…through offering it anyone by way of an inducement to leave the rest of you alone is to cease as of this moment. We do not know what manner of creature it is, or from what realm it has risen. But one thing we do know. It does not just want the girl, Little Hare. It did not come here for her alone, it came for you. Every single one of you. Understand that. It will not be satisfied until every one of you has suffered the torments it intends for you, and it has laid siege to your village with this end in mind. Not because of a single child. But there is hope of your escaping this fate if you continue to follow the orders I have issued. As you know, the Demon does not seem able to employ its power when confronted with oak. We do not know why. Perhaps it is linked to the magic of your forefathers. Whatever the reason, it seems to be true, and it is what we must use as the mainstay of our defences against it. That is why all gates remain shut, and the wall is guarded day and night. That is why some of you men have been practising with the oak shields. You all of you know what has been arranged. If it does get past the perimeter wall, all the women and children will come in here, into the hall. You hear the cry '*To the hall*', you know what has happened, and where you must come. The men chosen for the task will take their place in the shield wall. The others will do what they can to guard the hall entrance from inside. And if you have one of the oak crosses, I suggest you wear it. At all times. If you do not, stay near someone who does. The oak. It is our only proven defence. Your only hope. So, I say once more, you will offer no one as a sacrifice, and you will discuss it no longer. If you do, you will answer to me. The child, Little Hare, is now under my personal protection. If she is harmed in any way, I will punish whoever is responsible, directly and harshly. On that last point, I make you this particular promise. If anyone attempts to give her to the Demon, it is not the child but they who shall find themselves beyond the safety of the oak wall. Some of you have seen what that can mean. All of you have been told. Do not test me on this. That is all."

Eadred came forward again. "Those of you who wish to remain may do so. Otherwise, you are free to go back to your homes." As the villagers left, he called after them, "Remember to be sparing with food, and fuel for the fires. We have sufficient for several weeks, but only if we are careful." He saw Eadwig heading for the door. "Eadwig, lad. Get yourself over here. I wish to talk with you."

As he walked reluctantly back to his grandfather, Eadwig gave Alditha an accusatory look. She waited until he was nearer and said, "I did not betray you, Eadwig. I promised I would not, and I kept that promise." Eadwig wondered what, then, did his grandfather wish to discuss. At the same time, Eadred himself was wondering how he would introduce the subject of what had become of the boy's father, Wulfstan. For some time he had hoped to protect Eadwig from the knowledge, just as he had sought to protect Godgifu, Wulfstan's wife, and his own wife, Ceolwin, Wulfstan's mother. To his consternation, they had discovered somehow, and the news had been extremely hard on both women. Ceolwin had refused to believe it at first, but now she spent hours in the church praying for the immortal soul of her dead son. Godgifu had grown distant, retired to her chamber, and rarely spoke to anyone. If they could find out, Eadred reasoned, so could the boy. Better it came from him than by way of careless village gossip.

As Eadred explained about Eadwig's father - leaving out some of the more distressing details - the boy said very little. When Eadred had finished, the boy still sat there, surprisingly calmly, almost thoughtfully. Then Eadred noticed that his hand kept straying to the ankle where he had been grabbed and injured as he climbed the wall back into the village.

"Could it have been?" the boy asked.

"I don't know…It's possible," replied Eadred.

******

CHAPTER 18

Eadwig was on the wall again. The hour was very late, but still it seemed strange to him that there was apparently no one on guard close to where he was climbing. The wall was to be guarded at all points, and at every hour, day and night. Eadred and Orderic had been clear on that point. Only that morning Tosti had been knocked to the ground, and beaten near insensible by Walter the Bear when the big Norman had discovered him drunk on guard duty – some versions of events said he was actually asleep - with the warning that, if he were ever caught in that state again, it would cost him more than a few teeth and some bruises. The moon was full, and visibility good for so late an hour. However, straining his eyes in both directions, Eadwig could see no one. He listened. There were no coughs or clearing of throats to be heard, nothing at all to indicate a single soul was anywhere near him on the wall. Well, that was fortunate really. He might not be beaten quite as hard as Tosti if he were to be discovered, but there was no doubting the trouble he would be in, and the severity of the punishment his grandfather would mete out if Eadwig were caught up here again.

It was cold. Moonlight glittered from the crystals of frost gathering on the wood beneath his hands as he pulled himself up onto the wall, and his breath billowed white when he breathed out. Suddenly that breathing seemed very loud to him in the otherwise quiet night. He held his breath, and froze in position where he was. Then he shook his head. Why on earth was he worrying? Hadn't he just satisfied himself that there was no one near? But there *was*, wasn't there? There was the person he was climbing the wall to see. But why should Eadwig worry if *he* heard him? His father would not hurt him. His father would be glad to see him. He had made that clear when he called out to him, waking him from his sleep, and the dreams that haunted it. Eadwig's chest grew tight with emotion. His father was not dead like everyone had told him. Wulfstan was alive, and he was close by, somewhere out there in the forest.

Eadwig looked out at the trees. They were a wall of dark grey and black. Nothing to see there. He looked down below, towards the foot of the wall. Odd, but there was the body of Swein. Hadn't he died near the gate? Yes, he had heard his grandfather lamenting the impossibility of retrieving the body from where it lay out there on the track, saying it was a shameful way to treat the mortal remains of so gallant a Housecarl. Eadwig was sure he was nowhere near the gate or track, so how was it the body came to be here? The wolves in the valley this winter, had they moved it?

Eadwig had no time to give the matter any more thought. He was interrupted by a rustling of dead leaves and snapping of frozen twigs coming from the direction of the forest.

"Father?" he whispered, although somehow it sounded to him like a shout. "Father, is that you?" he asked again.

Nothing.

Then, "My son? My brave boy?"

"Yes, Father, yes!" Eadwig moved forward as if he were about to climb down from the wall, but his father's voice stopped him. "No, boy! Don't! Don't come down. Stay where you are."

"Why not?"

"You may fall and hurt yourself."

"But Father, it's easy, see…"

"Wait, boy!"

"I want to see you."

"You can. You will. But if you come down here, how shall we open the gate? We cannot get back in. And I so wish to see your mother…Your brother too…"

"My *brother*?" Eadwig frowned. "Hakon is dead, Father.

Don't you know that?"

"So he is, so he is. Now, climb back inside, and I will meet you at the gate. I will be waiting outside when you open it. Then we can go hunting again. Just like we used to. You, me, and Hakon. Together again."

"Hakon is…"

"Dead. Yes. I remember now. He's not with us. So just you and I, then. We will go. Would you like that? We'll take Gra along."

"But it's dark, Father."

"So it is. Well…? Why do you linger, boy?" The tone altered, became more insistent. "Open the gate, damn it!"

"No, boy, no!" cried Swein.

Eadwig nearly lost his grip on the wall. "*Swein*? But you're dead?"

Swein's body shuddered, rolled over, then stood. The arrow Walter had shot still jutted from the chest. "You should ask the same of your father. He has been dead this past year. This is not him, Eadwig. This is not him. It is something else that wants you to think it is your father. You must not open the gate to it."

Wulfstan stepped from the trees. He was still in the shadows, but there seemed to be the shape of another, much taller man, behind him.

"Who is that with you?"

"With me? There is no one with me. I am alone. I am come back to you, my son. And I am alone."

Even in the shadows, Eadwig could make out the battle-axe Wulfstan held in his hands - perhaps the same one he had carried with him when last Eadwig saw him, as he rode off to war. Wulfstan raised his arms above his head, swung the axe, felling Swein with one swift blow. A dark stain spread out onto the pale snow beneath him, and Swein lay still. Then vanished from sight.

"Where has he…? Father, that was Swein! Why did you hurt him?"

"He sought to turn you against me, boy. Confuse you with his lies. It was working, was it not? See, the gate remains closed because you listened to him. Time is short. Open it for us."

"No, I won't. Not yet. I don't think I should until I have asked Grandfather. I want to talk to Grandfather first."

"Your *grandfather*? It matters not what your *grandfather* would say. You are my son. I am your father. Duty and honour dictate that you must obey me before anyone else. Forget that timeworn fool. My father is a weak, pathetic old man. He is too fearful of the changes we will bring to his village. Forget him, and just do what I tell you, boy. Open the damned gate or face a whipping you will never forget for being so disobedient. Well, which will it be?"

"I know now what Grandfather would say," Eadwig shouted. "He would say I should not open the gate!"

Eadwig began to scrabble back inside. Wulfstan stepped forward, fully out of the shadows, and into the blue-white brightness of the moonlight. The boy screamed when he saw how his father was changed. The pale, lifeless skin stretched over the sunken features of the face, with its expression of pure hate. The whole thing made far worse by the unnatural glow in the otherwise dead-looking eyes. He screamed even louder when Wulfstan lunged for him, grabbing at his ankle, holding him fast, preventing him from getting down from the wall.

Eadwig awoke with a cry.

Anxiously, he reached down under the sheepskin and blankets for his ankle, half expecting to find the wound there that had previously healed was now warm and damp with fresh blood, and painful to the touch. Relieved to find this was not the case, he lay back and tried, unsuccessfully, to get back to sleep. There was a pressure in his bladder that he could not ignore, so he slipped out from under the covers.

******

Across from the hall, in Alditha's house, Little Hare was also troubled by bad dreams - as she almost always was since her experiences at Gyrtun. Despite Alditha reassuring her that this was only to be expected, and that things would get better in time, Little Hare herself had not been so convinced of it. However, it was true that she was getting more used to the nightmares. Often these days, once awake, she recognized the dreams for what they were, and it was becoming less common for her screaming to bring Alditha and the maid, Hitta, rushing in to comfort her. These days, she knew if she waited long enough, the terrors would pass. Only tonight, they didn't.

With the fading of her nightmares, Little Hare awoke, opening her eyes onto the darkness of the small chamber where she slept. Still not fully awake, she curled up into a ball, pulling the fleece covers more tightly around her, hoping to drift back into a less nightmare troubled doze. As she did so, she open her eyes again for an instant, closing them almost immediately. Then her eyes snapped back open. She had not really focused on anything much before. There was only darkness in front of her. Had that darkness, or something within it, shifted slightly?

She drew in a deep, shocked breath. Before she could let it out again as a scream, a rough hand clamped down over her mouth. It smelled of sour sweat. And something else. Something she did not recognise at first. Then it came to her. It smelled of the tavern, of the ale the men drank. Even in her terror this was some relief. These were the smells of a man. No demon smelled like this.

This gave her courage. She kicked out. Her foot must have found its mark. There was a grunt of pain. "Stop that!" hissed a man's voice she did not recognise. But then she still only knew a few of the adults in Elastun. So far, she had found all those she had met - even the Normans - to be kind. This, then, was not one of them. She did not know this person. She kicked again. This time her foot did not make contact with anything but air.

"I said, that's enough!" the man growled.

Little Hare bit down on the hand clamped around her face.

"Ouch! Little Hare? Little *bitch* more like! Do that again and you'll be sorry."

Before she had thought about it, Little Hare bit down even harder. Then came the fist. It felt like the roof had fallen in and landed on her. A loud thud, then nothing.

The child seemed unconscious, but Tosti did not trust her not to wake - she might even be pretending, the bitch - so he kept his hand clamped over her small mouth as he carried her from Alditha's house, stepping over the unconscious Hitta - also a victim of his rough fists - as he came out into the cold night.

The freezing air had the effect of sobering him a little, although not enough to make him think better of what he was doing. The more he had drunk in Cynric's tavern earlier that night, the better his plan had seemed, and the more justified he felt in carrying it out. So what if Eadred and that bully of a Norman had cautioned against harming the girl? They would all of them die if that thing that had killed Leofric did not go away - this girl included. Her fate was sealed either way. So why not at least discover if it was only really her the thing wanted? What difference if she died now instead of later? If there was some chance that by offering her as a sacrifice now, the rest of the village would be spared her fate, why not take it, however slim it might be? If they were all to die anyway, then she was lucky because she would get it over with ahead of the others. Tosti remembered the noises Leofric had made. The screams were bad enough, but it was the pathetic whimpering that he could not put from his thoughts. Leofric - his friend from childhood - had always seemed to him a strong man. A man who could take what life threw at him, and laugh - or drink - it off. To see him reduced to that whimpering thing had been unnerving. Tosti kept turning it over and over in his mind. He tried to imagine the pain, and was sure he would not be able to bear it should he himself be faced with the same fate. Anything - even the shame of arranging the death of this child - was better than that. Anything.

He missed his footing on the frozen earth, and skidded forward, almost dropping his burden. His hand had come away from the girl's mouth, and she let out a small moan. He clamped it back down quickly, braced himself for the pain if she bit him again, and was relieved to find she was still unconscious. He must be careful, though. She must not be allowed to alert the men at the wall to his presence beneath them when he crept with her to the gates.

It would have to be the gates. He had considered mounting the walkway, and simply dropping the girl down over the other side, but had decided against it. He was much more likely to be seen doing it that way. If there were any moonlight or starlight at all, he would be in danger of presenting a silhouette. Besides which, he had noticed the men on guard usually stayed fairly near the steps to the area they watched. He would never get onto the walkway unseen. Whereas, if he made his way below the walkway, and approached the gates from beneath it, there was a good chance he could remain in the shadows the entire way, and get to the gates unnoticed. Once there, it would merely be a matter of getting the gates open just enough to push the girl out onto the track, and closing them again before he was spotted. There was every chance he could do it all entirely unnoticed. The first the villagers would know of it would be the discovery that the girl was missing later that morning. By then, it would be too late for them to prevent what came next. And they might all be saved.

Tosti's part in the villager's deliverance might never be

known. Would he ever reveal it, he wondered. Maybe he would, one day. Then again, maybe not. Eadred was not always the forgiving type, even if the rest of the village might gladly have expressed their gratitude for what Tosti had done for them.

He had decided upon the gates opening onto the track through the forest rather than those at the far end of the village that opened out onto the fields because there were fewer buildings and, therefore, less cover that end of the village. Also, these gates were closer to Alditha's house, so there was less distance to travel with his burden.

Alditha. There was another bitch. Who did she think she was, anyway? So she had married Eadred's grandson, what of it? Before that she'd been nobody special. Now she was getting herself in with that Norman. Even though Hakon, wherever he was buried, hadn't been in the ground there much above a year! Disgusting. Shameful. Tosti wasn't the only one who had noticed, either. Others in the village had remarked upon it. You couldn't turn a corner nowadays without coming across Orderic and Alditha exchanging whispers. Her making sure she was under his protection when the time came, that's what that was all about, whatever that fool of a Norman might tell himself. Obvious to anyone with eyes to see it, really. It was typical. Always the same with these pretty women. They found a way to use their looks to make life that bit better for themselves. It had been no different with her mother. Despite suspicions that the woman was a witch, no one had dared say anything about it for fear of incurring the wrath of Swein. Exactly the same story when you thought about it. The woman marries above herself, and then the husband dies, so she gets herself in with another man to protect her. Typical, too, that it was Alditha who had been sheltering this girl. Appearing so smug about doing the right thing for this poor man's orphan, when all the while she was making a slut of herself with that Norman bully to ensure she was under his protection. Two-faced and deceitful, exactly as her mother had been. Well he, Tosti, knew better. Sheltering the child was what was putting them all in danger.

Little Hare gave a muffled whimper beneath his hand. Another time this might have encouraged Tosti to feel some pity for her. Not tonight. Tonight it only reminded him of the fate of Leofric, increasing his resolve to avoid such a fate for himself by whatever means were available to him.

It was not far now. Tosti was only yards from the gate, and no one guarding the wall had seen him approach. They were all concentrating on looking out from the village - the flames from their raised torches illuminating the frozen trees and the snow covered ground beyond the wall, turning the moonlit whiteness into a flickering dance of orange light and shifting shadows - to ensure no danger approached from the forest or the fields. None of them thought to look behind themselves.

A few more paces and Tosti found himself approaching a small pig hut at the corner of an enclosed pen. He would have to be careful not to disturb its inhabitants. He caught the smell of the animals inside on the breeze. Crouching low, he skirted the pen, heading for the wall near the gate, now only a matter of a few yards over to his left. Inside the small hut one of the pigs grunted, shifting position as it huddled for warmth next to its companions. Tosti stopped moving, holding himself as still as he could, although it was difficult, burdened as he was by the dead weight of the child. Once he was satisfied that the noise from the pig had not drawn any attention, he made a final dash forward until he was beneath the walkway, and safely hidden among the shadows there. The snow was deeper and less trampled here, gathered in drifts. It creaked and crunched underfoot, the sound amplified in the space created by the right angle of the wall meeting the walkway. Tosti was forced to move at a much slower pace if he was not to be overheard.

"Not long now. It will all be over soon," he whispered, partly to himself, partly to the still insensible child in his arms. "I promise it won't take long." As he said this, Tosti felt the first real pang of guilt he had experienced since he had thought up this scheme. He really didn't know what the Demon had planned for this girl, and he certainly had no idea how long whatever it was would take. Given that he himself was terrified of what pain might be in store for him were he to fall into the hands of the Demon out there, what right had he to condemn this child to that fate? He stopped where he was, glanced down at the dark bundle in his arms. For the first time, he felt the warmth of it - of her. He could smell her hair, her skin. She smelled of herbs. Or was it flowers. Doubtless some ointment or something of that kind mixed by Alditha. *By the witch's daughter.* Yes, he should remember that. It helped strengthen his resolve. This child was in the care of the daughter of a witch, who in turn was under the protection of the Normans. What did the likes of them care about the fate of the village? He was doing this for the village. "Remember that," he said, entirely to himself this time. It was this one child's life weighed against everyone else's. Put like that, it was a bargain anyone would gladly make. He was simply making it on behalf of the rest of village, because they themselves were being prevented from doing so.

He heard footsteps approaching overhead, voices he recognized. Alfred, talking quietly with Cynric. Alfred. He was guilty of being a little smug at times too. Cynric, however...Good old Cynric, he would understand. He would thank Tosti for what he was doing if he knew. Tosti wondered again if, when it was all over, he would ever dare reveal his part in it.

The flickering light from a torch shone down through the gaps in the boards of the walkway above, illuminating the girl's hair. There it was, that guilt again. Tosti hastily covered the child's head.

Alfred and Cynric finally stopped talking, and walked off in separate directions, their progress marked by the light of their torches. One of them - it was impossible to tell which now they were no longer speaking - walked back along the boards, away from the gate. The other took only a few paces, then stopped where he was. No matter. Nobody was watching the inside of the gate any more than they were watching for activity behind them. Tosti was sure he would be able to get the gate open, and the girl out beyond the safety of the wall, as long as he could remove the drawbar on his own.

Little Hare wriggled, moaned. If she were to wake up… start screaming..!

Tosti raised a fist, ready to knock her out again if she were coming round, but she fell silent, and was spared another blow. Tosti put his hand over her mouth once more, and it was then he felt something warm trickle between his fingers. Too much of it to be only saliva. Blood then, from where he had hit her before. There would be much more of it soon. How much blood did this small child have inside her? He could not think about that. He was doing this for the good of the village.

Tosti was nearly there. He shifted Little Hare so he held her entirely in one arm, leaving the other free to open the gates. Even then, with her body hanging down limply, either side of the arm that he wrapped around her waist, she was not really that heavy.

Not much blood, then.

He heaved her up a little so he had a better grasp, then, with his free hand, he reached out for the drawbar. It was coated with frost crystals that were so cold to the touch they stung the skin of his fingers. He gritted his teeth, pulled.

Nothing. No movement.

Tosti sighed. Just as he feared, he could not move it

with only one hand. He would have to put the child down, and use both. He crouched, laying Little Hare as much as possible on the blanket that she had been wrapped up in - not through compassion, but through concern that contact with the cold ground might bring her to her senses. He then took hold of the drawbar with both hands, his face grimacing at the coldness of the wood. He pulled, gently at first. Still it would not move. It had frozen in place. He cursed. There was no alternative. He was going to have to use all his strength to get the damn thing to move and, with it stuck like that, it might well be noisy. Everything would have to be done quickly. Wrench out the drawbar, throw open the gate, then throw out the child, all in one set of actions. Then get away, and out of sight. He needn't go that far, though. Once he was a decent enough distance - it need only be forty of fifty yards - he could turn about and run back towards the gate, on the pretence that he had been drawn by the shouts of the guards, and was coming to see what he could do to help.

******

On hearing the cries outside, Orderic had immediately hurried from the hall. Once in the open air, the direction from which the cries were coming was more obvious. The gates! He turned in that direction and ran. Eadred, older and slower, followed behind.

Walter, who had been on duty outside, came up alongside Orderic.

"The gates. They've opened the gates, the fools!" said Walter.

"Why, in God's name?" asked Orderic.

Both men arrived in time to see Alfred out on the track in front of the open gates, a torch in one hand, and using the other to drag some sort of bundle back into the village. A second figure watched from just inside the gates, leaning forward, reaching out, ready to help bring Alfred and the bundle back inside.

Alfred was only feet away from the gates when the noise began. The high-pitched whine and the low rumble beneath it that indicated the presence of the Demon and its followers. Alfred cried out and swung around, raising his torch, the light from it picking out several figures emerging from the treeline. The flames reflected from their helmets, the blades of their weapons and, on some at least, picked out their faces. Alfred gave another cry of fear, turned back, and ran towards the open gates, still dragging whatever it was behind him.

Had Alfred sensed, or just guessed that they were closer now? Suddenly, he dropped his torch, seized the bundle with both hands and, with a strength born of years as a blacksmith, he raised it above his head and tossed it through the gates, only moments before the figures closed in around him and began tearing at his flesh. He screamed and fell, writhing beneath them.

"Close the gates! Close them!" yelled Orderic, at the same time frantically gesturing with his hands, uncertain whether the order would be heard above the noise from beyond the wall. However, the other man - they could see now it was Cynric - simply stood there, gaping, unable to move, transfixed by what was happening to Alfred. When Orderic and Walter at last drew level with him, Orderic shoved the Welshman aside, grabbed at one of the gates, and began pulling it shut. Walter took hold of the other.

The gates were nearly closed when a figure that, to their horror, both men recognized, interposed itself between them, slashing its sword violently from side to side, preventing them from completing their task. It was Richard. Or what had once been Richard.

Orderic drew his sword, and parried one of the slashes, but Richard was peculiarly strong, and Orderic came close to losing his grip on his weapon. He stepped out of the way of the next blow rather than attempting to block it. A third swing of Richard's sword clipped Orderic's shoulder, nicking the chain mail. Before a fourth could do real damage, Walter had stepped up with his sword and deflected the blow, allowing Orderic time to step away, and swing at Richard's head. Although the sword blow sent Richard staggering back, it did not drop him, as it would any normal man.

In his peripheral vision Orderic could see movement out on the track. It was the other shadowy figures, stepping away from Alfred's torn corpse, now ready to join Richard in the attack. He felt a jolt of alarm. If it took both him and Walter to hold back Richard alone, what chance was there when they all came at them? Then, to Orderic's bewilderment, Richard leapt back, his sword falling from his hands.

Eadred was now in front of Orderic and Walter. Before him he held one of the oak shields made by Dunstan, the carpenter. It was having the effect they had hoped for. Richard staggered back, using his arms to cover his head.

"Back!" Eadred shouted. All three men fell back from the gates, which were then closed by Mark, Cynric, and a couple of villagers who had joined them.

Orderic scrambled up onto the walkway, and looked out. There was now no sign of Richard or any of the others, only two dead bodies. The fresh corpse of Alfred, torn apart, the pieces lying in a spreading pool of the dead blacksmith's blood, and the older body of Swein, Walter's arrow still protruding from the chest.

Catching his breath, Orderic climbed down, and glanced about. One of the village men had already scooped up the bundle Alfred had thrown through the gates. He was cradling the child in his arms. Orderic recognised Little Hare.

"Is she hurt?" asked Orderic.

The man looked up at him blankly, shrugged.

"Take her to Alditha," instructed Eadred.

"I'm here," said Alditha running over to join them. "What happened?"

"My question, also," said Orderic, scowling at the assembled villagers. "Which of you can tell me?"

"It was him," said Cynric.

"Who?"

"Him," repeated a visibly shaking Cynric. Orderic saw that he was pointing towards someone lying on the ground, in the shadows behind the gate. It was Tosti.

Tosti groaned, put his hands to his head.

"It was that one there," continued Cynric, the anger in his voice increasing. "He had the gate open before we knew it. I was further along the walkway. Alfred was closer. It was him knocked Tosti down. Only not before the coward had thrown the little girl out through the gate. From where I was, I couldn't see what it was at first. When I saw it was a child, I couldn't believe it."

"What happened then?"

"By the time I got near, Alfred had already rushed out to bring her back. You saw the rest of it." Cynric spat in the direction of the prone Tosti. "Piece of filth! Got Alfred killed."

Orderic snatched a torch from a nearby villager, and strode over to where Tosti lay, still groaning. Leaning forward, Orderic thrust the flames towards Tosti's face. The man shrank back, terrified. Blood ran from the gash in his forehead where Alfred had struck him.

Orderic tilted his head from one side to another, studying the frightened Saxon. "Tosti, is it? I'm curious...what manner of man are you to do such a thing?"

"For the village…" Tosti pleaded.

"For yourself," said Eadred, from behind Orderic.

"For the *village*…" Tosti wailed again. "I did it…"

"Say that one more time, I will cut your liar's tongue from your head before I have Walter here cut that off too!"

growled Orderic.

Tosti began to sob, grabbed imploringly at Orderic's ankles. "Please don't... don't hurt me...I can't...I didn't..."

Disgusted, Orderic shook his head, and grabbed Tosti by the scruff of the neck, pulling him close, so their faces were nearly touching. He could smell the alcohol on the other man's breath. "Drunk, bah! Is that where you find your courage, then? In the tavern? Tell me, exactly what kind of courage does it take for a grown man to sacrifice a small child to a monster? You'll need to find a different sort of courage now, though. You are going to die. I am going to have you killed. I must. Now, get on your feet. Meet death with the little dignity even a man like you may possess. I will allow you that much."

"No, please, I beg you..."

"Damn you, where is your shame, man?" Orderic let Tosti drop back into the mud and snow. Tosti whimpered, and began crawling on his hands and knees towards Eadred. Orderic brushed his hands contemptuously. "I will kill this worm, Eadred. No matter what excuse he gives you. So, save your words. You cannot prevent me."

When Tosti reached Eadred, he collapsed back, panting, looking up at the old man. "Eadred, you have to stop this," he pleaded. "You know I only did it so our village would be saved. *Eadred..?*"

Eadred had taken a step back, his features twisted with loathing. Alditha, who was tending Little Hare, glanced up, and caught his eye. The old man looked away.

"What would you have me do?" Eadred asked.

For a moment Alditha thought this question was addressed to her. Only when Eadred added, "Well, Tosti? Imagine yourself in my position. What would you suggest I do with you?" did she understand it was not.

Tosti stared up at Eadred. His mouth fell open, but he said nothing.

"Do as the Norman told you. Get up," said Eadred coldly.

Tosti looked confused.

"I said get up. On your feet."

With apparent difficulty, Tosti finally did as he was instructed. He stood there before Eadred, swaying unsteadily, his clothes caked in mud and damp with melting snow, his forehead and face bloodied from Alfred's blow.

"Eadred," said Alditha. "Eadred!"

The old man turned. "What is it?"

"Show mercy."

"For what he has done? Where was *his* mercy? Alfred is dead, girl. Do you not think someone should pay for that?"

"I do, you know I do. What Tosti has done is…" Alditha could not find the words to say. She was not sure what she felt about Tosti. She too loathed him for what he had attempted, and yet she could not bring herself to want him dead quite as easily as it seemed these men could. Eventually, she said, "I only ask that his end be instant," knowing that to ask any more than that would have been pointless. "Let us not become like the Demon we fear and despise. So much suffering. How are we to bear it? There is too much of it in this valley already."

Orderic stepped forward. "Instant? Very well…" His sword was raised, ready take off Tosti's head.

Tosti staggered back, raised his hands. "No, no!" He would have run, had Walter and Cynric not grabbed him.

"I have given you a chance at a little dignity," said Orderic, "and you will not take it. As you wish. If you refuse to meet death on your feet, then you can meet it on your belly." He turned to Walter. "Down with him."

Walter grabbed Tosti's shoulders and pushed down, at the same time kicking his legs out from under him. Tosti cried out as he collapsed forward. Immediately, Walter took hold of his hands, and forced them up behind his back, flexing the wrists, and leaning his weight onto him, forcing

Tosti's head forward so it was pressed into the ground.

Alditha had gone over to Orderic. "Instant," she reminded him.

"It will be," said Orderic. Then, in whisper only Alditha could hear, he added, "You have my word on it."

Satisfied, Alditha nodded, and stepped back. Orderic raised his sword once more.

"Wait!" cried Eadred.

"Argh! How many interruptions must there be?" complained Orderic. "You do nothing to help this man by them. Why is it you Saxons must always seem to dispute every death?"

"You will wait!" insisted Eadred, and knelt down beside the struggling Tosti. For a moment it looked as if he were going to say something to him. Then, instead of leaning in towards Tosti's head, Eadred slipped around behind Walter, and took hold of one of Tosti's feet. Before anyone knew what he was doing, Eadred had rammed his dagger home hard into one of Tosti's ankles, severing the Achilles tendon. Tosti shrieked, then shrieked again when Eadred lifted the other foot, and performed the same action.

Walter leapt up, looking to Orderic for instructions. Dumbfounded, Orderic found he had none to give.

"Over the wall with him!" shouted Eadred.

"What? Oh God, no!" cried Alditha.

Eadred gestured to some of the villagers. "You, you, and you. Pick him up. Then you take him up there, and you throw him over."

Tosti sobbed and pleaded as the men lifted him up.

Alditha hurried over, and stood in front of Eadred. "Listen to me. You must not do this! What Tosti tried to do was wicked and wrong. What do we become if we match his wickedness?"

"It is not the same thing, you know that."

"Yes, but…"

Eadred pushed her away. "No, Alditha! Out of my path!

I will not hear you say another word in his favour. A good man has met a terrible end because he sought to save the child. It is only fitting that this wretched excuse for a man meet the same end for trying to condemn her. Or would you have his fate be easier than that of the brave man whose death his actions have caused? Remember, it would have been the fate of the child too, had Alfred not prevented it." Before Alditha could think how to reply, Eadred strode past her, and addressed the men holding the terrified Tosti. "Take him up! An eye for eye. Was that not what you promised, Orderic?"

"It was," replied Orderic, his eyes straying to Alditha. "However, this is not necessary. I am content to take his head. "

"You may be. I am not!" said Eadred. "Take him up!"

By the time Tosti had been manhandled onto the walkway, he was close to passing out. Before he was heaved up onto the wall and pushed over the edge, Eadred rubbed snow into his face, and slapped his cheeks so that he came back to his senses again, and was fully aware of what was happening to him.

No one risked leaning out beyond the wall to see exactly what came for Tosti. His screams from the darkness below them were sufficient indication that the Demon's followers, or perhaps even the Demon itself, had arrived to claim him.

******

CHAPTER 19

Eadwig saw it all. His need to urinate had taken him out to his usual spot against the wall behind the great hall, and it was from there he had been returning when he heard the shouts from the guards. He had followed, only a few paces behind, when his grandfather and Orderic had run in the direction of the gates. He had watched what took place next. He had seen it all. And something else besides. Something everyone else seemed not to have seen. When the gates had opened, and the Demon's followers had stepped into the light of the torches carried by the men at the wall, Eadwig had thought he might still be dreaming. Then he remembered what his grandfather had said. So, this was no dream. It *was* Wulfstan's face he saw looking at him from the trees. It *was* his father.

Only his father did not seem like the one from his nightmare, nor could this be the one his grandfather had warned him against. The face he saw was that of the old Wulfstan. The real Wulfstan. His father, alive again, looking right at him. And he was smiling. No malice in the look, only affection. So, while everyone else had been focused on the incidents taking place by the open gates, Eadwig had been looking beyond them, at the face of his father. Not one of the Demon's men, not bewitched like the others, and not dead. It was the face of his living father he had seen out there. It was the voice of his living father he had heard in his head, letting him know his love for him. Asking to be saved. Asking to be let in.

That was why, when everyone had been so captivated and horrified at Eadred's choice of punishment for Tosti, when everyone had either been unable to look away as he was carried up onto the walkway and thrown to his fate, or had been unable to look, and so closed their eyes or turned their faces in the other direction, Eadwig had been able to creep unnoticed up to the gates, and wait there in the shadows until all the villagers and Normans gathered at the wall began to disperse.

It took all his strength, but eventually the drawbar dropped to the ground. It made more noise than he had expected. He glanced around anxiously. No one had heard. Even if they had, by then it was too late. The gate was open. Eadwig knew his grandfather was sure to be angry with him, but what was that compared to the joy he would feel when he saw his son alive again? Then it would all be forgiven and forgotten. The only thing that made Eadwig at all sad was the fact that he had not seen Hakon out there with his father.

With the drawbar removed, the gates swung open easily.

Eadwig's father stepped inside. He took his son in his arms, and lifted him high. Then his father pulled him close, and squeezed. Eadwig closed his eyes, rested his face against his father's chest, and squeezed back. His father squeezed harder. It was becoming a little uncomfortable. Eadwig tried to wrestle himself free, but his father continued to squeeze, harder still. It hurt now, it hurt a lot. "Please, Father. Stop it." Eadwig struggled, managed to pull his head free, strained his neck back, looked up and found himself staring into the grey and rotting flesh of a dead man's face, saw now the unnatural light in the eyes that looked down at him.

******

Mark was the first to see the gates opening again. The thin grey line appearing in the dark of the wall, expanding into an ever widening rectangle. He saw the silhouette of what appeared to be a child, then taller silhouettes, weapons in their hands. When he finally realised what was happening he cried out an urgent warning, but it was in Norman French, so only Walter and Orderic understood. They, in turn, relayed the warning to the Saxons.

By the time the alarm had been raised, the high whine and low rumble were beginning again, and Wulfstan, Turold, Richard, and six other similar undead warrior figures had entered the village. Close behind them, dwarfing them all, and issuing commands in a language none but they could comprehend stood the Demon itself. For a few seconds the sight froze all who saw it into inaction - particularly those among the villagers who had only previously heard the descriptions of what waited outside the wall, but had never before seen it for themselves. The delay was fatal to some of them. By the time the order to fall back to the hall was finally given, several of the villagers who had been standing nearest the gate at the time it was opened had already been overrun, and their ordeal had begun.

Orderic was the first to remember the actions that had been planned. "Eadred, the shield wall! Form the shield wall!"

"Yes, of course," said Eadred. He cupped his hands around his mouth, began to call out. "Shield bearers, to me! Shield bearers, to me! The rest of you get back! Back, *now*! To the hall." He grabbed at the two men nearest to him and, pushing them in the direction of the hall, said, "You two, gather everyone who is not already in there. Do it. Do it now!"

Orderic stopped another man. "You, are you a shield bearer?" The man shook his head. "Right," said Orderic, "you get to the church, and you tell Brother Edmund and the others to come at once. They are not safe where they are. Whatever they may believe, they are not safe. They must come."

Another man who came running past, on his way to the hall, was grabbed by Eadred. "Where are you going,

Wilfred? The shield wall…you stay with me, remember? As we practised it! Follow me. Bring your shield."

Wilfred looked panicked. He was looking around himself for something. It was then Eadred understood.

"Your shield…where is your shield, lad? Why do you not have it with you? My order was to keep it with you at all times. At *all times*, you young fool!"

Cynric ran up to them. "It's here, I have it, Eadred. He must have dropped it." He passed the shield to Wilfred. "Take it… and don't drop it again, eh."

"Well done, Cynric," said Eadred. "Where were your wits, lad?" he asked Wilfred, then saw how badly the young man was shaking. "Never mind now. Just do as we practised, and you'll be fine. Stay with me. Do as I tell you."

They had reached the front of the hall. By now other men had begun to join them, each one carrying one of the oak shields. Eadred counted. "Only seven?" He had to shout to be heard, even by those standing near. The noise that always signalled the presence of the Demon was growing in strength.

"Alfred was to have been part of the wall," shouted Cynric in reply, pointing out beyond the gates.

"Ah…yes…poor Alfred. But what of Harold? Where is Harold, curse him?" Eadred demanded. "Never mind. There is no time." He gestured for the men to draw close around him so they could hear, but most were distracted by what was happening at the gate. He punched their shoulders to get their attention, and read the fear on their faces when they turned to look at him, saw how their hands shook. Keeping his own expression as calm as he could manage, he said, "You are afraid. That is natural. I said you would be, remember? But you must look only to me now. Concentrate on my commands. Ignore everything else. *Ignore it.* You watch my arm, and you follow my signals…just as we practised. Think only about doing that, and nothing more. You will not be able to hear me soon, so you must use your eyes…watch for my signals. Understand? Now, form up. You know what to do. A line. Here."

As instructed, the men formed up. Shields locked together, they stood in a line at a right angle to the front of the hall, shielding the entrance from the direction of the gates, where the Demon and his followers were still finishing off the last of their victims.

"So, the time has arrived. We make our stand, eh?" shouted Eadred. "We protect our loved ones. Buy them some time to get to the safety of the hall. We keep this entrance clear, whatever it costs. That is our only purpose. Keep it clear so that others may get in. Then, when I judge the time is right, we close it up. Not before then. You wait for the command. Not before."

Eadred was not certain if they heard him at all now, the noise was so great. But they had practised the tactics he had shown them over and over, and he hoped that was enough. Everything depended on the wall not failing. And that in turn depended on the courage of these few men.

"Where are those damn Normans?" he grunted, not expecting anyone to hear the question, let alone reply.

"We are with you, old man," Orderic shouted into his ear, surprising Eadred by appearing right behind him. "There was no time to get to the horses, so we're going to have to fight on foot alongside you Saxons."

Eadred was about to shout something in reply, but Orderic pointed towards the gates. Any of the villagers who had been caught there were dead now or dying. In front of their torn bodies the undead warriors had formed a line - an echo of the shield wall they now faced - and at its centre stood the Demon.

******

Brother Edmund listened again to the noises outside. The first shouts and screams had come from the far end of the village. Now they were accompanied by that almost intolerable, high-pitch keening, and the jarring rumble. He had heard this before, and knew what it heralded. It was getting louder, which meant it was getting closer.

This was to be it, then? This was when he was to be tested. It had come much sooner in his life than he had expected, and was not at all how he had imagined it would be during those many long nights when he had lain in his cell at Menlac, dreaming of the day he would have the opportunity to proudly demonstrate the strength of his faith - always having to remind himself that pride was a sin, humility a true strength. Yet it *had* come. The Demon *was* out there. This night his faith would be tested, and the strength of it demonstrated.

He looked at the villagers gathered about him in the church, all eyes turned to him, seeking guidance and comfort. He saw the fear in those eyes, and felt a tremendous pity for them. And love. So, this was what it meant to be a father. He knew now what he must do. He must be their example. If there were any protection for them, it would surely be here, in this church. However, if the Lord decided that this was not to be, that they should not survive this night, then that should be accepted, and their fate embraced as His will. Therefore, whatever came through that door, Edmund must be the first to confront it. He must let these people see with what lack of fear he met his death. Let them be inspired by the courage his belief gave him. No matter what form that death took, he would not lose his faith, and the strength that faith gave him to endure it.

The doors flew open, crashed against the wall. Some of the women screamed. Edmund spun around. He was almost disappointed, even angry, to discover it was only one of the villagers. A frightened looking man, who spat out the message from Orderic that they were all to come to the hall right away, then left immediately the message was delivered.

"If the Norman says we are to go to the hall, then maybe we should go?" said someone.

"Don't be a fool! It's in the direction of the danger! You have only to listen," protested another.

"He would not summon us if he thought it the wrong thing to do."

Edmund took a breath, turned back to face his flock. "Yet it *is* the wrong thing to do. Listen to me. The Demon walks among us, bringing with him pain and death. Naturally, you are afraid, as am I."

As he said this, Edmund realised with wonder that it was not true. He was not afraid. He was excited - almost ecstatic, in fact - but he was not afraid. He told himself he must keep in mind that these people did not share his strength of faith. As with most people, theirs was weaker in nature. That was why it was his role to guide them. It would be an act of sheer will. He must use his own faith to raise and sustain theirs.

Stepping in among them, smiling, he said, "Your fear weighs heavily upon you. I see this, and understand it. It pulls you in one direction, then in another. But remember this...The Demon has his own fears. And what do you think he fears more, these walls, which are the walls of the house of God, or the walls of the hall because by chance they were built from the wood of a particular tree? You have an easy choice to make this night. It is between trusting in the mercy of the one true God, or in the misguided magic of the past. In your hearts you already know the answer. The Demon fears God." He looked into their faces, enjoying how they hung on his every word. "The Demon fears God!" he said again, more slowly this time, letting it sink in. "Here, in this church, is where God resides tonight. As he always has. Not in the hall. Here, in *His* house."

"It is not so simple, Brother," said a woman's voice Edmund recognised straightaway. Alditha was standing in the doorway. "I wish it were so, but it is not. These walls are not oak. There is no hope of protection here."

"To pray is to hope," replied Edmund.

"You are wrong, Brother. To stay when you should go is to throw away God's gift of life. His gift of the oak to protect us."

"Pray with us," said Edmund, offering his hand. "Come...You are frightened, we *all* are." That lie again. Edmund was not afraid, and it was wonderful. "Death is not such a terrible thing."

Alditha looked about her at the frightened faces. Hers, she knew, must look the same.

"Yes, I am afraid. Yet it is not death I fear, but pain. Our suffering is what nourishes the thing that is coming for you. Our pain. The harder to endure, the better. Would you condemn these people...even the children among them... to *that*? You imagine that God wants *that*? I will not believe it of Him. Well...? Answer me, monk!"

Edmund flushed with anger. "Who are *you* to say what He does or does not want? A mere woman..."

"Better than a boy whose only understanding of life is was he has been taught by others, most of whom have had precious little experience of life outside their stone walls themselves!"

Instead of answering, Edmund looked over her shoulder. Orderic had appeared at the door, Walter and Mark behind him in the shadows. Alditha wondered how much he had heard. She would not have to ask his opinion on whether the people here should remain or make their way to the hall.

Orderic took a step forward, now fully illuminated by the candles in the church. "We will do what we can to protect you if you come with us now, you have my word. Those who would come, come. The rest are free to take their chances in this place."

"The word of a Norman," scoffed Edmund.

"Believe what you will about that. Time is short. Do you

hear how the noise increases? It draws nearer. Your people are already suffering and dying out there. It will do the same to you when it gets here. This," Orderic gestured around at the church, "it will not protect you."

"Oh, and *you* will?" scoffed Edmund again.

Ignoring Edmund, Orderic addressed the people cowering behind him. "We are leaving this place now. Come if you will. Stay if you must. If you come, my men and I will do what we can to get you safely to the hall. Unlike this man of God, I make no promises beyond that."

"Please," said Alditha. "You *can* trust him on this. Please…"

Only an old couple and a young woman with two small children clinging to her sides came forward. Another woman who looked as if she might follow was pulled back by her husband. Walter stepped across, took the husband by the wrist. "Harold," he said, "Why are you not at the shield wall?" Harold did not reply. He looked at his wife, then back at Walter. "They're better off without you," said Walter, releasing his arm. "Where is your shield?"

"Wha..?" was all Harold could manage to say.

"Your shield, where is your shield? You were to have it with you at all times."

Harold only shook his head.

"There is no time for this," said Orderic. "We leave now."

When Alditha and her small party followed the three Normans out of the church, the noise from across the village had risen.

Orderic put his mouth close to Alditha's ear. "There must be a dozen more in there. They will all die, you know that."

"I tried," said Alditha.

"Easier to protect a small number," said Walter with a shrug, leaning in so they could hear him.

Mark put his mouth up to Orderic's ear, asked

something in French. Orderic shook his head. Even in the moonlight, Alditha could see Mark was perplexed.

Orderic beckoned for the little group of villagers to draw near. Raising his voice above the noise, and gesturing to emphasize his words he said, "Stay in-between us as we move. Walter and I will go ahead. Mark will look to the rear. You understand? If you see anything coming, you let us know. Woman, do not let the children stray. We will not go back. You understand?"

Orderic saw Alditha was watching him. She must know as well as he that, even if they were to make it safely to the hall, it was only likely to be a postponement of the inevitable end. How long could they really last inside with those things from the world of the dead outside. They had not left when there was the entire perimiter wall keeping them out. Why would they leave now, when their advantage was so greatly increased?

At least it was a fight, and that was what he knew how to do.

He glanced at the children. He and Eadred had already agreed that, should the hall be breached, the woman and children would die at the hands of the men rather than let them fall into the hands of the Demon and his followers. Orderic looked back at Alditha, imagined having to end her life. Mercy or not, he wondered if he could do it. Perhaps he would ask Walter if the time came. But then, if it must be done, he had much rather it were by his own hand. Though through what right? The woman was not his. Never would be. He looked away.

He did not attempt to shout above the noise, he simply beckoned for them to follow him.

******

The shields were proving effective. That was a small victory in itself, thought Eadred. Time and again the Demon's creatures had charged forward, their deathly grey faces contorted into scowls of rage, as if they intended to smash into the wall of shields, scattering or trampling the men holding them. But each time the oak had driven them back. As soon as they were closer than three or four yards they always veered away like someone running towards a huge wall of flames and being turned back by the intensity of the heat at the last moment. All the same, it was no easy thing, standing your ground against these fiends. It took discipline and courage not to fall back from such an onslaught. However, as long as Eadred and his men remained locked together, as long as they were agile, quick to react to any attempt to get around them - blocking the path of these unholy creatures from whatever direction they chose to come at them - the entrance to hall remained safe.

Eadred guessed that most of the villagers who were ever going to be were now safely within the walls of the hall. His heart grew heavy at the thought of those who were not. Those already among the bodies that lay out there by the gate, or had been among the unlucky ones who were overtaken and caught before they made it inside the great hall - their approach too slow or from too far off, despite the best attempts of Eadred and his men to create a safe passage for them. It was not something deliberate, but often there had been a terrible bargain of life for life. As one group of villagers fell into the hands of the Demon's creatures, another might take advantage of them being distracted to make it to the hall. If the Demon and his followers had been more disciplined, then far fewer villagers would have been successfully gathered in.

When Orderic returned with the stragglers from the church, Eadred decided, they would retire inside, close the huge oak doors, and shore them up with the oak planks he had had Dunstan set aside for that purpose.

The men of the shield wall had done well. He had seen their fear, and it had worried him that they might not overcome it. That they had was something of which they should be proud, whatever the outcome. It was not only for themselves they had stood their ground. It was for their families and friends, sheltering inside. These were fine men.

Fine men, but they were tiring. Eadred looked in the direction Orderic and the others would come if they had survived. How long should he wait? How much time should he give them? Not much more. Everything depended upon the possibility of closing the entrance swiftly and completely. For that, the shield wall must be intact. It should plug the gap as surely as a stopper in a barrel.

To his left he saw movement. Wulfstan again. So often it had been Wulfstan that attacked at the point in the small shield wall where Eadred stood. It had been unnerving at first, seeing his son like that. He had nearly been the one to cause the wall to fail, staggering back, shocked to see the face of his dead son looming up out of the shadows. Still, he had held his ground. It was what Wulfstan – the real Wulfstan, not this hollow mockery – would want. As soon as Eadred saw the expression of revulsion and fear on that face when it registered that the shield before it was made of oak, he had been reminded what it was that really stood before him.

There had been other close calls, other moments when the wall had been taken by surprise, but so far, by God's grace, they had always managed to move in time to prevent any of the creatures getting past them. That not all of the villagers had made it safely inside was a tragedy they would have to live with later. Some among the dead might well be relatives and friends of these men, standing with shields raised, on either side of him. And yet they had continued to hold their ground, for the sake of the ones who might still survive this night.

Eadred thought for a moment of his secret arrangement with the Normans. He had had his doubts when Swein first suggested it. But the Housecarl had been right. If it came to it, although the killing of the women and children would be hard, watching them tortured by these monsters would be far harder.

Suddenly, something had changed.

The noise, it had stopped.

The creatures in front of them drew back.

Eadred felt a slight slackening in the wall around him. "Hold the wall. Keep it tight!" he shouted. "Whatever happens, you hold this wall!"

The Demon came forward.

"Yes, yes. Hold the wall," it mocked. *"I am impressed, old man. Really I am. You discovered the oak. Held your ground. It won't last, of course. It can't. Your men look tired and afraid. Their will is ready to break."*

"I must disagree with you on that point. It will hold. Nothing you can do about that, so why not leave us be?" said Eadred.

"Nothing I can do? Leave you be? Hmm. Now it is I *who must disagree with* you. *Tell me, how do you feel about this young fellow?"*

For the second time Eadred came close to dropping his shield.

Eadwig twisted in the Demon's grip, squealing in pain and terror.

"This can go on and on for him. Or it can end now. He can be at peace, or I can claw and tear at his flesh, and shed his blood, drip by agonising drip. Your *flesh and blood, Eadred. Not some farm boy or tavern whore. Your flesh and blood, suffering instead of these villagers. These nobodies who you give your life to govern and protect, while in return they…they give you nothing. Really, who is serving whom? What is your opinion on the matter, young Eadwig? Speak up, so you grandfather can hear."*

The Demon squeezed, Eadwig screamed.

"I think that illustrates the boy's opinion very well, don't you? No? Shall I ask him again?"

"No, no. Please stop, I beg you," said Eadred.

"Hold the wall," shouted Cynric to the others. Then to

Eadred he said, "Eadred, you cannot agree to anything, you know that. The boy…"

"Is my grandson, Cynric! What would you ask of me? That I watch him die in agony?"

"I think we know that is exactly what your tavern keeper is asking. Flesh and blood, Eadred. Flesh and blood. Flesh and blood. Flesh and Blood."

The Demon raised the screaming Eadwig higher in the air, swinging him back and forth in time with his chanting. *"Flesh and Blood. Flesh and Blood."* Then he reached out a clawed finger and slashed it across the boy's abdomen, quick and sharp as a razor, creating a thin wound that slowly parted like a grin, and then began dripping blood in a row of splashes that showed black against the blue whiteness of the moonlit snow as the boy swung to and fro above it.

"Flesh and Blood. Flesh and Blood…" continued the Demon.

******

There it was again, that sin of pride. It was so difficult not to feel proud when he thought of what he was doing, and that he had been the one chosen for the role above all others who might have been. Although it could so easily have been any one of the other monks at Menlac the Abbot chose, in the end, it was he, Edmund, who had been sent into this valley, to this village, to these people. And God had surely guided the Abbot in the choice. Edmund smiled to think of it. Even Abbot Robert himself, who had risen high in the church, was not so blessed. There were things higher in the sight of God than abbots, there were….No, no, he must not. It was so hard, but he must not allow pride to undermine him. Gratitude. Gratitude was better than pride. He was grateful to God for choosing him above the other brothers, grateful that he had been selected to lead these members of the flock to grace. From where he knelt, Edmund looked up at the altar - that marvellously humble altar, nothing like it to be found within the decorated walls of Menlac. He clasped his hands in prayer.

What was it about his hands that made him feel something was wrong? He tried not to see it, tried not to remember. It was no good. He saw it again. His hands were stained red from where he had tried so desperately to help them, so utterly ineffectually to help them. He put his hands to his face, sobbing, remembering now. He breathed in, caught the metallic odour of the blood - not just on his hands, but all about him. Through his fingers, he stared up at the altar. It seemed to him now a pathetically simple thing. Not worthy of a place in the house of God. The smell of blood and the other odours of death came to him again, making him retch. He knew what he would see if he looked behind him. He was not ready to look. Not yet. He could not face seeing the bodies again so soon. He put his hands over his ears, remembering the terrible cries of the dying, and the hollow, unnatural laughter and howls of triumph of the things that had killed them. Killed them all, and yet let him, alone, live. Edmund, the only one not permitted the gift and glory of being a martyr to his faith. Edmund, the one who had misled these people - people who had not asked for that gift - because he alone had believed himself deserving of it, and wished for it. What manner of evil had there been present that could make of his faith this terrible, terrible joke? He had imagined himself prepared for anything, and he had been - anything but this.

The young monk curled up at the foot of the altar, pulled his cowl over his head, and began to scream.

******

'Flesh. Blood. Flesh…"

Walter raced forward, ignoring Orderic's shouted order

for him to stop. As he neared the Demon, Walter raised his sword and swung it round, expertly severing the screaming boy's head, and ending his suffering as quickly and efficiently as he knew how.

The Demon threw down the rest of the boy's body next to where the head had fallen.

"Brave man. Foolish man. Where is that shield of oak you have been hiding behind? You really should have listened to your captain."

Walter let out a sigh of resignation. In his haste to put an end to Eadwig's pain, he had thrown his shield aside without thinking. The Demon reached forward, lifted the large warrior as easily as he had lifted the child.

Walter refused to scream, even as he felt the bones of his ribcage snapping. Soon, he could not have screamed had he chosen to. He was gasping and dribbling blood as shards of his own splintered bones pierced his lungs.

Alditha did scream. Without looking at her, Orderic put his arm around her, all the while forcing himself to watch as his oldest friend was crushed to death.

Eadred had staggered back and collapsed, but foreseeing this, Cynric and the other men of the shield wall had been ready and immediately closed ranks in front of him. There was still hope.

"Norman, come to us," shouted Cynric.

Mark and Orderic joined their own shields in a small version of the wall, covering Alditha and the other villagers as they crossed to the hall entrance. Their route from the church had been surprisingly free of attack, although, at one point, Mark had shouted a warning that he saw something in the shadows, passing them by, heading towards the church. He had shouted in French and Orderic had chosen not to translate what he said for Alditha, although she guessed what it might be.

The children had been subdued and silent for most of the short journey, but now they were screaming and struggling in their mother's arms.

"Control them!" hissed Orderic.

It seemed for a time that between them the mother and Alditha had managed to do as Orderic ordered. It was as they reached the hall that things went wrong. One of the children broke free of his mother's grasp, throwing himself at what he considered was the greater safety of the shield wall, where he had spotted his father. This was enough to break his father's concentration. Like Walter and Eadred before him, the man dropped his shield, reaching for the boy, trying to prevent him from running into danger. The consequences were immediate and dire. The man next to him, seeing the space in the wall where the other's shield had been, lost his nerve and fell back, rather than attempting to plug the gap. From this point it became impossible for the few remaining men to form a solid line of defence quickly enough to hold back the ensuing attack. Wilfred crouched down behind his shield as the dead things rushed past, and Cynric leapt to one side. The others, panicked, fled inside or were killed before they could run.

Orderic and Mark had seen the breach happen, and correctly predicted the collapse of the entire shield wall, just as the Demon had. At the same time as the Demon and its followers were lunging forward, Orderic was pushing his own small group away, shouting for them to get back. He glanced over his shoulder in time to see the Demon wave the last of his followers into the hall then, before following them in, turn and give a snarl of triumph.

All order within Orderic's small group now collapsed. Having witnessed the death of her husband, the woman fell to her knees, still clutching her children who, like her, were screaming hysterically. The old couple made off for the far side of the village. Thinking they had made a mistake following Alditha and the Normans, they were making for the church once again

Worse than the screams of the woman and her children were the screams coming from inside the hall.

"If they move to the walls..." cried Alditha. "If they move near to the oak of the walls, there may be a chance for them. We must tell them.

Orderic grabbed her before she could run forward.

"Let me go!" insisted Alditha.

"It's too late. Even if your people pressed themselves right up against the walls, those things need only use a weapon to close the distance and reach them. The swing of an outstretched axe or a sword would be enough. The oak would not prevent them from doing that. Besides, there are too many people packed in there, and they are too panicked. They are beyond our help. We must leave, now."

"No! The oak, it will reduce the Demon's strength. It must. He and his kind will not be able to remain in there for long. They cannot linger there. Some of my people inside may still have a chance. We must try and help them!"

"*How?* What can we do? It has the upper hand now."

As if to illustrate this point, a body, stripped of its skin, was thrown from inside the hall, landing close to where they stood. Droplets of blood on the exposed flesh glistened in the moonlight.

At the entrance to the hall, Wilfred was now getting to his feet. He stepped forward, looked inside. "No, no, no!" he shouted. "Stop it! Leave them alone!" Raising his shield, he rushed into the hall, only to stagger back out again moments later, his arms ripped from his body, his face a bloody pulp. Alditha broke free of Orderic, and ran forward to help him, but Wilfred fell dead at her feet. She howled, leapt back, and began half running, half stumbling around the outside of the hall, her hands to her head, her cries a mixture of horror and frustration at not being able to do anything to prevent what was happening. She was coming back around the other side when a small child appeared at the entrance. Little Hare. Behind her was a teenage boy, Harfric, son of one of the farmers.

"You see?" shouted Alditha, scooping Little Hare up

into her arms, and hurrying over to Orderic. "You see? Some may yet live through this!"

At the same time, Cynric, having survived the collapse of the shield wall with only bruises, and a twisted ankle, had limped over to join them. "It doesn't matter, I'm sorry Alditha. We need to leave this place before they come back out," insisted the Welshman.

Orderic looked uncertain. He glanced down at Little Hare, thought for a moment before answering. "No, we wait... a little longer...help any who escape... like this child." Then added with a sigh, "Though I doubt there will be many."

"I doubt it too," said Cynric. "And I still don't want to be here when the Demon and his friends show themselves again."

"What if they can't?" said Orderic, suddenly.

"What?"

"What if they can't? The door! We close the door! It was meant to keep them out. Why not use it to keep them in? We have to do it right now, though. While we still can."

Cynric looked solemn. "Shut them all in with those things. You know what we would be doing?"

"Of course I do!" snapped Orderic. "We have no choice. Besides, they are dead flesh already."

Cynric nodded. "True."

"You can't!" cried Alditha. "What if more were to get free?" She pushed Little Hare forward. "You said it yourself just now, there could be more like this child...You don't have the *right* to do it."

"He doesn't have the right not to," said Cynric. "We must try. If there is any chance we can hold these creatures somewhere....Think, Alditha. There are other villages not yet ravaged by this. If we can save them...or just gain them some time. It is a price we must pay."

"You can say that because you are not from here, Welshman. Those are not your people screaming in there. If they were, and if you thought even one might yet survive…"

"Enough talk," said Orderic. He ran towards the entrance of the hall, followed by Cynric and Mark. Alditha quickly caught up, and began tugging at Orderic, begging him to wait.

When they drew near, they saw someone crawling forward, out from beneath the heaped bodies of the men of the shield wall. It was Eadred. He was covered in blood, barely alive. Alditha went to him. Orderic ignored him, grabbed at one of the doors, not letting himself look inside at the carnage he knew he would witness if he did. Cynric and Mark were at the other door. When they pulled them shut a great roar of rage erupted from within, drowning out even the screams of the dying.

"Should we burn it?" asked Cynric.

"And set them free?" replied Orderic. "No. Mark and I will hold them in place. Cynric, you break up those shields, fetch tools… hammers, nails. We must shore this up. It need not be strong, for they cannot approach it. But it *must* be secure."

Alditha crouched down, pulled Eadred up so he could see what was happening. He winced in pain, but she ignored this, turned his head so he could see. "Look! They are closing them in! Our friends, our people, Eadred. They are closing them in! We cannot allow it. We must stop them. How can I stop them? Tell me!"

A look of profound sadness came over Eadred's face. He looked away from her. "Orderic is right. Elastun is lost. Our people are lost. Gone. Others villages may yet be spared...that is what we must consider now. There is no other way…"

Alditha knew Eadred was right, but it did not make listening to the screams of the people inside the hall any easier. Nothing could. She knew the sounds would haunt her the rest of her days.

Little Hare came over. Eyes closed tight, the child wrapped her arms tightly around Alditha, who in turn had her own arms wrapped around the dead old man who had once been head man of the village.

******

CHAPTER 20

Orderic and Mark remained close to the hall for the rest of the night, pacing around and around, torches raised, watching for signs of anything escaping from inside. Every shadow, every flicker of light or unexplained noise was a cause for fear that something might yet be breaking free. But nothing did. Dunstan the carpenter and his sons - now all dead inside a tomb they had built with their own hands - had done their work well.

By the time daybreak came, all had long been silent within. No more growls of rage, no more cries of pain. That the Demon's victims were silenced forever was beyond doubt. As for the Demon, and its followers, there was no way of knowing. The fate of the followers must surely be inextricably linked to that of the Demon itself. The question was, had the oak merely weakened it, or had such prolonged exposure been enough to destroy it completely? If it were still alive in there, it seemed to be trapped. But for how long? It had been imprisoned at least once before, and had somehow freed itself. One thing was certain. The oak walls that currently enclosed it would not last forever.

Another question. Was it even a demon? That had been the monk's belief. He had been convinced of it. Orderic was still not.

Orderic looked from the hall to where Alditha sat, cradling Eadred's body, her head bowed forward, her hair falling onto the old man's face. Beside her, Little Hare was curled up asleep with exhaustion, her head resting in the lap of Harfric, the farmer's son. The teenage boy looked up at him, his grimy face streaked with tears. Orderic nodded as reassuringly as he could. The boy nodded back.

This whole group were now wrapped up against the cold in blankets and furs - something Cynric had seen to in the night.

Watching Orderic, huddled together inside the entrance of a nearby hut, were the old couple. They had reappeared shortly after the sun came up. With them was a pale and speechless Brother Edmund. Most of the time he simply stared ahead, barely blinking. He had been that way when they found him sitting among the dead in the church, the old couple explained, and he had said nothing since.

The woman with the two young children had run off with them into the night. They had not been seen since.

******

By midday, those dead who could be found had been stacked as respectfully as was possible inside the church. Edmund still refused to speak, and could not be induced to go near the old building, let alone say any words over them. So it fell to Alditha to say a prayer while the others looked on.

This done, the horses were then packed and saddled for the journeys that lay ahead. Cynric had agreed to stay behind in the village to ensure nobody who might come by attempted to open the hall. He would tell them the village had fallen victim to a dreadful pestilence, and the hall, which had contained the sick and dying, was not considered free of infection, and was therefore unsafe to re-enter. The truth, it was agreed, was not likely to be believed. The old couple said they had no wish to leave the village where they had lived all their lives. They were too old for that, so they would remain behind with the Welshman.

Alditha would take the monk and the two children - Little Hare and Harfric - to Menlac Abbey, where it was hoped they would be given sanctuary. She and Edmund would then attempt to persuade Abbot Robert of the need to take seriously the evil that had been visited upon the valley, and do whatever was in his power to ensure it was defeated should it ever break free. Edmund nodded in agreement when this was explained to him, so Alditha hoped his mind, and his voice, would be sufficiently recovered when the time came. At Orderic's insistence, Mark was to ride along with them for protection. He would also lend weight to their request for help by saying he spoke on behalf of Orderic who, the Abbot would know only too well, spoke on behalf of the Baron.

Orderic would not be going with them. He would return to Rylemont Castle, where he would try to convince the Baron of the truth of what had happened, and the need to take measures against it happening again.

As he mounted Malleus, Orderic nodded farewell to the others as they rode out of the village in the opposite direction. He watched them ride out of the far gate, then along the track towards the river, which would eventually lead them out of the valley, and north towards Menlac. Alditha did not look back. Orderic wondered how long it would be before he saw her again and if, when he did, he would still see the hate for him that now shone in her eyes every time she looked at him. It was not because she thought he was wrong to have done what he did - she had finally acknowledged that there was no other way - but because he was the kind of man who had been able to do it.

When they had gone, Orderic nodded a silent farewell to Cynric, turned Malleus, and rode towards the other gateway, and the track that would take him back to Rylemont. He would go there, talk with his brother, and then from there, perhaps, he would travel back towards Hastings, and the nearby site of the battle, where Swein had once encountered an old woman whose talk at the time everyone had thought mad. He would seek her out if he could, and ask for her help. He would begin by explaining why he, Orderic de Varaville, knew that she was *not* mad.

Printed in Great Britain
by Amazon